POWER
PLAY

POWER
PLAY

BEN BOVA

A TOM DOHERTY ASSOCIATES BOOK
NEW YORK

POWER PLAY

Copyright © 2011 by Ben Bova

A Tor Book
Published by Tom Doherty Associates, LLC
175 Fifth Avenue
New York, NY 10010

www.tor-forge.com

Tor® is a registered trademark of Tom Doherty Associates, LLC.

Library of Congress Cataloging-in-Publication Data

Bova, Ben, 1932–
    Power play / Ben Bova. — 1st ed.
        p. cm.
    ISBN 978-0-7653-1786-5
    1. Scientists—Fiction.   2. Energy development—Fiction.   3. Political fiction.   I. Title.
    PS3552.O84P58 2012
    813'.54—dc23

                                                                    2011024949

First Edition: January 2012

Printed in the United States of America

0   9   8   7   6   5   4   3   2   1

For the final time, to Barbara . . .

Jenny kissed me when we met,
>*Jumping from the chair she sat in.*
Time, you thief, who love to get
>*Sweets into your list, put that in.*
Say I'm weary, say I'm sad;
>*Say that health and wealth have missed me;*
Say I'm growing old, but add—
>*Jenny kissed me!*

—LEIGH HUNT

In the nineteenth century, a German-born engineer named John Fritz, working at the Cambria Iron Company in Johnstown, Pennsylvania, captured the [can-do] spirit when, after working for months to finish the first Bessemer steel machinery in this country, he came to the plant one morning and said, "Alright, boys, let's start her up and see why she doesn't work." The desire to find out what's not working, fix it, and then maybe get it to work is an American quality and our guiding star.

—David McCullough
American Heritage
Winter 2008

AUGUST

MHD?" asked Jake Ross. "What's MHD?"

Leverett Cardwell smiled his enigmatic little smile and replied, "It stands for magnetohydrodynamics."

"Oh, like Alfvén."

Jake was walking with the older man along the Hall of Planets, which ran the length of the museum's planetarium. They were passing beneath the model of Mars, a rust-red globe dotted with long-dead volcanoes. He had first introduced himself to Dr. Cardwell at almost this exact spot, more than a dozen years earlier.

"Alfvén dealt with astrophysics. The branch of MHD I'm talking about now is a way of generating electricity very efficiently," Cardwell went on, his tenor voice soft but perfectly clear. "An MHD generator can produce a lot of power in a relatively small piece of equipment."

Jake nodded. Lev was up to something, he knew. The old man didn't just chat to pass the time of day. He had some purpose in mind.

Jacob Ross had first come to the Van Allen museum on a mandatory class trip when he'd been in middle school. None of the guys wanted to go to a geeky science museum, Jake included. But once the teachers got the kids settled into the strange, round, domed room that housed the museum's planetarium, the lights dimmed slowly until the place was pitch black. And then they turned on the stars. Thousands of stars sprang out of the darkness, with the faint glowing ribbon of the Milky Way arching among them. Young Jake got turned on, too. Sitting in the darkness, watching the stars wheel in stately procession overhead, he became hooked on astronomy for life.

He rode city buses to the museum every weekend. He scraped together enough money from his after-school jobs to buy a student membership. He attended the planetarium shows so often he began to learn the lectures by heart.

And he discovered that the soft, clear voice that explained the stars in the darkness belonged to Dr. Leverett Cardwell, the planetarium's director. With some trepidation, Jake fumblingly asked Dr. Cardwell a question about his lecture one Sunday afternoon, out in the hallway under the model of Mars, while the rest of the audience streamed past after the planetarium show had ended.

"You've been coming pretty regularly, haven't you?" Cardwell asked the youngster.

Surprised and pleased that the director had noticed him, Jake stuttered, "Y . . . yessir."

Thus began a lifelong friendship. Cardwell took Jake under his wing, opened the planetarium's library to him, and helped him win a scholarship to the state university.

And now Lev was talking about something called MHD.

"Magnetohydrodynamics, huh?" Jake said.

Walking slowly toward the bright yellow globe of the Sun glowing above the museum's entrance lobby, Cardwell said, "There's a group of people in the university's electrical engineering department who are working on MHD power generation."

Why's he telling me this? Jake wondered. But he knew he wouldn't have to ask; Lev would explain it to him in his own time.

Jake had grown into a reasonably healthy young man. Scrawny as a child, picked on by the neighborhood bullies, he'd worked hard on homemade exercise equipment to build himself up. Now he stood just short of six feet tall, still on the lean side, but solid. His hair was dark and unruly, his face too long and horsy to satisfy him. Even so he'd been fairly popular with women, and married his high school sweetheart. But since his wife's fatal car accident he'd kept to himself.

Leverett Cardwell was a tiny man, round-faced, balding, so neat and carefully groomed that some thought him effeminate. His large, round, slightly protruding owl-gray eyes always seemed to Jake to be searching, inquisitive. Jake had never seen Lev wearing anything but a gray wool suit, winter or summer, and a jaunty little bow tie.

"I've been invited to a cocktail party by one of Frank Tomlinson's people," Cardwell said as they walked slowly toward the museum's entrance.

Frowning at the seeming change of subject, Jake asked, "Isn't he the guy they say might run against Senator Leeds?"

Cardwell nodded, his smile turning almost impish. "If Tomlinson decides to run, he's going to need somebody on his staff to advise him about science. I think you could do the job very well, Jake."

"Me?" Jake's voice squeaked with surprise. "I'm just an associate professor. I don't even have tenure yet."

"Aren't you up for tenure this year?"

Nodding gloomily, Jake answered, "Along with five other people, including a Hispanic woman. Besides, I'm the youngest. They'll give it to one of the others this time around."

Nonchalantly waving a hand in the air, Cardwell said, "Maybe not. Maybe they'll surprise you."

Jake made an unhappy grunt.

"I think it would be a good idea for you to attend the Tomlinson party," Cardwell said. "Meet the man. Let him meet you."

"I don't think so."

"You've been keeping to yourself too much, Jake. I know Louise's death was a blow, but that was more than a year ago—"

Jake stopped walking. He could feel his guts twisting. "It doesn't matter," he said. "Nothing matters much anymore. It's just . . . Lev, nothing's any fun anymore."

"You can't have any fun sitting by yourself watching old movies on television."

"I don't just watch television."

"What else do you do?"

"Prepare my lectures. Do my research. I'm working on a proposal for the imaging team on the next Mars lander."

"You need a social life, my boy."

Jake looked down at the man who'd been his mentor for so many years. Mentor? Hell, Lev's been more of a father to me than my old man ever was, he told himself. I wouldn't be here if it wasn't for him. I'd still be back in the 'hood, in those narrow streets and row houses, working some dumb-ass job and dodging the wiseguys.

Reluctantly he asked, "I won't have to wear a tux, will I?"

Cardwell laughed. "Heavens, no. This is just a cocktail party, not a formal occasion."

Jake capitulated. "Okay, I'll go, if you think I should."

"I do indeed, Jacob."

"When and where? What time should I pick you up?"

"Oh, for goodness' sake, I'm not going!"

"You're not?"

"No. This is an opportunity for you, Jake. They're not interested in an old geezer like me."

Jake felt stunned. Lev was past sixty, he knew. But that's not old! he told himself. There must be some other reason why he wants me to go without him.

TOMLINSON RESIDENCE

The afternoon was sultry, so glaringly hot and humid that Jake was sweating by the time he'd walked from his curbside parking space up the gently rising bricked driveway to the front door of the Tomlinson mansion. It was a quietly imposing house that spoke of old money, in a part of the city that Jake had never been in before. He saw a pair of youngsters lounging by the Bentleys and Porsches parked along the driveway and realized they would have taken his old Mustang and parked it for him. It'd look great, he thought, his beat-up old gray ghost alongside all those luxury cars.

An actual butler in a dark suit opened the glass-paneled front door and looked at him questioningly. Jake could hear muted laughter and the hum of many conversations coming from inside the house.

"Um, I'm Jacob Ross," he said. "Dr. Cardwell—"

"You are expected, Dr. Ross," said the white-haired butler, allowing himself a minimal smile. He opened the door wide and gestured Jake through. It was blessedly cool inside, cool and dry.

The foyer was bigger than Jake's apartment. Marble floor. Broad staircase. Big windows with brocaded drapes shutting out the August heat. The sounds of the cocktail party were coming from a half-open door across the way, between two large paintings of soft green landscapes.

Jake felt mildly puzzled. Lev had told him to be there by four P.M. It was still a few minutes before four, yet the party seemed to be in full swing already.

"This way, sir," said the butler in a quiet voice, not much above a whisper.

He led Jake across the foyer and pulled the half-open door all the way. The room beyond was crammed with people talking, laughing, drinking. Somewhere in the crowd someone was playing a piano. The men were mostly in suits, although Jake noticed some blue jeans and denim jackets among them. The women were young, fashionably dressed, glowing with jewelry and the self-assurance of wealth.

Feeling slightly shabby in his old gray slacks and navy blazer, Jake stepped into the crowd. At least I'm wearing a tie, he said to himself. A dark-suited waiter appeared at his side.

"What can I get for you, sir?"

Thinking about the drive back across town, Jake asked, "Do you have any ginger beer?"

"Of course." The waiter disappeared into the chattering crowd.

A young woman smiled at him. "You're Dr. Ross, aren't you?"

Surprised to be recognized, Jake replied, "Jake Ross, yes."

"I'm Amy Wexler. One of Mr. Tomlinson's volunteers."

She was pretty, with a lively smile and fresh, sparkling eyes. Like a cheerleader, Jake thought. Slim figure, strong cheekbones, beautiful honey blond hair cascading to her shoulders. Floor-length skirt of swirling blues and greens, soft blue sweater over a white blouse. Bracelets clattered on her wrist as she extended her hand to Jake.

Are those real gold? he wondered as he took her hand.

"Mr. Tomlinson wants to talk with you in private, so don't leave before the two of you have had a chance to chat, okay?"

Jake nodded, wondering what he should say, what he could say. The waiter reappeared with a tall glass of ginger beer on a silver tray and Amy Wexler melted back into the crowd. Jake looked around for a familiar face, knowing that there couldn't be anybody he knew in this bunch. These people come from money, he knew. They wouldn't be caught dead in my neighborhood.

"Some party, isn't it?"

Jake turned to see a man in a suede jacket and jeans grinning at him. Instead of a tie he wore at his throat a bolo with a jet-black chunk of onyx set in intricately worked silver.

"I'm Bob Rogers," the man said, extending his hand.

Jake shook hands with him. "Jake Ross."

Rogers was about ten years older than him, Jake judged. His face was seamed, as if he'd spent a good deal of his life out in the open. He had a lean, leathery look to him, emphasized by the suede jacket and bolo. Crinkly pale blue eyes and wispy sandy hair. He held a tapered pilsner glass in one hand, nearly empty.

"You think all these people will support Tomlinson if he runs?" Rogers asked.

Jake hesitated a moment. Then he replied, "If he runs, I guess they will. They must be his friends."

His grin widening a bit, Rogers said, "If Tomlinson decides to run for the Senate, he'll ask them to open their checkbooks. Then we'll see how many of them are really his friends."

Jake grinned back. "Yeah, I guess it's easy to be a friend when the guy's handing out free drinks."

Rogers pointed toward the big French doors on one side of the room. "Looks a little less crowded over there."

Jake edged through the crowd alongside Rogers. Through the tall glass doors Jake could see green hedges baking in the afternoon sunshine and a corner of a swimming pool.

"Bet that's an Olympic-sized pool," Rogers said. "Nothing halfway about the Tomlinsons."

"You know them?" Jake asked.

"I've met him and his father a couple of times. At university functions. They're big donors."

"Are you at the university?"

"Electrical engineering department."

Feeling relieved, Jake said, "Astronomy."

"No kidding?"

"Do you know—"

Jake felt a tap on his shoulder. Turning, he saw Amy Wexler standing beside him.

"I'm sorry to interrupt," she said, beaming that cheerleader's smile at him. "Mr. Tomlinson would like to see you now, Dr. Ross. In the library."

Jake gave Rogers a rueful look. Rogers hoisted his nearly empty glass of beer and said, "I'll see you later, Jake."

"Right." And he let Amy Wexler lead him through the oblivious crowd toward the library and his private chat with B. Franklin Tomlinson.

B. FRANKLIN TOMLINSON

The man radiated wealth. That was Jake's first impression of Tomlinson, as Amy Wexler ushered him into the library. She shut the heavy oak door behind Jake, cutting off the noise of the cocktail party and leaving the two men alone. B. Franklin Tomlinson stood at the far end of the richly carpeted room, smiling warmly at Jake.

Tomlinson was tall, with broad shoulders and a squarish, ruggedly handsome face, deeply tanned. The jacket of his three-piece suit was thrown carelessly over the back of the chair he was standing next to; his vest was buttoned over his flat midsection. Thick, wavy golden blond hair with just a hint of gray streaking through it that made him look distinguished, Jake thought. Sparkling sapphire blue eyes. And that smile could melt platinum.

For a moment Jake wasn't certain of what he should do, what he should say. The library was hushed, only the two of them in it. Bookshelves lined three of the walls, up to the ceiling. Every inch of the shelving was filled with books, all so neatly stacked and new-looking that Jake figured they'd never been opened. The fourth wall bore the room's only window and a half-dozen framed photographs of Tomlinson and others aboard sailing boats.

His smile unwavering, Tomlinson extended his hand toward Jake. "I'm Frank Tomlinson," he said, as if that explained everything.

Jake swiftly crossed the thick carpeting and shook Tomlinson's hand. "Jake Ross," he said.

"Yes, I know." Tomlinson's grip was firm and steady. With his free hand he gestured to a pair of bottle green leather chairs in the corner by the window. "Let's sit down, shall we?"

"Are you really going to run against Senator Leeds?" Jake asked as they sat facing each other.

"Somebody ought to," Tomlinson said lightly. "Chris has been in the Senate for more than twenty years. Time for a change, don't you think?"

With a nod, Jake said, "But beating an incumbent isn't easy."

Tomlinson chuckled softly. "I don't go after easy tasks, Dr. Ross."

"Jake."

"Jake," Tomlinson echoed. "My father always told me that the tough jobs are the ones worth tackling. That's where the fun is."

Unable to think of a response, Jake took a sip of his ginger beer. Then he noticed that Tomlinson wasn't drinking anything.

"Dr. Cardwell spoke very highly of you," Tomlinson said, leaning back easily in his chair.

"You know Lev?"

"My father put up the money to build the planetarium. He also personally picked Dr. Cardwell to run it. I've known Lev since he first came here. I was just a kid."

Feeling a little confused, Jake said, "But the planetarium isn't named after your father."

Tomlinson made a wry smile. "Despite his usual demeanor, my father is basically a modest man. He asked that the planetarium be named after an astronomer he respected, Bart J. Bok."

"Oh." Jake gulped at his drink again.

"Do you want another?" Tomlinson asked.

"No, I'm okay with this, thanks."

"What are you drinking?"

"Ginger beer. It's nonalcoholic."

"In Australia they take it with brandy. Brandy and dry, the Aussies call it."

Jake almost asked Tomlinson if he'd been to Australia, but stopped himself in time to save the embarrassment. Of course he's been to Australia, Jake told himself. He's probably sailed yachts there. Or raced cars in the Outback.

"Dr. Cardwell says I should have a science advisor on my team," Tomlinson said. "And he says you're the man for the job."

"He told me the same thing."

"So what do you think?"

"Well, Mr. Tomlinson—"

"Frank."

"Um, okay, Frank . . . I don't know much about politics, and even less about how a political campaign is run."

Tomlinson actually laughed. "That's no problem, Jake. I'm surrounded by campaign managers, aides, volunteers. They all tell me they know exactly how to get me elected."

"Uh-huh."

"What I need is somebody who knows about science. What I need is an issue, a new idea, something that will show that I'm different from Leeds. Different and better."

"A new issue."

"Sure! Like Jack Kennedy and going to the Moon. Something exciting. Something to get people stirred up."

"I see."

Tomlinson leaned forward in the chair, toward Jake. In a voice that suddenly was deadly serious, he asked, "Think you can find me a new idea that I can campaign on?"

And Jake wanted to do it. He looked into Tomlinson's sapphire blue eyes and saw that they were unwavering, deadly earnest. He realized that he wanted to help this man succeed.

"I can try," he said.

Tomlinson's smile returned. "That's all I can ask of you, Jake. Try your best."

"I will."

"Good. You come up with an electable issue and I'll name you as my science advisor."

"How quickly will you need it?"

Tomlinson cocked his head slightly, calculating. "It's August now. The election's next November. That gives us fifteen months."

"Fifteen months," Jake echoed.

Raising a warning finger, Tomlinson said, "But we'll need that issue long before then, of course. I've got to decide whether I'll file for the race by the end of the year. I'll need a good issue from you before then."

"In four months?"

"Sooner, Jake. In a few weeks, if you can."

"I'll do it," Jake promised.

"Good! Wonderful!" Tomlinson got to his feet and Jake hauled himself up to stand beside him. He realized that he was actually an inch or so taller than Tomlinson.

"I'll have something for you in a couple of weeks," Jake promised.

Tomlinson took Jake's hand in both of his own. "I'll look forward to it." He led Jake toward the door of the library. "In the meantime, enjoy the party."

"Thanks."

As he reached for the doorknob, Tomlinson said, with a sly grin, "You'll enjoy politics, Jake. Great way to meet women."

AMY WEXLER

The party was still going strong, dozens of people talking, laughing, drinking. Jake watched as a pair of older men, both portly, both in dark business suits, came up to Tomlinson.

"Where's your jacket, Frankie?" one of them demanded; he was bald, florid-faced. He had to raise his voice to be heard over the din of the others.

"I left it in the library," said Tomlinson, with a good-natured smile.

The bald man shook his head disapprovingly. "If you're going to be a United States senator—"

Raising a warning hand, Tomlinson said, "I haven't made up my mind about that yet."

The other old man smiled knowingly. "Yes you have, you just don't want to admit it in public yet."

"Now, really, Mr. McPherson . . ."

Jake felt a tug on his sleeve. Turning, he saw Amy Wexler standing beside him. She leaned toward him and said into his ear, "How did it go?"

"Okay, I guess."

"You're going to join the staff?"

"I don't know. Mr. Tomlinson wants a good idea to campaign on."

Her sculpted face looked somewhere between curious and skeptical. "A good idea?"

Jake nodded. The party seemed noisier than ever, and he didn't like shouting to make himself heard.

Amy seemed to understand. Taking his arm in her grip, she tugged him toward the French doors. As he meekly followed her Jake glimpsed Bob Rogers in the crowd, talking earnestly with a stubby little guy who looked vaguely familiar: maybe a news anchor from one of the local TV stations, Jake thought.

Amy led Jake through the French doors and out onto the patio. It was still blazing August hot outside, but mercifully quiet. She walked to a white-painted bench placed in the deep shade of a thickly leafed box elder tree. Brushing dead leaves off the wooden bench, she sat down. Dumbly, Jake sat beside her.

"That's better," Amy said.

He agreed. "It's pretty noisy in there, isn't it?"

"It gets noisier as they drink more liquor."

"I remember reading a paper once," Jake said, "that calculated the noise of a cocktail party, based on the number of people and the number of drinks served."

"A scientific paper?"

"Yeah. It was published in *New Scientist,* I think."

She smoothed her long blue-and-green skirt with one hand. It made Jake think of the sea: not that he had ever seen an ocean first-hand, but he pictured a softly billowing sea, far from land, alone on a sailboat with a beautiful long-legged woman. Then a memory of Louise flared in his mind and he felt guilty.

"What's the matter?" Amy asked.

He looked away from her. "Does it show?"

"Something's bothering you, that's obvious." She seemed genuinely concerned.

"It's . . . personal."

"Oh. I see."

Feeling even more miserable, Jake said, "I'm sorry. I shouldn't be such a sap."

"Let's talk about Franklin's campaign."

"He said he hasn't made up his mind to run yet."

She gave him a sly smile. "Don't believe that line. It's just his way of getting people to urge him to run. He wants them committed. He wants them to back him all the way to Washington."

"You think so?"

"I know so," Amy said. "He's been a lot more honest with his key volunteers than with his potential backers."

"You're one of his key volunteers."

"Yes, I am. And you can be, too. He needs a good science advisor. Senator Leeds is a nincompoop about science."

Jake laughed. "Not only about science. How he's managed to stay in the Senate for all these years . . ." He shook his head.

"He gets himself reelected," Amy said, quite seriously. "He has an organization that runs very smoothly. He gets support from the unions, from the construction industry, and from gaming. Even the car dealers back him, for god's sake! Franklin's going to need a better organization."

"And lots of money."

"Money's no problem," she said. "Franklin has family money, and the family's friends are all very well heeled."

"I guess," Jake said.

"What he needs is ideas, issues he can campaign on. Issues that Leeds can't co-opt."

"That's what I'm supposed to do," Jake said. "Come up with a science issue."

"Do you have anything in mind?"

"Not really," he admitted. "Not yet. This is all new to me. I haven't had a chance to think much about it."

Leaning slightly toward him, Amy said, "Please think hard about it, Jake. He needs you. I know he does."

The bright sunlight glaring down on the patio made Jake feel uncomfortable. Or was it the situation he was being maneuvered into? he wondered. "There are other scientists in the state. Probably better ones. I'm just an assistant professor of astronomy."

"But you're young, Jake. Young and good-looking. You'll look good on television."

"Me? On TV?"

"Of course. And if Franklin wins the election, you can go to Washington with us."

"Us?"

"We'll be working together on the campaign. If you join the staff I'll be your liaison with Franklin. You and I will work together, Jake."

He felt his eyebrows rise and heard himself say, "That'd be great!"

Amy Wexler smiled warmly at him. "Yes, I think it would be great."

And Jake heard Tomlinson's words: *You'll enjoy politics, Jake. Great way to meet women.*

ELECTRICAL ENGINEERING DEPARTMENT

The sign on the double doors said DO NOT ENTER WHEN RED LIGHT IS FLASHING. And the red light was indeed flashing.

Jake stopped, his fist poised to knock on the door. It had been easy enough to locate the electrical engineering building on campus, but once inside, finding the laboratory where the MHD work was being done had been a bitch. None of the students ambling through the hallways seemed to have ever heard of the MHD lab. Jake had to contact campus security on his cell phone and even the gravel-voiced officer who answered him seemed unsure of the laboratory's location.

"They moved it last year, after the explosion," the security officer said.

"Explosion?" Jake yelped.

"Yeah . . . wait a minute, I'm scrolling through on the computer. Yeah. Here it is. EEA-105 and 106. That's in the annex of the electrical engineering building. You go down to the building's basement and out the tunnel that connects to the annex."

After a few wrong turns in the basement, Jake finally stood at the double doors marked 105/106 and waited for the red light to stop flashing. The tunnel was narrow; insulated pipes ran along its low ceiling. Jake could hear water gurgling along one of them.

Dr. Cardwell had told him to look into the MHD work.

"If you want a good science-based issue for Tomlinson's campaign," Lev had insisted in his mild, soft-voiced way, "MHD power generation is just what you're looking for."

A sudden roar erupted from the other side of the closed doors, like a rocket taking off. Jake flinched with surprise. The doors rattled, and he could feel the floor vibrating beneath his feet.

Just as suddenly as it started, the howling roar cut off. And the red light went dark.

Jake rapped on the door. Nothing happened. He knocked again, harder. The door suddenly swung open and a sour-faced man frowned at him.

"Whattaya want?"

The guy was about Jake's height, wiry build, thinning sandy hair. He wore a checkered tan work shirt, cut-off jeans, and moccasins without socks. His light brown eyes looked pugnacious, almost angry.

"I'm Jake Ross," he explained. "I'm here to see Tim Younger."

"That's me." Younger did not move from the doorway. Past his shoulder Jake glimpsed a couple of technicians fussing over what looked like a pile of copper plates. A strange, almost sweet odor wafted from the lab; it was somehow familiar, yet Jake couldn't place it.

"Professor Sinclair told me that you're running the MHD experiments."

Younger's scowl eased a little. "The prof sent you over?"

"Yes. I want to—"

"Hey, Jake! What're you doing down here?"

Jake recognized Bob Rogers from the party at Tomlinson's house, several days earlier. He came up beside Younger.

"Come on in," Rogers said, pulling the door open wider. To Younger, he said, "It's okay, Tim. This is Jake Ross. He's in the astronomy department."

Younger stepped back, still looking slightly suspicious. "I thought you might've been another one of those pissants from the safety office."

"No," Jake said, stepping into the laboratory. "I'm an astronomer."

"So what are you doing down here?" Younger asked, almost truculently. "We don't do any stargazing here." His voice had an adenoidal twang and an accent that sounded to Jake like Boston or maybe Down Maine.

"I came to see this MHD generator you're working on," Jake said.

Rogers smiled boyishly and gestured. "Well, there it is."

The MHD generator was hardly impressive. The man-tall stack of copper plates stood in the middle of the lab. A squat cone-shaped contraption that looked to Jake a little like a rocket nozzle was stuck into one side of the pile and a stainless steel tube ran out from the other. A tangle of metal pipes and plastic tubing coiled all over the apparatus like the arms of an octopus. Thick wiring festooned the whole assembly, hanging from the ceiling, snaking along the floor. Jake recognized a big green tank of liquid oxygen off in one corner, a thin whiff of white vapor seeping from its top. Beside it stood what looked like a coal hopper, blackened with soot. That's the smell, Jake realized: burning coal.

"That's it?" he asked.

"That's the rig," Rogers said genially. Pointing, he explained, "Powdered coal and liquid oxygen in at this end, they're burned in the combustion chamber, the plasma shoots through the channel inside the magnet there and produces a dozen kilowatts or so."

"Fourteen, this morning," one of the technicians called from the other side of the generator.

"You said plasma?"

"Ionized gas," Rogers answered. "It's hot enough for some of the atoms to have their electrons knocked off them, so the gas becomes electrically conducting."

"I'm an astronomer. I know what plasma is," Jake said. "The stars are plasma. Most of the universe is plasma."

Roger chuckled good-naturedly. "Yeah, right. But the plasma we get from burning coal is only lightly ionized."

Younger spoke up. "We add potassium to the mix in the combustion chamber to increase the ionization."

"And the plasma gives up electrical energy as it goes through the magnetic field?" Jake asked.

Rogers said, "Right. The plasma's our armature, like the coil of copper wire in a normal power generator."

Jake looked from Rogers's friendly smile to Younger's cantankerous scowl. "An armature," he said, questioningly.

Patiently, Rogers explained, "In a conventional power generator, you spin a bundle of copper wires in a magnetic field. The copper conducts electricity, and as it spins through the magnetic field it generates an electrical current."

"Faraday figured that out in the eighteen-thirties," Younger added.

"And the bundle of copper wires is the armature," Jake said, a little uncertainly.

"Right," Rogers agreed. "In the MHD generator, though, the stream of hot plasma is the armature."

With growing understanding, Jake said, "I get it. But the conductivity of the plasma must be a lot lower than the conductivity of copper wire."

"Yeah, but the plasma blows through the magnetic field at supersonic speed," Younger said, jabbing a forefinger at Jake's chest.

"Like the exhaust from a rocket engine," said Rogers.

"Damned sight faster than any copper armature," Younger emphasized.

"I see," Jake replied.

"MHD generators are a lot more efficient than the generators that the electric utility companies run," Rogers said.

Younger huffed. "They're using the same technology Edison used, for crap's sake. Forty percent efficiency. Same as Edison got, within a couple of percentage points."

"This little baby," Rogers said, glancing at the MHD generator, "runs between sixty and sixty-five percent. And she's only a little experimental job. The bigger an MHD generator is, the more efficient."

"Wait a minute," said Jake. "You're telling me that this experimental rig is already fifty percent more efficient than the generators our utility companies use?"

Rogers nodded, smiling. Younger's face twitched into an expression that was as close to a smile as he could get.

"How'd you like to have your electricity bill cut in half?" Younger asked.

PROFESSOR ARLAN SINCLAIR

His head spinning from the facts and figures that the two men were throwing at him, Jake said, "Look, I'm supposed to have lunch with Professor Sinclair. Why don't you come along?"

Younger frowned. "I bring my lunch and eat here. I've got no time to go out to the cafeteria and socialize."

"I'll go with you," said Rogers. "I need to talk to the prof anyway."

As they walked along the low-ceilinged tunnel that connected to the main building of the electrical engineering department, Rogers said gently, "Don't get the wrong impression about Tim. He's a typical Yankee sourpuss, but he's a good man."

"If you say so," Jake replied.

"He was in charge of the rig when it blew up last year. Killed one of the technicians. Knocked the roof off the shed. They found pieces all over the campus."

"Geez!"

"We were lucky nobody else got hurt. The technician was a university employee, not a student."

Jake almost said, *Expendable,* but caught himself in time.

"Tim's a hands-on guy, not a *theoretiker* like me," Rogers went on.

"You're a physicist?"

Rogers nodded. "And Tim's an engineer. He's not on the faculty, he's an employee of the university. I don't pull rank on him or anything like that, but he feels the difference all the time."

Shrugging as they stepped through the door out into the late-morning sunshine, he added, "Then there's the family connection.

I'm descended from Major Rogers, of Rogers's Rangers. The French and Indian War and all that."

Jake felt awed. "Christ, I just saw an old movie on TV about that. Spencer Tracy played Major Rogers!"

Grinning, Rogers said, "Tim's from a working-class family north of Boston. Some of the guys kid him that he's descended from the Younger Brothers, the old frontier outlaw gang. It gets under his skin sometimes. That's why he can be kind of prickly."

"So I don't make any bank robber jokes in front of him."

"I wouldn't advise it."

As they walked across the campus to the faculty cafeteria, Rogers explained more about the MHD generator. A power generator's efficiency depends on three things: the conductivity of its armature, the speed with which the armature moves through the magnetic field, and the strength of the magnetic field.

"Our armature is the plasma flowing along the channel," Rogers said. "Conductivity's a lot lower than copper wire, but the supersonic flow speed more than makes up for that. And our big rig uses a superconducting magnet: a lot stronger field strength than the electromagnet we've got on the little baby."

"Your big rig?" Jake asked.

Rogers looked slightly surprised. "You don't know about the big rig?"

"No."

"If you've got some time after lunch I'll take you over to see it."

"I've got a lecture class at two," Jake said.

Tilting his head slightly, Rogers replied, "Okay, some other time."

They entered the cafeteria building, already noisy with crowds of students chattering away as they lined up at the counters, dishes and silverware clattering as they loaded trays from the displays of sandwiches, pizza, and hot meals. Jake followed Rogers up the stairs to the top floor and the faculty cafeteria, much quieter and less crowded. The woman at the reception desk showed them to a private room, where a table big enough for eight was set with four places.

"I guess the prof is bringing somebody with him," Rogers said.

"Should we go get our lunches or wait for him here?" Jake wondered.

Rogers thought it over for a few seconds, then suggested, "Whyn't you get what you want while I wait here for him?"

"Okay. Can I bring you something?"

"Diet Coke."

Jake nodded and left the private room. He passed several people carrying loaded trays coming the other way but didn't turn his head to see if any of them went into the room where Rogers was waiting.

He picked up an unidentifiable sandwich and two Diet Cokes, then found that he couldn't pass up the dessert table's apple cobblers. By the time he returned to the room where Rogers was waiting, Professor Sinclair was sitting at the head of the table, deep in discussion with the physicist. And a good-looking young brunette was seated at the professor's right.

Both men got to their feet as Jake put his tray on the table.

"Professor, this is Jake Ross, from the astronomy department," said Rogers.

Professor Arlan Sinclair was a big man, several inches taller than Jake, barrel-chested and broad in the shoulders. His hair was a thick leonine mane of silver that curled down to his collar. He wore a navy blue blazer and a rep tie of the university's red and gold. His face was fleshy, but handsome in a dramatic, movie-star way. He smiled guardedly as he took Jake's proffered hand in a firm grip.

"And to what do we owe the honor of your presence?" Sinclair asked, in a tone that was almost imperious. His voice was deep, resonant. The kind that won arguments.

"Dr. Cardwell told me to take a look at the MHD generator work," Jake said.

Sinclair's smile faded. He sank into his chair; Jake and Rogers also sat. The young woman looked curious, but said nothing.

"*Doctor* Cardwell?" Sinclair asked, practically sneering. "You mean the fellow who runs the planetarium?"

"Yes," said Jake. "Leverett Cardwell."

"He bought his doctorate from a diploma mill," Sinclair said, in a disgusted grumble.

"That's not so!" Jake blurted.

"Check it out for yourself," said Sinclair.

Jake stared at the professor, not knowing what to say.

Bob Rogers broke into the cold silence. "Cardwell does a damned fine job at the planetarium."

Sinclair nodded. "Oh, he's a good showman, I'll grant you that. But he's not a scientist. Not at all."

Holding on to his rising temper, Jake repeated, "Dr. Cardwell advised me to look into the MHD generator work you people are doing."

"For what purpose?"

The brunette spoke up. "Dr. Ross is going to be Franklin Tomlinson's science advisor." Turning to Jake, she added, "Isn't that so, Dr. Ross?"

She was really very good-looking, Jake realized. Oval face, dark brown hair that fell straight back past her shoulders, in a practical, no-nonsense sweep. Her eyes were dark, too, deep brown, calm and serious; slightly almond-shaped, kind of oriental, exotic. She was wearing a blue and white blouse with a cut-out neckline, deep enough to be interesting while still being modest. She impressed Jake as a sincere, thoughtful young woman: intelligent and strong-minded.

For a long moment Jake didn't reply. Not until she smiled slightly and repeated, "You *are* joining Tomlinson's campaign staff, aren't you, Dr. Ross?"

"Jake," he heard himself say.

"Jake."

Rogers broke the spell. "Jake's an assistant professor in the astronomy department."

"I'm Glynis Colwyn," the brunette said. "I'm from the business school. I'm working with Professor Sinclair, doing a case study of the MHD program for my thesis." Her accent was strange, intriguing: almost like a British inflection, but not quite.

Rousing himself at last, Jake said, "Uh . . . to answer your question, Ms. Colwyn—"

"Glynis."

"Okay . . . Glynis. To answer your question, I *am* seriously considering advising Mr. Tomlinson if he runs for the Senate next year."

Sinclair looked from Jake to Colwyn and back to Jake again. "I still don't understand what that has to do with our MHD work."

"Tomlinson needs a science issue to campaign on," Jake said.

"Our MHD work is a research program," Sinclair said, "not a political issue."

"But it could be," Glynis said. "You could get a lot of attention for the program if Tomlinson picks up on it."

Sinclair shook his head. "Do we want that kind of attention? I don't think so."

"But—"

"I don't want our work turned into a political football," Sinclair insisted.

"It might be helpful, you know," Rogers said. "We're going to need a big wad of funding to build a pilot plant one of these days."

"That's far in the future."

Glynis said, "Isn't it about time that a politician made scientific research one of his priorities? God knows that Senator Leeds wouldn't recognize a test tube from a . . . a . . ."

"Prophylactic?" Rogers suggested.

Jake, Rogers, and Colwyn burst into laughter. Sinclair stared at them coldly.

JACOB ROSS'S OFFICE

By the time he reached his own office in the astronomy building Jake was sopping wet. An afternoon thunder shower had brewed up while he was giving his Introduction to Astronomy lecture to an auditorium full of bored freshmen. Most of them were taking Astronomy 101 to fulfill their curricular requirement for a science course. They were more interested in texting and tweeting on their cell phones than in the Copernican theory.

It was pouring when he finished the lecture. Lightning flickered across the clouds and thunder boomed like artillery. Jake stooged around in the classroom building's entrance for as long as he could stand it, then decided to make a dash through the rain to his office.

Now he stood at his office window, wiping his face with a paper towel and trying to straighten his hair while he mulled over his lunch with Bob Rogers and the imperious Professor Sinclair. And Glynis Colwyn. She must be of Welsh descent, Jake thought.

How could MHD be made into a political issue? Jake wondered. Okay, they can build a more efficient power generator. Maybe. If it works. Rogers's little machine only produces a dozen kilowatts. That's not going to change the energy picture.

What the hell am I doing in politics anyway? I'm not a politician. That's Tomlinson's bag, not mine. I don't know why Lev thought it's something I should do.

He sat down in the springy little chair behind his desk. As usual it rolled backward on the hardwood floor until it bumped into the bookcase. Newton's first law of motion, Jake said to himself. Plant your butt on the chair and it rolls away from the goddamned desk whether you like it or not.

His office was little more than a cubbyhole, cluttered with books and journals and test papers waiting to be graded. Tenure, Jake thought. If I get tenure they'll move me to a bigger office, maybe the one in the corner that old Likiovick occupies. He'll be retiring next year. Yeah, like I've got a chance for tenure. In another five years, maybe.

Then his eye caught on the photo of Louise framed on the corner of his desk. Louise. She was smiling at him, that warm, happy smile of hers. Like sunshine. Like wonderful, glorious sunshine.

He turned to look at the office's only window. It was still raining hard. No sunshine out there.

A single knock on his door made him spin around. The woman from Tomlinson's party stepped into his office.

"Dr. Ross?" she asked, with a tentative smile.

He sprang to his squishy-wet feet and desperately tried to remember her name. Amy something . . .

"Ms. . . . uh, Waxman?"

"Wexler." She stepped into the office.

"Wexler," Jake said. "Of course. Amy Wexler."

"That's right."

She was wearing a short skirt that showed her long legs to good advantage. A dripping folded umbrella in one hand and a pocket-sized leather purse in the other. Her blond hair was pinned up, piled artfully on her head, off her graceful neck.

There was only one other chair in the office and a pile of astronomy journals was stacked on it. Jake hurried around his desk, banging a shin in the process, and scooped the journals up.

"Have a seat," he said. "You can just prop your umbrella against the bookcase by the door."

She looked doubtful. "It'll drip on the floor."

"That's okay." He was standing close enough to catch the fragrance of her perfume. Light, flowery. Her blouse was starched white, almost a man's shirt, but it looked awfully fine on her. So many of the students dress like refugees from a Dumpster, he thought; it's good to see a woman make herself look attractive.

Amy Wexler sat on the wooden chair and Jake retreated back behind his desk.

"Mr. Tomlinson sent you?" he asked as he sat down. The chair started to roll, but Jake grabbed the edge of his desk with one hand to stop it.

"Not really," she replied.

"Oh?"

She smiled again, brighter. "I just thought that if you and I are going to be working on Franklin's campaign, we ought to get to know each other."

"Oh."

"I mean, we'd work together much better if we weren't strangers, wouldn't we?"

Jake nodded. "That makes sense."

"So . . . what are you up to? Have you zeroed in on an issue that Franklin can use?"

Jake realized he was biting his lip. Forcing a smile, he said, "I think maybe I have, but it's going to take a little more study before I can tell for sure."

She waited for him to go on.

"It's got to do with power generation. You know, electricity."

"Energy?" she asked.

"That's right. Energy."

"That's a good issue. A strong issue."

Jake bobbed his head up and down. "Well, that's what I'm looking into."

Amy looked pleased. "Senator Leeds is vulnerable on energy. He voted for the cap and trade bill, and he gets big campaign contributions from the oil lobby."

Suddenly Jake felt confused. "I thought big oil was against cap and trade."

She shook her head. "Only on the surface. They know it won't be effective."

"Really?"

With a slightly pitying expression, Amy said, "In politics, Jake, things are not always what they seem. It's not like science."

"I don't know much about politics," he admitted.

"And I know very little about science."

"We both have a lot to learn."

"I guess so."

Jake didn't know what more he could say. He glanced at the photo of Louise, smiling at him.

Amy said, "So why don't we have dinner? You're not busy tonight, are you?"

Jake almost blurted that he hadn't been busy any night for months. But he caught himself in time and replied merely, "No, I'm open for dinner."

"Good." Amy fished in her purse and pulled out a card. "Here's my address and phone number. My e-mail address, too."

Jake took the card and asked, "What time do you want me to pick you up?"

She hesitated a moment. Then, "I'll meet you at the restaurant. Ristorante Amore, in center city. Do you know it?"

"I'll find it," Jake said. "What time?"

"Seven? Is that all right?"

"Seven is fine."

She stood up and put on her cheerleader's smile. "See you at seven, Jake."

Amy Wexler picked up her umbrella and stepped out into the hall-way, leaving Jake standing behind his desk as the office door slowly swung shut. After many minutes he turned and looked out his window. The rain had stopped and sunshine was breaking through the clouds.

RISTORANTE AMORE

'**ve** never been here before," Jake said as he and Amy Wexler entered the restaurant.

"I think you'll like it," she replied. "The food's wonderful and the service is really great."

Jake had expected that a posh midtown restaurant would have its waiters in tuxedos, but the maitre d' wore a tight-fitting black T-shirt and matching narrow-legged slacks. He was a suavely handsome young man who knew Amy well enough to give her a brotherly hug. She pecked at his cheek and said something to him in Italian.

"This is Stefano," Amy introduced. "He's the owner."

Stefano offered his hand and a gleaming welcoming smile.

"If there's something you want that isn't on the menu," Amy explained as Stefano led them to their table, "just ask our waiter and they'll fix it for you."

Jake was impressed. The restaurants he frequented down in his neighborhood were mostly hamburger joints. There was the local piano bar, but since Louise's death he hadn't been able to go there. Not alone. Not with Chuck playing the same old songs about love and loss and longing.

Ristorante Amore was indeed posh, Jake decided. Even though the waiters worked in their shirtsleeves. Not like the restaurants you see in the movies, he thought, but pretty damned classy. At least the waiters all wore ties. Soft music purred from speakers in the ceiling; the conversations from the other tables were a muted buzz. The place smelled of spices and strong coffee.

And Amy was right about the food. It was first-rate. At her urging he tried the calamari; he'd never eaten squid before. Then a steaming bowl of pasta.

As he clumsily twirled his fork in an attempt to wrap a few strands of spaghetti around the tines, Amy said, "You know, in all honesty, I ought to warn you."

Jake glanced down at his lap and saw that his napkin was in place. "Warn me? About what?"

She hesitated a moment, appraising him with shrewd, probing eyes. They were grayish green, Jake realized. Hazel eyes: cool, like a lake up in the mountains.

At last she said, "Politics can be a dirty business."

"So I've heard."

"It can get very unpleasant, Jake. Are you ready to face that?"

He put his fork down and stared at her across the table. "I'm just giving Mr. Tomlinson some advice about science. I won't be involved in the political side of things."

"Everybody's involved in the political side, Jake," Amy said, very gravely. "Once you're in, you're in all the way."

Jake shook his head. "I don't think—"

She interrupted, "Jake, you know there are gambling casinos in this state."

"On the Indian reservations, yeah, I know."

"Who do you think runs them?"

"The tribes, I guess."

Amy gave him a *don't be so naïve* look.

Jake caught her meaning. "Oh, come on. You don't mean the Mob."

"Straight out of Las Vegas," she said. "The Mafia. They don't call themselves that anymore, but it's the same thing."

He tried to shrug it off. "Even if it's true, it's got nothing to do with me. I'm just dealing with scientific issues." Then he tried to grin. "Unless calculating gaming odds is considered science advice."

"I'm serious, Jake," she said. And he saw by her expression that she was.

"The Mob."

"It's not like *The Godfather*, but these people are real and they're in Senator Leeds's camp."

Jake spread his hands. "I still don't see what that's got to do with me."

Leaning forward slightly, Amy explained, "Leeds supports their casino operations. They support Leeds. If you come up with an issue that gives Franklin an edge, they won't like it."

"Are you trying to scare me off?"

"I'm trying to show you the whole picture. You have a right to know what you're getting into."

He leaned back in his chair, staring at her. She looked completely earnest, intent.

"Look," Jake said, "I've lived with wiseguys all my life. In school they used to beat me up for my lunch money. Or because I got better grades than they did. Smart kids had to play dumb so they didn't show up those bastards."

"In school? You mean, like high school?"

"Grammar school. They start young. I stayed as far away from them as I could. One of the reasons I took to astronomy was that they had nothing to do with it. I could spend my time in the planetarium and be away from them."

Amy shook her head slightly. "If you work on the Tomlinson campaign you might not be able to keep away from them."

"Thanks for the warning."

"What are you going to do about it?"

Jake thought it over for all of two seconds. Looking into Amy's hazel eyes, he said, "Nothing."

"Nothing?"

"I can't let them run my life, Amy. And besides, I don't think I'll be important enough to Tomlinson for them to even notice me."

Very seriously, she asked, "But if you do become important enough . . ."

He shrugged. "We'll cross that bridge when we come to it."

Amy broke into a happy smile. "That's wonderful, Jake. You're wonderful."

Before he could think of something to say, their waiter came to the table and gestured to their half-eaten entrées. "Is everything all right?"

"It's fine," Jake said.

"Lovely," said Amy.

She didn't mention politics again for the rest of the dinner. When the check came, Amy insisted that the Tomlinson campaign would pay. Jake sat there feeling as if everyone in the restaurant were staring at him, allowing the woman to pay.

As they left the restaurant and walked across the dimly lit parking lot, Amy pointed out her car: a silver BMW.

"That's a lot of automobile," Jake said, impressed.

"My one extravagance," she said. "My apartment's just a one-bedroom flat."

Jake thought of his own seedy place downtown.

She unlocked the car with a beep of her remote key, then turned back to Jake. He realized that she was almost his own height in her heels. In the shadows of the parking lot, he could see her eyes gleaming.

"Thanks for a lovely dinner," she said.

"I should thank you."

"Thank Franklin."

"I'd rather thank you."

She stepped close enough to touch. "I really did enjoy this evening, Jake."

His arms slipped around her slim waist. "I did, too."

She lifted her face toward his and he kissed her.

"We'll have to do this again," Amy breathed. "Real soon."

"Next time I pay."

She laughed. "You're so serious about everything!"

"Yeah." He kissed her again. Then she disengaged and turned to open her car door.

"Okay, next time it's your treat," she said, then ducked into the car.

Jake watched as she backed the car out of its parking space and turned it past him toward the exit. He waved good-bye when her headlights swung over him. Then he walked to his own beat-up Mustang convertible. He wondered where he could take Amy for dinner. Not in my neighborhood, he realized. Not in my neck of the woods.

THE BIG RIG

Jake spent the weekend scrolling through every Internet source he could find for information about MHD power generation. He found it hard to concentrate on the words and data, though. His mind kept drifting back to Amy Wexler. Tomlinson had been right: Politics is a good way to meet women.

What he learned was that there had been abortive MHD generator programs in the United States, Russia, China, Japan, and even Australia. The American work dated back to the 1960s. None of the programs had amounted to much. The Russians actually fed power from their prototype MHD generator into the Moscow electrical grid—but not for long. For some reason, all of the previous MHD power generation programs had faded into failure.

Bob Rogers had invited him to see the "big rig," as the physicist called it, which was located off campus, up in a mining town in the foothills. So Monday morning Jake drove out of town, guided by the GPS system he had bought two years earlier at Circuit City's going-out-of-business sale.

Lignite was a gray, run-down town, little more than a crossroads between two secondary state roads, with a gas station on one corner, a dreary motel across from it sporting a faded sign that proclaimed VACANCY, a cinder-block post office, and a dilapidated diner rusting away under the summer sun. Sad, empty-looking houses and shops ran for a few blocks down both streets, then abruptly ended in wind-blown sagebrush. A forlorn bird circled in the empty bright sky: a hawk or maybe a buzzard, Jake didn't know which.

Feeling apprehensive, Jake parked in front of the diner and got out of his Mustang. The old clunker looks almost good compared to this dump, he thought. Two other cars were parked there, one of them a dust-coated highway patrol cruiser. A glance at his wristwatch showed he was almost ten minutes early for his meeting with Rogers. The sun felt warm enough for him to peel off his tan sports jacket and toss it back in the car, even though the breeze sweeping down from the hills was cool.

Jake looked around. Nothing much to see. A few buildings along the two streets, no traffic at all. The foothills rose off in the distance, turning brown from lack of rain. Beyond them were the bare granite mountains, purple-blue in the distance, shimmering with heat haze. Nothing but miles and miles of miles and miles, Jake thought. He half expected to see John Wayne striding down the dusty road, heading for a shootout at high noon.

Helluva place to put a high-powered research facility. Then he grinned to himself. Rent must be pretty damned low. And if anything blows up here the news media will never hear about it.

He spotted a rooster tail of dust approaching from the direction of the foothills. Jake watched it come nearer and resolve itself into a big, boxy Land Rover, caked with road dust. It pulled up into the parking lot, dwarfing Jake's Mustang, and out stepped Bob Rogers with a big grin on his face. He was wearing tan chinos stuffed into tooled black cowboy boots, and a splashy red and white western-cut shirt with snaps instead of buttons.

"Welcome to Lignite!" Rogers called.

Rogers led him into the diner for an early lunch.

"Tim won't start today's run until one o'clock," Rogers said.

The diner was almost empty, only an overweight state highway patrol officer sitting at the counter, a heavy pistol hanging at his bulging hip, two-way radio clipped to the epaulette of his shirt. Rogers slid into the nearest booth; Jake sat across the cracked, stained table. The bleach-blond waitress was plump, too, and bosomy, but the scrambled eggs and crisp bacon were surprisingly good, Jake thought. The coffee was weak, but what the hell. Rogers talked about the town all through the meal.

"Used to be a thriving mining town, back in my grandfather's day. Coal trains a hundred cars long would chug up the rail line every day. But then the country started switching to oil for heating, and the environmentalists found out that high-sulfur coal causes acid rain and old Lignite just faded up and almost blew away." Rogers didn't seem upset by the town's parlous history. "Great place to grow up, though. Especially if you like riding."

"You grew up here?"

"Yeah. We still have a rodeo, every Fourth of July."

Jake nodded. A rodeo. The big event of the year in swinging downtown Lignite.

"We're burning high-sulfur coal right out of the old Lignite mine," Rogers said.

"Despite the environmentalists?" Jake asked.

"That's the whole point. In the MHD generator we can extract the sulfur compounds in their gaseous state before they get out of the exhaust stack. The rig is environmentally clean!"

"So there's no pollution coming out the stack?"

"Nothing but some nitrogen compounds and cee-oh-two."

"Carbon dioxide is a greenhouse gas."

Rogers shrugged. "Yeah. The EPA has a program to sequester cee-oh-two; pump it underground so it doesn't get into the atmosphere and contribute to global warming."

"I've read about that."

"The big rig runs at almost seventy percent efficiency, calculating from the amount of fuel in and the amount of electrical power out."

"Seventy percent?"

Grinning, Rogers said, "We'll do better than that."

"Seventy percent is pretty damned good."

Rogers grabbed the check when it came, over Jake's faint protest. Then he slid out of the booth and said, "Come on, let's go check out the big rig."

Once outside again, Rogers told Jake to follow his Land Rover. "It's a straight shot out to the test shed. You can't miss it."

Jake went to his Mustang. It was baking hot inside. He thought about putting the convertible's top down but decided against it. Instead he rolled down the windows and turned the air-conditioning on full blast.

He watched Rogers carefully back his dust-caked Land Rover out of its parking space. Jake thought the big wagon looked as heavy as a tank. Suddenly Rogers gunned it up onto the road and took off like an Indy 500 racer. Jake pulled out of the parking lot, bounced up onto the road, and leaned on the Mustang's accelerator pedal to catch up. All he could see of the Land Rover was a cloud of gritty dust. It was so thick that Jake started to cough; he rolled his windows up.

They were past the town in a minute, out onto the flat, arrow-straight road. Nothing on either side but low-lying sagebrush, not even a tree. Then Jake saw in the distance a square structure; it looked something like an oversized shed made of corrugated steel.

They pulled up at the parking lot in a screech of gravel and dust. Jake saw that the facility was indeed a big corrugated metal shed. Must get damned hot in there, he thought.

"Here we are!" Rogers said, grinning like a kid as he stepped down from his van and led Jake toward the building.

Pointing toward the Land Rover, Jake groused, "That thing must burn a lot of gas."

"It's an LR-4," Rogers replied. "Plenty of cubes under its hood. Gets me through the snow when a car like yours would get stuck."

Jake nodded grudgingly as they entered the metal building. Inside, it was just one big open space, a test cell, with the bulky MHD generator and its associated gear almost filling it. Jake was surprised that the place was pleasantly air-conditioned. Half a dozen technicians in grimy lab coats that had once been white were gathered off to one side of the space. Rogers waved hello to them without bothering to introduce Jake.

"There she is," Rogers said, pointing like a proud father.

This MHD generator was much larger than the apparatus on campus. Its central core was nearly ten feet high and even more in length. Instead of a stack of copper plates the core was a glistening metal tube, studded with small protrusions that were connected by color-coded wires to an electrical bus standing on long metal legs above the rig. A much larger oxygen tank stood at the right, alongside what was obviously a coal hopper. Another tank, stainless steel, stood next to them.

"Liquid nitrogen," Rogers said, his voice strangely subdued. "For the superconducting coil. It doesn't need any electrical power input once it's activated. Saves us a big chunk of megawatts."

"How much power does this rig put out?"

"We've had it up to thirty-five megawatts. Our aim is fifty. Tim wants to goose it up to seventy-five."

Jake felt impressed.

"Over there, on the aft end of the rig, is the equipment for separating the sulfur compounds. Works like a spectrometer, same principle."

"Oh," said Jake, "like the GCMS on some of the Mars probes."

"GCMS?"

"Gas chromatograph mass spectrometer. They analyze the Martian atmosphere, samples of rocks, that kind of thing."

Rogers nodded, with a grin. "Yeah, sort of like that. Except we're dealing with tons of plasma flow, not milligrams."

"Off-the-shelf equipment?" Jake asked.

"Pretty much. We've had to tinker with it a little, but it's pretty much standard gear. No new inventions needed."

"And the carbon dioxide sequestering?"

With a slight shake of his head, Rogers replied, "We don't do that. But when we're ready for a prototype power plant, the EPA can supply us with a contractor for that part of it."

Jake's eyes followed the heavy cables snaking out from the core of the MHD generator. They led to a boxy metal structure: tall, square, grayish green.

"And what's that?" he asked.

"Inverter," said Rogers. "The generator puts out DC power. The inverter converts it to AC, the kind of electrical current that the utility industry uses. All your household appliances, electric motors, heaters— they all run on alternating current."

A new question popped into Jake's mind. "What do you do with all the megawatts you generate?"

"Dump it."

"Dump it?"

"Yeah. We run it into a bank of resistors out behind the shed. Heats 'em up pretty good."

"You don't use the electricity for anything?"

With a shake of his head, Rogers answered, "No. Not yet, anyway."

Rogers led Jake to a control booth set behind a thick glass partition. A metal panel studded with dials and switches stretched along the partition and a heavy wooden back wall carried dozens more gauges.

"When the little rig blew up last year," Rogers said cheerily, "the fire was so hot it melted the gauges on the wall."

Jake noted a single fire extinguisher standing in the corner. That won't do much good if this rig blows, he thought.

Pointing upward, Rogers said, "We put blast doors into the roof. If she blows, the doors swing open and let out most of the explosion's force."

Jake felt far from reassured.

For nearly an hour the technicians fussed and tinkered with the rig while Rogers chatted amiably and Jake wondered if he would live through an explosion. Precisely fifteen minutes before one the door from the parking lot banged open and Tim Younger came striding through. His boots were scuffed dusty brown, his jeans faded, his shirt wrinkled. He had a wide-brimmed, flat-crowned cowboy hat pulled down over his narrowed eyes.

Christ, Jake thought, all he needs is a six-gun strapped to his hip.

TRIAL RUN

Barely nodding at Jake, Younger asked, "We ready to run?" as he stepped into the control booth.

"Just about," said Rogers.

Jake watched, fascinated, at the play of personalities. Rogers might be the physicist who laid out the underlying concepts of the MHD generator, the man who designed the big rig, but Younger was the guy in charge here. The technicians followed him around like puppy dogs as he left the control booth and walked slowly around the apparatus, checking every inch of it, every wire and connection. Rogers remained in the control booth with Jake. They were both spectators now.

Finally Younger pushed his hat back on his head and nodded, satisfied.

"Okay," he said to the technicians. "Let's fire her up and see what she can do."

"You've run this rig before, haven't you?" Jake asked Rogers, almost in a whisper.

"A couple dozen times."

"He acts like it's the first time they've tried it."

With a wry little smile, Rogers said, "For Tim it's always the first time."

Younger came back into the control booth, faithfully trailed by the six lab-coated technicians. All of them male, Jake noted. The booth suddenly felt crowded with all of them jammed in, uncomfortably warm, despite the air-conditioning. Jake could smell the acrid tang of perspiration, and somebody had bathed himself in a heavy, musky aftershave.

"Power on the bus," Younger said, his hat pushed far back on his head. His tone was flat, subdued, but four of the technicians began flicking switches as if their lives depended on it.

"Fuel feed ready," said one of them.

"Oxygen feed ready."

Younger said, "Magnet?"

"Up and running. Full strength."

"Separator?"

"Ready."

Younger scanned the control panel, left to right, then looked through the thick glass partition at the rig, sitting silently before them.

"Start fuel feed."

Jake heard a slithering, grating sound: pulverized coal sliding down a chute.

"Fuel feed on."

"Start oxygen feed."

"Oxy on."

"Igniting burner," Younger said, pressing a stiffly extended finger onto a square red button.

The technician's reply was lost in a roar like a rocket taking off. The building rattled. Jake's hearing blanked out, the noise was so intense. Clapping his hands to his ears, he turned enough so that he could see the gauges on the wall behind them. Dials were ratcheting upward.

Rogers was grinning broadly, hands pressed to his ears. A couple of the technicians had donned earphones; the rest covered their ears against the immense, bone-jangling noise. Younger stood like a statue, though, staring at the rig as it roared with the throats of a million dragons. The seconds stretched. Jake saw that the technicians also stood frozen at their posts, gaping at the MHD generator through the quivering glass partition. He himself stood rooted, frozen, nailed to the floor by the sheer overwhelming *power* of the generator's roar. The MHD generator was unchanged to his staring eyes; Jake could see no flame, no motion at all except the trembling insistent vibration that made the very air shake and rattled his eyes in their sockets. His breath caught in his throat.

Then Younger stabbed the same finger at the same red button. The noise shut off abruptly. The vibrations stopped. All the gauges ran down to zero. Jake cautiously took his hands off his ears. Everything sounded muffled; Jake felt like his head was underwater. He squeezed his eyes shut and reopened them. Nothing had changed, and yet . . .

Younger was beaming. He turned to Rogers and they slapped a high-five.

"Forty-eight megawatts!" Jake heard Younger's delighted shout, but it was smothered, as if his ears were swaddled in cotton.

The technicians all looked happy, big grins as they flicked switches and pecked at buttons on the control board.

Rogers had pulled out a pocket calculator. He looked up and down the controls, tapping on its keypad.

Jake's ears were ringing. He remembered going with Louise out to a pistol range, years ago. Even with earphones clapped to his head the noise of the guns firing kept his ears ringing for days afterward. Louise had been impressed that Jake hit the target nearly dead-center with most of his shots. She punched three holes through the tin roof of their shelter when she tried to fire an automatic.

"Seventy-two percent," Rogers yelled, showing his calculator's tiny screen to Younger. It sounded to Jake as if the man was speaking from the bottom of an echoing well.

Younger was all smiles. "We're getting there," he said. "We're definitely getting there."

The outer door swung open, sudden sunlight flooding into the test cell. Glynis Colwyn rushed in, obviously distressed about something.

"I heard the noise from a half mile up the road," she shouted. "Don't tell me you've run the test already!"

GLYNIS COLWYN

A
s Glynis hurried across the test cell toward the control booth, Younger shot a sly grin at Rogers. Once she entered the booth his expression grew stern and he said to her, "Hey, I *told* you we'd run at one o'clock."

Looking upset, she said, "It's only a quarter past one."

Younger shrugged. "The checkout went smooth, so we fired her up."

"I wanted to see the run!"

Another shrug. "Then you should have been here on time."

Glynis frowned at him. She was dressed in a pair of deep blue slacks, with a white short-sleeved pullover that reached to her hips. Jake noticed she had a necklace of turquoise around her throat, and a turquoise bracelet on one wrist. Her long dark hair look disheveled, windblown.

"We'll probably run it again, around three, four o'clock," Younger said.

She looked from his face to Rogers and back again. "I've got to be back at Professor Sinclair's office at three thirty."

"Too bad," said Younger.

"Damn! I nearly broke my butt getting here. My blasted car's having ignition troubles again and I had to get it checked out this morning before I left."

Younger said nothing; he simply turned away from her and started fiddling with some of the knobs on the control board. Rogers looked embarrassed.

Clearly unhappy, Glynis said, "I might as well go back, then."

Rogers made an apologetic, "It's a shame you had to come all the way out here and miss the run."

"Yes," she replied, eying Younger. "Isn't it?"

Jake could feel the high-voltage tension between Younger and Colwyn. Rogers seemed to be in the middle of it.

Colwyn glared at Younger's back, then turned and headed out toward the door.

Once she'd left, Jake half whispered to Rogers, "What was that all about?"

With an uneasy smile, the physicist replied, "Tim thinks she's a spy."

"A spy?"

"From Sinclair."

"But this is Sinclair's program, isn't it?"

"It's *my* program," Younger snapped, looking up from the control board. "I run this fucking show. It's my responsibility. When something goes wrong I get the blame. Okay. But I won't have his fucking snoops sticking their tits into my work!"

Jake involuntarily backed away from Younger's blazing anger.

The engineer muttered darkly, "She sleeps her way into the fucking program and now she's coming up here snooping around."

Rogers gripped Younger's shoulder. "Take it easy, Tim. After all, Sinclair *is* the head of this program."

"So he gets to bed her, big fucking deal," Younger grumbled. "He wants me to produce test results so he can write papers about them and get his name in the journals. Well, if that's what he's after, he'd damned well better leave me alone so I can get the fucking results he wants."

Rogers raised both hands, palms outward, showing his agreement. "I'll talk to the prof about it."

"You do that," Younger growled.

Jake heard himself say, "Uh . . . I'd better get back to town. Thanks for letting me see the run. It's damned impressive."

Younger nodded curtly at him.

"Come on," Rogers said, gripping Jake by the arm, "I'll walk you to your car."

They walked across the now-silent test cell, footsteps clicking against the concrete floor.

"Like I told you, Tim's very proprietary about the test runs," Rogers explained, his voice low. "He still feels bad about the explosion last year. Some people blamed him for that technician's death and Sinclair didn't do much to protect him."

Jake nodded, but replied quietly, "He doesn't do much to make friends for himself, though, does he?"

Rogers chuckled. "No, not Tim. Making friends is not his style. Most definitely not."

They shook hands at the door, then Rogers turned back toward the control booth and Jake stepped outside. It was glaring hot under the bright, high sun. Jake saw Glynis Colwyn sitting disconsolately in her car, a sleek classic Jaguar XJ-S, forest green. Probably more than twenty years old, Jake estimated, but it still looked as if it was in mint condition, beneath its coating of road dust.

"It won't start," she said through the open driver's window. She looked close to tears.

Walking over to her, Jake saw that she was seething with anger and helpless frustration.

"What's the trouble?" he asked. Before she could reply he added, "With the car, I mean."

"The damned electrical system. Every time I turn off the engine the battery dies."

The older Jags have a reputation for electrical troubles, Jake knew. He remembered an old line to the effect that the only people who can afford a Jaguar are those rich enough to have a mechanic ride with them.

"I've got jumper cables in my trunk," Jake said.

"You do?"

With a weak grin, he admitted, "I've had my problems with my old Mustang."

Within minutes he had jumped the Jaguar's battery and Glynis had gunned its engine into a throaty purr.

"Better keep it running," Jake shouted as he disconnected the cables.

"Don't worry. I won't turn off the engine until I reach the dealer. The head of their service department knows my American Express number by heart."

"I'll follow you, just in case. Okay?"

"Terrific."

So Jake drove behind the sleek Jaguar all the way back to the city. Glynis pushed the speed limits and he worried that a highway patrol officer or city policeman might pull them both over. They wouldn't look twice at his old Mustang, he thought, but they love to give tickets to expensive cars.

She made it to the Imperial Jaguar service department's parking lot without being stopped. Jake parked near the street under a shady tree and watched her in earnest, hand-waving conversation with an older, bald, potbellied man. Jake glanced at his wristwatch: two forty-three. He'd get her to her meeting with Sinclair in plenty of time.

Glynis looked surprised once she spotted his drab gray Mustang still in the parking lot. She hurried over to him.

"You waited for me?"

"Sure. Get in. I'm going back to the campus anyway."

She climbed in and clicked on her seat belt. "What's the sense of having a convertible if you don't put the top down?" she asked as he started the engine.

He looked at her. "It's kind of hot, don't you think?"

"No. It's a pretty day."

Together they reached up and disconnected the latches holding the roof to the windshield, then Jake pressed the button and the fabric roof folded neatly back.

"There!" Glynis said. "That's better, isn't it?"

He nodded. She was smiling at him and those almond-shaped eyes of hers looked very enticing. Younger said she's sleeping with Sinclair, he thought. Sinclair had a reputation, despite being married. Can't say I blame him, Jake said to himself. She's a real looker.

He pulled his sunglasses out of the console between the seats as he eased the Mustang toward the driveway that exited onto the street.

"So where are you from?" he asked as they pulled out into traffic.

"West Virginia," she said over the wind and traffic noise. "Morgan-
town."

"Coal miner's daughter," said Jake, picturing another kid struggling to make her way up from poverty, just as he was doing.

Glynis was silent for a moment, then said, "Not exactly a coal
miner's daughter. My father owns the mine."

"Owns it?" Jake's voice went high with surprise.

"I happen to be the grandniece of the Earl of Cardigan. That's
back in Wales. He's impoverished nobility, of course, but the American branch of the family has done quite nicely for itself, thank you."

"Wow."

"How do you think I can afford a Jaguar?"

She was not quite laughing at him, but Jake felt embarrassed
anyway.

"I hadn't thought about that," he lied. The truth was that he'd
figured the Jaguar had been a gift, maybe from Professor Sinclair,
who was rumored to give expensive gifts to beautiful young women.

"I ought to trade it in for a VW," she said. "More reliable."

"But you look so good in the Jag."

"Thank you!"

"So what are you doing with Sinclair? I mean . . . what are you
doing with the MHD program?"

Her smile faded. "I'm working for my MBA, using the MHD
program as the subject for a business analysis." Suddenly she burst
into laughter. "Maybe I should switch to electrical engineering and
figure out what's wrong with my damned car!"

JACOB ROSS'S OFFICE

Jake spent the afternoon in his office, listening to students' problems and complaints. This must be what it's like for a priest when he hears confession, he thought. My mother was sick and I couldn't get to class all week. My computer crashed. I just can't seem to get the hang of the math, Dr. Ross; calculus is like a foreign language to me.

Jake had heard the same sad stories, the same excuses, time and again. He half expected one of the students to claim that his dog ate his homework.

Finally he closed his office door and leaned his back against it, as if afraid another distressed student would try to break in. Visiting hours are finished, he said to himself. The doctor is out.

The phone on his desk rang. Wearily he went over to it and picked it up as he sank into his wheeled chair.

Dr. Cardwell's voice said cheerfully, "Just reminding you that Alice and I are expecting you for dinner at seven tonight."

Relieved, Jake said, "I'll be there."

It was almost ten minutes before seven when Jake pressed the doorbell at Cardwell's snug little cottage. Lev and his wife had lived there for ages; the place always looked spanking new, as if it'd just been repainted. Colorful flower beds along the edges of the neatly trimmed lawn. Graceful shady linden tree leaning protectively over the gray slate roof.

Mrs. Cardwell opened the door and beamed at Jake. She was a tiny woman, with a charming smile and sparkling blue eyes. She had been a clothing model in her youth, and still looked strikingly lovely even though her hair had gone gray. She refused to color it, saying laughingly that she was too vain to try to hide her age. Her first name was Alice, and Lev often hummed the refrain of some old song about an Alice blue gown. Strange, Jake thought, that he could easily call Dr. Cardwell Lev, but he could never address Mrs. Cardwell by her first name.

"I know I'm early, Mrs. Cee," he began.

"Of course you are," she said cheerily. "You've never been late in all the years we've known you."

Jake nodded ruefully. It was a habit he couldn't seem to break; he was always fearful of showing up late, so he usually arrived a little early. Sometimes embarrassingly early. He tried to bolster his self-confidence by remembering Admiral Nelson's claim that he owed his success in life to always being a quarter of an hour early for everything. Some people were nettled when he showed up early; they *expected* their guests to be fashionably late. Jake had never learned how to do that.

Commenting absently on the seasonably hot weather, Mrs. Cardwell showed Jake into the living room. "Lev's in the kitchen," she said. "I'll fetch him for you."

The Cardwells' home always looked to Jake like something out of a children's tale: the rooms were small, ceilings low. There was a fireplace in the living room, dark and empty in midsummer. Bookshelves lined the walls. Upholstered old sofa and armchairs that felt more comfortable to Jake than the secondhand furniture in his own apartment.

Leverett Cardwell stepped into the living room with a pair of tall beer-filled glasses in his hands. He was in his shirtsleeves, but his usual jaunty little bow tie was knotted beneath his round chin.

"Sit down, Jake," he said. "Relax." Handing one of the glasses to Jake, he asked, "How did things go today?"

By the time Mrs. Cardwell announced dinner, Jake had told Lev about the test run and the tension between Tim Younger and Glynis Colwyn.

Cardwell shook his head. "Personalities. They always get in the way of progress."

They sat at the undersized dining room table, barely big enough to hold four, as Mrs. Cardwell brought in a platter of roast pork. It sizzled and smelled delicious. Jake suppressed a grin. In all the years he'd had dinner at the Cardwells he couldn't remember Mrs. Cee cooking anything but roast pork. He wondered if she knew how to cook anything else.

"So they're making progress with the bigger generator?" Lev prompted, once his wife had served out their portions.

With a fork in his right hand, Jake said, "Forty-eight megawatts this morning."

"That's good. How long did the run last?"

"About a minute or so."

Lev nodded absently. "They'll have to do some long-duration runs before they can get the utilities interested."

Jake swallowed a chunk of pork, then said, "If the MHD system really is more efficient than ordinary power generators, that could give Tomlinson an energy plank for his platform. If he runs."

"Oh, he'll run, all right," Lev said. "He's just being careful about when he announces that he's running."

"Politics," Jake muttered.

With his quizzical little smile, Cardwell said, "Politics is the way things get done, Jake. Remember that. A politician is someone who can get free people to work together. It's not always a dirty business."

"I guess so." Jake returned his attention to the food on his plate. The beets were just the way he liked them, slightly tart with vinegar.

"So what are you going to tell Tomlinson?" Cardwell asked.

A vision of Amy Wexler flashed into Jake's mind. "I'll work for him. If he'll have me."

"You have to give him something he can use."

Nodding, "Energy efficiency. MHD can produce more kilowatts per pound of fuel than ordinary generators. Twice as much. We could cut people's electric bills in half."

"That's an exaggeration," Cardwell said, "but not too big a whopper."

Jake disagreed. "Bob Rogers claims—"

Patiently, Cardwell said, "There's a difference between how efficient Dr. Rogers's generator is and how big a cut in electric bills that it might eventually bring about."

Mrs. Cardwell piped up, "But don't politicians always stretch things a little when they're campaigning for office?"

Her husband laughed. "More than a little, Alice, dear. More than a little."

"So energy efficiency is the issue I'll give to Tomlinson," Jake said.

"Energy efficiency," Cardwell echoed.

"And it'll be clean energy, too," said Jake. "No sulfur emissions. No carbon dioxide greenhouse gas."

Cardwell nodded as he picked up his glass of beer. "And what else?"

"What else?"

After a sip of his beer, Cardwell asked, "What did you think of Lignite?"

Mildly surprised at the seeming change of subject, Jake shrugged. "It's pretty much of a dump. Practically a ghost town."

"Lev and I honeymooned there," said Mrs. Cardwell.

"You did?"

Smiling at the memory, she said, "Lignite was a bustling town in those days. And the Main Street Hotel was a lovely place."

"The coal mines were prosperous then," said Cardwell. "My first job, out of college, was in the company's laboratory out there."

"Really?"

"We were developing products out of coal tar."

"That was more than forty years ago," Mrs. Cardwell said.

"You've been married that long?"

"I was barely out of my teens," Cardwell said, grinning across the table at his wife. "Alice was practically jailbait."

She blushed prettily.

"Yes, Lignite was quite a town back then."

Jake nodded and turned his attention back to the remains of his dinner. And then it hit him.

He looked up at Cardwell. "MHD can use high-sulfur coal!"

"That's what I've heard," Cardwell said mildly.

"I mean," Jake said, growing excited, "MHD could make the high-sulfur coal in Lignite profitable again. It could revitalize the state's coal industry!"

Obviously pleased that Jake had finally figured it out, Cardwell said, "Now that's an issue that can get Tomlinson elected to the U.S. Senate."

JACOB ROSS'S APARTMENT

Jake was still bubbling with excitement when he got home. That's what Lev was after all along, he told himself as he parked in his space behind the apartment building and bounded up the steps to the second floor. Push MHD power generation as a way to bring back the state's coal industry. Plenty of votes in that!

He unlocked his front door, flicked on the lights, and rushed to his desk to look up Amy Wexler's phone number. The apartment was small: one bedroom, a living room that Jake had turned into a paper-strewn office, and a kitchen that he barely used except for the microwave oven. When Louise died, he couldn't bear to stay in the home they'd built together, so he returned to the run-down part of town near his old neighborhood and took the first apartment he saw.

Amy's phone was ringing. Jake had her number and e-mail address on his desktop computer screen. After three rings her voice came on: "Hello. I'm not home at the moment. Please leave your name and number and I'll get back to you as soon as I can."

Jake nodded to himself. Of course she'd be out. She's probably having dinner at one of the nice restaurants uptown. She's a busy woman. She's probably got a dozen guys chasing after her.

"Uh, this is Jake Ross," he said, even while his mind was wandering. "I've got an important idea that I want to talk over with you, Amy. I think it could be a winning issue for Mr. Tomlinson."

He left his number and hung up. For a moment he considered calling her cell phone number, but decided he didn't want to disturb her if she was out having dinner with some guy. Sagging back in his creaking desk chair, he surveyed the room. A mess. Newspapers and magazines littered the sofa. The books in his makeshift bookcase were jammed in helter-skelter, with no rhyme or reason. Whenever he wanted a particular book he had to search through all the damned shelves from scratch. Through the open bedroom door he could see that he hadn't bothered to make the bed for several days.

Maybe I should get a housekeeper to straighten up the place once a week, he thought. But he shook his head, dismissing the idea. Not in this neighborhood. That'd be an open invitation to have the place looted.

Not that there's much to steal, he realized. The computer's good. And the TV was new: big plasma flat screen that he'd bought so he could watch football games. Alone. Nobody to disturb his concentration on the game's tactics and strategy.

Christ, I wish somebody was here to disturb my concentration. I wish—

The phone rang.

He snatched it up. Amy's voice said, "Jake, you sounded excited."

"Hi! I guess I am. I think I've got an issue that can get Tomlinson elected."

"Wow! That'd be great. What is it?"

He hesitated. "It's a little complicated . . ."

"Science stuff, huh?"

"It's not just that. It could bring back the state's coal industry, create lots of jobs."

"And votes!"

"I think so."

Her voice took on a new eagerness. "I want you to tell me all about it. I'll be right over."

"Not here! I . . . my place is a mess."

"Don't worry about that, silly. I've got your address. I'll be there in fifteen minutes, maybe less."

Jake swallowed hard. "Okay. It's . . . it's not the best part of town, you know."

"I'm not coming over to look at real estate."

"Well . . . um, there's a parking lot behind the building. Park there. It's safer. I'll meet you down there."

With a light laugh, Amy said, "You're very protective, aren't you?"

"I grew up here, Amy."

"All right. I won't get out of the car unless I see you. Deal?"

"Deal."

Jake launched himself into a frenzy of straightening up his living room. Most of the scattered papers and magazines he toted into the bedroom and stuffed into the clothes closet. He pulled the sheets up onto the bed and smoothed them a little. Shutting the bedroom door behind him, he looked over the place. Not all that bad. Needs a dusting, but what the hell.

Once he stepped out into the darkened parking lot he realized that the night had grown chilly. He looked up at the stars. Not much to see in the glare of the city's lights. He made out Orion's blazing Rigel and its belt of three blue giant stars. Sirius was hidden behind a factory tower. The Perseid meteor shower's due next week, he realized. I could see them a lot better out in Lignite.

A car swung into the parking lot. That's not her Jag, he said to himself. Then he remembered that it was Glynis who owned the Jaguar. Amy drove a silver BMW, and that was her car nosing into a parking slot by the building's rear wall. He hurried over to the car as she turned off the rumbling engine.

Amy opened the door and stepped out, almost bumping into Jake, he was standing so close.

"No muggers out tonight?" she teased.

"You park that BMW out on the street and it'll be stripped by the time you come back for it."

"Really? It's that bad?"

He shrugged, easing a little. "It can be. Sometimes."

"It's chilly," Amy said.

Taking her by the arm, Jake led her to the building's door, up the concrete stairs, and into his apartment.

She looked around. "Cozy."

Jake thought that "cozy" was her word for "rat's nest."

"Can I get you something?" he asked.

"Do you have any cognac?"

He almost laughed. "No. I've got some wine in the fridge. California, I think."

"That'll be fine." She went to the sofa and sat down. Jake saw that she was wearing a short-skirted black dress, with glittering jewelry at her wrists, her throat, and her earlobes. Her thick, dark blond hair framed her face. Her legs were long and shapely.

With an effort he turned his attention to the refrigerator and pulled out the half-gone bottle of chardonnay. He found a pair of clean wineglasses in the cabinet over the dishwasher and carried them to the coffee table in front of the sofa.

As Jake sat and yanked the plastic cork out of the wine bottle, Amy said, "Now tell me about this hot idea of yours."

"It's a way to produce more energy, cleanly, from the kind of coal we've got in this state."

"More energy? Cleanly?"

Nodding as he poured the wine, Jake said, "It's a better way to generate electrical power: MHD power generation."

"MHD?" she asked. "What's MHD?"

"Magnetohydrodynamics."

Her jaw dropped. "Oh my god."

Jake waggled a hand in the air. "Don't let the term buffalo you. Just call it MHD. It could be Tomlinson's ticket to the Senate."

For more than an hour Jake explained the MHD generator to Amy, stressing how it was much more efficient than ordinary power generators.

"And it can burn the kind of high-sulfur coal that we have here, cleanly. They take out the sulfur before it can get out into the environment."

Amy sipped wine and listened. She didn't ask many questions, but whenever she looked doubtful Jake explained that point more carefully. It was a skill he had learned from years of teaching classes. Most students are too embarrassed to ask a question and show their peers that they don't understand something. Jake had learned to recognize that hazy look of confusion or incomprehension and explain the doubtful point without the student having to raise a hand.

At last Jake finished. "That's it," he said, feeling excited about the idea again. He ticked off points on his fingers. "More electrical power. More efficient power generation. Lower electric bills. Clean power, no damage to the environment. Reopen the state's coal mines. Create thousands of new jobs."

Amy looked impressed. But she asked, "This device actually works?"

"I'll take you up to Lignite. That's where they have the big rig. It produced forty-eight megawatts this morning."

"That sounds impressive," she said.

"They'll have to show that it can run for thousands of hours continuously, the way regular generators do," Jake said. "That could be a big hurdle."

Amy shook her head. "Doesn't matter. It doesn't have to work, Jake. It just has to have the potential of working. If Franklin can offer the potential of reopening the coal mines, of creating all those jobs— that'll be good enough, believe me."

"But—"

"I know. You're a scientist and you want it to work. But this is politics, Jake. The promise is more important than the reality."

Even though he didn't want to, Jake frowned at her.

"Don't scowl," Amy said, tapping his cheek lightly. "If this helps Franklin to get elected he'll push for federal funding for the project. You help him, he'll help you."

"That's politics, huh?"

"Yes, it is." She leaned closer. "I think you've done something wonderful, Jake."

"Not me," he said, feeling flustered by the nearness of her. Her perfume was enticing, very feminine. "It's guys like Rogers and Younger . . ."

"You," she said, with a hand on his thigh.

Jake pulled her to him and kissed her. Her lips opened slightly and suddenly he was wrapping himself around her and he didn't give a damn if his bedroom looked like Hiroshima after the bomb.

SEX AND LOVE

Amy's naked body lay curled against Jake, both of them sweaty and sticky-wet beneath the tangled bedsheet. She nestled in his arms, murmuring in his ear.

Half drowsing, Jake blinked his eyes and asked, "What'd you say?"

"I have to go," Amy said, in a whisper.

For a moment he didn't understand. Then, "Leave?"

"Yes."

"Can't you stay?"

Amy pushed herself up on one elbow. Nodding toward the digital clock on the night table, she said, "It's past two. I have a big meeting at nine o'clock."

"So go to sleep," he said. "I'll set the alarm."

"No. I can't." She pulled free of Jake and sat up. "I've got to get back to my place."

"You can use my shower," he said.

"Thanks, but I'll shower when I get home." She slipped out of the bed and started searching in the dark for her clothes.

Jake flicked on the bedside lamp.

"Thanks," she said as she pulled on her panties.

He rolled out of bed and reached for his own clothes.

"You don't have to get up."

He grunted. "You're not going down to the parking lot by yourself."

She smiled at him. "You're very protective."

He said nothing, just watched glumly as she fastened her bra and pulled up the straps. She's really stunning, Jake thought. Trim as a racing yacht.

Once they were both dressed Jake led her down the concrete stairs to the building's back door. It was chilly outside, and the sky had clouded over. He couldn't see a single star.

Amy unlocked her BMW with a beep of the remote key, then turned and kissed Jake lightly on the lips.

"Thank you," she breathed. "It was lovely."

"Thank *you*," he said. And he watched her get into the car, gun the engine, and pull out of the parking lot.

Jake wearily climbed back to his apartment, fumbled with the key, then headed back to his thoroughly roiled bed. Lucky man, he told himself. As he undressed again he thought about Amy's smooth, lithe body. Sitting on the bed, he realized that this was the first sex he'd had since Louise had died. He expected a pang of remorse, but instead he merely said to himself, Well, at least you haven't forgotten how to do it.

But once he fell asleep he dreamed of Louise. He didn't realize he was dreaming. He was sitting in the living room of their home, watching football on television. Louise sat on the big, comfortable sofa beside him, her feet tucked up beneath her, just as intent on the game as he was. A commercial break came on, and she got up and headed for the kitchen.

"Beer?" she asked, over her shoulder.

"Sure," he said.

From the kitchen, Louise called, "Jake, can you come here a minute?"

He got up and went to the kitchen.

But it wasn't the kitchen. It was the morgue where her battered body was laid out on a metal table and the police had taken him there to identify her body and it was her, Louise, her skull bashed in, her face caked with blood, her deep brown eyes open and staring sightlessly.

"They'll have to perform an autopsy," the policewoman was saying. "It's mandatory in accident cases."

Jake stepped to the edge of the table and reached out to close Louise's eyes. The policewoman clasped his wrist.

"Sorry, sir. You're not allowed to touch the body."

"But she's my wife."

"I'm sorry, sir."

And Jake's eyes snapped open. He was soaked with cold sweat. He sat up in the bed, his head hanging, and wished he could cry. He wanted to cry, wanted to let the tears burst out and wash away his grief. But the tears would not come. He was alone, without even tears to ease his agony.

PROFESSOR SINCLAIR'S OFFICE

No," said Professor Arlan Sinclair.

Jake blinked with surprise. "No?"

They were sitting around the circular table that took up one corner of Professor Sinclair's spacious office. A corner office, with big windows that looked out on the distant blue-hazed mountains. Amy Wexler sat on Jake's left, Bob Rogers on his right. Tim Younger sat next to Rogers and Glynis Colwyn sat between Younger and the professor.

It was two days after Amy had gone to bed with Jake. Two days in which their only contact had been a couple of very proper telephone conversations to set up this meeting with the head of the university's MHD program. Two days in which Jake's head spun with the memory of her blithely unrestrained acrobatics in bed. Despite his misery of guilt, his insides quivered at the thought of her, and now she was sitting primly beside him, as if nothing at all had happened, wearing a no-nonsense navy blue business suit.

Sinclair looked as fierce as a flowing-maned lion standing guard over his cubs.

"As I told you before, I will not have the MHD program turned into a political football," he said, with a slight toss of his head. The gesture reminded Jake of films he had seen of President Roosevelt. Had Sinclair deliberately copied FDR's imperious body language?

"I don't think you understand," Amy began.

"I understand perfectly well," Sinclair said, almost truculently. "You want to use our work to get votes for Frank Tomlinson. You have no interest in MHD research itself."

"If Mr. Tomlinson gets elected to the Senate he will push for federal funding for your program. That could mean millions of dollars, Professor Sinclair. Tens of millions."

Sinclair's fleshy face darkened. "And it would turn a well-organized, carefully paced research program into a government boondoggle. I won't have it."

Younger spoke up. "Prof, we could use the Washington money to fund the long-duration tests."

"We can do long-duration tests on the Mark I, here on campus."

"At low power levels," said Younger.

"That's perfectly all right. The plasma physics is the same."

"But the engineering isn't," Younger insisted. "The electrode erosion isn't. The channel integrity isn't."

Rogers jumped in. "Professor, the utility companies won't be impressed by low-power runs. They'll want to see five thousand hours at fifty megawatts, at least."

Sinclair glared at him. For a long moment the big airy office fell coldly silent. Jake could hear the faint whisper of the air conditioner's fan.

At last Sinclair said, "Government funding will bring government regulations. Washington red tape. News reporters hounding us. Is that what you want?"

Rogers began to shake his head, but Glynis said, "What is it that *you* want, Professor? Do you see the MHD program as a perpetual research operation, or do you want to see MHD making an impact on the real world? Do you want to produce electrical power, or research papers for the academic journals?"

Sinclair's eyes flared. Younger looked surprised. Rogers bit his lip.

Amy said, "Professor, I'd like you to meet Mr. Tomlinson and discuss this directly with him. Perhaps he can convince you that he's sincere about wanting to help you to make a success of MHD."

"This is what we need!" Younger blurted out.

Jake spoke up. "I don't know about the rest of you, but I think that creating thousands of jobs is an important thing to do. This is more than politics and more even than research. It's helping people to find employment, to feed their kids, to raise their families."

"Coal miners," Sinclair rumbled.

"And the technicians who run the mining machines," Jake countered. "And the accountants and bookkeepers and secretaries who work in the mining company's offices. And the truck drivers."

"Butchers and bakers," Glynis added, with a grin.

"And supermarket workers," Amy put in.

Sinclair appeared unmoved. "Do you know how many people are killed each year in coal mine disasters?"

"Not as many as the number employed by the mining companies," Jake shot back.

"Won't you at least meet with Tomlinson?" Glynis pleaded.

"Talk it over with him," said Younger. "It won't hurt to talk to him."

Sinclair looked unmoved.

Then Amy said softly, "I would take it as a personal favor to me if you would meet Mr. Tomlinson and discuss the situation, Professor."

Jake turned toward her. The tone of her voice was almost like a little girl's. She had lowered her eyes demurely.

Sinclair squirmed in his chair for a moment, then replied, "I suppose it wouldn't hurt to talk to the man."

Rogers broke into a big grin. Younger nodded as if they had just accomplished an important milestone. Jake saw Glynis turn her attention from Sinclair to Amy and back again.

"Good!" said Amy, suddenly bright and smiling. "Thank you, Professor Sinclair."

Smiling back at her, Sinclair said, "It's nothing."

But Jake thought it was something indeed.

'll set up the meeting," Amy said, once they had left Sinclair's office and were walking down the hallway toward the building's exit and the parking lot out in the summer sun.

Rogers walked along with Amy and Jake while Younger and Glynis Colwyn headed in the other direction, she toward her office, he for his car and the drive up to Lignite.

"How much does Tomlinson understand about MHD?" Rogers asked.

"Not a thing, yet," Amy replied. "Jake's going to brief him."

"I am?" Jake said. "Wouldn't it be better if Bob did? After all, he knows a lot more about this than I do."

Amy shook her head. "No disrespect, Dr. Rogers, but I think you know too much about MHD. Franklin would be overwhelmed if you tried to tell him all the technical details."

Rogers looked hurt. "I can give him a stripped-down explanation."

"Let Jake do it," Amy insisted. Turning toward Jake, she spelled it out. "Go easy on the technical details, Jake. Emphasize that MHD could revitalize the state's coal industry. That's the important point. Franklin will be more interested in votes than kilowatts."

"And the fact that MHD will allow us to reduce our imports of foreign oil," Rogers added.

"Yes, that too," Amy agreed.

"See?" Rogers smirked. "I can be political, too."

The parking lot was baking in the noontime sun. Rogers said good-bye and walked back toward the electrical engineering building and more tests on the little rig.

"How soon can you brief Franklin?" Amy asked Jake.

"I've got to teach my planetary astronomy class at two," Jake said. "I'm free after that."

"Cocktails at the Tomlinson residence, then," she said, all business.

"And dinner afterward?"

She smiled at him. "We'll see."

Then she slipped into her silver BMW and revved the engine to life. Not even a peck on the cheek, Jake said to himself ruefully.

It was slightly after five P.M. by the time Jake got to the Tomlinson residence. It really is a mansion, he realized as he rolled up the paved driveway; an honest-to-god mother-loving mansion. He parked his Mustang on the circular driveway and by the time he'd walked to the front door the white-haired butler already had it open, waiting for him.

"Mr. Tomlinson is expecting you, Dr. Ross. He's at the pool."

"Um . . . is my car okay there?" Jake asked.

"Perfectly all right, sir," said the butler, in a ghostly whisper.

Jake glanced back at the gray convertible; it looked shabby and out of place. So do I, I guess, he thought. Jeans and a short-sleeved polo shirt. Campus informal. He felt decidedly scruffy as he followed the butler through the mansion.

Tomlinson was in orange bathing trunks, stretched out on a re-cliner by the pool, a tall glass of something that looked cool on the little table by his side. Amy sat on the edge of the recliner next to him, bent toward him in earnest conversation. She had shed the business suit for a golden yellow bikini. Her hair was glistening wet, pulled back off her face. At least she's thrown a robe over the bikini, Jake saw, although the short terry-cloth robe hung open as she talked animatedly.

He started to frown, but then he thought, What the hell, I've seen more of her than that. Then he wondered if Tomlinson had too, and his frown returned.

"Jake!" Tomlinson called as he approached them. "Want to take a dip? There are spare suits in the cabana."

It was hot out in the glaring sun, but Jake shook his head. "No thanks. I'm okay as is."

Without straightening up, Tomlinson reached out and picked up the phone on the table next to his recliner. "Charles, a piña colada for Dr. Ross, please."

Jake sat uneasily beside Amy on the edge of the recliner. She smelled of chlorine and cool self-assurance.

Tomlinson gave Jake one of his dazzling smiles. "Amy tells me you're going to win the election for me."

Jake felt his cheeks redden. "I don't know about that, Mr. Tom—"

"Frank. Remember? I call you Jake and you call me Frank."

Bobbing his head, "Okay . . . Frank."

"So tell me about it. Oh, wait, here comes Charles with your drink."

Jake accepted the tall frosted glass from the butler, took a sip, then put it down on the table between the recliners by the telephone.

"It's MHD power generation," he began.

"So Amy told me. And MHD stands for magneto something or other?"

"Magnetohydrodynamics."

Tomlinson reached for his drink without taking his eyes off Jake.

"Think of a rocket engine," Jake said.

"Like the space shuttle?"

Nodding, "Right. Think of those hot exhaust gases going down a tube, a channel. There's a powerful magnet wrapped around the channel. As the gases go through, they generate enormous amounts of electrical power: megawatts per cubic meter. More."

"Okay."

"MHD generators are more than twice as efficient as the generators the electric utility companies use today. MHD can cut consumers' electric bills in half, maybe more."

"Really?" Tomlinson was smiling but he didn't seem all that impressed.

"And MHD generators could burn the high-sulfur coal we have in this state cleanly, without damaging the environment."

"We could reopen the mines," Amy said. "Lots of new jobs. Lots of profits for the mine owners."

Tomlinson said, "Really?" again, but this time there was an edge of excitement in his voice.

"Really," said Jake. "Clean energy. Reduce our imports of foreign oil. Use the energy resources we have right here in the USA. Revitalize the state's coal industry."

Sitting up straighter, Tomlinson muttered, "Several western states have big deposits of high-sulfur coal that are just lying in the ground, unusable."

"We could use them!" Jake enthused. "Energy independence!"

His smile genuinely pleased now, Tomlinson said, "My god, Jake. This could mean more than the Senate. This could carry me to the White House!"

Amy raised a cautioning finger. "The Senate first, Franklin. One step at a time."

He chuckled. "Right. Right. One step at a time. And the Senate would be a good launching pad for a run for the presidency in a few years."

"Onward and upward," said Amy, grinning back at Tomlinson.

Jake wondered how far they had already gone.

DINNER FOR THREE

Tomlinson insisted that Jake stay for dinner, and the three of them ate in the mansion's spacious dining room, huddled at one end of the long polished table beneath a chandelier dripping crystal while the butler and one of the kitchen help brought in various dishes. Another servant poured wine for them, making certain no one's glass went empty.

Jake barely noticed what he was eating, he was too excited about the grand visions that Amy and Tomlinson were unfolding before his eyes.

"I'll get in touch with whoever's running Lignite Mining," Amy said. "You'll want the coal interests aboard your campaign."

"And the environmentalists," Tomlinson said eagerly. "Get their top people to meet with Lignite's top people."

"Great!" she said, waving a fork in the air. "With you in the middle, bringing them together in common cause. Terrific photo op!"

Jake said, "You'll have to meet with Professor Sinclair first."

"Professor Sinclair?" Tomlinson asked. "Who's he?"

Reaching for his wineglass, Jake said, "He's the man in charge of the university's MHD research. And, uh, I'm afraid he doesn't think much of using MHD as a plank in your political platform."

"Really?" Tomlinson looked more intrigued than alarmed. "Why on earth would he feel that way?"

With a shrug, Jake replied, "I'm not sure. He's an academic—"

"We can't have him standing in our way," Amy said.

"I'll persuade him," Tomlinson said easily.

"He's agreed to meet with you," said Amy.

"Good," Tomlinson said. "Fine." He took a forkful of rare roast beef and chewed thoughtfully for a few moments. Then he said, "Jake, could you set up the meeting for me? I'd like to talk to him one on one." With a grin he added, "Give him a dose of my charm."

"Right," said Jake. "Will do."

The conversation moved on to other subjects, other problems, other opportunities: extending the state's old-age benefits, genetically engineered corn, climate change. Amy wondered aloud how the United Mine Workers would react to the promise of MHD.

"They're not as important here as in West Virginia," Tomlinson said. "This is a right-to-work state, remember. No union-closed shops."

Amy countered, "Still, the union's endorsement could be a nice feather in your cap. It could get you national recognition."

Tomlinson nodded. Then he said, "We've got to bring the electric utilities on board."

"That might not be so easy. They've been in Leeds's camp for years."

"Then we'll have to pry them loose from Leeds."

Amy nodded. "We can try."

By the time they had finished the sherbet and fruit cups of dessert, Jake could see that Tomlinson was eager to make MHD not merely a part of his campaign, but the central plank in a platform that stressed change.

Well, he thought to himself, every outsider candidate talks about change. The tough trick is to make the changes real once you get elected.

As they got up from the dining room table Tomlinson excused himself. "I've got a couple of dozen phone calls to make. Get the ball rolling. No time to waste."

"Then you're going to announce that you'll run?" Amy asked.

"In due time. And I'm not just going to run," Tomlinson said, smiling warmly at her, "I'm going to win."

She looked like a true believer staring at the object of her worship.

Tomlinson headed for his office while Amy led Jake to the front door with the butler hovering a discreet few steps behind them.

"Isn't it wonderful?" she said, almost dreamily. "He's going to run. And he's going to win. I just know he will."

Jake shook his head. "Sinclair could be a problem. He seems dead-set on keeping the program out of politics."

Laying a hand on Jake's arm, Amy said, "You set up a meeting with Sinclair. Let Franklin talk to him. He can charm anyone into doing anything."

Jake stared at her. "What's he charmed you into?"

Amy's eyes went wide for a moment, then she laughed lightly. "Jake, you're jealous!"

Suddenly feeling flustered, he replied, "I guess I am."

"And possessive," she added, more gravely.

He had no response for that.

"Do you want me to go home with you? Is that it?"

Of course that's it! he shouted silently. But he couldn't say it out loud. One roll in the hay doesn't mean you own her, stupid. She probably just did it to get you to help Tomlinson.

He heard himself ask, "Are you sleeping with him?"

"Is that important to you?"

"Yes."

She was gazing steadily into his eyes, as if searching for something. Her eyes were almost greenish, he saw, with flecks of brown in them.

"Come on," Amy said. "Let's go to your place. I'll follow your car."

"Are you sleeping with him?" Jake repeated.

"No," she said firmly.

He thought it was a lie. But he didn't care. Not with her standing so close that he could feel her breathing, sense her perfume, take her for his own.

At least for this night.

DECEMBER

ASTRONOMY 101

The months flew by. Jake stayed as close as he could to Bob Rogers, absorbing everything the physicist had to tell him about MHD. They even started meeting at the gym every Wednesday afternoon for an hour of one-on-one on the basketball court. Although Rogers was ten years older than Jake, he was in much better condition; he delighted in running rings around Jake, leaving him puffing and sweaty.

After a few weeks Jake began to do a little better. By god, he told himself, I'm getting back into shape! On the rare occasions when he was on campus, Tim Younger joined them and ran both of them ragged. It was the only time Jake saw Younger laugh.

Jake had expected Tomlinson to declare his candidacy in October, but the man kept postponing the announcement. Part of the problem was that Professor Sinclair was being very evasive about meeting with him.

Glynis Colwyn was working as liaison between Jake and the professor. But while Bob Rogers and even the surly Tim Younger spent hours with Tomlinson and brought him out to Lignite to witness a run of the big rig, Sinclair sent one excuse after another through Glynis, postponing a meeting with the would-be candidate.

"What's the professor's problem?" Jake asked Glynis as they walked across the campus toward the lecture hall where Jake met with his Astronomy 101 class. He was toting his old laptop in its worn leather case on his shoulder; Glynis carried a thick sheaf of papers under one arm.

She shook her head, frowning slightly. "Damned if I know. Arlan just seems . . . well, almost afraid to meet with Tomlinson."

"Afraid?"

She shrugged. It was a bright sunny day, warm for early December with the thermometer almost touching fifty degrees Fahrenheit in the early afternoon. Students were strolling across the campus, some even stretched out on the fading grass, pecking at their cell phones or chatting quietly. Glynis wore a maroon hip-length leather jacket over dark slacks. Jake had pulled up the collar of his lined leather car coat. When Louise had surprised him with it, many birthdays ago, she said its color was called bone. Now Jake thought that it looked like a bone that'd been buried in the ground and dug up again, more than once.

"Bob is gung-ho for Tomlinson," Jake said. "So is Tim, in his way."

"I know. Tim says that Tomlinson can get us the money to build a demonstration power plant: fifty megawatts for five thousand hours. That's what we need to convince the utility companies that MHD can work for them."

"So why is Sinclair hanging back?"

With a shake of her head, Glynis replied, "I've tried to get him to tell me. He just says he's not ready to meet with Tomlinson yet."

"What's he waiting for?"

"If I knew I would tell you."

"We could build the demo plant in Lignite," Jake muttered.

"Couldn't Tomlinson go ahead without Sinclair's blessing?" Glynis asked.

"I suppose. But how would it look if the head of the MHD program comes out against Tomlinson?"

She stopped walking, shocked. "He wouldn't do that! He couldn't!"

"Then why won't he meet with the man? Hell, he won't even talk with me."

"He's refused to talk to you?"

Jake shifted the laptop case from one shoulder to the other as he said, "Every time I phone him, his secretary says I should talk to you."

Glynis smiled. "Well, that's better than nothing, isn't it?"

"A lot better," he admitted. But then, "Still, it's not moving the professor off the dime."

With a weary sigh, she said, "I'll talk to him again."

"Tell him it's urgent."

"I will." She put out her hand and he shook it. Then Glynis headed toward the electrical engineering building and Jake turned off toward the lecture hall.

But not before spending a few moments watching her walk away. She's really very pretty, he thought. I ought to ask her out to dinner or something.

Or what? he asked himself. She's got no interest in you. Why should she? If Tim's got it right, she's shacking up with Sinclair. Somehow, Jake realized that he didn't want to believe that.

Jake had been working closely with Amy Wexler, seeing her almost every day, sleeping with her some nights. Her apartment was in a downtown high-rise condo, very expensive. Jake buried the questions that nagged at him: Is Tomlinson paying for this palace? What does she do the nights she's not with me?

Now a new question arose in his mind: Is Glynis sleeping with Sinclair? No, he told himself. She wouldn't. Tim's wrong about her. He's probably come on to her but she wouldn't do it. She's too independent for that kind of fooling around. Besides, he's a married man. She doesn't need that kind of trouble. Then he added, And she certainly doesn't need an assistant professor of astronomy.

The lecture hall was half filled with listless, bored students, most of them tapping away at their cell phones. Only a handful showed any real interest in astronomy. Those few, those precious few, sat in the auditorium's front row as Jake climbed up onto the stage and set up his laptop's PowerPoint slide presentation.

A couple of the front-row female students were quite good-looking, and they knew it. Trouble on the hoof, Jake thought. Lay a finger on them and they'll scream sexual harassment. But in the meantime they wear low-cut sweaters and lean forward a lot.

"All right," he said into the lectern's built-in microphone. "Let's settle down, shall we? Cell phones off, please."

A palpable wave of discontent spread through the half-empty auditorium.

"Okay," Jake said, forcing a smile. "Today we're going to look at the king of the planets, Jupiter, and its major moons. If there's any place in our solar system that harbors life, it's most likely here . . ."

POLITICS 101

Jake's telephone message light was blinking when he returned to his cramped little office. He punched the button and heard Glynis's voice:

"Jake, I've talked with Professor Sinclair about his avoiding you. He seemed surprised. He said he's tied up for the rest of today, but he's attending a social function this evening and he could talk to you there, if you want to come."

Jake phoned her back immediately. "What's this social function that Sinclair's going to? Where is it? What time?"

She hesitated for a moment. Then he heard, "It's a cocktail party. For Senator Leeds."

"Leeds? He's going to a cocktail party for Leeds?"

"Don't get upset, Jake," said Glynis. "It's a university thing. The senator is dedicating a new wing to the library this afternoon, and the university is giving him a cocktail reception afterward."

"And Sinclair's going to be there."

"It's just a formality. After all, he *is* the dean of electrical engineering this year. It doesn't mean he's in Leeds's camp."

Jake sucked in a deep breath to calm himself. "When and where?" he asked again.

The cocktail reception was in the library's new wing, of course. Jake rushed home to change into a presentable pair of slacks, a fresh shirt, one of his three ties, and his best suede jacket. No time for a shower, still, he was nearly fifteen minutes late; the room where the reception was being held was already filled to overflowing. People were milling around in the hallway, others were strolling through the new wing, admiring the empty bookshelves.

Jake shook his head at the way the university did business. They raised all this money to build a new wing on the library but they hadn't bought the books to fill it. Different budget. Construction money comes out of one pocket, book purchases another—much smaller—pocket. It's stupid, he thought. Anyway, printed books are an anachronism, almost. The students use the Internet to research their assignments.

"There you are!"

Jake turned at the sound of her voice and saw Glynis Colwyn squeezing through the crowd toward him. With Tim Younger a half step behind her, a plastic wineglass in one hand and a relaxed smile on his face.

"Hi," he said to her. Then he added, "I didn't expect to see you here, Tim."

"Glyn invited me," Younger said, looking pleased about it.

Jake blinked with surprise.

Glynis said, "Professor Sinclair is in there," she pointed back into the jam-packed room, "talking with Senator Leeds."

Frowning, Jake said, "I guess this won't be a good time to talk to him about meeting Tomlinson."

"I'm afraid not," she agreed. "I think I've brought you out here for nothing, Jake."

Jake shrugged. "I might as well get a drink while I'm here."

"Follow me!" Younger said brightly, and he turned and plunged back into the crowd.

The noise inside the room was almost painful. Everybody talking at once, nobody really listening. Glynis grabbed Jake's hand and literally towed him along as Younger plowed through the partygoers like a blocking back leading his ball carrier.

And there by the bar was Professor Sinclair deep in conversation with Senator Christopher Leeds. No, not really conversation, Jake saw. Sinclair was talking earnestly, urgently, into the senator's ear. Leeds was nodding as if he were listening, but his eyes were surveying the crowd, swinging back and forth like a pair of radar antennas searching for contacts.

"What'll it be?" the bartender asked, almost shouting to make himself heard.

"Jack Daniel's on the rocks," hollered Jake.

"No Jack," the bartender yelled. "I got Beam or Turkey."

"Jim Beam."

Leeds was a strikingly handsome man, Jake saw. Photographs didn't do him justice. He reminded Jake of a classic statue from ancient Rome: dignified, poised, radiating power and authority. Thick silver hair perfectly styled. Chiseled features, strong jaw. He wasn't as tall as Sinclair, and his figure seemed stocky, almost bloated, as if he were wearing a bulletproof vest under his expensive dark blue suit. He kept nodding and the professor kept talking and Leeds kept scanning the crowd.

"I'm sorry I dragged you out here for nothing," Glynis said, her voice almost hoarse.

Jake took a swallow of whiskey. "Well, why don't we get out of this madhouse and go have dinner."

She glanced toward Younger, who had moved slightly away from the bar. "Tim's already asked me to dinner."

"Tim?"

She nodded. "You could join us. I'm sure he wouldn't mind."

Jake thought that if he had made a date with her he'd sure as hell mind having another guy butt in. "Naw, that's all right. You go along with Tim. Have fun."

Glynis gave him an odd look. "You're sure?"

"Sure."

She edged away, found Younger, and the two of them made their way toward the door. Jake stood there, sipping his whiskey, watching Sinclair and Leeds. A younger man came up and joined the professor and the senator. Slightly taller than the professor and a lot thinner, he still looked enough like Sinclair to be his son.

Jake gulped down the rest of his drink. What the hell, he said to himself. As long as I'm here . . .

He placed the plastic glass back on the bar and pushed through the crowd toward Sinclair. The professor didn't see him coming, he was still intently jabbering into Leeds's ear while the younger man stood uneasily at the senator's other side.

"Hello, Professor," Jake said heartily.

Sinclair turned and recognized Jake. A look of alarm flashed across his beefy face.

"And you must be Senator Leeds," Jake said, forcing a smile.

"That I am," said the senator, extending his hand.

Sinclair said nothing, so Jake introduced himself to the senator. "Jake Ross, astronomy department."

"Pleased to meet you, Jake." But Leeds's eyes were already looking beyond Jake, probing the crowd.

Turning to the younger man, Jake said, "Jake Ross."

"Arlan Sinclair the Third," he replied.

So the professor's a junior, Jake thought as he shook hands with the Third. "Are you with the university?" Jake asked.

Professor Sinclair replied before his son could, "Arly works in Senator Leeds's office, here in the city."

All Jake could think of to say was, "Oh."

PROFESSOR SINCLAIR'S OFFICE

The next morning there was a phone message from Glynis waiting for Jake when he entered his office. He plopped into his springy little chair and pecked out her number.

"He wants to see you," Glynis said, without preamble.

With a bitter smile, Jake said, "Oh, so now *he* wants to see *me*."

"What did you say to him?" she asked, her voice sounding almost hostile. "He's very upset."

"I didn't say sh . . . beans. But I met his son. Who works for Leeds."

"Professor Sinclair's son?" Surprised.

"Who is employed by Senator Christopher Leeds, in his local office here in town."

A long pause. "Well, the professor wants to see you. How is two o'clock this afternoon for you?"

"I'm teaching a class then. What about four?"

"Let me check . . . four thirty? Can you make it then?"

"Yep."

"Four thirty, then. In the professor's office."

"Will you be there?" he asked.

"Of course."

"Good. See you then."

As Jake placed the phone handset back in its receptacle, he wondered how Glynis's dinner with Tim Younger went. That's none of your business, he told himself. Still, he wondered.

He thought about putting in a call to Amy Wexler, to tell her about the Sinclair-Leeds connection, but decided to wait until after he'd talked with the professor. Get the facts first, he decided. Don't go off half-cocked.

Professor Sinclair was sitting behind his heavy mahogany desk when Jake arrived at his office. Jake got the feeling that he had barricaded himself in there as if he were preparing to fight a battle. Through the office's wide windows Jake could see there was a dusting of snow on the distant mountains. The ski resorts will be open for business this weekend, he realized. It's going to be a white Christmas for them.

Glynis had opened the door when Jake knocked on it and now she showed him to one of the university-issue steel-frame chairs in front of Sinclair's desk. Its thin pad felt like concrete. There was another man already seated in the chair beside him, a thin-faced middle-aged man in a light gray suit, balding, dark-jowled, sitting with his legs crossed and his crafty eyes studying Jake.

As Glynis went to the chair at the side of Sinclair's desk, the professor introduced him. "Dr. Ross, this is Ignacio Perez."

Jake turned to shake hands. Perez smiled warmly yet his dark eyes seemed anything but friendly. "Call me Nacho," he said, his voice rasping as if he had a sore throat. "Everybody calls me Nacho."

Jake smiled tightly. "I'm Jake."

"Good," said Nacho. "Good."

"Mr. Perez works with Senator Leeds's reelection campaign office," said Sinclair, with clear distaste.

"Me and the senator go back a long ways," Perez said, grinning. "A long ways."

Glynis spoke up, "Jake is going to be Franklin Tomlinson's science advisor, aren't you, Jake?"

"That's right." Tightly.

Perez broke into a staccato laughter. "That's all right. No problem. I won't hold that against ya."

Sinclair put on a pained smile.

To the professor, Jake said, "I take it, then, that you're supporting Senator Leeds."

Looking more uncomfortable than ever, Sinclair said, "I

wouldn't say 'supporting.' I don't intend to be active in anyone's political campaign."

"Tomlinson wants to make MHD a major issue in his campaign," Jake said. "Will you support that?"

As if reciting a line learned by rote, Sinclair repeated, "I don't intend to be active in anyone's political campaign."

Jake glanced at Perez, then said to the professor, "I imagine your son will be working for Senator Leeds."

"He already is employed by Senator Leeds," Sinclair replied.

"I mean, in his reelection campaign."

Sinclair drew in a deep breath, then replied, "Arly's a grown man. He makes his own decisions."

Glynis spoke up. "Jake, you said you wanted Professor Sinclair to meet with Mr. Tomlinson. . . ."

Nodding, "That's right."

"Tomlinson don't have a chance against the senator," Perez said knowingly.

"I'd still like you to meet him and talk about the issue of MHD power generation," Jake said to the professor.

"I'd be happy to meet with him," Sinclair said.

Surprised, Jake blurted, "That's great! How's your schedule look for the rest of this week?"

Waving a hand as though the matter was trivial, Sinclair said, "Check that out with my secretary. Or better yet, with Glynis, here. She's become indispensable to me lately."

Indispensable, Jake thought. What the hell does that mean?

Shifting his eyes from Jake to Perez, Sinclair asked, "How is your schedule for the rest of the week, Nacho?"

Spreading his hands, Perez said, "I got nothin' but time, Prof. You set your meeting with Tomlinson and I'll be there."

everett Cardwell smiled his quizzical little smile. "What a tangled web we weave," he quoted, "when first we practice to deceive."

Jake was not smiling. "It's a serious problem, Lev. Tomlinson wants to announce his candidacy before Christmas and he wants to make MHD a major issue."

Cardwell and Jake were in the planetarium. The round, domed room was empty between shows, half lit, shadowy, hushed. The soundproofed walls seemed to cushion the air; Jake always felt a little strange, special, in the planetarium, as if he were in a cathedral or a holy shrine. Jake and Dr. Cardwell were sitting side by side in plush reclining chairs on the last row, by the curving wall, next to the control booth, speaking in low, guarded voices. The acoustics in the planetarium were so good that they could have spoken in whispers from across the chamber and still heard each other perfectly well.

"And he doesn't want to come out for MHD only to have Sinclair speak out against the idea," Cardwell summarized.

"Right," said Jake. "I've finally set up a meeting between the two of them, but Sinclair wants to bring one of Senator Leeds's flunkies with him."

The older man's smile stayed in place, but he said, quite seriously, "Arlan Sinclair's always been a sonofabitch."

Shocked, Jake couldn't do anything but gape at Cardwell.

With a little chuckle, Cardwell said, "We've known each other for a long time. He was after Alice, you know. Even after she married me."

"Sinclair?"

"Sinclair."

"I'll be damned." Jake suddenly understood Sinclair's disdain when he had mentioned Lev's name to the professor.

"Oh yes, he and I go back a long way. A very long way. And here I thought he'd be delighted with your proposal to make MHD a major issue for Tomlinson."

"He's solidly in Leeds's camp," Jake said. "His son works in the senator's local office."

"I might have known."

"So now I've finally set up the meeting with Tomlinson but Sinclair's going to bring one of Leeds's people to it."

Cardwell rubbed his chin thoughtfully. "You're afraid that Leeds will preempt the MHD issue, snatch it away from Tomlinson before he even announces his candidacy."

"And I don't know what to do about it," Jake said, feeling increasingly desperate.

"Nothing."

"Nothing?"

"You do nothing, Jake. There's nothing you can do, is there?"

"But Leeds will take over the MHD issue! He'll make the voters think it was his idea all along!"

"That can't be helped," said Cardwell.

"It's not fair!"

Cardwell said nothing for several moments. Then, tapping Jake's knee, he pointed out, "You may be losing sight of the forest, Jake. What's important is that *somebody* takes the ball on MHD and runs with it. Tomlinson, Leeds, the Three Stooges . . . it doesn't matter who does it. What's important is that MHD gets the chance it deserves to help this state and the nation." Before Jake could say anything, the older man added, "And the world."

"But what about Tomlinson?"

Spreading his hands in a gesture of helplessness, Cardwell replied, "I wouldn't worry about Frank Tomlinson. It's you I'm worried about."

"Me?"

"If Senator Leeds comes out for MHD and preempts Tomlinson on the issue, where does that leave you?"

Jake huffed. "Out in the cold. A science advisor with nothing to advise about." And he thought of Amy Wexler. Would she bother with me if I'm out of Tomlinson's campaign?

"It seems to me," Cardwell said, "that the only thing you can do is to set up this meeting between Tomlinson and Sinclair and hope for the best."

"Even with Senator Leeds's man there?"

Nodding, Cardwell said, "What's important, Jake, is that MHD gets the political backing it needs to become a successful technology."

"You think so."

"I certainly do. Remember your history classes. In World War Two, when the Nazis invaded Soviet Russia, Winston Churchill immediately offered Josef Stalin all the aid that Britain could give to the Russians. When some members of Parliament criticized Churchill for becoming friendly with the Communist dictator, Churchill replied that if Hitler invaded hell, he would try to say a few good things about the devil."

Cardwell chuckled while Jake stared at him uncertainly.

Getting to his feet, the older man said, "Politics, Jake. It's the art of getting what you want out of people who generally don't want the same things you do."

As he pushed himself up from the comfortable chair, Jake muttered, "Sleeping with the enemy."

But he was thinking about sleeping with Amy Wexler. Yet it was Glynis Colwyn's serious, sensuous face that popped into his imagination.

SHERIDAN HOTEL

I t was the oldest hotel in the capital city, named, Jake thought rue-fully, after a general whose major contributions to the state were to nearly wipe out both the Native Americans and the buffalo. For those accomplishments, Philip Sheridan was revered by the movers and shakers of the state.

"The only good Indians I ever saw were dead." Some historians claimed that Sheridan never said that, but his actions in the Indian Wars certainly reinforced that image of him.

The hotel itself was an imposing pile of brickwork and Victorian ornate décor. A statue of the general on horseback adorned the front entranceway. Jake hurried through the lobby, nearly empty in mid-afternoon, and took the groaning old elevator up to the suite where Tomlinson was to meet with Professor Sinclair. And Nacho Perez, Senator Leeds's man.

Jake had briefed Tomlinson and Amy on Sinclair's position, barely hiding his disdain for the professor. The bastard chased after Mrs. Cee even after she had married Lev. Was he hopelessly in love or just mad to get his hands on her? The latter, Jake felt. Sinclair didn't impress him as the type to pine away for love. Lust, yes, but not love.

Amy opened the door to the suite and let Jake in. Looking bright and cheerful in a knee-length pale yellow chemise, she smiled at him, but nothing more. As he stepped into the room, Jake saw that the furnishings were slightly old-fashioned: overstuffed chairs, a pair of smallish sofas, and a dusty-looking little desk of dark wood. A bar had been set up by the draperied windows.

"Where's the man?"

"In the bathroom," Amy said. "He's a little nervous about this, you know."

"Nervous? Him?"

"He has nerves. He's not as cool as he pretends to be."

Before Jake could think of a reply the door to the bedroom opened and Tomlinson stepped in, looking perfectly relaxed in a pair of pearly gray casual slacks and an open-necked coral shirt beneath an ivory sport jacket.

"Where's Professor Sinclair?" Tomlinson asked.

Jake looked at his wristwatch. "He should—"

The phone rang. Amy went to the ornate little desk and picked up the receiver. She nodded once, then, as she replaced the receiver, she said to Tomlinson, "They're on their way up."

"Good," said Tomlinson. "Jake, you let them in, please. Amy, you can be in charge of the bar."

Jake started to ask why he didn't get the hotel to provide a bartender, but quickly realized that Tomlinson didn't want any extra witnesses to this meeting.

The doorbell chimed. Jake swiftly crossed the thickly carpeted room and opened the door to admit Sinclair and Perez. The professor looked tight-lipped, almost grim. He was wearing a dark brown three-piece suit with a patterned tie of red and gold. Perez, in a flowered shirt, baggy gray slacks, and a sports jacket flapping loosely, had a bemused smile on his thin, swarthy face.

Tomlinson lit up with a smile that could melt glaciers. "Professor Sinclair, I'm so glad to see you."

Sinclair took Tomlinson's outstretched hand and made a perfunctory smile back. "How do you do?" Turning slightly, he introduced, "This is Ignacio Perez."

"Call me Nacho," said Perez, in his throaty, almost hoarse voice. "Everybody calls me Nacho."

Gesturing to Amy at the bar by the window, Tomlinson asked, "Drinks?"

"You got any beer?" Perez asked Amy as he headed toward the bar.

Sinclair accepted a glass of tonic water. Tomlinson took a scotch on the rocks and Jake merely shook his head when Amy gave him a questioning look.

As he led Sinclair to one of the room's matching pair of love seats, Tomlinson said, "Jake has told you that I intend to make MHD power generation a major issue in my campaign for the Senate."

Sitting on the front three inches of the little sofa, clutching his glass in both hands, Sinclair nodded warily.

"And you have a problem with that." Tomlinson sat on the facing sofa, his megawatt smile still in place.

Sinclair glanced at Perez, standing near Amy by the bar, then replied, "I think it would be a mistake to oversell MHD at this point. You shouldn't get the people's hopes up too soon."

"But it's a promising technology. It could mean a lot to this state."

"We have a long way to go before MHD can be practical," Sinclair said.

With a nod, Tomlinson replied, "I want to help you to get to that point. When I'm in the Senate I'll be able to steer federal money your way."

Jake saw Nacho Perez slink off to a chair in the corner of the room, sipping his beer from the bottle and looking mildly bored. Professor Sinclair looked uptight, almost angry.

"We're not ready for a massive upswing in funding," the professor insisted. "We have a long way to go."

"But wouldn't additional funding help you to get where you want to go?" Tomlinson asked.

Sinclair fidgeted on the love seat, took a sip of his tonic water, and finally admitted, "Additional funding would be helpful, of course, but only up to a point."

His smile suddenly vanishing, Tomlinson said, "Let's cut to the chase, Professor. What's your problem?"

Sinclair's eyes flashed, but he immediately regained his self-control. "We pushed too hard last year and it resulted in an explosion that killed one of our technicians. I'm not going to rush things again."

Tomlinson said, "I can understand that. You'll be in charge of the program all the way, though. Nobody's going to rush you or try to control your research, I assure you."

"That's more easily said than done," Sinclair countered.

Tomlinson paled slightly. It was very subtle, but Jake thought that just for an instant Tomlinson took Sinclair's truculence as a personal insult.

Before either of the men could make things worse, Jake jumped in. "We could revive the state's coal-mining industry with MHD. There's a lot more riding on this than who controls the research program."

Sinclair glared at Jake, but Tomlinson eased back on the little sofa and said gently, "What's really bothering you, Professor? Just what's eating at you?"

LOYALTIES

For a long moment Sinclair didn't reply. Instead, he took a long gulp of his drink. Tomlinson sat stock-still, his face grave, his eyes probing. Jake, standing in the middle of the room, saw that Sinclair's eyes were on Nacho Perez.

At last Sinclair cleared his throat and said, "I'm . . . I am committed to support Senator Leeds."

"I understand that your son works in Leeds's office," said Tomlinson.

Wordlessly, Sinclair nodded.

"The senator is holding that over you."

"No!" Sinclair snapped. "It's not like that! God, you make it sound as if he's blackmailing me."

"Isn't he?"

"No, he is not." With some of his usual strength, Sinclair said, "I have supported Christopher Leeds in the past and I see no reason to change that support now."

Jake heard himself ask, "Has Leeds promised to put federal money into your MHD work?"

Sinclair's face flushed. "We haven't discussed that. Not at all. We haven't even talked about the MHD program."

"Why not?"

From his seat in the corner of the room, Nacho Perez spoke up. "Hey, the senator's got a lot of other things to worry about. This MHD stuff is small potatoes."

"Really?" Tomlinson asked. "Is that Chris's attitude?"

"He's not interested in helping the coal industry?" Jake demanded.

"He's got more important stuff to do," Perez said.

Turning back to Sinclair, Tomlinson said, "I can't believe that Senator Leeds hasn't shown any interest in your MHD work, Professor."

Squirming slightly, Sinclair replied, "I've . . . mentioned it to him. Once or twice."

"And he's not interested?" Tomlinson seemed incredulous.

Recovering his composure, Sinclair said, "I believe the senator has a more realistic attitude about MHD power generation than you do, Mr. Tomlinson. This is a research program, for god's sake. You can't go promising people pie in the sky. It'll be years before MHD becomes practical, if ever."

Shaking his head, Tomlinson said, "It looks as if I have more faith in your work than you do."

"That's because you don't understand it. You don't know what the problems are, what obstacles are facing us."

"Please enlighten me, then."

Sinclair glanced at Perez, then at Jake, and finally returned his gaze to Tomlinson. "You think we can just order a superconducting magnet from Home Depot? Like a piece of retail hardware? Nobody's made a high-temperature superconducting coil to the size we'd need in a practical generator."

Before anyone could react to that, Sinclair went on, "And the erosion rate inside the channel. We've lined the channel with the kind of heat shield material NASA uses on the space shuttle, but still the channel burns through. And the electrodes! How do you think we can produce electrodes that will stand up to that stream of five-thousand-degree plasma and the megawatts-per-stere electrical charge in the plasma?"

"I haven't the faintest idea," Tomlinson murmured.

"Well, it won't be done by a wave of a magic wand," Sinclair insisted. "It will take years of research, years of hard, hard work."

"Which will require money," Jake said.

"Which I will personally guarantee to provide you, once I'm in the Senate," Tomlinson added.

"You personally guarantee?" Sinclair scoffed. "What about the other ninety-nine senators? What about the White House and the House of Representatives?"

Hunching forward, hands on his thighs, Tomlinson said, "Professor Sinclair, that's what leadership is all about. When I'm in the Senate, I intend to be a leader. I intend to move ahead—with MHD as well as other programs. I don't want to be a drone, like Senator Leeds."

"Hey!" Perez yelled from the corner. "The senator ain't no drone!"

"What has he done?" Tomlinson challenged. "Except to help the casinos and the highway developers."

"He's done plenty," Perez said truculently.

Sinclair got to his feet. "This is getting us nowhere. I came here to meet you, Tomlinson, out of common politeness. I appreciate your interest in MHD, but I think it's premature." He eyed Jake as he added, "It's misguided."

Tomlinson rose, too. "I still intend to make MHD an issue in my campaign. Will you come out against that?"

With a glance toward Perez, Sinclair said, "I do not intend to be active in anyone's campaign. I'm a scientist, not a politician."

"But would you oppose my proposal to accelerate the MHD program?"

"If news reporters ask me what I think of your proposal, I'll have to tell them the truth."

"You'll tell them your opinion," Jake said.

Glaring now, Sinclair shot back, "The truth."

Tomlinson sucked in a deep breath, then put his smile back on. "Well, Professor, I want to thank you for taking the time to talk with me."

A little more gently, Sinclair said, "I'm sorry we don't see eye to eye on this."

"I am, too." Tomlinson offered his hand, Sinclair shook it limply, and then the professor headed for the door with Perez trailing behind him.

As the door closed, Tomlinson slugged down the remainder of his scotch and headed for the bar. Amy was already pouring him another.

Still standing in the middle of the room, Jake said, "That didn't go very well, did it?"

"Not hardly," said Tomlinson.

But Amy said, "Sinclair's hiding something."

"You think so?"

Handing Tomlinson his refill, she said, "It just doesn't make sense. Here you're offering him the chance to expand his program, to get to where he wants to go, to make MHD a success, and he's turning you down."

Jake went to the bar and reached for the fifth of Jack Daniel's. "He's an academic. He doesn't want a big, high-powered program. He's afraid he'll lose control."

Amy shook her head. "There's something more. He's hiding something, I'm absolutely sure of it."

"What could it be?" Tomlinson asked.

"Something about his son?" Jake guessed.

"Whatever it is," Amy said, "Leeds knows about it and is using it to keep Sinclair in his camp."

"And if we could find out what it is," Tomlinson said, his eyes narrowing, "we might be able to swing Sinclair over to our side."

"Or neutralize him, at least," said Amy. "Pull his fangs."

Tomlinson turned and laid a hand on Jake's shoulder. "Jake, you're our man on campus. We need you to ferret out Sinclair's secret."

Jake started to refuse, but then he thought, Ferret out Sinclair's secret. Yeah, the sonofabitch must be hiding something. I'll bet Mrs. Cee isn't the only forbidden fruit he's chased after.

FORBIDDEN FRUIT

Jake went home alone and that night he dreamed of Louise again. Nothing erotic. Nothing sad or remorseful. They were at home, in the house they had built together, getting ready to go out somewhere. Jake was putting on a sports coat and Louise had just stepped into the front hallway, beaming her radiant smile, happy, eyes sparkling, alive.

Jake woke up and turned toward her. The bed was empty; he was alone. He sat up and squinted at the red numerals of the digital clock on the dresser: 4:44. That must mean something, he thought. Yeah. It means it's sixteen minutes before five A.M.

The bedroom felt cold in the dark. Jake pulled up the covers he had kicked off in his sleep. He thought that if this was a movie he'd pull out a cigarette and puff on it in the shadows. Macho man. Jake had never smoked. As a kid he couldn't afford cigarettes. Later, he understood the medical warnings about tobacco and never allowed himself to take up the habit.

But now he felt alone and cold and miserable without even a cigarette to light his darkness. What's the use? he asked himself. What's the fucking use?

If I'd driven to the store instead of letting Louise go she'd be alive now. Maybe I'd be dead but she'd be alive. She didn't deserve to die. She was so full of life, so giving and caring. She brought happiness wherever she went. She—

Stop it! he commanded himself. She's dead and there's nothing you can do about it. Not a goddamned sonofabitch motherfucking thing you can do about it. Life belongs to the living. Get on with your life.

Yeah. Get on with it. Why? What for? You've just been going through the motions for the past year. That's why Lev pushed you into this Tomlinson business. To give you something to live for. Big fucking deal. Working for a rich bastard who's playing at being a politician. The wannabe senator. And he's already thinking about the White House.

Amy. The sex is good with Amy. Terrific, really. Jake shook his head, as if to clear his thoughts. I ought to feel guilty about it. Louise hasn't been dead for much more than a year and here I'm rolling in the sheets with a chick who looks like a football cheerleader.

And fucks like a rabbit, he added. Louise would understand, he thought. It's not love, Lou. It's just sex. The body takes over, like cruise control.

Just sex. Yeah, like oxygen is just something you suck into your lungs.

He lay down again on the wrinkled sheet, pulled the blanket up to his chin, turned on his side, and watched the digital clock's numerals change. When they reached 5:00 A.M. he rolled over on his other side and squeezed his eyes shut. Go to sleep, asshole. You've got a class to teach.

And some detective work to do.

Jake was bleary-eyed when he arrived in his office that morning, but the first thing he did was phone Glynis Colwyn and invite her to lunch.

"I'm rather busy . . . ," she began. Jake could hear the uncertainty in her voice.

"I really need to talk with you," he said, with more conviction than he really felt. "We had this meeting between Tomlinson and the professor yesterday, and I need to talk it over with you."

"Why me? I wasn't there."

He looked out his office window and saw big gray clouds building up. Snow clouds. We'll have a white Christmas even down here, looks like.

To Glynis, he said, "I need to know how the professor felt about the meeting."

"But you were there, weren't you, Jake?"

There was something in her voice, something he couldn't identify. Anticipation? Suspicion?

"Look, Glynis, the truth is I'd just like to have lunch with you. Yesterday's meeting gives me an excuse to ask."

For several long seconds she didn't reply. Then, "You don't need an excuse, Jake. I'd be happy to have lunch with you."

He drove the Mustang to the front entrance of the electrical engineering building. Glynis was waiting at the glass double doors, bundled into a quilted parka. Before Jake could get out of the car, she pushed through the doors and hurried to him. He leaned across and opened the passenger side door for her.

"It's cold!" Glynis said as she slid into the seat and reached for the safety belt.

"December in the foothills of the Rockies," he said. "It gets cold in West Virginia, too, doesn't it?"

"Oh yes, of course. But I've never liked it. If I had my choice I'd live in Hawaii or Guatemala or someplace where the temperature never gets anywhere near freezing."

Jake gunned the engine and headed off campus. "I thought we'd eat in a real restaurant, instead of the cafeteria."

"Fine by me," Glynis said. Then, with a grin, she asked, "What did you have in mind?"

DANNY'S SEAFOOD LOCKER

t wasn't much of a restaurant. The décor was mostly old fishing nets and travel posters on the walls. But when Glynis had expressed her preference for warm climates, Jake thought that Danny's was the best he could provide her.

Once inside the door, Glynis wormed out of her quilted coat, and Jake saw that she wearing denim jeans and a Christmas-bright red sweater. Practical clothing for the December cold but on her the outfit looked fresh and attractive. The dark-skinned young Hispanic hostess showed them to a booth in the rear of the restaurant. When a waiter pushed through the double doors of the kitchen, Jake could smell fish cooking and the distinctive odor of French fries sizzling in the deep fryer.

A sallow-faced, ponytailed waiter asked if they wanted anything to drink. Glynis ordered a glass of chardonnay and Jake asked for a dark beer. The waiter came back with a stemmed glass of wine and a green bottle of Dos Equis Especial: a pale lager.

"That's the darkest we got," the kid mumbled.

Jake sighed. "Okay."

The waiter started to leave their booth, but hesitated. "You want a glass?"

Jake shook his head.

"Not dark enough?" Glynis asked.

"Not dark at all."

She took a tentative sip of the wine, then got down to business. "There's not much I can tell you about Arlan's reaction to the meeting. He came back and closeted himself in his office with Nacho. He hasn't mentioned the meeting this morning."

Jake shrugged. "You know, I was sort of surprised to see Tim with you at that cocktail party last week."

She looked at him questioningly.

"I mean, last summer, when I first saw the two of you together, he sure didn't look like dating material."

Glynis cocked her head slightly to one side. "He was paranoid about me," she said, with a soft smile. "He thought I was spying on him for Professor Sinclair."

"Were you?"

"Certainly. I still am. The prof needs to know how things are going and Tim isn't the type to write out weekly progress reports."

"But . . ."

"But he's no longer suspicious of me," she said, her smile widening a bit.

"How'd you work that?" Jake asked, trying to keep his own suspicions off his face.

The waiter came back. "You ready to order?"

Jake frowned at the interruption. He grabbed at the wrinkled paper menu and asked for the fried oysters. Glynis nodded and said she'd take the same.

Trying to sound casual, Jake asked again, "So how did you get Tim to trust you?"

She almost laughed. "Jake, you are so transparent! You think I used my womanly wiles on Tim, don't you?"

That was exactly what Jake was thinking, but he answered, flustered, "I don't . . . no . . . it never crossed my mind."

"Not much." She seemed to find it all amusing.

Leaning across the table toward her, Jake said, "I just found it surprising to see the two of you at the party for Leeds. And then you went to dinner together."

"We're coworkers, Jake. I see Tim at least once or twice a week. There's nothing romantic about it."

"Really?"

She shook her head. "You men see everything in terms of sex. A woman can't even shake hands with a man without all the other men in the room thinking she's going to jump into bed with him."

"Maybe that's because they all want to jump into bed with her themselves." Jake was stunned to hear himself admit it out loud.

Glynis started to reply, hesitated, then merely shook her head again. Her face was utterly serious, her dark exotic eyes deep, steady. A lot going on behind those eyes, Jake thought.

"Tim thought you were sleeping with Sinclair," he said, practically whispering.

"I know," she answered. Jake waited for more, but Glynis just sat across the table from him, looking . . . he couldn't decide if the expression on her face was distress or simmering irritation.

The waiter brought their platters of fried oysters. Jake was glad of the interruption this time.

"Well, anyway," he said, trying to change the subject once the waiter had left, "I need to know how Sinclair reacted to the meeting with Tomlinson."

"I wish I knew," Glynis said, as she stuck a fork in one of the breaded oysters. "He hasn't said a word about it to me."

"You said he's been talking with Nacho Perez."

"Yes. Every day. Usually on the phone but several times the man has come to the prof's office." She frowned slightly. "I don't like that man. He's . . . he gives me the shudders. I think he could be terribly violent; I think he might enjoy violence."

Jake muttered, "I wish I knew what they were talking about."

"Beats me," Glynis said.

They fell silent. Jake chewed through three of his oysters, sipped at his bottle of beer. Some spy I'm turning out to be, he thought. I can't get any information out of her.

Glynis put her fork down and looked at him intently. "Jake . . . about Tim and me. I don't want you to get the wrong impression. I don't sleep around."

"Has Sinclair ever hit on you?"

"Now and then," she said lightly. "But it's nothing I can't handle. Actually, he can be rather sweet when he wants to be."

"He's married, isn't he?"

"Yes, but they've been separated for years."

"Separated?" Jake asked. "Not divorced?"

"I don't believe so," Glynis said. "Either way, he seems to be paying a lot for her support."

"Some marriages don't work out, I guess," Jake muttered, remembering all over again how lucky he had been with Louise.

Glynis shook her head. "It doesn't seem to bother him all that much. At least the prof has never tried the old 'my wife doesn't understand me' line."

Jake nodded.

"Tim's under a lot of pressure, too, you know. Underneath that dour Yankee hide of his, Tim is a good engineer who's taken on the responsibility of making the big rig work. Sinclair has been riding him pretty hard."

Jake felt his brows go up. "I thought it was the other way around: Tim wants to push hard and Sinclair wants a careful, cautious research program."

"Don't you believe that for a second," Glynis said. "Sinclair may give the impression that he's an ivory tower academic, but he's got a white-hot ambition burning inside him."

"He does? Then why isn't he jumping on Tomlinson's bandwagon? I would think—"

"Leeds has something on him," Glynis said flatly. "I'm convinced of it."

"His son's job?"

"No, I think it's something bigger than that."

Jake leaned against the back of the booth. Glynis was dead serious, he saw.

"What the hell could it be?"

"I don't know. But it's hurting him. Sinclair's no fool. He understands that Tomlinson's offering him a path to make MHD a success. But he's hanging back because Leeds doesn't want him to support Tomlinson."

Mulling over the possibilities for a moment, Jake asked, "Do you think you could find out?"

Glynis didn't answer for several heartbeats. At last she said softly, "Jake, I work for the man."

"But his attitude is hurting Tim, isn't it?"

"And Bob Rogers. Everyone on the program."

"So, if we could find out why Sinclair's doing this, if we could get him to swing to Tomlinson's campaign, we could help him and Tim and Bob and all the others."

"I suppose so," she said slowly.

"It would be good for everybody," Jake coaxed. "It would even be good for Sinclair, if we could get him out from under Leeds's control."

"I suppose so," Glynis repeated, more softly.

MONSTER

is real name was Benito Falciglia, christened such at the insistence of his granduncle, who stood as his godfather at the infant Benito's baptism. Before, during, and after World War Two, Granduncle Umberto had admired Benito Mussolini—from the safe distance of America.

Even in grammar school Benito hated being called Benny. Fortunately he was of such a large size that the other kids started calling him Frankenstein's Monster. He amiably took to the nickname, which was soon shortened to Monster. He was so big and could look so menacing when he wanted to that Monster seldom had to resort to violence. Just a scowl and a growl and the other boys forked over their lunch money or whatever else Monster demanded of them.

By the time he became the workhorse lineman for the high school football team, playing both offense and defense, Monster was recruited by the neighborhood gang. He was really a gentle soul beneath all that muscle, but he took orders from the wiseguys and broke a few legs here and there.

Jake had known him since kindergarten. In a perverse way he liked Monster. He had always helped the big guy with his homework. Not that Monster was slow or stupid; he simply found it much easier to get one of the bright boys to do his school assignments, rather than take the trouble to do them himself. Most of the teachers knew this, but did nothing about it—especially in high school, where the faculty wanted nothing more than to get this gang enforcer out their doors for good. The football coach felt otherwise, yet Monster graduated with the rest of his class.

In return for Jake's help with the schoolwork, Monster protected

Jake from the roughnecks and other gang members. "Jake's okay," he would tell them. "Leave him alone." And they did. Most of the time.

Jake's apartment was on the edge of his old neighborhood, far enough away from those narrow streets and row houses for Jake to feel surprised when he saw Monster lounging on the street corner as he pulled onto the driveway of his building. No mistaking that hulking form.

By the time Jake had parked behind the apartment building, he saw Monster ambling toward his car. Jake got out, locked the Mustang, and walked over toward him.

"Hi, Monster," he said, trying to make it cheerful. "Haven't seen you in a long time. How are you?"

Monster waggled a hand. "Mezza, mez'. Whatcha doin', Jake?"

"I'm still at the university."

Monster seemed to weigh this information as the two men stood in the parking lot in the lengthening shadows of late afternoon. Jake was bundled in his lined leather car coat and had a wool watch cap pulled down over his ears. Monster wore nothing heavier than a checkered sports coat.

"The word is that you're gettin' inta politics," Monster said.

Jake felt his pulse thump. He nodded, "A little, yeah."

Frowning a bit, Monster said, "The word is that some people don't like that."

"Some people?" Jake asked, working to keep his voice normal. Monster loomed over him like one of the Grand Teton mountains.

"Yeah. Here and there. You know."

"What don't they like about it?" Jake asked.

With a shrug of his heavy shoulders, Monster said, "I dunno, but they ain't happy with you, Jake."

"I'm not doing anything wrong," Jake said. "I'm just giving some advice to Tomlinson's campaign. Science stuff."

"Yeah. I know you're okay, Jake. But these guys, they ain't happy with you."

"What should I do?"

"Watch your step, Jake. Just watch your step."

With that, Monster turned and walked away, leaving Jake in the darkening parking lot. Monster had no ill feelings toward Jake, he knew, but he also knew that if he were told to, Monster would break every bone in his head. In his mind, Jake heard a stern voice telling him, *Remember, you have been warned.*

CLYDE'S BAR

A my Wexler frowned as Jake told her about Monster's warning. The two of them were sitting side by side at the bar, she sipping on a martini, he nursing a Negra Modelo.

"I told you that Leeds has some tough supporters," she said.

The bar was crowded with Happy Hour drinkers. It looked to Jake as though most of them were regulars; the two scurrying bartenders seemed to know what each new customer wanted the instant he or she sat on the stools. There was a restaurant farther inside the place but it seemed half empty at this early hour. The bar, though, was busy and noisy with conversations and laughter. Some golf game was showing on the TV up on the wall above the cash register. Muted.

"They must be worried about the MHD idea if they're showing muscle already," Amy said.

Jake made a wry grin. "Well, they've got me worried, that's for sure."

Amy reasoned, "Sinclair must have told Leeds everything about the MHD program. Now Leeds recognizes it as a threat to him."

"A threat to me, you mean."

As if she didn't hear Jake, she mused, "Why doesn't Leeds just come out and announce he's backing MHD? He could do it before Franklin does and he could start pushing for federal funding right away. Take the issue right out from under our feet."

"Maybe Tomlinson should make a statement about MHD right away," Jake suggested.

"Before his official announcement that he's running?" She shook her head. "That doesn't make sense."

Jake said, "He could say he's interested as a private citizen. A concerned voter and taxpayer."

"Jake, that's not the way the game works."

He saw, though, that there was something going on in her mind. Amy sat silently, idly twirling her long-stemmed martini glass in both hands. Those hazel eyes were looking past him, focused on some new idea taking form. Jake picked up his glass and took a healthy swallow of his dark beer.

Slowly, as if rehearsing the agenda for herself, Amy said, "Franklin's due to announce his candidacy in another ten days. . . ."

His Christmas present to the state's voters, Jake said to himself.

". . . And Leeds can make a statement about MHD anytime he wants to," Amy continued. "Either from his office here or from Washington."

Jake said, "If he does it from here he can have Sinclair standing beside him."

Amy nodded slowly. Suddenly she hunched toward Jake and said, "You're right! Franklin's got to make a public announcement about MHD now! Right away! Before Leeds can open his mouth about it."

"Before he announces his candidacy?"

"Yes!" Amy said, with iron certainty. "Tomorrow. It'll get him headlines, interviews on the news shows. Then, when he does announce he's running, he can say that the opportunity MHD offers this state is what made him decide to run."

"Instead of the other way around."

"Exactly. Jake, you're a political genius!"

He laughed out loud, thinking that a political genius ought to be rewarded in bed.

And so he was.

The regional Public Broadcasting System TV station was on campus. The university ran the PBS station and melded it with the courses they offered on television and journalism.

Franklin Tomlinson still looked doubtful about the whole business when he entered the bare little studio. The walls were blue-painted cinderblock, the ceiling festooned with dangling television lights. Three TV cameras stood in one corner, their cables snaking across the concrete floor.

His handsome face dead serious, Tomlinson sat in a far corner of the studio in what looked to Jake like a barber's chair, while a makeup specialist brushed a light powder across his jaw.

Standing well behind the cameras, Jake whispered to Amy, "He doesn't look happy about this."

"He will when the reporters come hounding after him tomorrow morning," she said tightly. She was wearing business attire: pearl gray slacks and a navy blue hip-length jacket. Jake was in his usual jeans and sport coat.

Tomlinson got up from the makeup chair and pulled on his suit jacket, then allowed the show's producer—a pudgy female student from the university's journalism department—to lead him to the set where he was to be interviewed. It looked threadbare to Jake: a single sofa, one armchair, and a coffee table. Behind them was a pair of fake bookcases. Turning to look at the monitor screen set up behind the cameras, Jake saw that the set appeared presentable: the backdrop for a serious interview.

The interviewer was an old hand: silver hair thinning, midsection going to paunch. Jake remembered watching him on one of the local commercial TV newscasts back in his childhood. Now the man had retired from commercial television and did these PBS interviews as a public service. And a tax deduction, Jake thought.

The overhead lights went on, bathing the set in glaring brightness. An amplified voice announced, "In five . . . four . . . three . . ."

Tomlinson's face suddenly lit up brighter than the overhead lights as the interviewer looked into the cameras and said, "Good evening, and welcome to *Face the Issues*. Tonight we'll be talking with B. Franklin Tomlinson, one of the state's leading citizens and—if the rumors are correct—a potential candidate for the United States Senate."

Turning to face Tomlinson, he said, "So let me start off by asking you straightaway, are you going to run against Senator Leeds?"

Smiling his megawatt smile, Tomlinson said, "I'm thinking of it, George. Thinking very hard about it." Before the interviewer could ask another question, Tomlinson added, "And let me tell you why."

Looking mildly surprised, the interviewer fell for the gambit. "Why?"

"MHD," said Tomlinson, as if speaking a magical word.

"MHD?" asked the interviewer. "What's MHD?"

HEADLINES AND PROPOSITIONS

The first thing Jake did when he woke up the next morning was to turn on the local news broadcast. Sure enough, there was Tomlinson—looking earnest even while he was smiling brilliantly—telling his interviewer how MHD could bring prosperity back to the state's coal mining industry.

As he showered and shaved and brushed his teeth, Jake clicked from one local station to another. Tomlinson was on every one of them. Amy's done her job well, Jake thought while he dressed. He's in the spotlight for sure.

While he munched on his breakfast of bran flakes and instant coffee, Jake turned to the cable news networks. No mention of Tomlinson on the national level. Well, he said to himself, they'll start to notice him when he announces he's running against Leeds. He got up from the kitchen counter and went to his desk. The digital edition of the local newspaper had Tomlinson splashed across its front page, with a long sidebar about MHD. Jake was only mildly surprised to see Bob Rogers's byline on the sidebar.

His morning class on planetary astronomy went well. The eight students were all motivated, interested. Two of them were helping Jake with his proposal for the high-resolution camera on NASA's next Mars lander. Somehow, though, Jake didn't find the class as exciting as the buzz about Tomlinson. Politics can be exciting, he thought, even while he was reviewing imagery from one of the little roving vehicles trundling across the frozen red desert sands of Mars. I helped to make headlines!

Once he got back to his office he phoned Glynis Colwyn to ask her to lunch.

She sounded wary. "I'm not sure I ought to be seen with you, Jake."

"Huh? Why not?"

"Professor Sinclair isn't happy about Tomlinson's spouting off," she said.

"Oh. I'm persona non grata, eh?"

"Decidedly."

"Are you sore at me?"

"Me?" She sounded genuinely surprised. "Why would I be upset with you?"

"Well, if Sinclair's pissed off . . ."

"Don't be silly. I think what you've done is fine. Tim's ecstatic about it." Her voice hesitated a moment. "Well, as ecstatic as he allows himself to be."

Jake laughed. "Okay, then. Come on to lunch with me. We can go back to Danny's, off campus."

Slowly, she replied, "I usually have lunch with Tim, you know. When he's not up in Lignite."

"Bring him along. Bring Bob Rogers, too. I need to talk with both of them anyway."

He could hear the relief in her voice. "All right. Danny's, you said?"

"Yeah. You know where it is, don't you?"

"I remember. And I have a GPS in the car. If I can get it to start."

"Good. See you at Danny's. Noon."

"Make it twelve thirty."

"Okay. Twelve thirty."

As he hung up, Jake realized that Glynis and Tim must be getting serious. And he felt his face hardening into a frown at the thought.

As usual, Jake was early for the lunch date. He sat alone in a booth at the far end of the restaurant, wondering if Glynis would actually show up. Why wouldn't she? he asked himself. She said she'd bring Tim and Bob with her. He checked his cell phone and then his wristwatch. Twelve thirty-two. Where is she?

Bob Rogers came into the restaurant and looked around. Before

Jake could slide out of the booth Rogers spotted him and headed his way.

"Your guy's made the headlines," Rogers said as he sat beside Jake.

"And you're on the front page," Jake replied. "I didn't know you wrote for the newspaper."

Rogers shrugged modestly. "Oh, that was a background piece they asked me to write more'n a year ago. They've been sitting on it all this time."

"It's a good piece. Clear. Anybody could understand it."

"The managing editor liked it," said Rogers. "I think maybe because he didn't have to pay for it."

"They didn't pay you?"

"Nope."

"Cheap bastards."

Rogers laughed. "That's the newspaper business."

The same ponytailed waiter asked what they wanted to drink. Rogers and Jake both asked for beer. Then Jake saw Glynis enter the restaurant, with Tim Younger right behind her. He waved to them and they came to the booth, hung their coats on pegs on the wall, and sat together across the table from him and Rogers.

Once they all ordered their meals, Jake asked Glynis, "You said Sinclair was pissed off about Tomlinson's interview?"

She pursed her lips before answering, "He tries very hard to keep his self-control, but he was very upset this morning. Very upset. He slammed the door to his office and was on the phone all morning."

"Talking to Leeds, most likely," said Younger.

Rogers said, "I got four calls from local news outfits asking about MHD."

"I sent them to you," said Glynis. "They called the professor but I knew he wouldn't talk to them."

"So where do we go from here?" Younger asked.

Jake said, "Tomlinson's going to announce that he's running against Leeds. It would be great if you two were there when he makes the announcement."

Younger's eyes flicked to Rogers and then back to Jake.

Rogers squirmed a little, sitting beside Jake, then said, "That would be kind of tough. I mean, we both work for Sinclair. It would be like a slap in the face for us to show up with Tomlinson."

"What can he do to you?" Jake asked. "You have tenure, don't you?"

Rogers nodded slowly, then pointed across the table. "Tim's an employee."

Younger huffed. "Let him fire me. Then we'll see how far he gets with his fat-ass program."

"Let's not get emotional about this," Glynis cautioned.

Jake saw the anger radiating from Younger. Rogers looked embarrassed, Glynis troubled.

"Now look," Jake said, "the worst thing we could do is snarl up the MHD work. Absolutely the worst. I don't want to cause a split among you."

Younger fixed his eyes on Jake. It was like being stared down by a frontier gunslinger. "There's already a split between him and me."

"I know you and Sinclair don't see eye to eye," Jake said.

Rogers tried to lighten the moment. "Eye to eye? It's more like tooth and nail."

"Fang and claw?" Glynis suggested.

Younger grinned minimally. "Look, the prof and I have our differences. But as long as he leaves me alone to run the big rig, we can get along."

Rogers said weakly, "With me in the middle."

"So you see, Jake," Glynis said, "why Tim can't make a public show of support for Tomlinson. Or Bob, either."

"It'd tear the program apart," Rogers agreed.

"The hell with the program," Younger growled. "I'll stand up for Tomlinson and Sinclair can go piss in his hat."

"You'll do nothing of the kind!" Glynis said sharply.

Nodding, Jake said, "It wouldn't do any of us any good to wreck the program. Tomlinson needs you guys to succeed."

"Which means you will continue to work like a good boy, Tim," said Glynis, "and keep your temper under control."

Younger gave her a look that was halfway between a guilty grin and an angry glare.

The waiter brought their lunch orders and they started to eat without any further talk about politics. As Jake dug into his fried fish platter, he realized that he was hips-deep in a snake pit. The MHD program has got to keep getting good results, which means that none of the people working the program can show in public that they support Tomlinson. Which means that Tomlinson's going to have to push MHD as a major plank in his campaign without any of the guys working on the program supporting him.

A real nest of snakes.

There's got to be some way around this, he told himself. But for the life of him, Jake couldn't see what it might be.

CARROT AND STICK

Jake was shocked to see Nacho Perez in his office when he returned from lunch. The man was stooped halfway over in front of his bookcase, peering at the journals and reports stacked on the shelves, his unbuttoned sports jacket hanging loose.

"What the hell are you doing here?" Jake demanded.

Straightening up, Perez replied, "Waitin' for you, doc."

"How did you get in? The door was locked."

With a shrug of his thin shoulders, Nacho said, "I didn't steal nuthin'."

Angry, Jake went to his desk and plopped into his little chair. It rolled backward and banged into the bookcase behind his desk.

Perez didn't seem to notice. "You read all them books?"

"Yes."

"You must be pretty smart."

"What do you want?" Jake snapped. "Why are you here?"

Still standing, Perez said, "He wants to see ya."

"He?"

"The senator. He wants to see ya."

"Well, I don't want to see him."

"Yes ya do."

Perez said it flatly, without a hint of malice, but Jake remembered his brief talk with Monster.

"Come on," Perez coaxed, "all he wants to do is talk with ya."

"Senator Leeds."

"Yeah."

Jake sat behind his desk glaring at Perez, thinking, Senator Leeds wants to talk with me. Why? What's he up to?

"Come on, kid. I got a car waitin' downstairs. We can do this the hard way or the easy way. Up to you. Either way, you're gonna talk with the man."

Slowly, reluctantly, Jake got to his feet. Perez took his topcoat off the hook on the back of the office door and Jake realized he hadn't taken his car coat off. He rummaged in its pockets for his cap while the two of them headed out into the hallway and toward the car Perez had waiting.

Monster was behind the wheel.

"Hi, Jake," he said cheerily as Jake climbed into the black sedan's rear seat. Perez ducked in and sat beside him.

They drove off campus, through the heart of the city, and out into the wooded countryside, heading away from the mountains. Visions of one-way rides and Mob assassinations flooded Jake's mind.

"Where're we going?" he asked, trying to keep his voice from shaking.

"The senator's place, out by the lake," said Perez.

It was a low, slant-roofed country lodge out on the edge of the lake that had been created when the river had been dammed to make a reservoir. In the summertime families came out for swimming and waterskiing. Jake had spent many moonlit evenings with Louise along the shore, watching the waves glittering in the silvery light.

Monster swung the car up to the lodge's front door and killed the engine. Perez slid out of the backseat and Jake followed him.

"I'll wait here," Monster said, leaning his beefy arms on the sedan's roof. "I'll drive you back to town when you're finished, Jake."

"Fine," Jake replied, trying to smile.

Inside, the lodge was decorated in rustic style: log walls, timber beams supporting the ceiling, comfortable armchairs grouped around a big stone fireplace, blackened from use although there was no fire crackling in it at the moment.

Senator Leeds was standing by the big sweeping window that looked out onto the lake, a tumbler of amber liquid in his hand. The late-afternoon sunlight glinted off the water. Even with most of the trees bare the scenery was spectacularly beautiful.

"You're Jacob Ross," the senator said as he turned his back to the view. He took a few steps across the oval rug and stuck out his hand. "We met at the dedication of the new library wing."

"Senator Leeds," Jake murmured as he took the senator's hand. It was cold and wet from holding his drink.

Leeds was handsome, Jake saw again, although his once-chiseled features were getting soft. He still looked like a marble statue to Jake, but the marble was starting to turn into something more like putty.

Gesturing to one of the armchairs, the senator called to Perez, "Nacho, see what Dr. Ross wants to drink."

"Just club soda, thanks," said Jake.

"You're not a drinking man?" Leeds asked.

Jake replied, "Not when I need to keep my wits about me."

Leeds raised his head toward the ceiling and gave out a hearty laugh. "I see. You think you're in the enemy camp so you want to be careful."

Jake nodded.

Quite seriously, the senator said, "I'm not your enemy, son."

You're not my father, either, Jake said to himself.

Perez handed Jake a tall glass tinkling with ice cubes. "Club soda," he said. "With lime."

"Thanks." Jake took a sip.

Senator Leeds stared at Jake for a long, silent moment. Then, "Jake, we have an awkward situation on our hands."

"Awkward? How so?"

"You've convinced Tomlinson that this MHD business can get him votes, but the people running the MHD program don't want anything to do with Tomlinson."

"I guess that is kind of awkward," Jake admitted.

"It would be best if you told Tomlinson to drop the MHD idea. It's pie in the sky, anyway."

"I don't think so," Jake replied. "I've looked into the technical details and—"

"Pie in the sky!" Leeds insisted. "You've gotten Tomlinson to promise more than he can deliver."

With the ghost of a smile, Jake said, "Isn't that fairly normal for a politician?"

Leeds's face went dark for an instant. But he quickly recovered and countered, "I deliver for the people of this state. I bring home the bacon."

The pork, Jake amended silently.

Leaning forward to tap Jake on the knee, Leeds added, "And I can deliver for you, too."

"For me?"

"My sources at the university tell me you're up for tenure this year."

Jake blinked in surprise.

"I can get the committee to grant you tenure. You'd be the youngest member of the faculty to get it. Quite a feather in your cap, career-wise."

For several moments Jake didn't know what to say. He simply sat there, open-mouthed, while Leeds smiled knowingly at him.

"All you have to do," the senator went on, "is tell Tomlinson that you were wrong about MHD. It won't work. Not for a long time. Ten years, at least."

"But I don't think that's true," Jake heard himself reply.

Leeds glanced up at Perez, then said, "It's true enough. Professor Sinclair himself told me."

"But—"

"Listen, son. You're not helping Tomlinson with this MHD crap. If he tries to make an issue of it I'll smash him flat with the facts."

Jake said nothing.

"But if you get Tomlinson to back off, I'll get you tenure at the university. A favor for a favor. Deal?"

Leeds was smiling but there was no warmth in it. His eyes were crafty, searching.

"I . . ." Jake heard Lev's voice in his head, warning him not to make a decision before he'd thought hard about it. *Engage brain before putting foot in mouth*, Lev would say.

"I'll have to think about it," he said.

The senator's smile disappeared like a lightbulb being snapped off. "All right," he said. "You think about it. You've got twenty-four hours. I want your answer by this time tomorrow."

Jake nodded and got to his feet. As he followed Perez back to the waiting car he thought, They're giving me the carrot-and-stick treatment. Tenure is the carrot and Monster's the stick.

Perez stayed at the lodge; Jake rode up front beside Monster back to the campus as the sun set behind the woods and the shadows of evening crept over the land. By the time they reached the city it was fully dark.

Monster was in a good mood as he drove, reminiscing about the old days in the neighborhood.

"You remember the time those spics tried to throw a picnic in our park?" he asked, grinning widely.

It was a public park and the Hispanic kids had a perfect right to use it, but the guys from Jake's school didn't want them there and a major battle ensued, kids belting each other all over the grass, picnic tables upended, baskets of food turned into bludgeons, the air filled with blood and screaming and bilingual curses. Jake had hung back at the edge of the fight but Monster had waded right in, jovially cracking heads. The wails of police sirens finally sent everybody scampering. By the time the cops arrived the only people in the park were unconscious or too battered to get up from the grass—plus some cranky old farts who told the cops what had happened.

"I remember this one guy in the park," Monster was giggling as he spoke, "pulled a switchblade on me. Thought that gave him the edge. I just grabbed his wrist and twisted his arm right out of his shoulder socket. I bet the poor jerk still can't use that arm."

Jake stayed silent. The happy days of youth, he thought. I wouldn't live through them again for all the money in the world.

But then he thought, Maybe Monster's trying to tell me something. Maybe he's trying to remind me of what he could do to me if Perez or Leeds tells him to. Jake shook his head. No, Monster's not that subtle. If they tell him to break my head he'll do it, but he's not shrewd enough to try psychological warfare on me.

"I seen your apartment building," Monster said as he pulled up in front of the campus garage. "Nice-lookin' place."

Compared to what? Jake asked silently. Maybe compared to the row houses they both grew up in the building looked pretty good, but next to Tomlinson's mansion or even Amy's swanky condo his apartment building was seedy, run-down.

Jake opened the car door and started to get out, but Monster grabbed his shoulder. Turning, Jake saw that Monster was smiling at him.

"Good to see you again, Jake," he said. "I always liked you."

"I like you, too, Monster."

They shook hands, Monster's big paw engulfing Jake's. Standing out on the sidewalk as the car pulled away, Jake realized that Monster had said he'd liked him. Liked. Past tense.

Once he got up to his apartment, Jake pulled off his coat and phoned Amy. As he punched the keys of her number he saw that his machine had no messages for him. Nobody had called. As usual.

"So I've got twenty-four hours to give Leeds my answer," Jake said. With a glance at his wristwatch he amended, "Twenty-one and a half hours, actually."

Amy had agreed to meet him as soon as Jake had called. The bar at the Roosevelt Club.

"Tell them at the door that you're Mr. Tomlinson's guest," she had instructed Jake.

"Right."

"And wear a tie or they won't let you in."

Opened when Theodore Roosevelt was president of the United States, the Roosevelt Club was the hangout of the richest men in the state. Business and political leaders. Old money. Franklin Tomlinson's father had served as chairman of its house committee for decades. Senator Christopher Leeds had never been invited to join.

The bar was a quiet, darkly paneled room at one end of a plush corridor that led to the club's spacious dining room. Jake was surprised at how small it was. Only half a dozen stools at the bar itself, and no more than four high-walled booths along the far wall. There was a rear door that opened onto a garden, where members could come in or slip out without going through the main area of the club.

No one was sitting at the bar when Jake entered, and only one booth was occupied, by three elderly couples sipping at cocktails and chatting amiably.

Jake pulled up a stool and angled it so he could watch the door to the corridor. Amy won't sneak in through the garden, he figured. The black bartender asked what he wanted to drink and Jake ordered Jack Daniel's on the rocks.

"Sir, are you a club member or a guest?" the bartender asked.

"I'm Mr. Tomlinson's guest."

"Mr. Tomlinson Senior, sir, or his son?"

"The son."

The bartender smiled brightly. "Jack on the rocks. Right away, sir."

At that moment Amy showed up at the doorway. With Tomlinson, who was holding her arm. She wore a cardinal red cocktail dress, its skirt mid-thigh, its neckline scooped low enough to show some cleavage. Tomlinson was in a dark gray three-piece suit, tailored perfectly.

They both smiled at Jake and Tomlinson pointed to one of the empty booths. Jake slid off his stool, then turned to the bartender.

"I'll bring your drink to your table, sir."

Without being asked, the bartender began to mix a pair of martinis. Jake realized that Tomlinson had brought Amy here often enough for the guy to know what she drank.

He slid into the booth opposite the two of them and shook hands perfunctorily with Tomlinson across the table.

"So Leeds actually met with you," Tomlinson said, by way of greeting. He seemed fascinated with the idea.

"He wants me to tout you off MHD," Jake said. "I'm supposed to give him my answer tomorrow afternoon."

Tomlinson looked up at the paneled ceiling, then asked, "What did Chris offer you?"

For some reason that he didn't understand, Jake felt a pang of guilt.

Misunderstanding Jake's silence, Tomlinson prodded, "Come on, Chris knows how to play the game. He wants something from you, so he offered you something in return."

With considerable bitterness, Jake said, "He offered me a choice: tenure at the university or a broken head."

Tomlinson broke into a grin. "He threatened you?"

"Not in so many words, but it looked damned clear to me."

Amy said to Tomlinson, "He must be worried if he's pressuring Jake."

"Worried about the MHD idea." Tomlinson's smile broadened. "We're on to something, all right. If MHD scares him, it's a card we can use to beat him."

With a glance at Jake, Amy said, "I don't understand why Leeds is being so blatant about this. He has Sinclair on his side. Tim and Bob Rogers aren't going to come out and openly support you. Why is he so afraid of the MHD idea?"

"Because it's a great issue," Tomlinson said, with growing excitement. "It's an issue that can decide this election." He reached across the table to bang Jake playfully on the shoulder. "By god, Jake, I think you've won the election for me."

Jake muttered, "I hope I live long enough to see election day."

"Don't tell me you're scared?" Tomlinson said.

"Damned right I am. I know the goons he'll use. I grew up with them."

With a wave of his hand, Tomlinson said, "We'll protect you. Don't worry."

Jake nodded uncertainly.

"And if it's tenure you want, that's no problem. My father built half the goddamned school's campus. He'll put in a word for you."

Just like that, Jake thought, staring at the man. His father puts in a word and I get tenure. If I live to enjoy it.

The bartender brought their drinks on a tray. Jake noticed that Tomlinson's martini was garnished with a twist of lemon, while Amy's had three little green olives on a plastic spear.

"Thank you, Kenneth," Tomlinson murmured to the bartender.

Tomlinson lifted his glass and Jake noticed that its stem was actually two curved arcs of glass: they looked like a cowboy's bowed legs.

"To MHD," Tomlinson proposed. Jake touched his glass and Amy's with his own.

After a sip, Amy said, "We have a problem."

"What might that be?" Tomlinson asked, taking a second swallow of his drink.

"With Sinclair in Leeds's camp, and Tim and Rogers neutralized, who's going to be our spokesperson about MHD? Who's going to explain it to the reporters and the public?"

Tomlinson nodded toward Jake. "My science advisor, of course."

"Me? I'm not a public speaker."

"Come on, Jake," Tomlinson said, "you speak before auditoriums full of students every day, don't you? Talking to reporters isn't that different—they're just a little dumber and a lot more aggressive, that's all."

"I'm not an expert on MHD."

"You know more about it than I do," Tomlinson countered. With a grin, he added, "That makes you our expert."

"But I don't have Sinclair's stature. He's—"

Amy interrupted, "This isn't academia, Jake. Nobody's going to compare your curriculum vitae against Sinclair's."

Tomlinson agreed. "He's got a Ph.D., you've got a Ph.D. As far as the news media is concerned, you're both scientists and that's that."

"I don't know . . ."

"You can do it, Jake," Amy said, fixing him with her hazel eyes. "I know you can."

He nodded reluctantly. *This is just what I need, shooting my mouth off to the news media. Great way to get a visit from Monster or some of his pals.*

ANNOUNCEMENT

J ake fretted and fidgeted all the next day, worrying about what he was going to tell Leeds and what the senator's reaction would be. Finally, after his afternoon class, he hurried across the chilly campus to his office and looked up Senator Leeds's phone number.

Leeds's voice came up immediately, strong and measured: "This is Senator Christopher Leeds. I'm sorry that I can't take your call at the moment, but if you'll leave your name and number—"

Jake hung up. He'll know what my answer is when he doesn't hear from me, he told himself. Then he remembered an old aphorism: Not to decide is to decide.

The deadline for filing for the Senate race was the last day of the year, so on the Monday after Christmas B. Franklin Tomlinson scheduled a news conference in the main ballroom of the Sheridan Hotel.

"The week between Christmas and New Year's is a slow news period," Amy explained to Jake. "Franklin will get plenty of coverage: local, state, even national."

The two of them were in bed in Amy's condo, celebrating Christmas together. Jake had bought her a pendant of Russian amber set in silver: he thought it complemented her dark blond hair. She cooed over it and wore it in bed. She had given him a set of solid gold cuff links and shirt studs. "For the tuxedo you're going to wear at Franklin's victory party," she said.

They had both been at Tomlinson's house for his family's Christmas Eve party. It was a huge bash, centered around a Christmas tree that scraped the lofty ceiling of the mansion's living room. It was dripping with ornaments and lights; Jake had never seen such an opulent tree, except in old movies.

Tomlinson introduced Jake to his father, Alexander. The man must have been at least eighty, but he was erect and slim as a cavalry saber. His hair was iron gray, cropped in a flat military buzz cut. His skin looked almost waxy, like old parchment. But his handshake was firm as he greeted Jake in front of the tree.

"You're my son's science advisor, are you?" His voice was surprisingly deep and strong.

"Yessir," Jake managed to reply.

"Stay away from nuclear energy," Alexander Tomlinson said sternly. "It's a lousy issue; nothing but trouble."

Jake nodded dutifully. "I will, Mr. Tomlinson."

"Good. Make sure that you do."

And Jake began to realize what was driving B. Franklin Tomlinson into politics. This old man had all the single-minded determination of a charging bull—and about the same amount of finesse.

Amy was at Tomlinson's side through much of the evening, dressed in a low-cut gown of white and gold that dripped with sequins. At precisely eleven thirty, Tomlinson asked everyone to be quiet.

"I'm going to be making a public announcement in a couple of days," he said as the crowd gathered around him. "But I wanted you—you who've been friends to my family and me for so many years—to hear it first."

He paused dramatically. Everyone stood in their tuxedos and fine gowns and jewels, silent, expectant. Amy was standing next to Tomlinson, looking glitteringly beautiful; the elder Tomlinson stood at his son's other side.

Tomlinson crooked a finger in Jake's direction. "Jake, you come up here, too. You're a major part of my team."

Feeling shabby in his old blue suit, Jake came up and took his place beside Tomlinson's father.

"I want you all to know," Tomlinson said, his eyes sparkling as if he were handing out Christmas presents, "that I will be a candidate for the United States Senate in next November's election."

It came as no surprise, but everyone gasped and then cheered and applauded. Jake saw that Amy was clutching Tomlinson's arm with both her hands, gazing up at him adoringly.

Just as Amy had predicted, the ballroom of the Sheridan Hotel was jammed with news reporters and photographers the next Monday morning. Jake saw that all the local TV stations were there, together with the major cable networks. Most of the camera crews and photographers were male, although there was a healthy number of women among the reporters.

Jake was standing off to one side of the stage, beside Tomlinson's public relations aide, a bespectacled, crew-cut young man dressed in a tweed jacket. He looked young enough to be a freshman. According to Amy, though, he was a top man in the biggest PR firm in the state.

Amy was nowhere in sight as a technician from the hotel fiddled with the microphones up on the lectern. The camera crews were setting up their equipment, kidding around and jostling each other for the best positions up in front of the assembly. She's with Frank, Jake knew. They're going over the last-minute details.

The big ballroom was buzzing with dozens of conversations. Somebody cracked a joke and a burst of laughter erupted from the back of the room. Jake felt jittery, his hands sweaty. The room felt hot to him, stuffy. Too many people too close together, he thought.

Alexander Tomlinson was over in the far corner of the room, surrounded by men his own age: his cronies, all smiles and expectations. The elder Tomlinson looked stern and uncompromising, however. I wonder if he ever smiles, Jake asked himself.

"Testing, one, two, three . . ." The technician's voice boomed across the room. Looking startled, he ducked down to adjust the audio equipment hidden inside the lectern.

The technician hurried off the stage and the room suddenly fell silent, expectant. After a few moments, the door at Jake's side of the stage opened and B. Franklin Tomlinson came striding into the room. He bounded up onto the stage, beaming his megawatt smile, looking dashing and youthful even in his conservatively dark blue three-piece suit.

"Good morning," he said into the microphones. His voice sounded strong, self-assured. "I hope Santa Claus was good to all of you."

A scattering of chuckles. Jake looked around for Amy. She slipped quietly through the doorway and came to Jake's side, beaming up at Tomlinson.

"I think you already know why I've asked you here this morning," Tomlinson went on. "I have decided to be a candidate for the United States Senate in November's election."

A sort of sigh gusted through the room. The announcement was expected, of course, but now it had actually become a reality. Cameras clicked and whirred, and Jake saw that while most of the reporters were holding up digital recorders to take down Tomlinson's announcement, a few were actually scribbling on notepads.

"I'll be running on the Republican Party's slate, and look forward to engaging the Democrats' candidate in a meaningful discussion of the issues."

"What about the primary?" someone asked.

Tomlinson shrugged good-naturedly. "I don't expect to have any serious opposition within the party." With a grin, he added, "At least, that's what the state's party chairman told me."

Jake noticed the elder Tomlinson scowling darkly.

The newspeople waited for more.

Tomlinson didn't disappoint them. "One of the issues that I intend to pursue deals with energy. There's lots of new technology that we can use to end our dependence on the oil that we import from overseas. One of those technologies is being explored right here at our state university. It's called"—he grinned—"don't let the name scare you: it's called magnetohydrodynamics."

Before anyone could complain, Tomlinson said, "That's MHD, for short."

He took a breath, then continued, "MHD is a very efficient way of generating electricity—cleanly, without polluting the atmosphere. It could ultimately cut a household's electric bills in half."

That seemed to make an impression, Jake thought.

"What's more, MHD can use this state's abundant supplies of

coal and revitalize our coal industry. It could mean thousands of new jobs across our state."

A voice from the mass of reporters called out, "But our coal has too much sulfur in it to be usable, doesn't it? It would cause acid rain, wouldn't it?"

Smiling broadly, Tomlinson nodded as he replied, "Our state's high-sulfur coal can't be used for ordinary power generators, that's true. But MHD power generators could burn our coal cleanly, without releasing those sulfur compounds into the atmosphere."

That opened a barrage of questions. Tomlinson dealt with them smoothly, like a big-league shortstop handling ground balls.

Suddenly, though, Tomlinson said, "I want you to meet my science advisor, the man who's educated me about this MHD process." Jabbing a finger in Jake's direction, Tomlinson called, "Dr. Ross, come on up here."

Stunned with surprise, Jake stood rooted to the spot until Amy nudged him gently. "Go on up," she urged.

Reluctantly, Jake climbed the three steps and walked across the stage to stand beside the brightly smiling Tomlinson, who wrapped an arm around Jake's shoulders as cameras clicked and whirred.

"This is Dr. Jacob Ross," said Tomlinson. "Jake's a professor at the university. He can fill you in on all the details of the MHD process."

Great, Jake thought. I'll be on all the news broadcasts tonight and in the papers tomorrow. Leeds and Nacho Perez will see me. So will Monster.

FEBRUARY

ROGERS'S RANGERS

Jake woke up to the sound of snowplows chugging along the street. Pulling his terry-cloth bathrobe around his naked body, he went to the window and saw that more than a foot of snow had fallen overnight. Great, he thought. I'll spend the morning digging out my car.

By the time he drove through the campus's only cleared entrance Jake felt sweaty beneath his heavy sweater and coat, his back ached, and he was certain his palms were going to blister from the shoveling he'd done, despite his leather gloves. But the clouds had blown away and the sun was shining brightly out of a crystalline blue sky. The campus was eerily quiet and empty, covered in white. Only half of the parking lot nearest Jake's building had been plowed out; the rest was covered with mountainous piles of snow that were hardening into rock-solid ice. With his wool cap pulled over his ears and his lined car coat zipped to his throat, Jake mushed his way across the nearly empty lot toward the astronomy building. Nobody else was in sight.

Jake was scheduled to meet with the three graduate students who were assisting him on his proposal for the next Mars lander; then he had his regular lecture class in the afternoon.

Inside, the building seemed deserted, and somebody had posted a garish ALL CLASSES CANCELED notice on the bulletin board. Big black stenciled letters on sunshine yellow paper. An anonymous graffitist had drawn a smiley face in the lower right corner of the sheet and scrawled *Hooray!* along its edge.

I should have checked my e-mail before I left the apartment, Jake berated himself. The university must have sent out a notice.

All classes canceled, Jake said to himself. Great. But my meeting with the Mars probe grad students is still on. At least, as far as I'm concerned.

Jake's office felt chilly once he'd hung his coat on the back of the door. They're saving on fuel, he thought. They don't expect anybody to come in on a day like this so they're keeping the thermostat dialed down.

No classes. Wondering if his grad students would show up anyway, Jake sat carefully in his desk chair, planting his booted feet firmly so it only rolled a foot or so. He checked his phone: no messages. Then he powered up his desktop computer. Just the usual spam, some university announcements. And a message from his grad students: Snowed in. See you first thing next week. Okay?

Jake knew he didn't have any recourse. They weren't coming in. Probably having a snowball fight on the dorm's parking lot. I got here through the snow but they're not coming in. Dedicated seekers of knowledge, the three of them.

So now what? he asked himself. You've got the whole day to yourself. Tomlinson's campaign is running smoothly enough, Jake thought. Some right-wing group had put up a candidate to challenge him in April's primary, but Amy didn't think that was going to be a problem. Tomlinson had both the coal industry people and the state's environmental movement in his camp. Leeds was ten points ahead in the opinion polls, although the professionals predicted that the gap would close significantly once the campaign heated up, after the primaries.

Jake realized he hadn't done a damned thing about his proposal for the sensor on the next Mars lander for the past several weeks. This meeting today was supposed to get the proposal back on track. But the kids weren't going to show. Leaning back in his spindly little chair, he told himself that there was still plenty of time for the proposal. After all this political stuff is finished, he thought. Once I get Tomlinson out of my hair I'll dive into the proposal full time.

Sinclair. Jake steepled his fingers and sunk his chin to his chest. Sinclair hasn't uttered a peep all this time. According to Glynis, the newspeople have been after him for a statement about the MHD work, but Sinclair's avoided them all. Younger and Rogers have kept quiet, too. As far as the news media is concerned, Jake told himself, I'm the expert on MHD.

Some expert. All I know is what Bob and Tim have told me.

On an impulse, he picked up his desk phone and called Rogers. The physicist answered before the phone could ring three times.

"Don't tell me you want to go down to the gym," Rogers said, chuckling. Caller ID, Jake realized.

"Hi, Bob. I thought I was the only one crazy enough to come in on a day like this."

"I slept on campus. Decided not to drive all the way back to Lignite in the snow."

"You live in Lignite?"

"All my life," said Rogers.

Jake hadn't realized that. "Are you busy? Got time for a chat?"

Rogers answered, "I'm talking things over with a few of my grad students. You want to come up here? Might be interesting for you."

"Sure," Jake said.

"Better walk," said Rogers. "Our parking area hasn't been plowed out yet."

Nodding, Jake said, "Right. I'll be there in ten, fifteen minutes."

"I'll have some hot coffee waiting for you."

Most of the campus walkways hadn't been cleared yet, either. Jake's boots were soaked through by the time he struggled across the final snowdrift in front of the electrical engineering building's main entrance. From off in the distance he could hear a snow shovel scraping on pavement. Maybe they'll get all the walkways cleared off before the spring thaw, Jake thought sourly.

There were more of the ALL CLASSES CANCELED notices plastered on the corridor walls; Jake wondered who was on campus to put them up.

Rogers's office was on the top floor and, sure enough, there was a big stainless steel coffeepot perking cheerfully atop the bookcase next to the physicist's desk. A sleeping bag was half rolled up between the desk and the office's only window, with a sturdy pair of thick-soled work boots beside it, next to the heating grill on the floor.

But no one was in the office. Jake heard voices coming from the glass-paneled door in the wall to his right. Stepping up to it he saw that somebody had Scotch-taped a sheet of paper marked WORKSHOP— ENTER AT YOUR OWN PERIL.

He recognized Rogers's voice coming from the next room, so he rapped on the flimsy door once and opened it. Rogers and a half-dozen others were bent over a big circular oak table, which took up most of the room's floor space.

"We've got to do better than this," Rogers was saying, his back to Jake and the door.

Five of the grad students were young men. The sixth was Glynis Colwyn, who smiled as she recognized Jake. She looked freshly scrubbed and perky in a thick woolen turtleneck sweater and form-fitting jeans.

"Hi, Jake," she said brightly. "Welcome to Rogers's Rangers!"

"Rogers's Rangers?" Jake asked.

Bob Rogers turned around with a self-deprecating little smile on his leathery face. "My grad students," he explained, waving a hand at the five of them. "We're a sort of think tank these days."

His grad students showed up this morning, Jake groused to himself. Then he thought, Maybe they all slept here through last night's snowstorm.

Jake looked questioningly at Glynis. Before he could ask, she said, "No, I haven't taken up EE. I'm doing liaison for Professor Sinclair."

"Oh," said Jake.

"Take your boots off and put them over by the heating grill," Rogers said. "Dry them out." Jake noticed that the physicist was in his stocking feet: brightly patterned argyles.

As Rogers introduced his grad students, Jake saw nine tubular objects laid out on the round table. They looked about the same size as a night watchman's flashlight, but they were blackened on one end; two of them seemed to have been melted almost halfway down their lengths.

Rogers gestured toward them. "That's our problem," he said. "This might stop the whole program in its tracks."

LIGHTNING RODS

What do you mean?" Jake asked, peering at the objects on the table.

"Electrodes," Rogers said, almost dolefully.

One of the grad students raised his head and sniffed loudly. "I think the coffee's done," he said. Jake had already forgotten his name.

"I'll get it," said Glynis. With a wry grin, she added, "Woman's work, you know." A couple of the male students hooted derisively.

As she slipped out of the room, Rogers explained that the electrodes were fitted into the channel of the MHD generator.

"The plasma goes through the channel at supersonic speed. It's more than five thousand degrees Fahrenheit. It's loaded with potassium salts to buck up its conductivity and a lot of sulfur compounds from the coal."

With a nod of understanding, Jake said, "So the channel takes a beating."

Rogers shook his head. "The problem's not with the channel. It's lined with ceramic tiles, like the heat shield material on the space shuttle. The channel's okay. It's the damned electrodes."

Jake looked down at the blackened tubes.

"The electrodes have to be electrical conductors. We can't make them out of ceramic. They have to tap the electrical power in the plasma and carry it out to the transformer."

"I get it," said Jake. "If they don't work well you can't get the power out of the plasma."

Rogers nodded glumly as he hefted one of the tubular objects in one hand. "They stick out into the plasma stream while it's roaring down the channel, five thousand degrees hot and in supersonic flow, with megawatts per cubic inch of electrical power crackling in there."

"Like lightning rods," Jake muttered.

"Exactly!" said Rogers. "Lightning rods that're getting zapped constantly, as long as the generator's running."

"They erode," said one of the young men.

"A lot," added the student beside him.

Jake picked up one of the electrodes. It was much lighter than he had expected, judging from its size. But he could see that one end of it had been melted as if it had been stuck into a blast furnace.

"And the erosion rate is too damned high," Rogers said.

"How long do they last?" Jake asked.

"That one in your hand was in the little rig downstairs for just over a hundred hours."

"They're all from the little rig?"

"Yep. These are all from low-power runs. We haven't even tried any long-duration runs on the big rig yet."

One of the other students said, "We're moving the separator from downstream of the channel to upstream, between the combustion chamber and the channel."

The young man beside him said, "That'll let us separate out the sulfur compounds before the plasma streams into the channel."

"Which is where the electrodes are," Jake said.

"Right."

Rogers took up, "Separating out the sulfur upstream of the channel will help reduce the erosion rate. Lowers the plasma's enthalpy a bit, but we can live with that."

Before Jake could ask about enthalpy, Glynis pushed through the door with the big stainless steel coffeepot in one hand and a tower of Styrofoam cups swaying in the other.

"Coffee break," she announced.

After a sip of the scalding-hot coffee, Jake asked Rogers, "How serious a hang-up is this electrode business?"

"Pretty damned serious. When electrode performance degrades the generator's power output nosedives. We haven't been able to run for much more than a hundred hours without the damned buggers crapping out on us. And that's at low power levels."

Glynis, standing between them, said, "The professor is very worried about this."

"He ought to be," Rogers muttered.

"You're melting the lightning rods," Jake said, eying the blackened electrodes on the table.

A little more brightly, Rogers said, "I think if we could build them like mechanical pencils—you know, screw them into the plasma stream while they're wearing down, like the lead in a pencil—we might be able to solve this problem."

"Can you do that?"

"Tim's working on it, up at the big rig. That, and moving the separator upstream of the channel."

Glynis said, "He's snowed in up there."

"They're okay, though?" Rogers asked. "Lignite hasn't lost electrical power, has it?"

"They had an outage overnight," she replied. "The power's back on now. I talked with Tim over his cell phone first thing this morning."

"Well," Rogers said, holding his steaming Styrofoam cup in both hands, "we're not going to solve this problem by staring at the little buggers."

Raising his voice, he said to his grad students, "I want a survey of all the potential materials we can use for the electrodes, with their conductivities and their calculated erosion rates."

The young men moaned a little. One of them asked, "How soon?"

"Yesterday," said Rogers.

The young man shook his head. "I knew you'd say that."

Rogers grinned at him. "Then why did you ask?"

He gestured toward the door, and Jake followed Glynis back into Rogers's office. The physicist sat behind his desk; Jake and Glynis took the two plastic bucket seats in front of it.

"What's Sinclair doing about all this?" Jake asked.

Rogers shook his head. "Not a damned thing. He seems paralyzed."

Glynis agreed. "He's been in something of a daze for the past several weeks. He canceled the one lecture he was supposed to give this semester. He spends most of his time cloistered in his office, all by himself."

"He doesn't see anybody?" Jake asked.

"Hardly anyone. His secretary, of course. And me." She hesitated, her eyes flicking away from Jake for a moment. Then she went on, "But he hasn't really had much to say to me lately."

"Me, either," Rogers said. "He used to want daily reports on how the runs are going. Last week he told me to e-mail a report to him every Friday."

Looking uncomfortable, Glynis said, "It's as if he's . . . well, as if he's in a stupor or something."

"Something medical?"

"No," Glynis said. "Psychological."

Jake tried to sort this out in his mind. "And he doesn't talk to anybody? Not even on the phone?"

"He's spoken with Senator Leeds a few times."

"Ah!"

"And his son. The professor talks to his son almost every day."

"He's letting Tim and me run the program," Rogers said. "That's not like him. Not like him at all."

"What the hell could be wrong with him?" Jake wondered.

Glynis said, "Whatever it is, I think it's got something to do with Leeds. The senator is just about the only person Professor Sinclair's spoken to in the past month."

Then she added, "And his son, of course."

Two weeks later Jake attended the public debate between Tomlinson and his only Republican rival for the primary election, a local businessman named Harmon Dant. Amy had told him that Dant was a far-right conservative who neither knew nor cared about technology.

"He'll talk about taxes, taxes, taxes," Amy had said.

The debate was set for seven P.M. in the gymnasium of the city's oldest high school. The basketball hoops at either end of the room had been folded up against their backboards and tiers of portable benches had been carried in. As usual, Jake was early; hardly a dozen people were there when he came in out of the frigid early March evening. As he climbed to the top tier of benches, where he could rest his back against the cinderblock wall, Jake pulled off his watch cap and lined coat. It felt chilly in the converted gym, but nowhere near as bad as the sub-zero winds gusting outside.

One local television crew was setting up a pair of cameras. Down in the middle of the floor stood two lecterns with a small desk between them.

Leaning against the wall, Jake realized that he hadn't seen Amy in more than a week. They talked almost every day on the phone, but she was with Tomlinson almost all the time now. Jake wondered if she were sleeping with him, too.

As he watched the auditorium slowly fill up, Jake remembered Henry Kissinger's remark that power was the ultimate aphrodisiac. He grinned ruefully. Well, that lets me out.

Then he saw Glynis Colwyn enter the auditorium, wrapped in a bulky hooded parka and muffler. She pulled the hood down, and her dark brown hair spilled down her back.

"Glyn!" he shouted, his voice echoing off the bare walls. "Up here!"

She looked up and saw him. So did just about everybody else in the place. Jake felt embarrassed yet glad as Glynis climbed up the benches toward him.

"It's freezing out there," she said by way of greeting as she sat next to him.

Jake had a sudden inspiration of wrapping his arm around her shoulders, but he figured he'd already called enough attention to himself, and besides she wouldn't appreciate his gesture.

Instead, he helped her struggle out of the parka. She folded it neatly and slipped it beneath her rump. Jake did the same with his coat. It made a lumpy cushion but it was better than the hard bench.

"How's Tim doing?" he asked.

She shook her head. "I haven't seen him in a week. He's ensconced himself up there in Lignite, working on the electrode problem. I think he sleeps with that stupid generator."

And not with you, Jake added silently.

"Uh . . ." He tried to focus on the moment. "What brings you out here on a freezing night like this?"

"Professor Sinclair asked me to come to the debate and tell him how it went."

"He's feeling better?"

Glynis tilted her head slightly to one side. "He's still pretty much a recluse. But he wants to know how Tomlinson does in this debate."

"And you have no idea of what's bugging him?" Jake probed.

"Tomlinson, of course. For some reason he's terribly upset about Tomlinson making MHD such an issue."

Jake looked into her dark, troubled eyes. This is my fault, he thought. But she doesn't seem to blame me for it.

"Oh, look!" Glynis said. "Here they come."

The auditorium was only half filled. Who wants to come out and freeze their butt on a night like this? Jake asked himself.

Tomlinson came striding out of a side door, all smiles, with a platinum-haired woman that Jake recognized as one of the anchors on the local PBS news station. Behind her came Harmon Dant, a bulky figure with thinning hair and a slightly uneasy expression on his apple-cheeked face. Tomlinson was wearing a perfectly tailored three-piece suit, as usual; Dant was in casual slacks and a navy blue blazer, unbuttoned and flapping around his ample middle.

The audience—such as it was—rose to its feet and applauded tepidly. Then Jake saw Amy Wexler hurry across the polished oak floor and take a seat on the front row of benches.

As the two candidates stood at the lecterns, the TV woman sat daintily at the little desk and looked directly into the camera with the red light glowing.

"Good evening," she said, "and welcome to the first of what we hope will be a series of debates between the two candidates for the Republican Party's nomination to run for the U.S. Senate."

She introduced Tomlinson and Dant, then told the audience that Tomlinson had won a coin toss and would speak first. Of course Tomlinson won the toss, Jake thought. The rich always get their way.

"Dant doesn't look like much, does he?" Glynis whispered.

Jake nodded his agreement as Tomlinson began his thoroughly rehearsed statement. Jake knew it by heart. Change. New hope for the state. Use our natural resources, both human and economic. Use the state's best minds. Develop a new energy system that can lower the taxpayers' electricity bills, cut the nation's dependence on oil imported from foreign countries, deliver electricity cleanly, and rejuvenate the state's coal industry. Jobs, energy efficiency, economic growth, and more jobs.

The audience applauded politely when he finished. Then the moderator turned to Harmon Dant.

With a rueful shake of his head, Dant began, "It's fine for Mr. Tomlinson here to talk about pie in the sky. He's so wealthy it doesn't matter how high your taxes go; he's got all sorts of fancy accountants and numbers jugglers to protect his money.

"Me, I'm just a businessman. I wasn't born with a silver spoon. I worked for what I got, and I'm still working. But I know what's important to you folks. Just like me, you're worrying about taxes, about gang violence in our schools and on our streets, about teenaged girls having babies before they finish high school, for cryin' out loud, about abortionists murdering unborn children. *That's* what important to you, and by golly, it's important to me, too!"

The audience broke into thunderous applause. Stunned, Jake heard hoots and whistles of approval.

"It's going to be a long evening," Glynis said over the noise of the ovation.

Alexander Tomlinson was furious.

"You let him wipe the floor with you!" he raged at his son. "He ran rings around you and you just stood there!"

As planned, Jake had driven to the Tomlinson residence after the debate for a debriefing session, leaving Glynis in the frigidly cold high school parking lot. He had waited, though, to make certain Glynis's cranky Jaguar started. To his surprise, it purred to life with no trouble. Glynis waved to him as she swung out of her parking space, leaving Jake alone in the dark, cold night.

Now, in the library of the Tomlinson mansion, it was blazingly hot.

Tomlinson and Amy were already there by the time the butler showed Jake into the library. The senior Tomlinson was pacing up and down the book-lined room, a blue vein in his forehead pulsing visibly.

"He's a *nobody*!" the old man bellowed. "And you let him make you look like a fool!"

Tomlinson had stripped off his suit jacket. Sitting in one of the library's capacious armchairs, his long legs crossed, he looked tired, frustrated, and bitterly unhappy.

"He didn't say anything specific," the son said. "He just talked in wild generalities."

"I watched the whole thing on TV," the father snapped. "I saw the applause he got."

Amy spoke up. "Dant packed the hall with his own supporters. That crowd doesn't represent the voters of—"

The elder Tomlinson spun on her. "Why wasn't the hall packed with *our* people? That's your job, lady!"

"It's just the primary—"

"Those people will go out and vote! A dedicated group of crazies can swing a primary election!"

"I'll do better next time," his son promised. "I'll know what to expect from him."

"I don't think there should be another debate. No sense looking like an ass all over again."

Tomlinson slowly got to his feet and faced his father. Jake saw that their profiles were alike, their postures straight and rigid, their fists balled at their sides.

"I'll beat him," the younger Tomlinson said. "That's a promise."

His father backed away half a step. Then he said, "We need to know more about this man Dant. Why he's running. Who's backing him."

"I'll put some of my people on that right away."

"No," the old man said. "Not your campaign people. Keep their noses out of it. I'll get some people I know to look into his background. Even if they're caught snooping nobody will be able to trace it back to you."

Amy asked, "Do you think Leeds has put him up to it? As a straw man, to take the nomination away from Franklin."

Alexander Tomlinson glared at her for a moment, but then he muttered, "I wouldn't put it past the sneaky sonofabitch."

As he drove home through the bitter night, Jake wondered if he should have asked Tomlinson's father to have some professionals look into Sinclair's background. There's something fishy about the professor's attitude, his behavior. Something's going on, and I can't figure out what it is.

Maybe Glynis knows, he mused, but she's too loyal to Sinclair to spill the beans. Or maybe she's afraid he'll cut her off from the program. That'll kill her master's thesis, ruin a year or more of work.

Somehow, the idea of hiring professional investigators to look into Sinclair's life disturbed Jake. If they find anything they'll take it straight to the old man, not to me. He'll ruin Sinclair if he thinks it'll help his son. He'll run right over him like an eighteen-wheeler.

As he pulled into his parking space and killed the Mustang's engine, Jake decided he'd have to work harder at finding out what was making Sinclair tick. But where to start? The professor won't see me. His son works in Leeds's office; I can't barge in there and start questioning him.

That leaves Glynis, he thought. I've got to get closer to her and find out everything she knows about the professor.

Somehow the idea of getting closer to Glynis didn't bother Jake at all. He smiled at the thought of it. But then he remembered that she was going with Tim Younger. A vision of a shootout in a frontier saloon popped into his mind: Younger gunning him down in a blaze of fury.

Jake pulled in a deep breath—and realized that it was well below zero, sitting in the post-midnight darkness in his unheated car.

HACKING

ake sat alone in his office the next morning, still wondering how he could pry into Sinclair's reason for refusing to back Tomlinson. Glynis is the key to it, he told himself. Yet somehow the thought of trying to use Glynis to ferret out Sinclair's secrets bothered him. Too damned sneaky, he told himself. It wouldn't be fair to Glynis. She's too nice a woman to use that way.

Besides, he admitted ruefully, she's too smart to allow me to use her. She'd see right through me. And if I came on to her, Tim would come after me.

Leaning back in his little wheeled chair, Jake asked himself, What do you mean, if you came on to her? She's going with Tim and you've got something going with Amy. Who's also letting Tomlinson sleep with her, most likely.

What a mess, he thought. What a tangled, bollixed-up freaking mess.

Then he thought of Cardwell. Ever since he'd been twelve years old Jake had brought his problems to the planetarium director. Maybe Lev can show me which way to go.

Half an hour later he was in Leverett Cardwell's office on the top floor of the museum. It was a spacious, airy room, with a wall full of bookshelves and a trio of windows that looked out across the domed roof of the planetarium. The windows were rimed with frost, even this late in the morning.

". . . so I just don't know what I should do," Jake was saying. He sat at the round conference table in the corner of the office, as he had so many times, with Cardwell sitting next to him in his prim little bow tie and neatly-pressed suit.

Cardwell hiked his eyebrows a bit. "You're not cut out to be a detective, Jake."

"You mean a spy."

"Whichever. It's not in your makeup. Drop the matter right here and now."

"But Tomlinson—"

Cardwell silenced him with an upraised hand. "Tomlinson can hire professionals to dig into Sinclair's life. Stay clear of it. If there's any dirt to be uncovered, let them do it. Keep your hands clean."

"I'm not being much help to Tomlinson, then."

"You've already helped him immensely," said Cardwell. "You've given him an issue that's so good that Leeds is backing this man Dant in an attempt to knock Tomlinson out of the running."

"You think Leeds is backing Dant?"

"Who else?" Cardwell smiled his odd little smile. "Oh, the senator's working through other parties, I'm sure. Straw men. But ask yourself: Who will benefit if Tomlinson is defeated in the primaries?"

Jake nodded. "I guess you're right."

Hunching closer, Cardwell asked, "Now what about this electrode problem? What are they doing to overcome it?"

For the better part of an hour Jake went over everything Bob Rogers had explained to him about the MHD generator's electrodes.

"Screwing them in like the lead in a mechanical pencil," Cardwell mused. "That's ingenious."

"Younger's going to set it up on the big rig, up in Lignite."

"I hope it works."

"If it doesn't, MHD will flop."

Cardwell shook his head. "No, Jake. It won't fail. It's too good an idea to fail."

"I wish I had your confidence, Lev."

The older man's smile widened a bit. "It's just a matter of perspective, Jake. You're thinking about the election in November. I'm thinking about the next century. MHD will work, eventually."

"After we're dead and gone."

Cardwell said, "You know, Charles Babbage invented the

programmable computer back in the nineteenth century. It was a mechanical monster—they didn't have electronics then, not even electricity. It never worked quite right, either. But it was a real computer, and it could have worked. It eventually led to today's computers. He's the grandfather of our modern computer age. He died a bitter old man, but his work was seminal."

Jake hunched his shoulders. "I'd like to see MHD a success while I'm still here."

"So would I, my boy. But the important thing is that it becomes a success, becomes useful, someday. Doesn't matter if we're here to see it. I'd like to be, but in the long run that doesn't matter."

"It matters to me."

"Good!" Cardwell said, with a grin. "Impetuous youth. Every new idea needs that kind of enthusiasm, that kind of vigor. You can't build new ideas with old farts like me."

Jake stared at him. "Lev, sometimes you're weird."

Laughing, Cardwell said, "Stick to the technical side of the game, Jake. Let Tomlinson and his father root around in the dirt. That's not your field of expertise."

Feeling far less than satisfied, Jake got to his feet. "I guess you're right."

Standing beside him, Cardwell said, "Of course, if you're determined to do something, you might try checking out Sinclair's file on some of the computer search engines. There might be something there that could help shed light on his behavior."

"You think so?"

As he walked Jake to his office door, Cardwell said, "There's a lot of information floating through the Internet. Who knows what's in there about Sinclair?"

"I wonder."

"It might be worth a try."

"Might be," Jake agreed.

As he reached for the doorknob, Cardwell said, "One thing, though. If you find anything that looks interesting, useful, would you bring it to me before showing Tomlinson? I'd like to see it first."

"You would?"

His face hardening, Cardwell said, "I'd like to know what he's up to. I've got an old score to settle with Arlan Sinclair."

Jake had never seen Leverett Cardwell look so grim.

That evening, Jake found that there was indeed plenty of information on the Internet about Professor Sinclair. He decided to search the Net from his computer at home, rather than his office desktop. Too easy for other people on campus to poke into his files. Do it at home, he told himself. Less chance of being found snooping.

But there was damned little useful material among the megabytes of data. By midnight Jake was bleary-eyed and more respectful of Sinclair than he had been before. There was plenty of information about Professor Arlan Sinclair available on various search engines. His early work in high-temperature gas physics. His patents on laminar flow regenerative cooling systems for rocket engines. Awards and honors for everything from artificial heart pump designs to research papers on shock waves in interstellar plasmas.

But nothing useful.

According to his standard biography in the university's files, Sinclair was still married. One child, a son, Arlan III. Tell me something I don't know, Jake grumbled to himself.

Google. Yahoo. Wikipedia. Jake even looked up the state government's site on prominent citizens.

Arlan Sinclair II. So he's not a junior, Jake saw. Married 1983 to Olivia Vernon. One child . . .

Feeling sleepy and cranky, Jake logged off, got up from his desk chair, and headed for the bathroom. By the time he had finished brushing his teeth, though, he went back to the computer and looked up Olivia Sinclair, née Vernon.

There wasn't much in the files about her. She was from old money, apparently, and lived upstate, in the town of Vernon. She was listed in the social registry. No e-mail address, but there was a phone number given.

Jake yawned as he shut down his computer for the night. It was nearly one A.M. Maybe I'll phone her tomorrow, he thought as he went to the bedroom. Nothing ventured, nothing gained.

OLIVIA SINCLAIR, NÉE VERNON

t was very good of you to see me," Jake said as he sat in the front parlor of the Vernon house.

It had obviously been a palatial residence, once, but now it seemed faded, dusty, a relic of bygone years. Mrs. Sinclair was a chubby woman with a round, dimpled face. Her hair was the shade of ash blond that older women achieve when they try to glamorize their gray. She was wearing a long-skirted print dress, two different shades of dull brown, as she sat primly on an armchair facing Jake.

He felt awkward. All during the drive up to Vernon Jake had wondered what he would say to Mrs. Sinclair, how he could explain his reason for visiting her. During the two-hour drive, the car radio had played seven ads for Harmon Dant. Jake had counted them. Seven. Dant's ads were on every radio station, pushing his conservative message of cutting taxes, ending legalized abortion, cracking down on crime. Fishing around the radio dial, Jake could find no ads for Tomlinson. Not one.

Mrs. Sinclair smiled vacantly at Jake. "Would you like some tea?"

It was past time for lunch, but Jake answered, "No, thank you. I'm fine."

She had greeted him at the front door when he'd rung the bell. As far as Jake could tell, the house was empty except for her. No servants in sight. No relatives. Does she live in this mausoleum all by herself? he wondered.

"You said you worked with my husband?"

Jake started to shake his head, caught himself, and replied, "I'm working with Franklin Tomlinson on his campaign to be elected to the U.S. Senate. Mr. Tomlinson thinks that your husband's MHD power generation program could be very good for this state—and the nation."

"That's nice," said Mrs. Sinclair.

Wondering what on earth he should be saying, Jake blurted, "You have a very nice house here."

She nodded pleasantly. "It was built by my great-grandfather. He founded this town, you know. It's named after him."

"Really."

"He was a great man: a very successful businessman, a civic leader, a true philanthropist."

"I see."

Silence stretched between them. At last Mrs. Sinclair asked, "And how is Arlan these days?"

"Oh, he's . . . he's fine, Mrs. Sinclair. He's very busy at the university, of course."

"Of course."

"Um . . . do you see much of him?"

Her smile remained undiminished. "Now and then. He comes up here once in a while."

"That's nice," Jake said, feeling like an idiot.

Mrs. Sinclair got up from her chair and walked slowly to the window. Pulling the lace curtain back, she asked mildly, "Is that your car? It's lovely."

Jake hopped to his feet and went to the window beside her. Yes, she was actually looking at his beat-up old Mustang.

"It needs to be washed," he apologized.

Turning to him, Mrs. Sinclair asked, "Could you do me a great favor, Mr . . . eh . . . oh dear, I can't recall your name."

"It's Ross, ma'am. Jake Ross."

"Could you do me a great favor, Mr. Ross?" she asked, her fleshy face puckering into a girlishly beseeching expression.

"A favor?"

"I have an appointment on the other side of town, but my car's in the shop. Would you be kind enough to drive me?"

"Sure," Jake said. "Of course."

"I won't be a minute." And she turned and hurried out of the parlor.

She came back muffled in a floor-length fur coat. It looked a little bedraggled to Jake, the fur shiny. Could it be mink? he asked himself. Awfully expensive, if it is.

Mrs. Sinclair led Jake to the front hall closet, where she pulled out a long wool scarf and wrapped it over her head. All smiles, she nodded that she was ready to leave the house. Jake zipped up his car coat, pulled his watch cap out of its pocket and, with his free hand, opened the front door.

The afternoon was clear and crisp, although there were clouds building up over the mountains. Jake followed Mrs. Sinclair's directions through the town of Vernon and out into the brown frozen countryside. Patches of snow covered parts of the fields, although the road was clear and dry.

"Are we heading the right way?" he asked as they drove beneath an overpass for the interstate highway.

"It's just another little bit," she said, her eyes aimed straight ahead. "Less than a mile."

Sure enough, in a minute she pointed excitedly. "There it is! Turn off here!"

Jake saw a fair-sized single-story building, fake adobe style. A dozen or so cars were in the wide parking lot. A garish electronic sign by the side of the road proclaimed, BLUE MOUNTAIN CASINO.

A gambling casino.

"This is the place?" Jake asked, incredulous.

"Yes," said Mrs. Sinclair. "You can park right by the front entrance, there, in the breezeway."

He helped her to struggle out of the Mustang's bucket seat. Once on her feet Mrs. Sinclair almost ran to the heavy double doors of the casino's main entrance.

"Come on!" she insisted, waving impatiently to Jake. "My treat!"

Almost dazed with confused surprise, Jake followed her into the casino. Mrs. Sinclair slipped out of her coat and handed it to a stocky, bored-looking Native American woman tending the coat room. Jake took off his wool cap and stuffed it back into the pocket of his coat. He unzipped the coat but left it on.

The casino's lobby was lined with slot machines. Down three thinly carpeted steps, the main room was already busy with customers. Jake saw that most of them were middle-aged women sitting in front of slot machines that whirred and dinged incessantly. Farther into the room a few stolid-looking men were sitting at a table playing cards. Others were huddled around another table. Craps, Jake guessed.

"See?" said Mrs. Sinclair grandly. "See how much fun everyone is having!"

It didn't look like fun to Jake. All the customers looked grim, almost bellicose. The women at the slot machines seemed determined to hand all their money to the one-armed bandits as fast as they could.

"Come on!" Mrs. Sinclair urged. "My treat!"

Bewildered, Jake followed her down the three steps and onto the main floor. The place looked threadbare, worn out; it smelled of cigarette smoke and stale air.

"Let's try the blackjack table," Mrs. Sinclair said, grabbing for Jake's arm and pulling him down the aisle between the clanging slot machines.

A stern-looking elderly man, gray-haired and gray-faced, stepped into the aisle in front of her. He wore a dark suit and a weary expression.

"Mrs. Sinclair," he said, his face stony. "You know we're not allowed to let you play."

She gave him a girlish smile. "Oh, just for a little bit. I won't stay long."

The man shook his head. "I'd lose my job, Mrs. Sinclair."

"You're the manager, aren't you?" she wheedled. "You don't have to tell anybody that I was here. I won't tell on you."

Looking past her to Jake, the manager asked, "And who is this gentleman?"

"He's from the university. He works with my husband."

"My name's Jacob Ross," Jake said, as if that explained anything.

From behind him, Jake heard a young woman's voice say, "You'll have to come with me, sir."

Turning, he saw a uniformed police officer. She was short, round-ish, looked like a Native American. The patch on the shoulder of her bulky windbreaker said VERNON POLICE DEPARTMENT. She had a two-way radio clipped on her belt and a wicked-looking automatic pistol holstered at her hip.

Her right hand hovered near the butt of her pistol as she stared unsmilingly at Jake.

BUSTED

The police officer led Jake and Mrs. Sinclair out of the casino, while the manager walked a few steps behind them.

"I'll tell my husband about this," Mrs. Sinclair threatened as the officer bundled her into a Vernon PD squad car.

"Yes, ma'am," said the officer sweetly. "I'll drive you home. You can phone him from there." To Jake she called, "Please follow me in your car, sir. Unless you want to leave it here."

Jake followed the squad car back through town to Mrs. Sinclair's house. The policewoman got out of the squad car and walked to his Mustang. "Stay in your car, sir. Once I've got Mrs. Sinclair back inside her house, you'll have to follow me to the station."

Jake felt his brows hike. "Am I under arrest?"

"Nosir. Not exactly."

Wondering what "not exactly" meant, Jake watched as the policewoman led Mrs. Sinclair up to her front door. The older woman was jabbering away, obviously complaining, but the police officer paid no attention, as far as Jake could see. The cop pushed on the bell, and the door was immediately opened by a blocky, middle-aged woman in a black housemaid's outfit. Mrs. Sinclair went inside the house with her and the policewoman returned to her squad car.

As she opened the car door she called to Jake, "Just follow me, sir."

He meekly followed her to Vernon's police station. It was a small building, but made of solid stone. To Jake it looked like a fort that might have been built during the Indian Wars. He parked beside the squad car and followed the officer into the Vernon Police Department station.

Inside, it looked surprisingly modern. Clean, efficiently laid out with new-looking metal desks that each bore flat computer screens.

One wall was covered with TV monitors. Jake realized that just about every intersection in the town was covered by surveillance cameras. He even noticed a pair of screens that displayed the parking lot and front entrance of the Blue Mountain Casino.

So that's how they knew she went to the casino, he realized. They can watch the whole damned town twenty-four/seven.

The policewoman threaded through the desks toward the back of the squad room, glancing over her shoulder twice to make certain Jake was following her. She stopped at a glass door marked CAPTAIN HARRAWAY—PRIVATE. She rapped on the glass panel once, then opened the door and gestured Jake inside.

Captain Harraway rose from behind his desk like a dark cloud. His skin was deep brown, yet his features looked to Jake more Native American than African American. He was big, in all directions, thick arms bulging the sleeves of his blue uniform shirt, heavy midsection straining its buttons.

With a minimal smile, he pointed to the chair in front of his desk. "Have a seat, Dr. Ross."

Jake was impressed that the captain knew he had a doctorate. They've looked up my file during the time it took us to go from the casino to here.

Settling himself in his squeaking swivel chair once Jake was seated, Harraway clasped his hands in front of him and said, "We've got a sort of situation on our hands."

Jake said nothing.

Leaning forward on his beefy arms, Harraway went on, "Y'see, Mrs. Sinclair's from one of our most prominent families. And she's got this problem."

"Gambling?"

With a weary nod, the captain said, "Hooked like an addict. She'd blow what's left of the family fortune if we didn't keep her out of the casino."

Jake began to understand. "So you keep an eye on her."

"We sure as hell do. Her uncle's the mayor of this town and just about everybody on the town council is related to her, one way or the other."

"Does she live alone in that big house?"

"She has a couple of servants. Gave 'em both the day off just be-fore you arrived."

So she planned to have me drive her out to the casino all along, Jake realized. As soon as I phoned her this morning she started hatching her little plot.

Harraway interrupted his train of thought. "Now, what I need to know is, what're you doing here? Why'd you come all the way up here from the university to see her?"

How much should I tell him? Jake wondered. How much can I tell him?

Harraway sat hunched over his desktop, his eyes focused on Jake like a pair of hunting rifles. The expression on his dark face seemed to say, *I know just what you're thinking, buster. Make your story a good one.*

Jake sucked in a breath, then said, "I'm working with Franklin Tomlinson on his election campaign. I'm his science advisor."

"What's that got to do with Mrs. Sinclair?"

"Professor Sinclair runs the MHD program at the university and—"

"MHD? What the hell's MHD?"

"It's a new way to generate electrical power. Professor Sinclair heads the university's program and Tomlinson is interested in its pos-sibilities."

"So?"

Thinking as fast as he ever had in his life, Jake said, "So I came up here to pay a call on Mrs. Sinclair. It seemed like a polite thing to do."

"You drove two hours to pay a social call on Mrs. Sinclair." Harraway's voice rumbled with suspicion.

Jake nodded. "That's right." It was weak, but it was all he had.

The phone on the desk buzzed. Harraway glanced past Jake, out through his office window to the clerk sitting out there, then picked up the phone in his massive paw.

"Harraway," he said. "Yes, Professor. Good of you to call. Yes, she tried to sneak out to the casino again, but the manager wouldn't let her play. We got her home again all right. No trouble."

He listened for several moments, his eyes flicking from Jake to the squad room beyond his office windows, then back to Jake again.

"She had a visitor and got him to drive her to the casino. Guy from the university, says he's working with you. Dr. Ross. Ja—"

Even from across the desk Jake could hear Sinclair's furious outburst on the phone. Harraway's eyes went wide, then narrowed again.

"Yes, sir. Yes, I agree. I'll tell him. He's right here in my office, right this minute."

More angry chatter from the phone. At last Harraway said a polite good-bye and hung up.

"The professor wants me to lock you up and throw away the key."

Jake swallowed hard. "I only wanted to meet her . . ."

"He's damned pissed at you, boy."

"I didn't do anything wrong."

Harraway pointed a finger at Jake, like a pistol. "Let me give you some advice, Dr. Ross. Get out of Vernon. Get out *now* and don't *ever* come calling on Mrs. Sinclair again. If we see you in this town again we'll find a reason to arrest you. Vagrancy, littering, child molesting: we'll find some charge and make it stick. Do you understand?"

Jake nodded dumbly.

"Now get the hell out of here and don't come back."

Jake scrambled to his feet.

"And you'd better go see Professor Sinclair as soon's you get back to the university. He wants to talk to you."

REVELATION

Jake was only half surprised to see that Nacho Perez was in Sinclair's office. He was standing by the window, looking out at the snowy peaks of the distant mountains, hands clasped behind his back, rumpled suit jacket hanging loosely on his spare frame.

Jake had phoned Sinclair from his car as he drove back to the university. Even in the cell phone's tiny speaker he could hear the fury radiating from the professor's voice.

"You get yourself to my office the instant you reach the campus. Do you hear me? The very instant!"

Starting to feel angry himself, Jake had replied tightly, "I'll be there."

And Perez was there, too. As he stepped into the professor's sizeable office, Jake wondered if Monster were downstairs in the parking lot, waiting for him.

Sinclair was in his shirtsleeves; he had pulled his tie from his unbuttoned collar. He shot out of his desk chair the instant Jake walked into the room.

"How dare you intrude on my wife's privacy?" Sinclair bellowed before Jake could say hello.

"She invited me to visit her," Jake said.

Leveling an accusing finger at Jake, the professor snarled, "You had no right to see her. I'll charge you with criminal trespass, goddamn you! I'll get you fired! I'll break you!"

Jake glanced at the stubble-jawed Perez, who looked more bemused than annoyed.

Turning back to Sinclair, he said as calmly as he could, "Your wife is a gambling addict and you don't want anyone to know about it. Well, now I know and if you try to make good on your threats the rest of the world will know, too."

Sinclair's fleshy face turned flame red. His chest heaved visibly. Before he could say anything, though, Perez took a step from the window toward Jake.

"Now wait a minute, kid. You saying you'll keep your mouth shut about Mrs. Sinclair?"

"I'm saying that I understand why the professor here is under Senator Leeds's thumb. Leeds will keep quiet about her addiction as long as the professor doesn't support Tomlinson."

Sinclair seemed to crumple. He sagged into his desk chair, mouth hanging open, hands fluttering purposelessly. He took in a deep breath and pressed both hands firmly on the desktop.

"It's more than that," Sinclair muttered, staring down at his hands. "She nearly bankrupted me before I could . . . make the arrangements to keep her under control. The senator has been . . . helpful . . . financially."

"Your son's job," Jake said.

"More than that," said the professor.

"So it's your move, kid," Perez said, his voice scratchy, harsh. "Whacha gonna do about this?"

To Sinclair, Jake said, "I'll have to tell Tomlinson why you can't back his campaign."

"And he'll splash it all over the news media," Sinclair moaned.

With a shake of his head, Jake replied, "No, there's no point to that. It won't help anything. Tomlinson will understand that."

Perez said, "The best thing for you, kid, is to keep yer big mouth shut."

"I'll have to tell Tomlinson," Jake insisted.

"Would you keep quiet for ten grand?"

Jake blinked at Perez. "Ten thousand dollars?"

"Tax free." Perez's lean, swarthy face broke into a knowing grin.

"No thanks."

The grin disappeared. "You tryin' to hold us up for more money?"

"I don't want your money."

"You're gonna make things hard on yourself, kid."

"Is that a threat?"

"Could be."

Jake drew himself up as straight as he could and tried to keep Monster's image out of his mind. "Beating me up is the surest way to break this story to the news media."

"Who said anything about a beatin'?" Perez countered, with exaggerated innocence. Then he added, "But you could have an accident. Icy roads, too much to drink—"

"No!" Sinclair shouted. "I won't have any part of that."

Perez shrugged. "It ain't your department, Prof. You got nothin' to say about it."

"I've already told one of Tomlinson's aides about my visit with Mrs. Sinclair," Jake lied. "Told her on the cell phone while I was driving back from Vernon. If anything happens to me, she'll go straight to the news reporters."

Perez started to say something, then thought better of it. Sinclair sat at his desk, bowed over like a man loaded down with a burden that threatened to overwhelm him.

Jake turned around and headed for the door, thinking, I hope they believe me. I hope Monster's not downstairs waiting to break my legs. I've got to tell Tomlinson about this while I have the chance.

SURPRISES

As soon as Jake got to his own office he phoned Tomlinson. An aide told him in a haughty, know-it-all tone that Mr. Tomlinson was across the state, campaigning in the small farming towns.

"Amy Wexler, then," Jake said into the phone.

"Ms. Wexler is with Mr. Tomlinson."

Of course she is, Jake thought. Of course she is.

"Is there anyone else I could connect you to?" asked the aide.

"No," Jake said. "I'll try her cell phone."

All he got was the cell phone's message service. She doesn't even have the phone turned on, Jake said to himself. Looking out his office window, he saw that the sun was low on the horizon. Long purple shadows were creeping across the campus.

I wonder what motel they'll shack up in tonight, Jake grumbled silently.

His phone rang. Grabbing it, he blurted, "Amy?"

"No, it's me," said Glynis Colwyn's voice. "I need to talk to you." She sounded cold, grim.

"Sure. Where are you, I'll—"

"You stay where you are," Glynis said. "I'll come over."

Jake fiddled about the office for a few moments, then went back to his desk and phoned Tomlinson's office again. The same reedy, superior voice answered.

"This is Jake Ross again."

The aide asked, "And what can I do for you now, Dr. Ross?" He sounded slightly exasperated.

Jake realized he was biting his lip. "Uh, Mr. Tomlinson told me he would get someone to . . . uh, well . . . sort of watch out for me. You know, like a bodyguard."

"Bodyguard?" Jake could hear the surprise in the guy's voice.

"That's right."

"How . . . unusual."

"Do you know if he's contacted anyone about that?"

A hesitation. Jake got the feeling that the aide was suppressing laughter. Finally, "No, Dr. Ross, I haven't heard a thing to that effect."

"Oh."

"The Fain Security Company provides security for Mr. Tomlinson. You could ask them, I suppose."

The aide's smugly superior tone irritated Jake. "All right. That's what I should do, I suppose."

"Yes, it is."

"Do you have their number?"

"They're in the book, I'm sure."

You self-important little prick, Jake thought. Aloud, he said, "Thanks. You've been a big help."

"Just doing my job, Dr. Ross."

Jake slammed the phone back into its slot, fuming. Now he'll spread it all over campaign headquarters that I want a bodyguard. Damn!

A single rap on his door made him look up. Glynis Colwyn stepped into his office, her dark eyes snapping at him. She was wearing a knee-length dark wool coat over a maroon sweater and faded jeans, and clutched an expensive-looking leather purse in one hand.

"What did you do to him?" she demanded before Jake could get up from his chair.

"Sinclair?"

"Of course!" Glynis said, stepping up to his desk.

"I visited his wife, up in Vernon," Jake said. As they both sat down, he added, "She's a gambling addict and Leeds has helped the professor to cover it up."

Glynis's expression softened. "A gambling addict?"

"That's what Leeds has on the professor. Apparently he's put up a good deal of money to help pay Mrs. Sinclair's gambling debts."

Glynis shrugged out of her coat and let it drape over the back of her chair. "So that's why the professor won't go with Tomlinson."

"That's why."

More sharply, she asked, "And what do you intend to do about it?"

Jake spread his hands. "I'll have to tell Tomlinson, of course."

"Jake, you can't!"

"Why not?"

"It will ruin the professor. It'll be a scandal."

"That his wife's a gambling addict? Nobody's going to be ruined over that. Lots of people have the same problem. For god's sake, Glynis, the state has counseling programs for gambling addiction. They even put up billboards advertising the programs."

"But you don't understand! The professor will be humiliated."

Thinking of Cardwell and his wife, Jake said, "So what."

"That's cruel, Jake."

He sighed. "Yeah, I guess maybe it is. But Sinclair's no saint, you know."

"And the fact that he's taken money from Senator Leeds and now Leeds is holding that over him . . ." She shook her head.

"It'd be a good way to blacken Leeds's eye," Jake mused.

"Jake, don't."

"Sinclair has it coming."

"Because his wife is sick?"

"Because he's a pompous ass who's hidden his wife up there in Vernon while he hits on every woman he sees," Jake snapped.

Her chin went up. "That's not so."

"Isn't it? You told me he tried to hit on you."

"Oh, that," Glynis said. "That wasn't serious."

"Wasn't it?"

She didn't reply.

Thinking of Cardwell and Alice, Jake said, "It's not just students, Glynis. He's gone after married women, too."

"That's no reason to be so . . . so . . . vindictive."

She's trying to protect him, Jake said to himself. Why? She's going with Tim Younger and Tim's being held down by the professor.

He heard himself ask, "Whose side are you on, Glynis?"

"Side?" she asked. "Why do there have to be sides?"

"We're in the middle of a political campaign, for god's sake. I'm working for a man who's running for the Senate, remember?"

"And I'm working for a man who has a problem with his wife," she countered.

"What about Tim? What about the way Sinclair treats him?"

Her eyes flared. "Tim's a big boy. He can take care of himself."

"Like he's taking care of you?"

She stared at him for a long, silent moment. At last she said, "My relationship with Tim is none of your business."

"But why are you trying to protect Sinclair when he's treating Tim like some migrant farm worker?"

"Arlan needs protection from opportunists who'd ruin his career and his marriage just to help win an election."

Arlan? Jake thought. She's calling the bastard by his first name?

"I'm not an opportunist, Glynis," he said, surprising himself by how softly he spoke the words. "But I'm working for Tomlinson and I've got to tell him about Sinclair and the hold that Leeds has over him."

"No matter what," she said bitterly.

"Tomlinson won't go public about it," Jake tried to assure her. "It wouldn't do him any good." But inwardly he knew that Tomlinson could hurt Leeds by making this story public.

Slowly, Glynis got to her feet. She pulled her coat off the back of the chair, then said, "I had expected better of you, Jake."

He got up from his chair, too. "Tomlinson won't go public about it," he repeated. But it sounded lame, he knew.

"I hope you're right. I hope you're not going to ruin the professor just to score a political point."

Standing, Jake said, "You're forgetting the real goal here, Glynis. I want the MHD program to succeed. I want Tim to be a success."

"Over Sinclair's dead body," she said coldly.

Jake shook his head, thinking, If there's going to be any dead body around here, chances are pretty good it'll be mine.

CARDWELL RESIDENCE

A s soon as Glynis left his office, Jake phoned Cardwell.

"I have news about Sinclair," he said into the phone.

Lev didn't answer for a heartbeat. Then he asked, "What is it?"

Glancing at the twilight shadows engulfing the campus, Jake said, "Maybe we'd better talk face-to-face."

"That bad?"

"It's . . . complicated."

Cardwell's voice sounded strangely flat. "Alice and I have a dinner engagement at seven o'clock. Why don't you come over to the house for a beer, around five thirty?"

Jake said, "I'll be there."

Cardwell met him at the front door of his little doll's house, in a tuxedo complete with black bow tie, although his jacket was off and Jake could see the fire-engine red suspenders he was wearing.

He led Jake to the tiny room tucked beneath the stairs that led up to the second floor. Jake had always suspected that the space had originally been a closet, but Lev had turned it into a compact little study for himself, with a minuscule desk, the flat screen of a computer on the wall beneath the slanted ceiling, and even a narrow set of bookshelves on the one full-height wall. With the two of them sitting knee to knee, Jake felt as if he were in the captain's cabin on a submarine. The compartment felt stuffy with the door tightly closed. The promised beers were nowhere in sight.

"Gambling addiction," Cardwell muttered. "Poor woman."

"Apparently she went through a lot of their money. Senator Leeds has helped Sinclair financially—enough to control the professor."

His owl-eyed face wrinkled with concern, Cardwell asked, "Hasn't he gotten her some professional help?"

"I don't know. If he has, it isn't working. She trotted me out to the casino on the reservation as soon as I arrived at her house."

"And the casino manager wouldn't let her play?"

Jake nodded. "They've got the whole town staked out, Lev. She's like a prisoner up there."

"Poor woman," Cardwell repeated.

Jake got to his feet carefully, his hair brushing the slanting ceiling. "So now I've got to tell Tomlinson as soon as he gets back—"

"No," Cardwell said, so softly that Jake barely heard it.

"No?"

Waving Jake back to his little ladderback chair, Cardwell said, "You should keep this to yourself, Jake."

"But I thought . . ."

With a sigh and his strange little smile, Cardwell said, "You thought I was after Arlan's scalp. Well, I am. But not like this."

Jake sat there, dumbfounded.

"What good would it do?" Cardwell asked. "You could embarrass Sinclair and humiliate his wife. You could hand Tomlinson a smear he could use against Leeds, I suppose. But would that change Sinclair's opposition to Tomlinson?" With a shake of his head Cardwell answered his own question. "No, it would simply cement his position, force him to stand with Leeds. And the senator might even appear as something of a humanitarian, helping a man who has a problem with a sick wife."

"But . . . I thought . . ."

Shaking his head gently, Cardwell went on, "It wouldn't change anything, Jake, except to dirty up the campaign. Slinging mud is a nasty thing to do."

"I suppose it is," Jake admitted.

Patting Jake's knee, Cardwell brightened a bit as he said, "I'd like to catch Arlan with his pants down. I'd love to show the world what a womanizing SOB the man can be. But not this. This is below the belt."

"So I should keep this to myself?" Jake asked.

"If it would help Tomlinson's campaign, I'd say go ahead and tell the man. But this won't help. It might even make Leeds look a little better."

Jake felt as if his head were spinning. Politics, he thought. It's so damned convoluted.

Abruptly, Cardwell asked, "So what's going on with the campaign? How's Tomlinson really doing?"

Jake waggled one hand. "Dant's been a big surprise. Tomlinson's people keep telling him that Dant's backing is very narrow, just the ultraconservatives, but they're worried that it might be enough to snatch the primary away from us. If those crazies come out and vote in a solid block they could carry the election and leave Tomlinson out in the cold. Voter turnout in the primaries is usually pretty low. A strong, determined bloc of fanatics could beat us."

Rubbing his chin thoughtfully, Cardwell murmured, "And give Leeds a much easier opponent in the general election."

Jake nodded. "That's right."

"And MHD? What's happening with the MHD program?"

"The work's proceeding, mostly out in Lignite. Tomlinson's people are trying to get the chairman of the National Association of Electric Utilities to meet with him and endorse MHD."

"That's good," Cardwell said softly. "An endorsement could be helpful."

Jake recognized the pensive expression on Lev's face. "But . . . ?"

"But some active undertaking would be even better."

"Active undertaking?"

"An endorsement is merely lip service," Cardwell explained. "You should try to get the Utilities Association to *do* something concrete to show they're behind MHD."

"Do something?" Jake asked. "What?"

Cardwell smiled at Jake. "You're the science advisor, my boy. You think of something concrete for the association to prove its faith in MHD."

"Something concrete."

His gentle smile broadening, Cardwell said, "Always make the victim a party to the crime, Jake. Bind them to you."

Jake nodded. "I'll try."

"Good!"

Cardwell got to his feet and Jake went with him to the front hall, taking in a deep breath of air, as if he'd been submerged for the past twenty minutes. Alice came downstairs, all smiles and dressed for dinner in a lovely lilac gown. Jake said good night to them both and drove home through the early evening darkness.

He thought the car behind him was following him. Black Cadillac. Jake was pretty sure that was the kind of car that Monster drove.

"IF IT DOESN'T WORK . . ."

It was two days before Tomlinson and Amy returned, two days in which Jake struggled with his conscience about Sinclair and stewed inwardly at his suspicion that Amy was sleeping with Tomlinson. Two days of Jake looking over his shoulder for a sight of Monster or some of his pals.

She must be sleeping with him, he realized. They're together night and day for weeks on end. Why wouldn't she? I've got no claim on her. I never did. What happened between us was strictly fun and games. I'd be an idiot to expect anything more.

Still, he felt hurt. Betrayed.

He went through his classes like an automaton. Students dropped into his office for counseling sessions and he couldn't remember what he'd told them five minutes after they'd left.

Jake looked up the number of the Fain Security Company and spoke to a woman who identified herself as Micky Fain's daughter, Michelle.

"Our files don't show any record of Mr. Tomlinson asking for a security detail for you, Dr. Ross," she said, in a singsong kindergarten teacher's tone.

"Oh. I see. Mr. Tomlinson must have forgotten about it."

"He's a very busy man, of course."

"Yeah. I'll talk to him about it when he gets back to town."

Just after lunch of the second day Bob Rogers phoned. "We're going to do a ten-hour run on the big rig," he announced cheerfully. "Test the new electrodes. Want to come up and take a look with me?"

"Why not?" Jake responded. It was an excuse to get off campus, out of town, away from his troubles.

Rogers insisted on driving. "No sense taking two cars. We'll just pop in for an hour or so and see how things are going. Besides, the weather forecast is for snow and my beast can handle that better than your little convertible."

"But then you'll have to drive all the way back to Lignite, won't you?" Jake asked.

"Nah. If the snow gets too bad I'll get a dorm room on campus."

So Jake climbed into the heavy van and Rogers put it in gear and headed for the highway.

"Does Tim know we're coming?" he asked.

Rogers nodded without taking his eyes off the road. "You bet. I wouldn't pop in on him unannounced. He doesn't like that."

"He's an ornery so-and-so."

With a laugh, Rogers agreed. "There's an old bit from history I think about whenever Tim gets really stiff. World War Two, just after Pearl Harbor. Most of the U.S. Navy is sunk at Pearl Harbor. President Roosevelt needs somebody to run the Navy, build it up again, win the war."

Jake wondered how this related to Tim Younger.

Rogers went on, "Roosevelt picks Admiral Ernest King. Everybody's stunned. King was a drunk and a womanizer who had made a lot of enemies for himself. But he was tough, and smart."

"We did win the war," Jake said.

"Damned right. But when King heard that he'd been picked to run the Navy, which was mostly at the bottom of Pearl Harbor, you know what he said?"

Jake shook his head.

"He said, 'When they get into trouble they call for the sons of bitches.'"

Rogers laughed. It took Jake a moment to understand what the story meant. When you have a really tough job to do you need a tough man to do it.

Jake grinned a little. Tim Younger is a tough man. I'm not, he realized. I'm a cream puff.

Clouds were piling up over the mountains, dark and ominous, as they drove through the town of Lignite. They could hear the generator's roar while they were almost a mile away from the big rig's facility, even with the Land Rover's windows rolled up.

"Still running," Roger said, smiling. "That's a good sign."

By the time he parked the van the noise was like the thunder of a formation of fighter jets. Rogers leaned across and fished a pair of earphones out of the glove compartment. With a grin he handed them to Jake.

"What about you?" Jake shouted.

"I'll find a pair inside."

Once inside, even with the muffling cups pressing against his ears Jake could hear the generator's roar, feel the vibration in the air; a thin mist of dust was jittering across the quivering concrete floor of the test cell. Younger and the technicians were in the control booth, behind the glass partition, all of them wearing earphones.

Jake saw Younger mouth hello as he and Rogers squeezed into the already crowded booth. Tim wasn't smiling. Just a curt nod and the one word, to Rogers actually. I'm an interloper here, Jake told himself. A tourist.

Rogers pulled on a set of earphones. Tapping Jake's shoulder, he pointed to the gauges on the control panel.

"Fifty-two meg!" he shouted, loudly enough to get through the muffling.

"How long has it been running?" Jake hollered.

Younger must have heard him because he pointed to a digital clock on the back wall of the booth. It read 2:47:59, and as Jake looked at it the numbers changed to 2:48:00.

Rogers was grinning broadly and bobbing his head up and down. Almost three hours, Jake thought. At better than fifty megawatts. Good. Really good.

There wasn't much to do. While Younger and the technicians seemed fully absorbed in monitoring the gauges and dials of their control panel, Jake soon began to feel edgy. The generator just sat there, blasting away, but it didn't do anything visible. The whole building seemed to shake; Jake saw dust motes jiggling in the air. The generator seemed unperturbed, like a long-distance runner loping along in easy rhythm.

Inside the generator, Jake knew, gases heated to more than five thousand degrees were roaring through the channel at supersonic speed. Enormous electrical energy was crackling inside that channel, and just outside it was the superconducting magnet, cooled down to a couple of hundred degrees below zero.

Fifty-some megawatts coming from what was essentially a small piece of equipment. Jake had visited electric utility power plants, back when he'd been a student. He remembered the enormous turbines spinning away. They dwarfed the big rig. And the turbines at the hydroelectric dam, up in the mountains. They were even bigger.

If this rig can put out fifty megawatts, Jake calculated mentally, an MHD generator that can equal the power output of a regular power plant wouldn't be half as big as the regular plant.

Rogers had told him that MHD generators become more efficient as they get bigger. That's because the losses in the system come from the friction of the hot gas—plasma, really—rubbing against the channel walls. But the power output comes from the total volume of plasma in the channel. Make it bigger and the losses go up as the square of the channel's size, but the power output increases as the cube of the size. The bigger the better. Rogers called it "the three-halves law."

He tapped Rogers on the shoulder. When the physicist turned toward him, Jake yelled, "How're the electrodes holding up?"

With an exaggerated shrug, Rogers leaned close to Jake's ear and hollered, "Must be okay. The rig's still running, still putting out power."

Suddenly one of the technicians yelled something and gesticulated at the control panel. Looking down at the gauges, Younger hammered a fist against the control panel.

"Cut it!" he screamed, so loud that Jake heard it clearly even through his earphones. Technicians jumped in a flurry of pushing buttons and flicking switches.

The noise and vibration suddenly stopped. The needles on the dials all spun down to zero. The clock stopped at 2:51:44.

Younger was ranting. Jake yanked off his earphones and heard Tim bellowing, ". . . stupid motherfucking goddamned shitfaced sonsofbitches!"

Rogers was standing beside Jake, looking suddenly downcast, his earphones hanging around his neck.

"What happened?" Jake asked.

"Magnet developed a hot spot."

"And that stopped the test?"

Younger was still ranting. Over his tirade, Rogers explained, "It's a superconductor. It's got to be cooled down by liquid nitrogen. If a hot spot develops it could grow fast enough for the magnet to dump all its energy."

"Then the generator stops working," Jake surmised.

With a pained grin, Rogers said, "Then the generator blows up."

"Blows up? You mean it would explode?"

"Like a ten-ton bomb."

Jake rocked back, remembering a set of definitions that a visiting professor had given him when he'd been a freshman: "If it stinks or pops, it's chemistry. If it scratches or bites, it's biology. If it doesn't work, it's physics."

The MHD generator—with its superconducting magnet—was definitely in the realm of physics.

BITTER REALITIES

Rogers and Jake beat a hasty retreat from the big rig facility. Younger was howling with fury as the technicians scampered to keep out of his way.

Outside, it was starting to snow. Just a few flakes, but Jake was happy that they would probably be safely back in town before the storm got heavy.

"Well," said Rogers as they drove down the empty road, "the generator itself was working fine. The problem was with the magnet."

"It's got to be cooled," Jake said.

"Right. Two hundred below zero, Celsius." Then he amended, "One hundred ninety-six, actually."

"Cryogenic."

"That's the word for it."

"And when a hot spot develops . . ."

"All the energy in the magnet dumps into it, unless you shut it down damned fast."

"It could explode."

"It sure as hell can explode."

Jake thought about it as they drove through the thickening snowfall.

After a few minutes he asked, "Then why do you use a superconducting magnet? Why not an ordinary copper magnet, like the one on the little rig?"

Rogers glanced at him, then turned his focus back to the road as he explained, "You have to keep feeding electrical power to a copper magnet. A superconductor doesn't need any power input once it's activated. That means a lot of megawatts that we don't have to waste running the magnet. More net power output."

"But if it causes this kind of trouble . . ."

"Besides," Rogers went on, "a superconductor produces a much stronger magnetic field than a copper magnet can. We need the strongest magnetic field we can get to help make up for the plasma's low conductivity."

"But still . . ."

Rogers broke into a wry grin. "Tim will fix the problem. He's boiling mad now, but once he cools down he'll figure out what went bad with the magnet and fix it."

"You think so?"

Nodding, Rogers said, "That's what experimental physics is all about. You push the envelope until you run into a problem. Then you fix the problem and push some more."

Jake nodded back at him. But in his mind he pictured Tim Younger pushing the envelope until the big rig blew up in a fiery, fatal explosion.

It was snowing hard by the time Rogers dropped Jake off at the campus. Dark clouds pressed low, blotting out the sunset, and a strong wind gusted between the university buildings. Bending against the wind, Jake mushed through a few inches of wet snow and slid into his Mustang. The wipers cleared most of the snow off his windshield; he let the car's engine run for a few minutes, then turned the heater on to the defrost mode to finish the job.

By the time he got home, the university's radio station was devoting itself completely to the impending blizzard. Jake got a vision of children all across the state leaping with glee at the thought of not going to school the next day.

Once in his apartment, Jake checked his phone machine. Nothing. He flipped open his cell phone and saw that there were no messages waiting for him there, either.

Tomlinson's probably stranded somewhere out in the boonies, he thought. Shacked up with Amy in some roadside motel. He thought about phoning Amy again, decided against it, and went to bed, miserable and alone.

The phone woke him up. Groggily, Jake reached for it while squinting at his digital alarm clock: 7:32 A.M.

"Jake?" Amy's voice.

He snapped awake. "Amy! Where are you?"

"At home. We got back last night."

"Through the blizzard?"

"It wasn't that bad. We had a state highway patrol escort. The roads were plowed pretty well."

"That's good." He slowly pulled himself up to a sitting position. "I was worried about you."

"Franklin wants to talk to you. How soon can you get over to his house?"

Jake thought swiftly. "I've got a class at ten. Don't know how many will show up for it, though."

"Come over for lunch, then."

"Okay. I'll be there between twelve and twelve thirty."

"Good."

The snowfall was much less than Jake had expected. Listening to the radio as he shaved and brushed his teeth, Jake heard that the dire warnings of the night before had been replaced by more sober forecasts: The storm had blown through quickly, now it was clear, with high temperatures in the teens, overnight low near zero. No announcements of school closings. The kids are disappointed this morning, Jake thought.

Both before and after the weather report the station played advertisements for Harmon Dant. "A vote for Dant is a vote for our traditional values. A vote for Dant is a vote for *your* own way of life."

Jake shook his head and wondered why there weren't any ads for Tomlinson.

Snow had crusted into ice on his Mustang; it took nearly half an hour before Jake had cleared the windows enough to drive to campus.

His ten A.M. class was filled: an even dozen students exchanging ideas about the extent of the frozen underground seas of permafrost beneath the iron-red deserts of Mars.

Jake had been to Tomlinson's mansion often enough to park on the driveway, within a few yards of the front door. The butler knew him by sight and, after a whispered "Good afternoon, Dr. Ross," ushered him into the family dining room.

Compared to the grandeur of the formal dining room, this chamber was smallish, almost intimate. The table could seat only eight—ten, Jake thought, if they wanted to squeeze a couple more in. A big window at one end of the room let in bright sunlight. On the opposite wall stood a portrait almost as big as the window: some elderly Tomlinson of yore, frowning petulantly down at his descendents.

Tomlinson was already at the table, in his shirtsleeves and tieless. Amy sat beside him, wearing a pale yellow double sweater set and big gold hoop earrings.

Alexander Tomlinson sat at the head of the table, the expression on his face remarkably like the grouch in the painting. The butler showed Jake to the chair at the elder Tomlinson's left.

"All right," Tomlinson Senior said, in a loud, commanding voice. "Now that we're all here you can start serving."

A door to his right swung open and two uniformed servants carried out trays of food and a decanter of white wine.

The elder Tomlinson sampled the wine, nodded to the servant, then turned to his son.

"This man Dant is making a nuisance of himself," he grumbled.

Tomlinson nodded, almost meekly. "He's gaining in the polls, I know."

"If you don't do something—and soon—you're going to lose this primary."

"I'm not going to lose," Tomlinson said tightly.

His father harrumphed.

Jake blurted, "Dant's all over the radio. You can't turn to any station without hearing his commercials."

"Radio ads are cheap," Tomlinson quickly replied. "We've put most of our money into television. TV gets more response."

"You hope," said his father.

Amy said, "Dant is playing the right-wing card. Family values—which is a code phrase for antiabortion."

"He also talks about crime in the streets," Jake said.

"But there isn't any crime in the streets!" Tomlinson countered. "Crime statistics are down, not up."

You ought to try walking in the streets in my neighborhood, Jake thought. But he kept it to himself.

"Family values," the elder Tomlinson muttered.

"And lower taxes," said his son.

"Well," the father demanded, "what are you going to do about it?"

Before Tomlinson could answer, Amy replied, "Meet him head-on."

"Eh? What do you mean by that?"

"Come out strongly for women's rights. Let Dant talk to the ul-traconservatives. We'll talk to the biggest voting bloc in the state: women."

Tomlinson stared at her. "Do you really think . . . ?"

"You tell the voters that you support a woman's right to decide for herself about family planning. There're more women in this state who'll vote for that than there are who'll vote against it."

"Meet him head-on," Tomlinson mused. He turned to his father. "What do you think, Dad?"

The old man fixed his son with a stern gaze. "You've got to do *something*."

Amy smiled warmly. "You come across so beautifully on TV, Franklin. Just look into the camera and smile that handsome smile of yours and tell the women of this state that you're on their side. They'll vote for you. I know they will. Even the Catholics."

Jake wondered how much of Amy's certainty was based on her personal feelings for Tomlinson. But then he remembered Tip O'Neill's dictum about all politics being local. No, Jake said to himself, all politics is personal.

"And what about this MHD business?"

Jake stirred, realizing that the elder Tomlinson was talking to him.

"It's . . . making progress, sir," he equivocated. "They're testing a new electrode design on the big machine up in Lignite."

"What about this Professor Sinclair?" Tomlinson Senior demanded. "Is he going to make a public statement supporting Leeds?"

"No, sir, he is not."

"Are you sure of that, Jake?" Tomlinson asked.

Jake nodded. "Sinclair will stay quiet. He won't say anything, one way or the other."

"He's neutralized, you mean."

"That's one way to put it."

"Good work, Jake," said Amy, beaming at him.

"How did you do it?" Tomlinson asked.

With a shrug, Jake replied uneasily, "That's between the professor and me. He agreed to stay quiet through the whole campaign, right through to November. I agreed to trust his word."

The elder Tomlinson made a noise that was little short of a growl.

As he left the mansion, Jake thought he'd better call Sinclair and tell the professor that he hadn't told Tomlinson about his wife's addiction. That ought to satisfy Leeds and Nacho, he thought.

As he drove back toward campus, Jake turned on the car's radio. For once, he heard no ads by Dant. But the news broadcast opened with:

"There's been a double homicide in Vernon. Police report that Mr. and Mrs. Arlan Sinclair have both been shot to death in their home. According to Vernon police chief Peter Harraway, Sinclair shot his wife and then turned the gun on himself. Police are trying to determine his motive. Sinclair was a professor of—"

Jake snapped the radio off so hard the knob fell off in his hand.

REPERCUSSIONS

Jake drove straight to Bob Rogers's office. The electrical engineering department's secretary looked harried and drawn as she sat at her desk, phone to her ear. She half rose from her chair and held up a hand to stop Jake.

"Professor Rogers is in conference with the heads of the—"

Jake brushed right past her and strode down the hall to Rogers's office. The poor woman watched, open-mouthed, the phone still in her hand.

Rogers wasn't in his office, but Jake heard voices from farther down the hall, coming from the conference room. He walked to the door. Rogers was sitting with half a dozen older men and women: Jake recognized the university's top brass, deans and administrators. Rogers saw Jake and raised a cautionary finger. Jake retreated back to the physicist's office and waited there.

About fifteen minutes later Rogers came into the office, looking dismal. The others from the meeting paraded past the open office door, equally grim-faced.

"Well," Rogers said as he slid into his desk chair, "I'm now the dean of the electrical engineering department, pro tem."

"What happened?" Jake asked, dropping into one of the steel-framed chairs in front of the desk.

"They elected me to run the department," Rogers said, his face still gray, bleak. "For the time being. Until—"

"No. I mean what happened to Sinclair?"

Rogers shook his head. "Lord knows. I never took him for the kind that commits suicide."

"And his wife?"

"I don't know. I met her once a few years ago. She seemed like a nice enough person."

"This is terrible," said Jake.

"It's a shock."

That's when the realization hit Jake. It's my fault! If I hadn't gone up to Vernon, if I hadn't confronted Sinclair about his wife . . .

My fault. All my fault.

Rogers was talking but Jake barely heard the words. The enormity of his responsibility felt like an immense weight pressing down on him, making it hard to breathe.

He struggled to his feet, made some lame words to Rogers, and tottered out of the office, past the same secretary, who gave him a vicious stare, and out into the cold, snow-covered quadrangle.

By the time Jake got to his office, Glynis Colwyn was standing at his locked door. She looked blazingly angry.

"There you are," she said.

"Yeah," said Jake as he unlocked the door. "It's terrible, isn't it?"

He ushered Glynis into his tiny office. She was wearing a heavy gray turtleneck sweater and faded jeans tucked into fur-trimmed black boots beneath a leather thigh-length coat, which hung open.

Jake gestured to the office's only spare chair as he leaned tiredly on the edge of his desk.

"I know this is all my fault," he began. "I feel awful about it."

"Your fault?" She looked up sharply at him.

"You were right," he said, feeling wretched. "I pushed him too far."

Glynis shook her head. "That's nonsense."

"Is it? I confronted him about his wife, told him I was going to tell Tomlinson about it, and the next day he shoots the woman and kills himself."

"Arlan Sinclair did not kill anyone," Glynis said quite firmly. "He certainly did not commit suicide."

Jake stared at her. "What are you saying?"

"Arlan didn't kill himself. Both he and his wife were murdered."

"But the police—"

"The police force in Vernon? I'd sooner believe Osama bin Laden."

Jake saw that she was absolutely certain. And something else, there was something more, something that was making her tremble. Anger? Fear?

He looked into Glynis's dark, exotic eyes and suddenly understood. "My god, you were in love with him!"

She nodded once and her eyes filled with tears. "He loved me," she said, her voice breaking. "He loved me."

She buried her face in her hands and broke into sobs as Jake sat there on the edge of his desk, stunned. All her talk about being able to deal with Sinclair's hitting on her—it was all talk, a sham, a cover-up.

He heard himself say, "I thought you and Tim . . ."

"That was nothing," she said, her voice muffled. "I needed to get Tim's trust. Nothing really happened between us. I did it for Arlan . . . for him . . ."

Jesus H. Christ, Jake thought. All this time she's been Sinclair's lover, his mistress. She even came on to Tim to help Sinclair. The bastard used her like a piece of Kleenex. Lev was right: Sinclair's an unfeeling, totally self-centered sonofabitch. Then he amended, Was. Was.

He looked down at Glynis again, her body wracked with sobs. Leaning toward her, Jake put an arm around her shoulders.

"I'm sorry, Glyn," he whispered to her. "I'm really, really sorry."

She looked up at him, close enough to kiss. Tears runneled her cheeks. Her eyes were swollen, red.

"We've got to find out who did this, Jake. We've got to find Arlan's murderer."

Jake let Glynis stay in his office all afternoon. She seemed to pull herself together: dried her eyes, went to the bathroom. When she returned she began pacing the cramped office. Six steps in one direction, then turn. Six steps back, turn. She talked of nothing but finding who murdered Sinclair and his wife.

"He didn't even own a gun," she said, pacing. "He wouldn't know how to use one."

There's nothing much to it, Jake thought. Especially at point-blank range. But he kept that to himself.

He took Glynis to dinner at the first place he could find, the Taco Bell just off the campus. She said very little, picking at the guacamole dip and chili that Jake had ordered for her. Maybe she's all talked out, Jake thought. But her eyes were staring, looking far away from the here and now. She seemed stunned, unfocused, adrift.

Jake drove her to her apartment, a few blocks farther away. It was a decent building on a tree-lined street, although the trees were bare, dead-looking against the gray sky. Her three-storied building was the tallest structure on the block, flanked by older clapboard houses, several of them converted into offices for various university organizations.

As Jake walked her to the building's front door, Glynis muttered, "My car . . . it's still on campus."

"I'll come over tomorrow morning and pick you up," Jake said. "Phone me when you're ready."

"I . . . Have they appointed someone to take . . . take Arlan's place?" It seemed to take a teeth-gritting effort for her to get the words out.

"Bob Rogers," Jake said softly.

She nodded. "Of course. Bob. I'll be working for him now."

"Maybe you ought to take tomorrow off. Nobody's going to mind."

"No," she said, as she reached into her coat pocket for her keys. "No, I'll have to go in. I'll need my car."

"Take the day off," Jake suggested, more strongly.

Glynis shook her head. "No! I have to drive up to Vernon. I want to talk to the police there."

Jake saw that she had regained her self-control. Despite her grief and turmoil she was utterly determined. She had a purpose to fulfill.

"Okay," he said. "I'll go with you."

He walked up the steps with her to her second-floor apartment. It was a neat, no-nonsense place: sitting room, kitchen, bedroom. Everything tidy and clean. A slinky gray cat took one look at Jake and scampered into the kitchen.

Glynis went straight to the bedroom, pulling off her coat and letting it slip to the floor. She sat on the edge of the bed and curled into a fetal crouch and began quietly weeping again. Jake fidgeted in the sitting room, watching her through the open bedroom door, feeling helpless, useless.

He went into the bedroom, sat beside her, and put his arms around her.

"I loved him, Jake," she sobbed. "He loved me. He was so gentle . . . so . . ." The rest was lost in tears.

He held her close and she buried her face in his shoulder. He wished that he could cry, that he could let all the remorse and loneliness inside him wash itself away.

Resting his cheek on her head he whispered, "It's all right, Glyn. It's all right. I know what it is to lose somebody you love. I know the pain."

Jake realized he couldn't leave her. Not like this. He held her close, felt her body shuddering from the sobs, held her until his arms ached. Until her crying finally stopped.

"I'll stay here tonight," he told her. "You shouldn't be alone."

Glynis looked up at him.

Jake got up and went to the sofa in the sitting room. It looked comfortable enough. Then Glynis came in and handed him a pillow and a nubby blue blanket with a crocheted edge.

"Thank you, Jake," she said. "I . . . it's good of you to stay."

"Nothing to it," he said, taking the blanket from her hands.

"I must look a mess," she said. She turned and headed back to the bedroom. At the doorway she stopped. "The bathroom's in here."

Jake went in, did his business, and went back to the sitting room. Glynis was sitting on the bed, silent, lost in her thoughts.

As Jake sat on the sofa and began to take off his shoes she called from the bedroom, "Tomorrow we go to Vernon, remember."

CAPTAIN PETER HARRAWAY

Captain Harraway was not pleased to see Jake again. Jake got the feeling that Harraway somehow blamed him for the double murder. But the Vernon police captain was stiffly polite toward Glynis, in a strictly professional manner.

Jake and Glynis sat before Captain Harraway's desk, in the Vernon Police Department station house. The police captain was standing between his desk and a row of filing cabinets, looming over them like a dark mountain.

"It's open and shut," said Harraway to Glynis. "We found them in the living room. She was shot through the chest at point-blank range. Powder burns on her blouse. Then he shot himself through the right temple, scorched his hair."

"Who found them?" Glynis asked. She was all business now; the tears and misery of the night before had been replaced by dry-eyed, iron-hard determination.

Harraway frowned at her. "What's your interest here? Why've you come up here?"

"Ms. Colwyn worked directly with Professor Sinclair at the university," Jake said before Glynis could reply. "Naturally, the administration wants to know as much as possible about the circumstances of Professor Sinclair's death." Then Jake added, "He had many friends among the faculty and students, you know."

Harraway nodded minimally. "I guess he did."

Glynis repeated, "Who found the bodies?"

"The cleaning woman. She came in in the morning and found them in the living room. She called us."

Jake asked, "Where'd the gun come from?"

With a patient sigh, Harraway replied, "Apparently Mr. Sinclair bought it for his wife's protection, several months ago. It's registered in her name. Twenty-two caliber automatic. A woman's gun."

So it went, for nearly an hour. Harraway answered every question Glynis threw at him. He pulled photos of the dead bodies from a file drawer and spread them over his desk for Jake and Glynis to inspect.

"But why would he do this?" Glynis demanded. "Why would he drive up here and kill his wife and then himself?"

Harraway huffed like an old steam engine coming to a reluctant stop. Settling his bulk in his squeaking swivel chair, he clasped his massive hands together and stared at Glynis for a long moment. Jake thought he looked nettled, almost angry.

"I don't like having strangers poking around in the town's business," he said.

Jake felt surprised. "The town's business?"

"Mrs. Sinclair was one of this town's most important citizens. We went out of our way to take care of her, to protect her."

Yeah, Jake thought. Some protection.

"She had cancer," Harraway said, so softly that Jake wasn't entirely sure he'd heard correctly.

"Cancer?" Glynis asked.

"Inoperable. From what Dr. McGruder told me, she'd been on chemotherapy for more than two years, but it wasn't working. She was going to die. In a lot of pain."

"So Sinclair ended it for her," Jake said.

"And himself."

Jake turned to Glynis. "That's the motivation."

"I see," she said. Abruptly, Glynis stood up. "Thank you, Captain Harraway. We appreciate your taking the time to talk with us."

Harraway got up, too, slowly, like a tidal wave rising. "Just doing my job, Miss."

Jake got to his feet and walked with Glynis out of the office, through the quietly busy station, and out onto the street where his Mustang was parked next to a Vernon police cruiser. It was bitingly cold, thin gray clouds hiding the sun.

He helped Glynis into the car, then went around and slid in behind the wheel.

It wasn't until they were well out of town that Glynis hissed, "He's lying through his teeth."

"What?"

"Captain Harraway is a liar. Arlan didn't shoot his wife. He couldn't have. And he certainly didn't kill himself."

Jake kept his eyes on the highway, remembering Nacho Perez's threat about icy roads and accidents. But he could hear the absolute certainty in Glynis's voice.

"Don't you think you might be a little biased about all this?" he asked.

"Why would Arlan buy a pistol for his wife? What did she need to be protected from? The whole town was watching out for her, from what you've told me."

Jake had to admit, "Yeah, that's true."

"And how could Arlan shoot himself in the right temple? He was left-handed."

"He was?"

"He was."

Jake drove for more than a mile before he heard himself ask, "You think Harraway's claim that Mrs. Sinclair had cancer was a lie?"

"I wouldn't be surprised."

Before Jake could think of anything more to say, Glynis told him, "We've got to get to this Dr. McGruder, whoever he is."

The weeks flew by. Jake hardly saw Glynis; she was grimly trying to track down Dr. Ernest McGruder. Apparently he no longer lived in Vernon, not even in the state. He'd been a general practitioner, not an oncologist, and had retired a few months earlier to Florida.

As spring approached, Tomlinson's primary campaign swung into high gear. All the local radio stations were saturated with spot ads for him, as were the TV stations. Money talks, Jake thought, as Tomlinson pulled steadily ahead in the polls. Tomlinson's father talked grimly about how much this campaign was costing him, but Jake knew that the family money was augmented heavily by contributions from the family's wealthy friends. Amy complained that the mining and utilities industries "aren't putting their money where their mouths are," but Jake thought that finances were the least of Tomlinson's worries.

The MHD concept was all but lost in the candidate's new emphasis on women's rights, although Tomlinson did hammer on the point that the best way to keep taxes low was to create more jobs in the state.

Jake saw plenty of Amy Wexler, but always with Tomlinson or others. There were a couple of occasions when he might have asked her to bed, but he found that he couldn't. I'm not into sharing, he told himself. That didn't help much during the long nights of late winter, alone in his apartment or some dingy motel on the campaign trail.

Harmon Dant had carved out an impressive challenge at first, but as February gave way to March and the April primary elections edged nearer, Tomlinson's numbers climbed steadily. The analysts that Tomlinson's father had hired claimed that Dant had a solid base among the far-right segment of the party, but Tomlinson was holding his own within the party and drawing most of the independents to him.

"It's the women," Amy crowed. "Keep smiling at them, Franklin. They'll win this election for you."

Jake didn't know what was happening between Glynis and Tim Younger, but the long-duration tests at the big rig were gradually progressing. Seven hours without stopping. Then fifteen. Twenty-eight. Forty.

It was the last day of March when Jake returned to his office after his afternoon class just as his phone began to ring.

It was Amy. "Can you come with us to the big rig tomorrow afternoon?" Her voice sounded excited.

"What's happening?"

"Franklin's going to show the generator to Francis X. O'Brien!"

His brows nettling slightly, Jake asked, "Who's Francis X. O'Brien?"

"He's *merely* the chairman of the National Association of Electric Utilities," Amy said, as if she were pulling a rabbit out of a hat.

"So they've agreed to come out for MHD."

"They've agreed to come out and look," Amy said, more guardedly. "But, Jake, if he speaks up in favor of MHD it'll bring national recognition to Franklin! It'll cinch the primary!"

"You think so?"

"Really!" she enthused. "Be at Bob Rogers's office at noon tomorrow. We'll have a picnic lunch on the way to Lignite."

"I'll be there." As Jake hung up the phone he remembered Lev Cardwell's advice: *Make the victim a party to the crime.* That's what they're doing: The electric utilities will benefit from MHD, so make them support us publicly. Make them a party to the crime.

Amy's "we" turned out to be Tomlinson, Amy herself, one of the publicists from the campaign staff, Bob Rogers, and Francis X. O'Brien—with two of his own public relations men, all crammed into a monstrously long black stretch limousine.

The others were already in the limo when Jake crawled in behind Bob Rogers. Tomlinson introduced them both to O'Brien and
ignored the man's two PR aides and his own publicist.

Francis X. O'Brien was a tiny man, lean and narrow-jawed, with
a hooked nose and a toothy smile. A rat's face, Jake thought. His hair
was so luxuriantly dark and perfectly coiffed that Jake thought it had
to be a toupeé. It didn't match the wrinkled, faded pallor of his face,
nor his cold gray eyes. He had a reedy nasal voice with a flat midwest-
ern accent. Jake got the feeling that despite his pasted-on smile,
O'Brien probably had a volcanic temper. He wore a dark three-piece
suit with a pale blue tie knotted perfectly. His two PR flacks were in
identical dark suits, although their ties were striped burgundy and pearl
gray, respectively.

Despite the limo's size, Jake felt uncomfortable, wedged in between Rogers and Tomlinson's publicity guy—who was in a suede
sports jacket, not much different from the one Jake was wearing.
Tomlinson and O'Brien sat on the rear bench, with Amy between
them, showing plenty of leg in a mid-length slitted skirt.

Lunch was awkward. Amy asked the PR man sitting closest to
the raised partition that sealed off the limo's driver to hand her the
wicker basket and plastic cooler that had been stowed by the partition. He passed it from one set of hands to another until they were
resting at Amy's feet. It was difficult to eat the sandwiches she pulled
out of the basket without getting crumbs everywhere, despite the
checkered paper napkins Amy handed out. The cooler was deposited
between Jake and Rogers, and the men pulled out cans of beer and
soft drinks.

One of O'Brien's aides lifted a cut-glass tumbler and a decanter
from the rack on the side of the limousine's compartment. The other
hauled out an ice bucket. Between them they poured a stiff shot of
whiskey for O'Brien. They offered the same to Tomlinson, but he
shook his head and asked for a beer, instead.

By the time they had rolled through the town of Lignite, Jake
was swabbing his hands with a weird-smelling moist paper towelette
and trying hard to suppress a burp.

They could hear the roar from the big rig even through the limo's closed windows while they were still more than half a mile away from the test facility.

Rogers grinned and looked at his wristwatch. "Approaching seventy-five hours," he said, beaming.

Francis X. O'Brien nodded vacantly.

Tomlinson said, "They're aiming for a hundred hours of continuous operation."

"At fifty megawatts," Rogers added.

O'Brien nodded again.

Inside the test cell they all wore earphones as they crowded into the control booth. Tim Younger was all business; he barely shook hands with O'Brien and Tomlinson. From the strained expression on his face it looked clear to Jake that Tim regarded them as an interruption, tourists poking their noses into the very serious business of making the MHD generator run properly.

The trouble was, Jake quickly realized, that there was nothing much to see. The big rig was running smoothly and once the visitors had been shown the dials that indicated all was going well they quickly lost interest. When everything's going right, it's dull, Jake thought. Disasters are where the excitement is. After less than ten minutes Tomlinson led them all back outside again.

Younger looked relieved to see them go. Amy seemed subdued, almost worried.

Outside, it was cold despite the pale March sunshine. O'Brien made a beeline for the waiting limousine. Tomlinson trailed after him.

Once they were all jammed in and the limo started the long ride back to the city, O'Brien's flacks poured him another shot of whiskey.

Tomlinson put on his best smile and asked, "Well, Mr. O'Brien, what do you think?"

O'Brien took a gulp of his drink. "Seems to be running all right."

"The goal is one hundred hours of continuous operation," Amy said, still sitting between the two men.

"At fifty megawatts," Rogers added once again.

O'Brien said, "Impressive."

"It's the wave of the future," Tomlinson said. "And you can put the National Association on the bandwagon."

O'Brien glanced at his two aides, then asked, "What bandwagon?"

"The MHD bandwagon," Tomlinson said, with some surprise in his expression. "The National Association of Electric Utilities can position itself as being in favor of a new, more efficient way of generating electrical power. You can show the American consumer that—"

"Why should we be in favor of a more efficient way of generating electrical power?" O'Brien asked, almost crossly.

Tomlinson blinked. "You can show your customers that the association is working to lower their electricity bills."

"Why would we want to lower their electricity bills?" O'Brien's reedy voice was beginning to irritate Jake.

Amy Wexler said, "Your association members could score a public relations coup by showing that you're working to help your customers."

"And you could still make more profits," Tomlinson said, "even while you're lowering your rates."

O'Brien shook his head. "You don't understand, fella. We're a regulated industry. A board of politicians and other noble citizens set the prices we can charge for electricity in each and every state of the union. Why should we go for a new generating system that's more efficient? Those goddamn regulators will just force us to cut our rates."

Tomlinson looked shocked; Amy fell silent. Jake glanced at Bob Rogers; he seemed positively angry.

For long moments no one spoke. O'Brien took another slug of his drink. Tomlinson seemed at a loss for words. The limo rolled along the interstate under a thin gray cover of clouds.

At last Jake spoke up. "Your association should support MHD because it will show the people who pay their electric bills that you're trying to help them."

Before O'Brien could respond, Tomlinson jumped in. "That's right. You'll be on the side of the angels. You'll be showing your customers that you *want* to lower their electricity bills."

"And the regulatory boards—"

"The regulatory boards will go easier on you because they'll get pressure from the voters."

O'Brien shook his head. "The only time the voters put pressure on the boards is to stop us from raising our rates."

"But this time," Tomlinson said, reaching across Amy to jab a finger into O'Brien's shoulder, "you'll be going to the boards to ask them to *lower* your rates! Think of how that'll go over with your customers. And their political leaders."

O'Brien's eyes shifted to his two aides, who nodded in unison. Jake thought of bobble-head dolls.

Tomlinson added, "Lowering your rates will make your customers *and* the regulators happy with you. Of course, you won't lower them so much that you won't make an indecent profit out of the new system."

Everyone chuckled, except O'Brien.

Very reluctantly, he admitted, "Maybe you're right."

"You're damned right I'm right," Tomlinson snapped.

They drove on in silence for several miles. At last Amy asked, "Then can we count on your support for MHD, Mr. O'Brien?"

He looked her up and down, smiled, and replied, "Yeah, why the hell not? It's all so far in the future that it doesn't really matter one way or the other, does it?"

"The future becomes the present sooner than you think," Rogers said.

Make the victim a party to the crime, Jake told himself.

"Mr. O'Brien," he said, "maybe the National Association ought to do something specific to show that it's backing MHD."

"Do something?"

"Something that clearly shows you're in favor of MHD."

"Something?" O'Brien repeated, his voice like fingernails on a chalkboard. "Like what?"

Jake said, "Like building a transmission line that connects the big rig to the state's power grid."

Rogers's eyes lit up. "Wow! Instead of just dumping the power we generate we could put it into the grid—like the Russians did in Moscow."

O'Brien's eye narrowed. "You want us to pay for connecting your doohickey to the grid."

"We could add fifty megawatts to the local power availability," Tomlinson said, warming to the idea.

Amy jumped in, "That would be enough to light up the whole county of Lignite!"

"And then some!" Rogers said.

Jake explained more calmly, "It would be concrete evidence of your support for MHD. A gesture of goodwill. It would help the electricity consumers of the state. And it wouldn't cost much: just a few miles of a high-capacity transmission line."

O'Brien muttered, "A gesture of goodwill, eh?"

"That's right," said Jake.

O'Brien glanced at his aides. Their bobble-heads nodded in unison once again.

pril brought cold rain and winds that gusted down out of the mountains. The accumulated snow of winter melted away at last while Tomlinson raced across the highways in a final whirlwind tour of the state.

Tim Younger growled and groused when Jake told him that the National Association was going to hook the big rig to the state's power grid. But Glynis helped to calm him down and, once the rig had completed its hundred-hour run, Younger grudgingly allowed a construction team to connect the transmission line.

"You'll be adding fifty megawatts to the state's generating capacity," Glynis told him.

"When the rig's running," Younger pointed out. "Which it isn't while they're hooking up their line."

"Don't be a grouch," Glynis commanded. Younger grinned sheepishly at her.

Amy worried about the weather. "If it's raining on election day the turnout will be small. That could help Dant."

But election day dawned bright and sunny, unusually warm and springlike. Money talks, Jake reminded himself. Tomlinson's even buying the weather.

Election night the campaign staff and key volunteers gathered at the double-sized suite that Tomlinson's aides had taken at the Sheridan Hotel. Downstairs people were beginning to fill up the ballroom, but up in the suite Tomlinson stood unmoving in front of the wall-screen TV, watching the returns with single-minded intensity. He wore a charcoal gray pinstripe suit, no vest, with one of his own red-white-and-blue campaign buttons pinned to his jacket's lapel.

Amy was at his side, in a lilac cocktail dress and plenty of diamonds. Tomlinson's father, in a pompous old-fashioned tuxedo and black tie, prowled restlessly among the growing crowd, looking as if he wanted to kill somebody. Jake recognized many of the campaign workers and volunteers in the suite. News reporters and camera crews were filtering in, too—they clustered near the bar, Jake noticed.

Tim Younger came in, with Glynis. He looked out of place in cowboy boots, jeans, and a bolo tie among the city slickers in their three-piece suits. But if that bothered Tim he didn't show it. Glynis wore an off-white ball gown. She intends to go dancing, Jake thought. Jake was in his best and only blue suit, feeling stiffly uncomfortable with his maroon tie knotted at his throat.

Happy to see her, Jake made his way through the growing crowd toward Glynis and Younger.

"I'm glad you could make it," he said to them.

Before they could reply, the crowd whooped. Turning toward the TV screen, Jake saw that Tomlinson had built up a commanding lead.

"That's just the returns from the city," Tomlinson Senior barked, gesturing for the onlookers to calm down. "Dant's main strength is out in the rural areas. Don't go breaking out the champagne just yet."

Amy Wexler looked more than pleased, though, as she hung on Tomlinson's arm. "Dant won't be able to overcome that big a lead," she said to Tomlinson's father. The old man gave her a cold glare and walked away.

"How're you doing?" Jake asked Glynis. He hadn't seen much of her for the past few weeks.

"I'm all right," she said.

Younger excused himself and headed for the bar. Jake pulled Glynis toward one of the heavily draped windows and asked, more quietly, "Have you located Dr. McGruder?"

Nodding, she replied, "He's retired to a town called Cape Coral, in Florida. No e-mail address, so I've written him a letter. He hasn't responded to it."

"Can you phone him?"

"I have, several times. I get an answering machine, but he hasn't returned my calls."

Jake thought a moment, then said, "Looks like he doesn't want to talk to you."

"Then I'll have to go out there and face him in person."

Jake saw that Glynis was deadly serious. "Glyn, if your suspicions are anywhere near being right, going to see McGruder could be . . . well, dangerous."

"I don't care."

"But I do!" Jake blurted.

Her eyes went wide, but before she could say anything Younger came back with a pair of plastic champagne flutes.

As he handed one to Glynis, he said, "Sorry, Jake. Only got two hands."

Jake was staring at Glynis. She accepted the champagne from Younger, but as she raised the glass to her lips the crowd roared.

Turning back to the TV, Jake saw that the news station's election team had placed a red check mark next to Tomlinson's name on their election scoreboard, with the words: PREDICTED WINNER.

Amy stood on tiptoes to give Tomlinson a congratulatory kiss on the cheek. Cameras whirred. Tomlinson pulled loose, grinning, then raised both arms in a victory wave for the crowd. Tomlinson's father almost smiled. Everyone was cheering; somebody even threw a handful of confetti into the air.

But as Jake looked down at Glynis he saw that she was serious, somber, not even smiling. She's thinking about going to Florida to find Dr. McGruder, Jake knew.

Tomlinson made an impromptu thank-you speech to his campaign workers, finishing with, "Now on to November . . . and the United States Senate!"

Everyone yelled. Even the news reporters and camera crews joined in. Jake felt suddenly tired, as if he'd run a hard race and needed to cool down. Glynis smiled minimally and nodded, but her eyes were gazing past the crowd, past the celebration.

Tomlinson's father raised his hands for quiet. "If you'll all go down to the ballroom now, my son and I will join you there in a few minutes."

They all filed out, all except Tomlinson and his father. And Amy, who stood between the two men. Jake left the suite with Glynis and Younger.

In the ballroom a dance band was in full swing, belting out an old rock tune while couples in dark suits and bright gowns gyrated across the polished floor. Champagne was flowing freely. Jake spotted Bob Rogers and his wife thumping along with more energy than style. Glynis and Younger headed for the bar, leaving Jake standing alone, the blare of the music hurting his ears, thinking that he might as well go on home.

Then the band began a country-and-western waltz and Jake saw Leverett Cardwell and Alice come out onto the dance floor, looking like two animated china dolls, he in a tux and she in an honest-to-god Alice blue gown. They glided gracefully among the other couples, smiling at each other as if there were no other people on the planet.

Once the music ended, Jake weaved through the crowd toward the Cardwells. Lev saw him approaching and gave him a fatherly smile. Jake went with them to one of the round tables that had been set up along the periphery of the ballroom.

"You've done a good job, my boy," Cardwell said as they sat down. "You got the electric utility industry, the coal mining industry, and the environmental movement all to endorse MHD. That's grand."

Jake felt a flush of pleasure. "I'd rather hear that from you than get elected to the Senate myself, Lev."

Cardwell's round face grew more serious. "Now the job will be to keep your man from forgetting about MHD. You've got to keep the issue at the forefront of his campaign."

"I know. I will."

"What do you think Senator Leeds's main campaigning issues will be?" Alice asked.

Jake turned toward her. "I really don't have the faintest idea."

"It's too late for him to preempt the MHD issue from Tomlinson," Cardwell mused. "He'll probably stay away from anything dealing with energy."

"Then we ought to hammer him about it," said Jake.

Cardwell nodded. Looking past him, Jake saw Glynis dancing

with Younger. On an impulse, he asked, "Lev, would you mind if I asked your wife to dance with me?"

Cardwell's owl-gray eyes widened for an instant, then he turned to Alice and smiled at her. "Can I trust you with a younger man, dear?"

Alice giggled and got to her feet. Jake led her out onto the floor, wondering why he was doing this.

As they swung into the Latino beat of the music, Alice said, "You know, Lev was very upset about Arlan's suicide."

Tensing, Jake replied, "The police in Vernon claim that Mrs. Sinclair was suffering from terminal cancer."

"Really?"

He shook his head. "She didn't look like a cancer patient when I saw her."

"Ah, you never know, Jake. Some people look healthy even though they're dying inside."

Suddenly the music cut off in mid-beat. Jake looked up at the bandstand, then at the giant TV screen hanging to one side of it.

Harmon Dant was standing before a battery of microphones, cameras clicking and whirring at him. Despite his attempts to smile, Dant looked bitterly unhappy, his plump cheeks sagging, his eyes baggy.

He cleared his throat noisily, then leaned toward the microphones slightly as he began, "We fought the good fight, and I want to thank every one of you who fought it with me. We haven't really been defeated, only delayed."

Applause and cheers rang from the TV speakers.

Dant continued, "I want to congratulate Frank Tomlinson on his winning this primary. He had a lot more resources on his side than we did, and that's what counted."

He paused, and for a moment Jake thought the man might break into tears. But then Dant continued, "Despite tonight's disappointment, we will continue to battle for the things we believe in: less government interference in our lives, lower taxes, an end to murdering the unborn . . ."

"He's not going to offer his support to Tomlinson," said Leverett Cardwell. Jake hadn't noticed Lev's coming onto the dance floor to stand beside his wife.

"Some support," Jake sniffed. "It's not much past eleven o'clock and he's conceding the election."

Cardwell raised his eyebrows, then said, "Well, at least with Arlan Sinclair out of the picture you can get support from the people actually running the MHD program."

Jake nodded, realizing that Lev was right. Bob Rogers and Tim Younger had no qualms about backing Tomlinson.

Now that Arlan Sinclair was, as Lev put it, out of the way.

CAPE CORAL, FLORIDA

I t was hot in Florida. Summertime hot and humid, although it was only late April.

Glynis had insisted on going to Florida to see Dr. McGruder and question him about Mrs. Sinclair's cancer. Jake thought it was a wild-goose chase, at best, but once he realized how utterly deter-mined she was, he decided to go along with her. So on the Friday after Tomlinson's victory in the primary, the two of them flew to the Southwest Florida International Airport, in Fort Myers, and drove a rental car to McGruder's home in Cape Coral.

"What do you expect to find?" Jake asked, as he followed the car's GPS directions through the unfamiliar streets. The sun was glaring, the car's air-conditioning up to maximum. Jake was surprised at the traffic. Fort Myers was a considerable city. The people ambling along the streets were all in ultracasual T-shirts, tank tops, shorts, sandals. Just about everyone wore sunglasses.

"I want to know if she actually had cancer," Glynis replied. "And if she did, who her oncologist was. McGruder's just a GP. She must have been attended by a specialist—if she really had cancer."

"You think Harraway was lying," Jake said. It wasn't a question.

"I *know* he was lying," Glynis said, absolutely certain. "I just don't know if he was telling the truth about her condition."

The address turned out to be a modest bungalow on a palm-lined street that ran along a canal. Jake could see boats moored behind sev-eral of the houses, mostly small outboards for fishing, although there was one sleek cigarette boat hanging from davits across the waterway.

Feeling uneasy about this expedition, Jake rang the bungalow's doorbell. In the Florida humidity, he felt as if a hot, wet towel had been wrapped around him. Glynis seemed unaffected by the heat; she had had the foresight to dress for the climate in shorts and a sleeveless blouse.

A thickset swarthy woman opened the front door a crack. She was short and blocky as a bag of cement.

"*Que?*"

"Dr. McGruder, please."

The woman frowned. "No here. They take him away."

"Away?" Glynis asked. "Where?"

"Two days ago."

"Where? Where is he?"

Jake searched his pitiful Spanish vocabulary. "*Dónde está?*"

That brought a burst of rapid-fire Spanish. Overwhelmed, Jake made a pacifying gesture with both his hands. "Slower! Uh . . . *lentamente, por favor.*"

It took several minutes, but at last they figured that McGruder had been taken to the Alhambra Hospital, in Cape Coral.

As they slid back into the car and Jake revved up the engine—and the air-conditioning—Glynis said, "I didn't know you speak Spanish."

"Just a few words. Comes in handy now and then."

"I'm impressed."

"*Dos cervezas,*" Jake said. "That's my favorite Spanish phrase."

Glynis looked up the hospital's address with her cell phone and Jake punched it into the oblong gray box of the GPS system.

Alhambra Hospital turned out to be a hospice center, a place where people went to die.

"I hope we're not too late," Glynis muttered as they hurried across the cool lobby to the front desk.

They were.

"Dr. McGruder died last night of a coronary infarction," said the elderly woman at the desk. "He was suffering from Alzheimer's, poor man."

"Coronary infarction?" Glynis echoed.

"Heart attack," said Jake.

Looking at her computer screen, the receptionist shook her head sadly. "Poor man. He had no family at all."

"Who brought him here, then?" Glynis asked.

"A friend of his, apparently. From back in his hometown."

"And he had a fatal heart attack last night."

"Yes," the woman answered. "His friend was visiting with him at the time. Poor man, his Alzheimer's was so advanced he didn't even recognize his friend."

Jake asked, "He didn't recognize the man who was with him when he had the heart attack?"

"That's right."

"Who was he? How can we get in contact with him?"

The receptionist shook her head. "He's probably gone back north by now. He just left instructions for the body to be cremated and then he headed for the airport."

"Has the body been cremated?" Glynis asked.

The woman said, "In two days. State law."

"We've got to stop the cremation," Glynis said urgently. "Get an autopsy."

"Why?" Jake asked.

"To see if he really had Alzheimer's!" she snapped. "This is all too damned convenient to be true."

"You don't think that—"

But Glynis was already asking the receptionist, "What's the friend's name? How can we get in touch with him?"

The woman tapped at her computer's keyboard. "No information on his address. He must live back where Dr. McGruder lived, though."

"His name?" Jake repeated.

"Um . . . Perez," the woman said. "Ignacio Perez."

Jake still felt stunned as he sat beside Glynis in the cramped coach section of the flight out of Florida. He was in the middle seat, Glynis on the aisle. The middle-aged woman drowsing in the window seat was grossly fat. Jake hoped she wouldn't awaken and have to get up during the flight.

Leaning so close their heads nearly touched, Glynis asked again, "And this Perez person works for Senator Leeds?"

"I got the impression that he works for somebody who supports Leeds," Jake said. "Somebody connected with the casinos on the reservations."

"Someone connected with gambling."

Jake nodded. "There are five casinos across the state, all owned by Native American tribes."

"I wonder how much money they rake in," Glynis mused. "I suppose I could look it up."

"It's not how much they report," Jake pointed out. "It's how much they skim off the top. The money that doesn't get reported. The money that they don't pay taxes on."

"But that's illegal!"

With a crooked smile, Jake told her, "Amy Wexler told me that the casinos are actually run from Las Vegas. Big-time operators."

"Mafia?"

"They don't use that term, but—yeah, the Mob, organized crime. Big time."

"And this Perez person was sent to Florida to silence Dr. McGruder," Glynis said.

Jake sighed. "Nacho didn't go to Florida to inquire about Mc-Gruder's health."

"He must have murdered Arlan and his wife, then."

"He, or somebody like him."

"I was right," Glynis whispered. "We're dealing with murderers!"

Jake nodded, knowing that the closer they got to uncovering what really happened, the closer they came to facing their own deaths.

Once back home, Jake tried to reach Nacho Perez. The man was nowhere to be found. Nobody in Senator Leeds's office even admitted to knowing his name.

Sitting in his messy little office, Jake thought about the possibilities. There was one person he knew who would know where Perez was, but contacting that person would open a can of very dangerous worms.

Jake tussled with the possibilities for the better part of a day. He sleepwalked through his class, graded exam papers like a robot, his mind turning over the risks of what he knew he had to do.

As the sun was setting on a perfectly splendid day in late April, Jake picked the phone off his desk and called Monster.

To his surprise, Monster not only answered the phone on the second ring, but cheerfully agreed to meet Jake for dinner.

"Zorba's, okay?" Monster suggested.

The Greek restaurant in the old neighborhood. Sure, Jake thought. Nobody's been shot in Zorba's for a couple of years.

"Zorba's," he agreed. "Seven o'clock good for you?"

"Make it seven thirty, Jake. I got business to take care of first."

"Seven thirty, then."

"And come alone. Just me and you, Jake. We got things to talk over."

Jake's blood ran cold.

Zorba's was the best restaurant in the old neighborhood. Also the only restaurant, unless you counted the fast-food eateries on a couple of street corners or the Chinese joint that had been there since the Lewis and Clark expedition passed by.

It was a quiet place. No bouzouki music, no belly dancers, just the muted murmur of conversations and the occasional shout of "Oopah!" as men tossed down thimble-sized glasses of ouzo.

It got even quieter when Monster came in. All the conversations stopped in mid-sentence; everyone seemed to hold his breath. Monster spotted Jake at the table where he was sitting and strode across the half-empty restaurant to him.

People started talking again as Monster sat down and said, "Hey, Jake."

An elderly waiter in a stained white apron immediately placed a menu the size of a newspaper's double sheet in front of him.

Without even glancing at the menu Monster ordered the braised lamb. Jake did the same.

"And to drink?" wheezed the waiter.

Monster looked at Jake questioningly. "I'll have a glass of red wine," Jake said. Monster shook his head. "Water's okay for me."

Once the waiter left their table Monster hunched forward and said in a lowered voice, "Jake, you're headin' for trouble, you know."

"Me?"

"You. What're you snoopin' around for, tryin' to find Nacho?"

Jake ran the possibilities through his mind in a millisecond. What the hell, he thought. Monster already knows a lot more about this than I do. No sense holding back anything.

"Monster, the guy might have murdered somebody. Maybe more than one."

Monster straightened up in his chair, his face suddenly stony. "So?" he said. "What business is that of yours?"

"Did he kill Professor Sinclair? And Sinclair's wife?"

"You think I know?"

"Do you?"

Monster stared at Jake in silence. As if to break the tension, their waiter brought two dishes of braised lamb to the table, steaming with the aroma of spices and fresh green beans.

"Jake," Monster said, "eat your dinner and forget about this whole business. I like you, Jake, but you're messin' with things that're gonna get you in trouble. You and that girl you went to Florida with."

Jake's insides clenched. They know every move I make! he realized. They're watching me.

He wondered who "they" might be. It's not just Senator Leeds, he thought. There's more to this. A lot more.

But he said nothing further. He followed Monster's advice and ate his dinner. They talked about old times, high school days. Monster merrily recounted the fights he had been involved in. He went into some detail about the bones he had broken.

JUNE

April gave way to May and then to June. The weather warmed to pleasant summertime temperatures and Jake followed Monster's advice. He stopped asking about Nacho Perez, paid attention to his classes and his students. He even started working again on his proposal for the Mars lander's sensors.

Political activities had slowed after the primaries. Both Tomlinson and Senator Leeds were making preparations for the campaign that would culminate in November's election, spending most of their time raising money. Jake saw Amy Wexler once or twice a week, but only to talk about the science planks in Tomlinson's platform.

Dant's concerns during the primary about abortion forced Jake to work out a position for Tomlinson on stem cell research. After talking it over with the biomedical scientists on campus and a private company spun off from the university, Jake advised Tomlinson to emphasize two things: one, that stem cell research held enormous promise for future treatments of everything from Alzheimer's to heart disease, and two, that stem cells were being produced from ordinary blood and skin cells; there was no longer any need for harvesting stem cells from human embryos.

Once she heard that, Amy Wexler clapped her hands joyfully. "That should quiet the right-to-life people!"

Genetically engineered corn was another issue that sent Jake scurrying to the biology labs. Corn was a major crop in the state and improving its resistance to frost and insect pests was highly desirable. But conservatives raised specters of uncontrolled mutations that could ruin the corn crop. Even Tomlinson's father huffed about "Frankenstein on the cob." Jake worked out a reasonable approach that, he hoped, would allay the fears of the farmers and the general public.

Climate change, space exploration, even a controversy between archeologists digging into the state's past and Native American activists who protested their intrusions into sacred ground—Jake had to work out positions for Tomlinson that would alienate the least number of voters and perhaps even help to get some science accomplished.

And, of course, there was the MHD program.

"They've finished the transmission line from the big rig to the grid," Jake reported to Amy in mid-June.

She nodded uncertainly. "How does that help us?"

They were sitting in one of the booths at the Roosevelt Club's bar. Jake hadn't been to Amy's apartment since before the primaries, nor had she come to his place. The quiet, darkly paneled bar was as intimate as they had been for months.

"Whenever the generator runs, they can send the power into the state's electrical system. The local utility companies get fifty mega-watts for free."

"As long as the generator is running," Amy said.

"Tim's had it going for a hundred hours at a stretch," Jake said. "He's talking about going for two hundred hours."

"More than a week," Amy muttered.

"A little over eight days," said Jake.

She shrugged. "I suppose that's good progress for you science jocks, but what does that mean to the average voter?"

"Progress," said Jake.

"We need something more than that, Jake. Something that will make the voters realize that MHD is important. Something that will get votes for Franklin."

Jake said, "I'll try to think of something."

"The Fourth of July will be here in a few weeks," she said. "We're trying to think of something special that Franklin could do, something to get him headlines and really get the campaign off with a bang."

Jake figured that she and Tomlinson were getting themselves off with a bang fairly often.

Amy gave him an impish smile. "Don't look so sour, Jake."

"Sour? Me?"

"You wear your heart on your face. Whenever I ask you to do something you don't like, you frown like a gargoyle."

Jake said nothing, but he thought that if she could really see what he was thinking she'd stop smiling and go to bed with him. Yet he couldn't tell her that. Not now that she was so wrapped up with Tomlinson.

Still, the germ of an idea had popped into his mind. He didn't mention it to Amy, not there at the bar. He had to work out the idea in all its details. He knew he'd have to get Tim Younger's cooperation, and to get that, he'd have to go through Glynis.

He hadn't seen much of Glynis since their trip to Florida and Monster's warning about trying to find Nacho Perez. Yet he worried about her; she was determined to prove that Sinclair had been murdered, regardless of Jake's warnings.

But now he found that he was actually glad of an excuse to see her again.

Two days later, with all the details of his idea firmly in his mind, Jake invited Glynis to dinner.

She sounded wary when he called. "Dinner? Tonight?"

"You're not busy, are you?"

"No . . ." She drew the word out.

"I've got an idea I want to talk to Tim about," he explained. "But first I'd like to bounce it off you, see what you think of it."

For several heartbeats Glynis said nothing. Then, "Very well. Where do you want to go?"

Jake arrived at Danny's Seafood Locker a few minutes early, as usual. Feeling somewhat apprehensive, he slid into a booth and ordered a beer. "The darkest you've got," he told the young waitress.

To his surprise, she brought him a bottle of Negra Modelo. And a tall glass. Maybe the management heard my grumbling, he thought. Or maybe they have a better class of waiters working the dinner shift.

Jake was pouring the beer when Glynis entered the restaurant, wearing a soft pink blouse and dark slacks. She looked over the half-empty restaurant, spotted Jake getting up from his booth, and hurried over to him.

"Hi!" Jake said, glad to see her. For a fleeting instant he thought about kissing her, but Glynis gave him a perfunctory smile and slid into the booth on the opposite side of the table.

Her expression was serious. "I was surprised when you called."

"Oh?"

"You've been avoiding me since we got back from Florida."

Jake had told her about Monster's warning. "Look, I tried to locate Nacho Perez, you know."

"You told me about this goon's warning you."

"You ought to stay clear of it, too."

Strangely, Glynis smiled. "But don't you see, Jake? We must be on the right track; we're worrying them."

"They're worrying me, all right," Jake admitted.

"Are you scared?"

"Damned right. And you should be, too. If they've already murdered three people, they're not going to let the two of us get in their way."

Glynis started to reply, but the waitress interrupted to ask what she wanted to drink. She asked for a glass of chardonnay.

As the waitress left their booth, Glynis said, "I've talked it over with one of the state's assistant district attorneys. She's an old friend of Arlan's—one of his girlfriends, actually, from years ago."

Jake asked, "And?"

Looking disappointed, Glynis said, "She told me that all I have is suspicions." She hesitated a heartbeat, then went on, "And we're dealing with a very rough crowd."

"I know that," Jake said.

"But what are we going to *do* about it?"

He wished he knew. "Maybe," he started, "maybe the best thing to do is lay low until Tomlinson gets elected. He could ask for a full investigation. As a U.S. senator he might even be able to bring the FBI into the case."

Glynis looked disappointed.

"Look, Glyn, these guys are professionals. Gambling, prostitution, loan-sharking . . . they all run together. They use strong-arm tactics the way you and I use toothpaste. It's an ordinary, everyday thing to them."

"And you're going to let them get away with it?"

Leaning across the table, Jake said urgently, "I'm not going up against them by myself. That would be stupid."

She nodded. "I suppose so."

"And don't you try it, either. You'll get hurt."

"I suppose so," she repeated. But she didn't sound convinced. Or convincing.

The waitress brought Glynis's wine and a pair of menus. They sipped and studied the menus and ordered: filet of local trout for Glynis, fried oysters for Jake.

She gave Jake an odd little smile as the waitress left for the kitchen.

"Oysters again?" Glynis asked. "Do you need them?"

He nearly sputtered the beer he had just drunk. Coughing, he replied, "Uh . . . I like oysters."

"There's an old joke about them, you know. A fellow tells his pal that oysters aren't aphrodisiacs, as they're supposed to be. He says he had a dozen of them the night before and only nine of them worked."

Jake laughed weakly. He'd heard the joke before. He wished he could get one of them to work.

Once they'd started on their meals, Glynis asked, "So what's this idea you wanted to tell me about?"

Glad to be talking about something else, Jake said, "Tomlinson's people want some kind of demonstration to show the public that MHD works."

"So?"

"So the Fourth of July is coming up. Suppose we supply the town of Lignite with holiday lights. You know, red, white, and blue. The Statue of Liberty in red, white, and blue lights. Every house in the town, every store, the hotel, every building all decked out in patriotic lights."

"The way people decorate their houses for Christmas," Glynis said.

"Yeah. But this'll be for the Fourth of July. And all the electricity to light up the whole town's decorations will come from the big rig!"

Glynis's face lit up with enthusiasm. "That's wonderful! I love it!"

"Fireworks, too," Jake added. "Invite the whole state to come up to Lignite for the big Fourth of July celebration. Tomlinson can give a speech—"

"No. Let him push the button that lights up the town and sets off the fireworks."

"Yeah! It'll make a big splash in the news media for MHD," Jake said.

"Yes, certainly."

"Keep the lights on all night long."

"Powered by the big rig."

"Right."

Her expression dimmed suddenly. "But suppose something goes wrong? It could be a terrible black eye for us."

"That's why we've got to get Tim behind this. He's the one who'll have to make sure it works right."

"It would only be for eight hours," Glynis mused. "Maybe less."

"It could work," Jake insisted. "Tim could make it work."

"If he agreed to it."

"Do you think he would?"

Glynis looked thoughtful. "We'll see. Let me talk to him about it."

Jake nodded, thinking that all the women he knew were wrapped up with other men. He looked down at his fried oysters. A lot of good they're doing me, he thought.

t was almost a week later before Jake heard from Glynis again. She must be having a hard time convincing Tim about my idea, he thought. He could picture Younger adamantly refusing to use the big rig for a publicity stunt.

One morning, though, after a sweaty hour on the basketball court with Bob Rogers, Jake returned to his office and saw that Glynis had phoned to ask if he would take a ride out to the big rig with her. Jake immediately called her back.

"Bob's asked me to tell Tim about your idea for the Fourth of July," Glynis told him.

"You mean nobody's told him about it yet?" Jake snapped into the phone. "For chrissakes, we've only got less than two weeks to—"

She interrupted, "Bob thinks Tim will be more receptive to the idea if I spring it on him." Before Jake could think of a reply, she added, "Well, at least he'll be less negative about it."

Sure, Jake thought. He won't get sore at her. Smart move, Rogers. To Glynis he said, "Okay. I'll go with you."

That afternoon he hopped into her Jaguar and they started for Lignite.

"How's the car behaving?" Jake asked as they hit the interstate.

Glynis glanced at him. "Haven't had a lick of trouble with it for more than a week."

Jake felt far from reassured. Should have taken the Gray Ghost, he said to himself.

They made it to the big rig with no difficulties, though, Glynis pushing the powerful Jag well past the speed limits. Jake kept his eyes peeled for the highway patrol, knowing that the cops loved to ticket sleek, expensive cars. Especially red ones, according to local wisdom. He felt glad that Glyn's Jag was forest green.

The big rig was silent as they entered the oversized shed. Tim Younger was bent over the heart of the apparatus, a trio of technicians hovering at his side.

"Hello, Tim," Glynis called out.

Younger straightened up and turned toward her, a big smile on his normally dour face.

"How's it going?" Jake asked.

"We're inspecting the channel for erosion after our latest run," Younger said. "Everything looks good, even the electrodes. We'll be going for two hundred hours, starting tomorrow."

Glynis said, "Jake has an idea that could bring a lot of political support to MHD."

"An idea?" Younger immediately looked suspicious.

"A stunt, kind of," said Jake.

Younger started walking slowly across the concrete floor, toward the control booth. Matching him stride for stride, Jake explained his Fourth of July idea.

"Some stunt," Younger huffed.

"It could make everyone in the state aware of MHD, Tim," said Glynis.

"Yeah, especially if we have to shut the rig down in the middle of the show."

"It would only be for a few hours," Jake said. "Six, eight hours at the most."

"Keep the whole town lit up all night? How're people going to sleep?"

"They can pull their drapes closed," Glynis said.

"I don't like it," Younger groused.

Glynis looked him squarely in the eye. "You don't have to like it. Can you do it?"

"Yeah, sure . . ."

"Then let's go ahead with it," she said firmly.

"Look," Jake said, "you've already had the rig running for a hundred hours at a time. This'll be easy for you."

"Easy for *you*," Younger countered. "I'm the guy who has to make it work."

"You can do it, Tim," Glynis coaxed. "You know you can."

Younger tried to frown at her, but his expression quickly melted into a boyish grin. "Yeah, I guess we can."

"Fine," said Glynis.

"But I don't like it. It's sticking our chin out. If anything goes wrong . . ."

Jake heard himself quote, " 'Behold the lowly turtle: He only makes progress when he sticks his neck out.' "

Younger shook his head. "Politics. Sometimes I think the prof was right. This is nothing but a stunt for political reasons."

"So was landing on the Moon," Jake snapped.

The following day Jake drove Bob Rogers to a meeting at the Tomlinson residence. He wanted to explain his Fourth of July idea to the candidate and his aides, and Tomlinson wanted to map out their plans for the campaign against Senator Leeds.

"Tim agreed to it?" Rogers's voice was high with delighted surprise.

"Reluctantly," Jake replied, keeping his eyes on his driving. "But he agreed."

Rogers chuckled. "Glynis can get him to agree to anything."

Jake felt a flare of resentment in his gut. But he said nothing. I don't have the right to say a word, he told himself. What Glynis and Tim do together is none of my business. Still, he thought that Younger was taking unfair advantage of her, catching her on the rebound after Sinclair's death. But she doesn't seem to mind it, Jake had to admit to himself. She seems to like Tim. And he certainly seems to want to please her.

He parked the Mustang on the edge of the Tomlinson mansion's curving driveway. It was a warm and bright June afternoon, although thunderheads were building up in the west. We'll have showers before sunset, Jake thought, just like the forecast said.

The butler led them into the library, where Tomlinson was sitting beside Amy on the leather couch, looking tired, somber. His father stood by the window, eyeing the buildup of dark clouds. No drinks in sight, Jake noticed. But then the butler came back pushing a serving cart that rattled with bottles and glassware.

The elder Tomlinson nodded, and the butler silently withdrew. Amy went to the cart. "I'll be mother," she said, cheerfully. "Scotch for you, Franklin?"

Tomlinson pulled himself up from the couch and went to the cart, where Amy splashed scotch over a tumbler filled with ice cubes. Jake and Rogers both accepted frosted bottles of beer from the cooler beneath the cart's tabletop. Tomlinson's father took bourbon and Amy poured herself a glass of white wine.

As they all stood around the serving cart, Amy lifted her glass and toasted, "Here's to a successful debate."

Surprised, Jake blurted, "Leeds has agreed to a debate?"

"Three of them," said Amy, looking satisfied.

Rogers said, "I thought an incumbent didn't like to debate a challenger; gives the challenger too much recognition, makes him look important."

"Franklin already has plenty of recognition," Amy explained. "Leeds knows that Franklin is as well known now as he himself is."

"Leeds is no dummy," Tomlinson Senior said sternly. "Frankie didn't do that well in his first debate against Dant. Leeds is probably planning to ambush us, just the way Dant did."

"He thinks he can outscore me in a face-to-face," Tomlinson said, holding his drink in both hands as he walked slowly back to the couch.

"Outscore you how?" Jake asked. "What issues is he going to run on? I haven't heard anything from him except the old 'vote for experience' line."

"It's been a strong enough line for him for the past eighteen years," the elder Tomlinson pointed out.

"Leeds hasn't had to say much, so far," Amy explained. "He wasn't challenged in his party's primary, so he could just keep his mouth shut and wait."

"And hand out patronage," said Tomlinson's father.

"Pork," Jake said.

Easing back onto the couch, Tomlinson said, "Jake's raised an important question: What issues will Leeds push? We've got to be ready for him, whichever way he goes."

"Who's backing him?" Rogers asked.

Amy went to the couch and sat beside Tomlinson. His father gave the two of them a look that was somewhere between disapproval and disgust. Jake felt much the same way.

Turning to Rogers, the elder Tomlinson put his glass down on the serving cart and ticked off on his fingers, "Leeds is in bed with the unions, including the teachers' union. He's always had great support from the state's construction industry. And the car dealers; they think he saved them when GM and Chrysler needed bailouts. He's in solidly with the political structure, down to the ward levels."

"And the gaming industry," Amy added.

"The casinos," said Rogers.

"The guys from Vegas," Jake added. "They can play rough when they want to."

Tomlinson Senior h'mphed. "You watch too many TV shows, young man."

Jake fought back the response that flashed in his mind, about three murders and the threats he'd received. No, he told himself. They'll just think I'm going off the deep end. Not unless I've got proof. I'll just look like a scared idiot unless I can show them some proof.

"So what issues will Leeds run on?" Tomlinson asked again.

"Construction jobs," his father replied immediately. "More highway construction."

"And more graft for the construction companies," said Tomlinson.

"Education reform," Amy said. "Leeds has been in bed with the education bureaucracy for years."

Rogers shook his head. "It's a crock. They don't reform anything—except maybe lower standards so they can claim more kids are getting better grades."

"There's a lot of votes among those teachers and school administrators," Amy said. "Plus the parents who think their children are doing better in school."

The elder Tomlinson pointed a bony finger at his son. "Don't you go out and criticize the school system! They'll crucify you!"

"But Bob is right, Dad. All this folderol about reform is just so much bullshit."

"Keep out of it!"

Jake said, "I'd like to see a positive campaign, for once. You can use MHD as an example of what you intend to do: push for new ideas, new ways to inspire smart students to get into science and engineering."

Tomlinson nodded thoughtfully. "That could be a good way to handle the education issue." His father said nothing, which Jake took as a tacit vote of approval.

Rogers prodded Jake's shoulder. "You going to tell them about the Fourth of July?"

Jake looked from Tomlinson to his father and then back to Amy. "Tell them, Jake," she prodded.

"I . . . uh, I got this idea about decorating the whole town of Lignite with patriotic light displays and having the whole thing powered by the big rig. Fireworks and everything. Keep the lights on all night."

Rogers broke into a wide grin. "You'd be able to see the town on satellite photos, if it's a clear night."

"I could give my campaign kick-off speech at Lignite," Tomlinson said, his face lighting up.

Jake realized that Amy had already told Tomlinson about the idea. Now they were springing it on the old man.

Tomlinson's father grumbled, "Give your kick-off speech in that one-horse town? Nonsense! The speech should be made here in the capital, with a big crowd and all the news media."

"Bring them all to Lignite!" Amy said, suddenly excited. "Busloads of people! All the news media."

Rogers laughed. "That'll put Lignite on the map, all right."

"It'll put MHD on the map," Jake said.

Even Tomlinson Senior cracked a tight smile. But then he said, "If your generator works."

"It'll work," Rogers said. "We'll make it work!"

Jake thought that they'd have to get Tim Younger to make it work. And to do that, they needed Glynis to make Tim make it work.

T he hardest part was keeping all the preparations secret. There was no way to disguise the hullabaloo in Lignite. Trucks trundled into the quiet little town laden with long strings of lights and other patriotic decorations. Tomlinson's campaign office started sending out invitations all across the state to attend the Glorious Fourth in Lignite. The news reporters were amused by the idea that Tomlinson was trying to make the sleepy old town the launching pad for his election campaign.

Okay, Jake conceded. But no one was to mention the MHD connection to the upcoming holiday festivities. Bob Rogers worked as liaison between the Tomlinson campaign and the city fathers of Lignite, but that was explained by the fact that Rogers was a native son of Lignite, the local boy who went to the big city, got himself an education, and made good.

Lignite's mayor was an accommodating soul, cheerful and outgoing. But Jake insisted that he shouldn't be told about the MHD connection until the very last possible moment. The man had been the town's undertaker until he'd run for town council, eleven years earlier. Once on the council he'd handed his funeral parlor business to a cousin and got the council to elect him mayor—which it had faithfully done every year since.

Jake felt almost paranoid about security. "No leaks," he said to Rogers at least once a day, even while they were puffing and sweating on the basketball court. "No talking about MHD to anybody."

Rogers grinned good-naturedly, but muttered, "They should've put you in charge of the CIA, Jake."

At least once a week Jake drove up to the big rig facility, where

Younger was testing the MHD generator on runs of up to twelve hours.

Growing more nervous with each passing day, Jake insisted to Younger, "If you've got the slightest doubt about this, Tim, we can call it off. Just have the celebration and buy the electrical power from the utility company."

"Don't worry, Jake," Younger told him. "The generator's working like a charm."

Surprised at the dour Yankee's uncharacteristic optimism, Jake sputtered, "Like a charm?"

"Yup," Younger said, straight-faced. "We have to pray over it."

Humor from Tim Younger? Jake asked himself, almost dumbfounded. Yet he felt better that Younger was still as doubtful and reluctant as usual. It's good to be careful, he told himself.

Amy Wexler kept Tomlinson away from Lignite. "Franklin's too outgoing to keep our secret for long," she explained. "He'll start schmoozing with the mayor or somebody and let it drop that the whole town's going to be lit up by the MHD generator."

Jake agreed. Tomlinson was getting enough coverage from the news media, giving speeches around the state about creating new industries and new jobs.

Senator Leeds was giving speeches, too. He held a mammoth rally in the capital to announce a new federal grant for education.

"This will allow us," he said, from the steps of the capitol, "to hire hundreds of additional teachers and reduce the teacher/student ratio in our state's classrooms."

The crowd roared its approval.

Jake watched Leeds's speech on the TV in the faculty lounge on campus. Glynis had come in to watch it, too, sitting on the faux leather couch beside Jake. Hardly anyone else in the faculty had bothered to watch; there were only half a dozen others in the lounge.

Jake sighed as the crowd's applause went on and on and Leeds stood at the podium, smiling handsomely, his arms raised above his head.

"I'll bet most of the people in that crowd belong to the teachers' union," said one of the professors.

"Maybe so," the woman sitting next to him agreed, "but you've got to admit, Leeds brings home the bacon."

The pork, Jake corrected silently.

Glynis looked somewhere between contempt and disgust. "Have you read the details of the grant he's talking about?" she asked Jake.

He shook his head. All the others were getting up and leaving the lounge, heading back to their offices or classrooms. Glynis hadn't budged and Jake didn't move from her side.

"Well, I have," she said. "Most of the money will go to hiring administrators and staff: counselors, school nurses, librarians, positions like that. Very little is devoted to new teachers."

Jake shrugged.

"It's the old game," Glynis went on. "Tell the voters you're giving them what they want, when in reality you're giving the special interests what *they* want."

Pushing himself reluctantly up from the couch, Jake asked, "You see the educational establishment as a special interest group?"

Glynis stood up beside him. "Don't you?"

"I guess you're right," he agreed, "now that I think about it."

As they walked down the corridor toward Jake's office, Glynis said, "By the way, I think I know where Perez has hidden himself."

"Nacho?" Jake stopped in mid-stride and grasped Glynis's arm. "I don't want you to have anything to do with Nacho Perez!"

She pulled her arm free. "Jake, he's a murderer."

"We don't have any proof of that. And if it's true, it's all the more reason to stay away from him."

"I'm not afraid."

"You should be," Jake insisted, ignoring her unspoken implication that he was frightened.

"I think he's up in Vernon," Glynis said.

"Vernon?"

"It's the logical place for him to hide away. The whole town's controlled by the gambling casino. I'll bet that Captain Harraway is protecting him up there."

Jake had to admit that she could be right. But he said, "You stay away from Vernon. If you're right, the whole police force up there must be in on the deal."

"We can't let him get away with murder, Jake! If we can show that he was in town on the day Arlan and his wife were shot—"

"You could join the list of casualties."

Glynis looked at Jake for a long moment, her face solemn, cold. At last she said, "Very well, Jake. I'll have to go it alone, then."

Before he could think of anything more to say, before he could reach out to her, to stop her, to protect her, Glynis wheeled around and strode down the corridor, away from Jake.

Cursing himself for seven kinds of a fool—and a coward, to boot—Jake went through the motions of the final preparations for the big Fourth of July celebration in Lignite. He phoned Glynis every day, getting her answering machine most of the time. When she did speak to him, it was brief and cool.

"No, I haven't gone up to Vernon," she said, her voice steady, steely. "I'm calling the hotels and boarding houses, trying to find out if Perez is staying in one of them."

"You can't expect them to tell you anything," Jake objected.

"I tell them I'm from Senator Leeds's office. That makes them cooperative."

"Christ, Glynis, you're heading for trouble!"

"I don't care, Jake. He killed Arlan. I can't just sit here and let him get away with that."

Meaning that I can, Jake understood her unspoken accusation.

"For god's sake, be careful," he pleaded.

Glynis hung up.

Jake tried to concentrate on his university work and Tomlinson's campaign, but he kept worrying about Glynis. He thought about calling Tim Younger and telling him about the situation, but couldn't make up his mind to do it.

Meanwhile the election campaign was swinging into high gear. Senator Leeds had a twelve-point edge in the statewide polls, but Tomlinson was inching up. In his campaign speeches, Leeds hammered away at how well the state's economy was doing: Employment was holding steady, thanks mainly to new construction jobs that depended heavily on federal funding.

Tomlinson pointed out that outside of the construction and gaming industries, employment in the state was actually in decline.

"And what kind of an economy do we want?" Tomlinson asked in his typical stump speech. "Full employment for card dealers from Las Vegas while honest, hard-working men and women in local industries are being laid off?"

As June turned into July the gap between incumbent and challenger narrowed slightly, but only slightly, and slowly, very slowly.

Tomlinson's father complained to Jake, "This stunt of yours up in Lignite had better give my boy a big bump in the polls. Otherwise he'll never catch up."

Amy Wexler helped to arrange a convoy of buses to take VIPs and news teams on the nearly two-hour drive from the capital city to Lignite on the Fourth. Newspapers and TV broadcasts showed the preparations for the big patriotic celebration. Veterans of wars from Iraq and Afghanistan down to the elderly men from World War Two were invited to Lignite for the big day. Amy even located the state's last living veteran of World War One and made arrangements to bring the centenarian up to Lignite in a paramedic van.

Tomlinson's campaign people enlisted all sorts of civic and service organizations in their preparations: the American Legion and Veterans of Foreign Wars, the Elks and Moose, Boy and Girl Scouts, statewide police and firefighters groups. All promised to send delegations to Lignite on the Fourth of July.

Jake grew more antsy with each day. He drove to the big rig regularly, where Younger seemed strangely confident.

"Soon as Tomlinson presses the button, we'll fire up the rig and the town will light up," the engineer said as he stood by the silent generator.

"Don't you have to warm it up first?" Jake asked.

"Nope. The plasma equilibrates in five, ten seconds. She'll put out full power before you can blink an eye."

"But if something goes wrong . . ."

"We've interlocked with the power grid," Younger told him. "If anything goes wrong with the rig we can switch over to the regular grid within a second or two. Hardly a flicker. Nobody would notice."

Jake nodded, waiting for the other shoe to drop.

Sure enough, Younger added, "Of course, Tomlinson will get the bill from the electric company."

"Of course," Jake murmured.

Jake thought about inviting Glynis to drive up to Lignite with him for the big day. Amy had rented rooms at the town's hotel for him and other key people on Tomlinson's staff. Jake wondered where Amy would be spending the night. With Tomlinson somewhere, he supposed.

Several times he picked up the phone to ask Glynis, and each time he decided against it. She thinks I'm a coward. Besides, she'll want to be with Tim, not me.

So Jake drove to Lignite alone and checked in at the hotel. Somebody had given the old clapboard building a fresh coat of paint. The lobby still looked seedy, its carpeting threadbare, but there was a huge vase of fresh flowers just inside the revolving door and the desk clerk was a cute young woman with a bright cheerful smile.

The town was bustling with visitors. The streets were crowded with people walking up and down in the late afternoon sunshine: old men in faded uniforms, families with children clutching American flags in their fists, laughing teenagers sipping sodas and eating ice cream cones, their faces painted red, white, and blue. Parked cars lined the curbs, and several empty lots had been converted into parking areas for long lines of buses.

As Jake stood on the sidewalk outside the hotel, perspiring in the setting sun, he saw that Amy and her cohorts had done their job well. Lignite was swarming with eager, expectant visitors from all around the state. Half a dozen TV news vans were in view, reporters were interviewing people on the street.

Leverett Caldwell and Alice were strolling leisurely across the street. Lev spotted Jake and waved to him. Gesturing to the crowd swarming along the sidewalk, Lev made a circle of his thumb and forefinger. *Good job*, he was saying. Jake grinned like a schoolboy being praised by his teacher.

A blare of police sirens turned everybody toward the far end of town where B. Franklin Tomlinson had arrived, not in a limousine, but in a blocky Hummer painted red, white, and blue. Led by a pair of local police cruisers, Tomlinson's Hummer paraded through town, flags waving from its fenders, and stopped at the freshly painted city hall. The mayor and entire city council stood at the front steps to welcome Tomlinson. He bounded out of the van, all smiles, and began to shake hands with the politicians. Tomlinson's father climbed stiffly out of the Hummer behind the candidate, looking doubtful about this whole affair. Amy came right behind him, beaming beautifully in white slacks and a blue blouse with a red scarf around her throat.

Now all we need is for the MHD generator to work, Jake thought. He suppressed an urge to cross his fingers.

As Tomlinson and the mayor led a procession of VIPs and campaign workers from the steps of city hall, across the town's main street, and up to the platform that had been erected on the edge of the town square, Jake scanned the crowd for Glynis. She was nowhere in sight. She's up at the big rig with Tim, Jake told himself.

The sun was setting, but the streets of Lignite were still hot and dusty. Jake shuffled along with the crowd thronging around the speakers' platform in the square, sweaty and more nervous with each passing instant. The people were in a holiday mood, laughing, happy. Children ran through the crowd. Somebody popped a string of firecrackers and everybody jumped, startled for a moment.

The town's high school band—in uniforms that looked spanking new—broke into "Stars and Stripes Forever," drowning out the hundreds of conversations buzzing through the crowd. Jake stood in their midst, feeling alone, searching for Glynis even though he knew she wouldn't be there.

Jake had given Amy the precise time for sunset, and at that moment Tomlinson, his father, Amy, the mayor, and the city council and their wives all slowly climbed the wooden steps of the platform.

The band crashed to its conclusion and the mayor stepped up to the lectern. He was a pudgy man with bulging frog's eyes and a wide, accommodating smile. The last rays of the setting sun made his face look florid. Then he mopped his forehead with a big white handkerchief and Jake realized that the man was perspiring.

"Friends, neighbors, and visitors," the mayor began, his voice booming from loudspeakers placed around the square, "welcome to America's birthday celebration!"

The crowd roared.

The speeches droned on as the shadows of dusk inched across the square. Each and every one of the city council members got to say a few words. Portable lamps that had been placed at the corners of the platform began to glow. Jake spotted the planet Venus gleaming beautifully in the darkening sky.

At last the mayor took the lectern again and began to introduce Tomlinson. "We are very privileged tonight to have with us . . ."

Jake felt as tense as a bowstring. He knew that a mile or so away, Tim Younger and his crew were going through their final countdown with the MHD generator, listening to the speeches piped to them through a direct radio link, waiting for Tomlinson's cue to turn the generator on. He crossed the fingers of both his hands.

". . . and here he is," the mayor said, his sweaty face beaming, "our next United States senator, Benjamin Franklin Tomlinson!"

The band blared the first few bars of the Marine Corps hymn and Tomlinson stepped to the lectern, tall and handsome and smiling. The crowd cheered as he shook hands with the mayor, then raised his arms above his head.

Suddenly everything hushed. Tomlinson adjusted one of the microphones on the lectern, then began, "Thank you, Mr. Mayor. And thank all of you for coming here tonight for this wonderful celebration."

While Tomlinson spoke on and the evening grew darker, Jake's whole body tensed with anticipation. It'll work, he told himself. It's got to work. Tomlinson talked about new industry and new jobs for Lignite and the entire state. He ostentatiously held up the box with the big red button that was supposed to turn on the MHD generator.

". . . and every light, every decoration, every watt of electricity to power the entire town," Tomlinson was saying, "will come from the MHD generator that stands just a mile or so up the road from this spot."

Total silence. No one moved. It seemed to Jake that no one even breathed. It was dark now, the only light coming from the lingering twilight glow in the western sky.

"All right, then," Tomlinson said, "let's turn on the lights!" And he stabbed at the big red button.

Jake's heart stopped. And then the whole square, the entire town lit up. Huge beautiful lights of red, white, and blue. The Statue of Liberty stood outlined in lights on one side of the square, the marching men of *The Spirit of '76* on the other.

The crowd gasped, then applauded and roared its approval. Jake started to breathe again.

Fireworks erupted into the sky. The crowd loved it, oohing and aahing with each colorful burst. It went on and on, until Jake's neck became stiff from watching.

The square was brilliantly lit, and after the final burst of multicolored fireworks, the mayor grabbed the microphone again and invited everybody to the barbeque that was waiting on the far side of the square.

Jake pushed through the surging, laughing, chattering crowd toward the platform, where Tomlinson and the others were coming down the steps.

Tomlinson spotted Jake and waved to him. As Jake got within arm's reach, Tomlinson grabbed his hand and pumped it happily.

"You did it, Jake!" he bellowed over the noise of the crowd. "It's marvelous!"

"Tim did it," Jake yelled back. He saw that even Tomlinson's father looked pleased.

Amy came up and kissed him on the cheek. "Wonderful, Jake," she said into his ear. "Just wonderful."

As they trudged slowly through the crowd, Tomlinson shaking hands with every step, Jake spotted Tim Younger heading their way.

"What're you doing here?" Jake yelped.

Younger laughed. "The rig's running fine. I came for the barbeque. Going to take some back to the guys. They've earned it."

"Isn't Glynis with you?"

"No," Younger said. "Haven't seen her since yesterday. I thought she'd be with you."

GLYNIS

S tanding there in the middle of the swirling, boisterous throng, Jake's blood turned cold. "When's the last time you saw her?" he demanded of Younger.

The engineer thought a moment. "Day before yesterday. She came up to the rig, spent an hour or so."

And she's not here, Jake realized. My god, she's gone up to Vernon. That damned Harraway's probably tossed her in his jail. Or worse.

Catching the frightened expression on Jake's face, Younger asked, "What's the matter?"

"Glynis," Jake said, hollering to be heard over the crowd's din. "She might be in trouble."

"Glyn?"

Jake pawed through the pockets of his jeans to find his cell phone, shouldering his way toward the edge of the crowd as he did so. Younger came along beside him.

"What trouble?" Younger asked.

"She thinks Sinclair was murdered and she's trying to find out who did it." Jake pulled up Glynis's number and called it as he kept striding toward the edge of the town square, away from the noise of the crowd.

One ring. Two. Younger was watching intently.

"Hello." Glynis's voice!

"Glyn!" Jake's heart leaped. "Are you okay?"

"Of course I'm okay." She sounded puzzled by Jake's near-frantic question.

Feeling as if he'd just stepped off a high cliff, Jake stammered, "I . . . that is . . . you didn't come out to Lignite. . . ."

"I watched the ceremony on television," Glynis replied, her voice calm, curious.

"Why didn't you come here?" he asked into the phone.

"You didn't ask me."

"I thought Tim . . ." Jake glanced at Younger, who seemed curious, also.

"Actually, I'm packing a few things. I'm driving up to Vernon tomorrow."

"No!" Jake snapped.

"Yes," she said coolly.

"Stay right where you are," Jake said, his heart thumping. "I'm driving down to your place."

Sounding almost amused at his consternation, Glynis said, "I'll be here."

Clicking the cell phone shut, Jake told Younger, "She's okay. She's all right."

"What the hell's going on?" Younger was starting to look irritated.

Heading toward the hotel across the street where his car was parked, Jake explained, "I was scared that Glynis might be going up to Vernon and getting herself in trouble."

"What's going on with you and Glyn?"

"Nothing," Jake said. Then he added, "She's got this notion that Sinclair was murdered and she wants to prove it. I'm trying to stop her from making a fool of herself—or worse."

Younger looked very unconvinced.

"Look, Tim, I'm not trying to get between you two."

"You'd better not."

Jake raised both his hands, palms out. "Believe me, Tim, I'm not."

But Jake knew he was lying.

Leaving a decidedly suspicious Tim Younger at the town square, Jake hurriedly checked out of the Lignite hotel, dumped his travel bag on the back bench of his Mustang, and peeled out of the parking lot, heading back to the capital and Glynis's apartment.

It was after eleven o'clock by the time he nosed the convertible into the quiet, tree-lined street where Glynis's apartment building stood. He found a curbside parking space and hurried across the street to her building.

His insides were quivering. You're worried about her, he told himself. About her safety. But a voice in his head countered, Who're you trying to kid? You care about her. You want her.

She's going with Tim, he told himself as he pushed the buzzer for her apartment. She doesn't have any interest in me.

But you have an interest in her.

Yeah, he admitted to himself. Fat lot of good it's doing me.

"Jake?" Glynis's voice sounded harsh, grating in the intercom's tiny speaker.

"It's me," he said.

The front door buzzed. Jake rushed in and loped up the stairs. Glynis was at her half-open door, a questioning smile on her face.

"Jake, you look as though you're being chased by the whole Apache nation," she said, pulling the door wide so he could step into her apartment.

"I . . ." Jake felt relieved, flustered, yearning, all at the same time. "I was worried about you."

Glynis closed her door and eyed Jake warily. The same slinky gray cat also stared at Jake briefly, then walked regally into the kitchen. Glynis was wearing a shapeless T-shirt several sizes too big for her and baggy sweat pants. Her hair was pinned up, off her neck. Her feet were bare. She looked beautiful.

"Worried about me?"

"About you running up to Vernon. You'd be heading into a nest of snakes. Poisonous snakes."

She shook her head. "I don't care, Jake. They murdered Arlan and I'm going to prove it."

"You loved him enough to get yourself killed?"

Glynis looked away for a moment, then straightened up and admitted, "Yes. I did."

"Getting yourself killed isn't going to help him."

"They wouldn't hurt me," she said. "They can't afford another dead body on their hands."

He reached out and grasped her by the shoulders. "For god's sake, Glyn! You're dealing with the people who run Las Vegas! They know how to deal with dead bodies. They know how to *make* dead bodies!"

She shrugged out of his grip. "Jake, I'm frightened enough as it is. You don't have to scare me more than I'm already scared."

"Don't go to Vernon!"

"I'm going." There wasn't a shred of doubt in her voice, not a scintilla of hesitation. Jake saw that her mind was made up.

And so was his.

"All right," he said. "I'll go with you."

"You don't have to—"

"That Jaguar of yours might get temperamental again. We'll go in my car."

Glynis smiled at him.

CONFESSIONS

Jake drove home, spent the night telling himself he was an idiot, then drove back and picked up Glynis before either one of them had eaten breakfast. They headed out toward Vernon, the convertible's top down, the warm morning wind feeling good on their faces. The day was bright and clear, the sky a nearly cloudless blue.

"I'm not hungry," she said when he suggested they stop at an IHOP on the interstate.

"Neither am I," he admitted. Too nervous to be hungry, he realized. Too scared. Too . . .

Without taking his attention off the eighteen-wheelers whooshing past them, Jake raised his voice above the noise of the wind and asked, "How serious are you and Tim?"

Out of the corner of his eye Jake saw her blink with surprise.

"I know it's none of my business, but—"

"We're friends, Jake. A woman can have male friends without having a romance, you know."

He had to struggle to keep from smiling. "Yeah, I guess so."

"Tim's already married."

"He is?"

"To that machine of his. The generator."

"Oh."

"Besides, he's not my type."

Jake started to ask what her type might be, but stopped himself. You might not like the answer, he told himself.

They drove in silence for miles. The traffic thinned out and Jake put the Mustang on cruise control.

Turning toward him, Glynis said, "Jake . . . that night . . . when Arlan was killed and I was so upset . . ."

The night I stayed over at your place, Jake remembered.

"You said you knew what it was like to lose someone you love."

"My wife," Jake said, feeling that old hollow void inside. "She was killed in an auto accident. About a year ago, little more. Nearly two years, come to think of it."

"I'm sorry."

"Me too."

"I shouldn't have pried."

"It's okay," he said. "I met Louise in high school. She was the most popular girl in the school—and she fell for me!"

"Why not?"

Shaking his head at the memories, Jake said, "I was the luckiest guy in the world. And then . . . and then, all of a sudden, she was gone."

"It's so . . . final," Glynis said.

After several miles of silence, he glanced at her and saw that Glynis was lost in her own memories, her own sorrow.

Then Jake heard himself say, "That's why I'm so worried about this business with Perez, Glyn. I don't want to lose you."

She stared at him in wide-eyed silence. Jake felt just as surprised as she looked.

VERNON

As Jake swung the Mustang off the interstate and headed toward Vernon he asked Glynis, "How did you find Perez?"

"I phoned the hotel downtown, the motel at the casino, and every boarding house and B and B in the area and asked for him. I said I was with Senator Leeds's office and it was urgent that I find him."

It was almost noon and the sun was baking hot. Jake had pulled his old baseball cap out of the car's utility console but Glynis remained bareheaded. Her sleeveless blouse and short skirt exposed plenty of skin, too. He wondered if she would get sunburned despite her slightly olive complexion.

"So you tracked him down," Jake said.

"People were very kind, especially after I told them I was from Senator Leeds's office. Most of them had never heard of Perez, but the room clerk at the casino's motel said she thought he was staying in town at a bed-and-breakfast. The third one I called told me he was staying there. Or was it the fourth one?"

"You found him."

"I didn't talk with him. He wasn't in when I called. But they admitted that he was staying there. Had been for several weeks."

Jake felt puzzled. "What's he doing in Vernon?"

With a shrug of her bare shoulders, Glynis replied, "Hiding out. In Vernon he's protected from snoops like us."

Thinking of the massive Captain Harraway, Jake muttered, "And we're walking right into the lion's den."

His GPS box faithfully guided them to the address Glynis had given him. It was a beautifully maintained old three-story Victorian house, with a veranda stretching across its front and little balconies at both the upstairs windows.

"How quaint!" Glynis said.

Looks like a good place for a murder, Jake thought as he parked the Mustang across the street and pulled up its top.

When he started to get out, Glynis grabbed his sleeve. "Wait. Let's see if he's in first."

She fished her cell phone out of her purse and pecked out a number.

"Yes. Hello. It's Glynis Colwyn again. . . . Yes, that's right, from Senator Leeds's office. Is Mr. Perez in? No? Do you expect—oh, yes, I see. Thank you."

Clicking the phone shut, she told Jake, "He's out for the day. They expect him back this evening."

"Might be at the casino," Jake mused.

Glynis arched a brow. "Do you feel like gambling?"

"No," he said firmly. "It's bad enough being here, where Harraway or one of his cops can spot us. Going to the casino is just asking for trouble."

With a slightly mischievous smile, Glynis said, "Yes, I suppose you're right."

So they spent the day in Vernon, ate lunch in one of the town's three restaurants, strolled up and down its main streets, window-shopping like an old married couple while Jake expected Harraway or one of his officers to come roaring down the street and cart them off to the lockup.

Glynis actually bought a ridiculously garish oven mitt, decorated to look like a bright orange dragon. Jake shook his head when she picked it up off the shop's counter, but Glynis wormed it onto her hand and made its mouth open and shut.

"I could do a puppet show with this," she said, laughing.

Jake wished he could laugh, too, but he kept looking over his shoulder for one of Harraway's police cars.

As dinnertime approached, Glynis phoned the B and B again. Perez hadn't shown up. They ate dinner in the restaurant across the street from where they'd had lunch, Jake too nervous to eat much,

Glynis apparently blithely unconcerned about anything except the steak on her plate.

As the sun was setting they walked back to the bed-and-breakfast. The Mustang was still sitting at the curb across the street.

They slid into the car.

"Now we wait for him to show up," Glynis said.

"Like a police stakeout," said Jake.

"Yes."

They chatted about inconsequential things as the shadows of evening engulfed them. Jake found himself telling Glynis about his hopes to be on the team building the next NASA probe of Mars.

"Does that mean you'll have to leave the university?"

Nodding in growing darkness, Jake said, "I'll take a sabbatical. I'll probably have to go to the Goddard center, in Maryland."

"I see." She sounded disappointed.

"That's close to West Virginia. Your family lives there, don't they?"

"Yes, but I seldom get back there."

"You could come and visit."

"I suppose I could," Glynis said, sounding a little brighter.

Jake reached for her and she leaned toward him.

Her cell phone broke into "Flight of the Valkyries."

Jake straightened up as Glynis fumbled in her purse for the phone. "Yes? Yes! Oh! I see. Yes, we'll be right up."

Before Jake could ask she said, "It's Perez. He's in his room and he's waiting to see us."

"Glynis, are you sure you want to do this? If you're right, the guy's pretty dangerous."

"I'm right, Jake," she said, with utter certainty. "That's why I have to face him."

IGNACIO PEREZ

So what's this all about?" Nacho Perez asked, as soon as Glynis and Jake stepped into his room.

It was a fairly sizable bedroom, clean and neat, with a canopied bed and white-painted furniture. It looked to Jake like the kind of room a family would have for a couple of daughters. Two windows flanked a glass door that led out onto one of the house's upper balconies.

Perez was in his shirtsleeves and suspenders; his trousers looked baggy, overdue for a pressing. His jaw was stubbled, his thinning hair slightly awry. He was smiling, but Jake thought his eyes looked guarded, tired, dark with baggy sleepless rings beneath them.

"We want to ask you a few questions," Jake began.

Glynis snapped, "We know that you murdered Professor Sinclair and his wife, and also Dr. McGruder."

Perez stared at her for a wordless moment, then broke into a harsh, barking laugh.

Shaking his head, Perez said, "You kids been watchin' too much TV."

"We can prove that Sinclair didn't commit suicide," Jake said.

"So what?" Perez countered.

"You killed him," said Glynis.

"In your dreams, kid." Perez gestured to the sofa on the other side of the room. "Siddown. Take it easy and let me explain a couple things to ya."

Jake led Glynis to the sofa, keeping a wary eye on Perez, who pulled a wooden chair from the corner by the windows, turned it around backwards and straddled it, arms on its straight back, facing them.

"You kids got a lot to learn," he said. "You're stickin' your noses in places that could get you hurt."

"You're the one in trouble," Jake retorted.

Shaking his head more in sorrow than in anger, Perez said, "I oughtta be sore at you two. I gotta sit here in this hick town 'cause you're playin' detective."

"Senator Leeds sent you up here?" Glynis asked.

"Leeds?" Perez snorted disdainfully. "He's just a front. He works for the big boys, same as me."

"What big boys?" Jake asked. "Who are they?"

"Guess."

"Las Vegas," said Jake.

Perez grinned at him. "And L.A. And Chicago. They got their hooks in a lotta places."

"Why did you kill Professor Sinclair?" Glynis demanded. "What did—"

"I didn't kill nobody!" Perez snapped. "When they want somebody offed they bring in professionals."

"But they did have Sinclair murdered," Jake said.

"I didn't say that."

"Why?" Glynis asked. "Why murder a university professor. And his wife?"

"And her physician," Jake added.

Perez heaved a patient sigh. "Look. You two are nice enough kids. Don't get yourselves in this any deeper. Lemme give you some good advice. Go back home and forget about this. Leave the dead dead. You ain't gonna bring 'em back."

"But we can bring their murderers to justice," Glynis said.

His expression hardening, Perez jabbed a finger at Glynis as he said, "All you're gonna do is get yourself hurt, kid. You could wind up dead. Or maybe get shipped to Mexico, Honduras, someplace like that. They'd have a good time with you."

Jake jumped to his feet. "If anybody tries to hurt her I'll—"

"You'll do what, college boy? Nuthin', that's what you'll do. Because you'll be dead. Siddown and take it easy."

Jake plopped back onto the sofa.

"You realize that you've just admitted that Professor Sinclair and his wife were murdered," said Glynis.

"So what?"

"So I can get the state's attorney to arrest you."

Jake added, "Harraway can't protect you from the state police."

Perez shrugged. "So I'll be in Las Vegas. I'd like that better than this hick town anyway. Or maybe I'll take a vacation in Mexico. We got good connections down there."

"You're not above the law," Glynis said.

"Lady, we *are* the law. Why do you think we keep guys like Leeds in our pocket? We don't just run little towns like Vernon. We got whole states organized. And there's nuthin' you can do about it."

"But if Tomlinson gets elected—" Jake began.

"We'll buy him out, just like we bought out Leeds and a lotta others."

Glynis said, "Tomlinson doesn't need your money."

"Maybe not," Perez admitted. "But there's other ways of buyin' people. Women. Drugs. Power. If Tomlinson beats Leeds and goes to the Senate, we might help him move up and become president. That'd be neat, huh?"

Before Glynis could reply, Jake gripped her wrist tightly and said to Perez, "I see what you're telling us. I understand how the game is stacked." Turning to her, he said, "Come on, Glyn. It's time for us to leave."

"But—"

"Time to go home," Jake said firmly. He got to his feet and pulled Glynis up beside him.

"Thanks for the education, Nacho," Jake said. "I appreciate it."

"Just go home and forget this business," Perez said, rising from his chair. "You're a couple of nice kids. I wouldn't want to see you get hurt."

"I understand. Come on, Glyn. We've got a long drive ahead of us."

Glynis looked from Jake to Perez and back to Jake again. The expression on her face was halfway between puzzlement and frustrated fury.

ON THE INTERSTATE

Jake could feel Glynis's cold rage as he drove out of Vernon. She sat in the darkness beside him like a statue of ice, unmoving, silent as death. Neither of them said a word until he got onto the interstate and set the cruise control at seventy.

"You let him bully you," Glynis said, her voice hard and low.

Feeling more than a little angry himself, Jake shot back, "You don't realize what he told us, do you?"

"He told us to stop bothering him and you walked away."

"Before we got ourselves killed," Jake muttered.

"You don't believe—"

"Do you want to end up in some whorehouse in Mexico?" Jake snapped. "Bombed out on cocaine or heroin or whatever they pump into you?"

"I'm not afraid."

"Well, you should be. You don't understand what he was telling us."

An eighteen-wheeler roared past them, well above the speed limit, making the Mustang shudder in its slipstream.

"He told us that the Mafia would kill us," Glynis said, sounding sullen about it, reluctant to admit it.

Jake shook his head. "He told us that this is all about drugs. Narcotics. Those big boys he talked about aren't just into gambling. They're bringing narcotics into the state and Leeds and god knows who else in the state government is in with them."

Glynis was silent for several minutes. Another semi rig whooshed past them. On the median between the sections of the divided highway Jake saw the lighted sign of a gas station. He glanced at his fuel gauge and decided they could get back to the city without filling up.

"Do you think Mrs. Sinclair was hooked on drugs?" Glynis asked.

"Maybe. I don't think they'd kill her because she was a gambling addict."

"And the state police, the district attorney's office, the whole government . . ." Glynis sounded lost, bewildered as she began to recognize the size of the problem.

"Not everybody," Jake said. "But enough. They've got the state in their control and Leeds is part of it."

"I know that!" Glynis snapped. "What are you going to do about it?"

"Me?"

"You. Us. Whoever."

"Nacho wants us to drop the whole business. That would be the safest thing for us to do."

No reply. She sat beside Jake, her face profiled by the dim dashboard lighting. She looked tense, rigid—but filled with anger, not fear.

Jake gripped the steering wheel tightly, peering ahead into the darkness, and heard himself say, "I'm not going to drop it, Glyn."

"You're not?"

"All my life those wiseguys have pushed me around and I've let them do it. I ran away from them, tried to hide myself, buried myself in astronomy, as far away from them as I could go. And they've followed me. They're here, still pushing me, still telling me what I can and can't do." He felt resentment boiling up inside him, a hot unreasoning anger that he had kept bottled inside himself since childhood. "Guys like Nacho and Monster, they think they can get whatever they want. Just crack a few heads and everybody lays down for them. Well, fuck that! I'm not letting them walk over me anymore."

"But Jake, you said they could be dangerous," Glynis said, suddenly cautious, worried.

"Yeah. I'll have to deal with that."

"*We'll* have to deal with that."

Shaking his head, Jake told her, "You're going to West Virginia."

"I am not!"

"I want you out of here, Glyn. I want you where you'll be safe. Back with your family."

"I most certainly will not run away from this, Jacob Ross. Anymore than you would."

"There's no sense in both of us getting hurt."

"I'm staying," Glynis said, iron-hard.

Jake sucked in a deep breath, then replied, "Let's talk this over with somebody who can give us a better angle on the problem."

"Somebody? Who?"

"An old friend of mine. He's been like a father to me."

LOVE AND WAR

D r. Cardwell sat in stony silence as Jake told him what he and Glynis had learned. It was early morning; Cardwell's office was bright with the newly risen sun. Jake had phoned him the night before, as soon as he had returned Glynis to her apartment.

Now they sat at the round table by the windows, Glynis on Jake's left, dressed in a butter yellow short-sleeved blouse and dark green skirt, Cardwell on his right, in his inevitable gray suit and sprightly bow tie.

"So you believe Senator Leeds is part of this?" Cardwell asked, in his soft, curious voice.

"He has to be," Jake said. "He's fronting for them. Perez said as much."

His high forehead furrowing, Cardwell suggested, "Perhaps he doesn't know what's really going on."

Glynis snapped, "If he doesn't, it's because he doesn't want to know."

Cardwell took in a deep breath. "They murdered Arlan? And his wife?"

"And Dr. McGruder," Glynis added.

"It's all a cover-up," said Jake.

"But what are they covering up?" Cardwell asked, almost pleadingly. "What's the reason for it?"

Hunching closer to his old mentor, Jake said, "It's narcotics. Got to be. Mrs. Sinclair must have been hooked and the professor was going to crack up over it."

Cardwell shook his head. "That doesn't make sense. There's got to be something deeper than that."

Glynis said, "The MHD issue."

Cardwell's round eyes widened. "The MHD issue?"

"Professor Sinclair was forced to come out against Tomlinson's plan to push MHD," she explained. "But he didn't want to. He wanted to support Tomlinson. He wanted all the support for MHD that he could get. But they wouldn't let him."

Jake looked at her questioningly. "Are you sure?"

Her voice lower, Glynis answered, "Arlan told me things that he wouldn't tell anyone else . . . when we were together, alone."

In bed, Jake realized.

Cardwell said, "I still don't see . . ."

"They were holding his wife's problems over his head," Glynis continued. "But the professor was under terrific strain. It was tearing him apart. His wife, the MHD program . . . he was cracking."

"So they got rid of him," Jake said.

Shaking his head ruefully, Cardwell said, "It makes some sense, I suppose, but you don't have a scintilla of evidence, do you."

"No," Jake admitted. "We don't."

"And we apparently have the whole state's apparatus against us," Glynis added.

"Not the entire state," said Jake. "Just the police, the courts, and the district attorney's office."

"Plus Senator Leeds," Cardwell added, with a wry smile.

"So what do we do, Lev?" Jake asked.

"Tell Frank Tomlinson about it," Cardwell replied without hesitation. "I'm not sure what he can do, or even if he'll want to do anything, but you've got to tell him about this."

Jake nodded.

"At the very least," Cardwell went on, "he ought to be able to provide you with some protection."

It wasn't until late that night that Jake was able to meet with Tomlinson. The candidate had spent the day on the campaign trail, giving speeches at rallies in three different towns across the state.

He looked tired when the butler ushered Jake into the mansion's library. Tomlinson was sitting in one of the leather armchairs in his shirtsleeves, tie pulled loose, a whiskey in his hand, neat. Amy stood next to him, looking elegant in a knee-length black skirt and scoop-necked black blouse.

Tomlinson smiled wearily as Jake crossed the book-lined room and shook hands with him. "Pardon me for not getting up, Jake," he said from his chair. "I'm pretty bushed. I'm putting in more flying miles these days than an airline pilot."

"But ever since the Fourth of July your poll numbers have been climbing," said Amy, smiling brightly.

"Not all that much," Tomlinson said.

"But they're climbing," Amy insisted. "That's what's important."

Turning back to Jake, Tomlinson asked, "What would you like to drink, Jake?" Then he added, "How's the generator behaving?"

"Younger's giving it an overhaul," Jake replied. "In a few days he'll start a five-hundred-hour run."

"Sounds impressive." Turning to look up at Amy, Tomlinson said, "See what Jake wants to drink."

Jake shook his head and sat on the front few inches of the arm-chair facing Tomlinson's. "I've got a lot to tell you, Frank."

"About MHD?"

"About the drug traffic in this state and Leeds's involvement in it."

Tomlinson glanced up at Amy again. "Better get my father in here," he said.

"He's probably gone to bed by now."

"Call him. He'll want to hear this, I know."

Amy went to the phone on the desk as Tomlinson asked guard-edly, "Drug traffic?"

"We think it's behind the murder of Professor Sinclair and—"

"Murder? I thought he committed suicide."

"We think otherwise."

"We? Who's with you on this?"

"A grad student named Glynis Colwyn. She and Sinclair . . ." Jake found it hard to say, but he choked out, "They were lovers."

Tomlinson's brows went up. "The professor and the graduate student."

His lips pressed tight, Jake nodded.

Alexander Tomlinson's voice rang out, "What's this all about?"

Turning, Jake saw the elder Tomlinson standing in the library doorway, his fleshless face set in a demanding scowl. He was in a floor-length maroon robe that accentuated his slim, rigid figure. Even his stiff bristle of hair looked angry.

"Narcotics, Dad," said Tomlinson. "Jake here thinks Leeds is tied to organized crime."

Eyeing Jake disdainfully, Tomlinson Senior said, "Tell me something I don't already know."

Jake felt resentment simmering inside him. Getting slowly to his feet, he said to the old man, "Leeds is involved in three murders, and I've been threatened myself."

Still frowning, the elder Tomlinson turned to Amy. "You'd better fix me a single malt, on the rocks. Make it a big one. This sounds like a long night coming."

Alexander Tomlinson brushed past Jake and sat in the armchair next to his son while Amy went to the rolling table in the corner that was set up as a portable bar and poured a stiff whiskey for the elder Tomlinson. Still on his feet, Jake started telling them what he and Glynis had found out.

Tomlinson Senior sipped his whiskey as they listened. Once he muttered, "Narcotics." His son sat and watched Jake without comment. Amy sat on one of the Ethan Allen chairs near the bar as Jake ran through his story, pacing across the library floor the way he often did when lecturing students.

When Jake finished, Tomlinson Senior said to his son, "The casinos are a good way to launder drug money."

"I hadn't thought of that," Tomlinson replied.

Looking up at Jake, the old man said, "You've just confirmed what we've known for a long time. The gambling interests are backing Leeds, and they're into drugs as well."

"So we can make organized crime a campaign issue," Jake said.

With a worried glance at his son, Alexander Tomlinson shook his head. "That could be . . . risky."

"I know it's risky," Jake snapped. "They've threatened me, and Glynis, too."

"We can protect you," Tomlinson said.

"It's risky politically," his father said. "It could boomerang on us."

"The fact that Leeds is financed by organized crime?" Jake yelped. "How the hell could that boomerang?"

"You don't have any evidence."

"But you said you've known about this for a long time. Now they've murdered three people! What more do you want?"

"Jake, you've got nothing but hearsay," said Tomlinson. "There's no proof."

"We can't accuse Leeds of anything unless we have ironclad proof," Tomlinson Senior said sternly. "Without proof Leeds could accuse us of a smear, a desperate politically motivated smear."

From her chair by the bar, Amy said, "That could cost us votes."

"And it could be dangerous for you personally, and the graduate student you told me about," said Tomlinson, looking weary of the whole business.

"Graduate student?" his father demanded. "What graduate student?"

"The late Professor Sinclair's mistress, apparently," Tomlinson said.

"Oh, for Christ's sake! You mean this is all built on the word of some kid the professor was shacked up with?" The old man looked thoroughly disgusted.

Feeling resentful of the elder Tomlinson's dismissal, Jake said, "You make it sound smutty."

"Well, isn't it?" the elder Tomlinson snapped. "We'd look wonderful, wouldn't we, making unproved accusations based on some lovesick student's pillow talk."

"So you're going to do nothing about it?"

"There's not much we can do," said Tomlinson.

Amy said, "Franklin, you've got to get some rest. And start preparing for the debate."

"That's not for another two weeks," Tomlinson said.

"But the first debate is the most important one. It fixes your image against Leeds's in the public eye. It's your big chance to jump past him in the polls."

The elder Tomlinson, toying with the cut-crystal glass in his hand, murmured, "You know, there might be something else we can do."

"Something else?" his son asked.

"You can't come out openly and accuse Leeds of being involved in murder and dope dealing."

"Of course not."

"But we could start some rumors circulating around the state," Alexander Tomlinson mused, almost smiling. "Just a few whispers here and there. Undermine Leeds's image as an upright citizen."

Tomlinson looked shocked. "I can't do that!"

"You wouldn't have to do it," Amy said, enthusiastically. She got up from her chair and scurried to Tomlinson's side. "You won't have to say a word about it."

"But it's . . . unethical."

"All's fair in love and war," his father pronounced. "You think about it. Think hard."

"Three murders," Jake muttered, feeling stunned at how they were ignoring him.

Tomlinson looked up at him, his eyes baggy with fatigue. "We'll provide you with protection, Jake," he said. "And your grad student, as well."

"Thanks."

The elder Tomlinson started for the door. "It's been a long night. You think about what I said, son."

Thanks for nothing, Jake thought. But he didn't say it aloud.

As if he could hear Jake's thoughts, the old man turned back toward him. "The head of the FBI's regional office is the son of an old friend of mine. I'll tell him about this. He might make himself a few brownie points with the Justice Department if he could bring in a few big-time organized crime people."

Jake nodded. It wasn't much, but it was better than whispers.

THE FIRST DEBATE

Jake could see that Tomlinson was nervous. The man had been holed up with his advisors and spin masters for two days, his campaign activities suspended, out of contact with everyone else while he prepared for this debate against Senator Leeds. Jake had handed a sheaf of talking points about MHD to Amy; he hadn't been allowed to see the candidate himself.

Now, as the candidate and his closest aides walked down the concrete tunnel that led out to the arena, Tomlinson was fairly quivering with nervous energy. Jake remembered a classmate of his, Vince Tortoni, back in their freshman year at the university. Vince had been on the verge of failing their mandatory class in English literature, and had disappeared for several days before the final exam. Cramming, Jake knew. When Vince showed up for the exam he was bubbling with quotations from poetry. But as he grabbed his blue exam book and pencil, he turned to Jake and asked, agonized, "Dammit, what's my name?"

Jake hoped that Tomlinson hadn't overstudied the way Vince had.

The debate was staged at the university's hockey rink, an arena big enough to hold more than a thousand spectators jammed in on tiers of benches. Jake knew that Amy had done her best to get Tomlinson supporters to pack the place. He supposed Leeds's people had done the same.

The skating rink itself was covered with wooden flooring, yet the place still felt cold and clammy to Jake. The crowd was restless, impatient, voices buzzing in an expectant background hum. But as Tomlinson and his retinue stepped out of the tunnel and into the bright lights illuminating the arena, the throng got to their feet and applauded, cheered, whistled. Tomlinson turned on his gleaming smile and waved nonchalantly to them. The applause seemed to calm him, steady him.

Tomlinson went straight to one of the lecterns set up in the center of the floor while Jake took a seat on the front row, reserved for Tomlinson's staff and volunteers. Across the floor, Leeds's people sat facing them. Amy Wexler hurried over to the bench and squeezed in beside Jake.

The audience cheered even louder as Senator Leeds sauntered in, grinning and nodding. He stopped to shake hands with a few people in the crowd and Jake wished Tomlinson had been smart enough to think of that.

Instead of a single moderator, three news anchors from the state's three major television stations took up the seats between the two lecterns.

The audience quieted and sat down. Three television cameras were set up around the periphery of the floor; one of them was close enough for Jake to almost touch the guy operating it. The only woman among the three news anchors welcomed the audience and introduced the two candidates. Leeds had won the coin toss an hour ago; he would speak first.

Leeds smiled handsomely as he turned slowly to survey the crowd. Then he began:

"Thanks for coming out tonight. You all know me and you know what I stand for. For nearly eighteen years now I've served you in the United States Senate. I've worked hard to bring jobs to you, to improve our schools, to see to it that our state is a fine place to live and bring up your families.

"Okay. Now we're facing an election again. You have a choice. Are you going to vote for experience and solid accomplishment, or are you going to vote for an amateur who has nothing to offer but vague promises of pie in the sky, of technological miracles that won't benefit anybody but a tiny group of elite scientists?"

Leeds hesitated a heartbeat, trying to gauge the impact of his words on the crowd.

"My opponent has never run for political office before, yet now he wants to be a U.S. senator. And what does he represent? Not you! Not the honest, hard-working people of our fine state. He represents a narrow elite, a group of very wealthy old men who want to protect *their* interests, not yours. And an even smaller group of intellectuals and scientists. He's a playboy who's being put forward as a serious candidate when in fact he doesn't have the experience, the knowledge, or the interest to represent you in Washington.

"What's his big accomplishment? A gimmick with an experimental power generator that lit up some decorations for a few hours. We need solid experience and accomplishment in the Senate, not gimmicks. I know! I know how to get things done. All he can do is talk about some wild scheme that can't possibly be of any real use to you or me for another ten or twenty years!

"Vote for him and you vote for his wealthy family and his elitist friends and his crazy ideas. Vote for me and you vote for experience and accomplishment. You'll be voting for yourselves and your own interests."

The crowd got to its feet and applauded wildly. Jake glanced at Amy. Over the noise of the cheering he hollered in her ear, "Did you have any idea that Leeds would take this approach?"

"No," she yelled back, looking worried.

The crowd quieted and sat down. Tomlinson stood there, his face stern, solemn. He reached into his jacket and pulled out a small packet of papers. His notes, Jake realized.

"I guess I won't be using these," he said, and let the papers flutter to the floor.

Jake swallowed hard.

"It's true I've never run for political office before," Tomlinson said. "So why am I running now? I'll tell you. I'm running to make this state better, to make your lives better, to bring new industry and thousands upon thousands of new jobs to our state. I'm running to end the politics-as-usual complacency that's got our state in its death grip."

Turning to face Leeds, Tomlinson said, "Senator, I'm not ashamed of my family or my friends. They've done a lot for this state. Over past generations they founded the university, they financed research programs that have helped our farmers to be the most productive in the world. Far more workers in this state owe their jobs and their careers to what they've accomplished than to the federal pork barrel projects that soak up our tax dollars."

Looking up at the tiers of packed benches, Tomlinson said, "I want to move us forward. If we don't go forward we sink into complacency and corruption. We have tremendous opportunities ahead of us. We can use the knowledge coming out of our university to improve the properties of the state's corn crop. We can use new technology to generate electrical power more efficiently and cleanly and reopen our moribund coal industry.

"The good senator talks about a small group of scientists. What he hasn't told you is that this group of dedicated men and women can produce jobs for engineers and technicians, for store clerks and truck drivers, for coal miners and small business owners all across our state, all across our nation.

"We have a bright future ahead of us, if we can only recognize the opportunities that lie ahead and work to reach them."

Glancing back at Leeds, he repeated, "I'm not ashamed of my family or my acquaintances. I've been blessed with great parents and wonderful friends." Smiling brightly, Tomlinson said, "You know, they say that of those to whom much is given, much is expected. I've been given so very much. I want to use the gifts that have been granted to me to make your lives better."

Pointing at the crowd, he added, "Much has been given to you, too: a land of freedom and opportunity, a state that is rich in natural resources, a tradition of hard work and solid achievement. Now, in this election, much is expected of you. You—and only you—have the power to move us forward into a brighter and better future. It's not pie in the sky. It's bread and butter. It's the jobs and careers and new ideas that will feed your children and your children's children."

The crowd roared. They shot to their feet and yelled, whistled, stamped their feet until Jake had to clap his hands over his ears. The arena reverberated with the clamor.

Amy leaned close to Jake and hollered, "I guess he did all right!"

Jake nodded, grinning. He didn't need the notes, Jake said to himself. He came through without them.

SUMMER OF DISCONTENT

A nd then nothing happened. As July melted into the sultry days of August, the political campaign seemed to settle down into a routine. Tomlinson raced around the state, speaking at barbeques, libraries, PTA meetings in town after town. Smiling handsomely, outwardly full of youthful vigor, he seemed tireless. But Jake saw him at home, away from the other campaign workers and aides. He knew how much energy was being drained from the candidate.

Senator Leeds ran a much more relaxed campaign, appearing at huge rallies in the state's major cities. Mammoth crowds turned up for his appearances.

As they watched one of Leeds's speeches on television from Tomlinson's living room, Amy said, with grudging admiration, "His people know how to turn out a crowd."

"Union rank and file," murmured Tomlinson, leaning back on a big, plush sofa.

"They vote, dammit," his father growled.

"Organized labor," Amy said.

Organized crime, Jake thought.

Tomlinson's numbers were inching upward, but Leeds still had a seven-point lead in most of the polls. The Fourth of July stunt at Lignite had bumped Tomlinson's numbers higher briefly, but they settled back within a week. The debate had gone well, Jake thought. The news reports were generally favorable. But Tomlinson's poll numbers inched upward only slightly. At least they haven't gone down, Jake told himself thankfully.

Leeds kept hammering on his experience and derided Tomlinson's "elitist pie-in-the-sky fantasy" based on "an unproven and possibly dangerous technology, which at best will take ten or twenty years to do anything useful."

If Tomlinson's people had indeed started a whispering campaign about Senator Leeds's links to organized crime, Jake saw and heard nothing about it. No news stories, no hints in the political blogs and Web sites, no discernable whittling of the senator's lead in the election polls.

Jake saw Bob Rogers regularly, usually on campus at their basketball exercises, and he drove up to Lignite at least once a week. Tim Younger had the big rig purring along smoothly, putting out fifty megawatts for hundreds of hours without interruption.

"We're going for seven hundred fifty," Younger said, over the constant roar of the generator.

Calculating mentally, Jake hollered, "That'd be more than a month."

Younger nodded, a hint of a smile cracking his dour expression. "A month without interruption. Then we take her apart and see how she stood up to it."

At least Tomlinson got the Fain Security Company to detail a couple of men to watch Jake and Glynis.

"You don't have to look around for us," said the agent who showed up in Jake's office. "We'll be watching you and the young lady."

The agent looked like a wimpy little insurance salesman to Jake. Nondescript, spindly. Nothing like the tough guys he'd seen in movies and television.

Jake had dinner with Glynis as often as he could. Just to make sure she's okay, he told himself. Just to see that nobody's bothered her. But he knew that it was merely an excuse. He wanted to be with her. Talking with her, even if it was only over the table of some second-rate restaurant, was the one bright spot in his life.

Glynis seemed oblivious to his desires. "If the FBI is looking into this," she complained over dinner, "they're invisible to the human eye."

Trying to put a good face on it, Jake countered, "Come on, Glyn, do you think they'd come charging in with guns blazing? They're not a SWAT team, after all."

She smiled dubiously at him. "I suppose you're right."

It was on one of his late August visits to the big rig that Younger took him outside for a walk around the building. It was a blazing hot August afternoon, and there wasn't a tree or a scrap of shade anywhere in sight once they'd walked a few yards out into the dusty scrub. The distant mountains shimmered hazily, as if they were trying to pull themselves up and get away from this baking summer heat.

"Glyn tells me you two have been seeing each other," Younger said, his voice tight, his face grim.

"Um, well, yeah," Jake stammered. "Nothing serious. Just dinner now and then."

For several moments Younger said nothing. Jake saw the stony expression in his eyes. The muted roar of the MHD generator drowned out the whisper of the slight breeze. Nothing seemed to be moving on the sun-scorched land, not even a tumbleweed. The sun felt like a hot iron pressing down on his head, his shoulders. Perspiration trickled down Jake's ribs.

At last Younger said, "She's not serious with me, either. Not yet, anyway."

Jake wondered if Younger knew about Glynis and Sinclair.

Trying to smile, Jake said, "The first time I saw you two together, up here at the rig, I thought you were going to throw her out."

Younger shook his head. "She's a good kid. I like her a lot."

"I know," said Jake.

"I don't want you getting in my way," Younger said.

"Tim, I don't—"

Jabbing a finger at him, Younger said, "Just keep away from her."

"Now wait a minute . . ."

"She told me she's got a bodyguard." Younger looked incredulous.

"She's convinced that Sinclair didn't commit suicide. He was murdered. And Senator Leeds is mixed up in it."

"The two of you have been threatened?"

Jake nodded.

"Well, just keep away from her. I'll look out for her."

"You're up here at the rig most of the time."

"Just keep away from her," Younger insisted. "Understand me?"

"That's for her to decide, isn't it?" Jake retorted.

Younger took a step toward Jake, his hands balling into fists. "It's for me to decide, godammit! I don't want you near her."

Holy Christ, Jake thought, we're going to have a fistfight out here in the desert.

Raising his hands, palms out, Jake said, "Tim, calm down. This is a decision Glynis is going to make, one way or the other. There's nothing you or I can do about it."

Younger glared at him for a long moment. Jake could feel his heart thudding beneath his ribs, but he stood his ground, wondering what he'd do if Younger took a swing at him. He remembered the description of a fight from high school: Two blows were struck; he hit me and I hit the ground.

At last Younger muttered, "Just leave her alone. Stay away from her."

Jake shook his head, thinking he was too stubborn for his own good. He heard himself say, "There's nothing going on between Glynis and me except having dinner once in a while. We *are* both working on the MHD program, you know."

Younger looked unconvinced, but his body relaxed and he took a deep breath. "Don't try to beat me out, Jake."

Jake started to reply, thought better of it, and simply turned away and started walking back toward his car. Younger stood there in the high sun; Jake could feel Tim's eyes boring into his back, hear the throaty roar of the MHD generator blasting away.

DINNER FOR THREE

I t was a week later when Glynis phoned Jake at his office.

"An FBI agent called me," she said, sounding excited. "She wants to meet with both of us!"

Jake glanced at his phone's screen. He had two calls on his voice-mail list.

"What did you tell her?" he asked.

"I said we'd see her this afternoon."

Grimacing slightly, Jake said, "I have a class at two. How about later? After four o'clock?"

"I'll call her back."

Jake checked his voicemail and, sure enough, one of his two callers had been Special Agent Sheila Mankowitz. The other was one of his students, asking for a makeup date for the test he'd flubbed.

He called the student and settled on a date with him, then phoned Special Agent Mankowitz. Her line was busy, so Jake left his name and number. Telephone tag, he thought as he hung up.

His phone rang immediately.

It was Glynis. "We're going to have dinner with Agent Mankowitz tonight," she blurted, without preamble. "Seven o'clock. It's the only time she had available. That's all right with you, isn't it, Jake?"

He nodded as he replied, "Seven is okay." *As if I had anything else on my calendar.* "Where?"

"O'Brian's Irish Pub," Glynis answered. "On Maple Street."

"Okay. Seven o'clock." As he hung up, Jake wondered why Agent Mankowitz would want to eat at an Irish pub. Then he thought about how Younger would react to his having dinner with Glynis again— even with an FBI agent as a chaperone.

The pub was crowded and noisy when Jake arrived, nearly ten minutes before seven. People were piled at the bar three and four deep. Irish ballads were bleating out of the speakers in the ceiling, the volume way too high for Jake's comfort. The waitresses and barmaids were dressed in off-the-shoulder blouses and kelly green skirts: the management's idea of what Irish lasses wore, Jake reasoned.

He asked the head waitress for a booth, was given a buzzer and told to wait either outside on the sidewalk or at the bar. Jake squeezed through the crowd at the bar and spotted a bottle of Negra Modelo among the display behind the busy barmaids. Mexican beer in an Irish pub, he thought. The evening was filled with incongruities.

The buzzer went off when he was halfway through the dark beer, and as Jake carried his glass to the head waitress's station, Glynis came in the door, looking fresh and hopeful. She was wearing a coral red patterned summer knit dress, sleeveless, knee-length.

Jake smiled at her, although he couldn't help looking past Glynis to see if Tim Younger had followed her.

"Is she here yet?" Glynis asked, smiling expectantly.

Jake shook his head. "Not yet."

A waitress led them through the noisy mob thronging the bar to a booth toward the rear of the room, near the double swinging doors of the kitchen. Jake could smell corned beef and cabbage whenever a waiter pushed through the doors.

A short, chubby woman in a dark pants suit and starched white blouse came to their booth. Her face was round, framed with short-cropped dark hair. The jacket of her suit hung open. Jake wondered if she could button it over her ample bosom.

"Glynis Colwyn?" she asked, in a crisp, no-nonsense voice. "I'm Special Agent Mankowitz."

Jake half rose from behind the table as Agent Mankowitz slid in beside Glynis. "You must be Jacob Ross," said the FBI agent.

A real detective, Jake thought as he took her proffered hand. Her grip was strong, firm.

"Now then," said Agent Mankowitz, "I've been assigned to look into your allegations of murder associated with drug trafficking and money laundering."

"Good," said Glynis.

"So why don't you tell me what you know."

Jake sat as Glynis explained about their suspicions that the murders were a cover-up for narcotics and gambling operations. She was interrupted by a waitress who took their orders for drinks: chardonnay for Glynis, iced tea for Mankowitz. Jake nodded when the waitress asked if he wanted another beer.

Mankowitz listened without comment, without even nodding. The waitress brought their drinks and handed them stiff oversized menus.

". . . And that's about it," Glynis finished. Looking across the table at Jake, she added, "Unless you have something more."

"Just that all three bodies have been cremated, so you won't be able to get much forensic evidence," Jake said.

Mankowitz smiled condescendingly, then took a careful sip of her iced tea. "Forensic evidence is important on television shows, Mr. Ross. In the real world . . ." She shrugged.

"That man Perez as much as admitted that Professor Sinclair and his wife were murdered, along with Dr. McGruder."

"Your word against his," Mankowitz said.

Jake pointed out, "Perez also said he could leave the state, maybe even leave the country."

"It's not much to go on," the FBI agent said. She picked up her menu and began to study it.

"I know we don't have any firm evidence," Glynis admitted, "but doesn't it seem obvious to you that they were murdered?"

Mankowitz put down her menu and turned in the booth to face Glynis. "Ms. Colwyn, to begin with, murder is a state or local offense, not federal. We've known for some time that the gambling casinos are used to launder narcotics money, but that gets us involved in the tribal governments of the Native Americans who own and operate the casinos."

"They're operated by people from Las Vegas," Jake said.

Ignoring him, Mankowitz went on, "There's not much we can do about this, except add your suspicions of murder to a file that's already pretty damned thick."

"But Senator Leeds is involved!" Glynis insisted.

Mankowitz gave her a look that was little short of disgusted. "Yeah, open an investigation on a United States senator. During his reelection campaign. That would be a swell career move for me."

Jake said, "But you're missing the point. Why did they have to murder Sinclair and his wife? What's the connection to their drug and gambling operations?"

"Look," Mankowitz said, her dark brows knitting, "I'm just a very junior player here. I've only been in the field a few weeks and this is my first assignment. My boss told me to listen to what you had to say and report back to him."

"And then?" Glynis asked.

Mankowitz shrugged again. "That's up to my boss. But going after a U.S. senator? Get real."

Jake looked at Glynis. "Now you know why they keep Leeds on their payroll."

Glynis nodded glumly. They ate dinner in almost total silence. Someone started singing Irish ballads to a guitar accompaniment as they finished their meals. Jake was glad to get up and leave.

Glynis looked close to tears.

LABOR DAY

ake didn't see Glynis at all for the rest of the month. As Labor
Day approached he thought about inviting her to the big rally
that Amy was planning for Tomlinson. He told himself he
wasn't afraid of Younger, and if he wanted to invite Glynis to
the rally, she could always bring Tim along if she chose to.

He hoped she wouldn't choose to.

But somehow or other he kept delaying his call to her. She's not
interested in me, Jake told himself. And after that fiasco with the FBI
she doesn't even want to talk to me, most likely.

Tomlinson's poll numbers hovered five or six points behind
Leeds's. In the words of the local news media, "Senator Leeds has a
slim but comfortable margin over the challenger." Not a hint that
Leeds was tied to organized crime, to drugs and gambling and murder.

The MHD issue dwindled to a minor affair. Tomlinson's support
from the mining industry and the environmentalists couldn't overcome
Leeds's backing by organized labor and the state's political machine.
Jake tried hard to wheedle money out of the electric utility people, but
their support was little more than a public relations gesture.

A second debate between the candidates was scheduled for the
Saturday after Labor Day, but the two campaign staffs were at log-
gerheads as to where the debate should be staged. Tomlinson wanted
a venue that couldn't be packed by Leeds's cadres of union people.
Leeds wanted an outdoor setting, where thousands of people could
pour in.

It was during an all-night planning session with Tomlinson's staff
that Jake blurted, "Why don't we hold the debate in the planetarium?"

They were meeting at Tomlinson's campaign headquarters, a

former supermarket in the heart of the capital city that had been closed for more than a year. The owners had been happy to rent it to the candidate for little more than a song. The floor was now covered with desks, each with its telephone and computer, all unattended, so late at night. The walls were plastered with huge posters of Tomlinson, smiling confidently.

Jake wished that Tomlinson looked that confident in reality.

Amy Wexler gave Jake a quizzical look. "The planetarium?"

Before Jake could reply, one of the aides shook his head. "Too small. Leeds won't go for it."

There were an even dozen of them sitting around a long table in the middle of the cavernous room. The high overhead lights glared on the rows of empty, silent desks.

Jake countered, "The planetarium can seat two hundred and fifty people. And it's got TV links to the rest of the museum. We could even pipe the debate live outside, to the park. You could accommodate a thousand people or more out there easily."

Amy looked at him thoughtfully. "You know, that might work. Leeds claims he supports education—"

"He supports the teachers' union," one of the aides grumbled.

"Staging the debate in the planetarium," Amy continued, "might appeal to him. The education angle."

"It's worth a try," said the young man in charge of Tomlinson's news media relations.

It was nearly one A.M. when the meeting finally broke up. Amy walked with Jake out into the dark parking lot behind the former supermarket.

"That was a good idea, Jake," she said.

"Thanks."

The other staffers were heading for their cars. Amy walked beside Jake as he went toward his Mustang.

"It's been a while since we've had a chance to be alone together," she said.

In the shadows of the parking lot, he couldn't make out the expression on Amy's face, but her voice sounded light, almost amused.

"Yeah," he replied, uncertainly.

"I've neglected you, haven't I?" she murmured.

"Yeah," Jake repeated.

"I've been awfully busy with the campaign and everything," Amy said.

"And everything," Jake muttered.

"He needs me, Jake," Amy said, her voice suddenly pained, urgent. "He comes across so strong and confident in public, but he's tired of it all. It's so demanding! He's exhausted."

Jake said nothing.

"I mean, there are times when I think he'd like to give it all up. He never wanted to go into politics. It's his father, his father's pushed him into this. That old man thinks his family ought to run the world."

"So he needs your help," Jake said.

They had reached Jake's Mustang, parked under one of the light poles. A swarm of insects danced in its feeble light high above. Jake saw that Amy's silver BMW was parked next to his own car.

"He needs your help, too," Amy replied. "He needs all the help he can get."

With a weary sigh, Jake said, "I suppose he does."

"I need to talk to this graduate student of yours," Amy said, her voice suddenly strong, firm.

"She's not *my* grad student," Jake said, thinking, Truer words were never spoken.

"I've set up an interview with a political blogger and she—"

"No!" Jake snapped.

Surprised, Amy said, "What do you mean, no?"

"It's too dangerous. I don't want her to be at risk."

"Jake, from what you've told us they already know who she is."

"Yeah, but as long as she stays quiet she'll be okay. No interviews. No public appearances."

"They won't show her face."

"No."

"Jake, we *need* her to make a statement."

"For your whispering campaign."

"You make it sound dirty."

"Isn't it?"

"And murder is okay? You're willing to let them get away with murder?"

He had no answer for that.

Stepping closer to him, Amy said, "All right, if you want to be so protective of her, would *you* talk to the blogger?"

"Me?"

"You won't be named. Nobody will see your face or know who you are. All you have to do is say you think that Professor Sinclair and his wife were murdered and Senator Leeds is part of the cover-up."

"That's libel, isn't it?"

She laughed. "You can't libel a politician."

Thinking of Perez and Monster, Jake said, "No way, Amy. I won't be part of it."

She rested her hands on his shoulders and looked up at him, her cool hazel eyes glinting in the wan light. "Jake, you do want Tomlinson to win, don't you? You do want MHD to succeed?"

"Not like this."

"It's always like this, Jake," Amy said. "Politics is hardball. The softies lose."

He could feel the warmth of her, see the promise in her eyes.

"I'm sorry I've neglected you, Jake," Amy said, her voice softer, almost sorrowful. "I've missed you. But we're together now. Tonight I'm all yours."

"And tomorrow?"

"Tomorrow you get interviewed for the blog."

Jake nodded and kissed her. So she lets me screw her if I screw Leeds, he thought. That's politics.

Jake spent the night at Amy's apartment and enjoyed every moment of their time in bed together. In the morning they showered together and she treated him to oral sex while the steaming hot water sluiced over their naked bodies.

All the while a voice in the back of his mind was telling him that she was buying him, getting him to do what she wanted by giving him what he wanted. And Jake wanted it. His body took control of his brain, instinct over intellect, need over knowledge. You think with your balls, Jake berated himself. You know she's been sleeping with Tomlinson. But that didn't stop him.

And what about Glynis? he asked himself. How would she feel if she knew you were sleeping with Amy? Hell, she must know already. And she doesn't care. She doesn't care what I do. Why should she? I don't mean a damned thing to her.

After a quick breakfast in the apartment's minuscule kitchenette Amy made a phone call, then announced, "It's all set. He'll see us at nine thirty."

Jake realized it had been all set up from the night before, maybe even earlier.

Jake followed Amy's BMW to the other side of the city, a rundown street near the interstate, where trucks rumbled along the elevated highway past rows of five-story apartment buildings, gray bricks grimy with soot.

The blogger turned out to be a badly overweight young man with a two-day growth of ginger-red beard on his round, many-chinned face. He reminded Jake of an orangutan, with cheek pouches and sad, heavy-lidded eyes. He worked out of his basement apartment, a one-room lair with a single window set up by the ceiling, curtains pulled shut, although Jake could see through the slit between them the hubcaps of a car parked at the curb outside. The place was dark, damp. It smelled of perspiration and stale pizza and soy sauce. The sofa bed was open, sheets rumpled and soiled-looking. The rest of the furniture looked like junk recovered from a flood or a secondhand sale. A table by the sink was littered with cardboard food containers.

But standing on the rickety desk in the corner was a spanking-new computer, bright and clean.

Jake took this all in with a single glance once the blogger had opened his apartment door.

"Jake, this is Freeforall," Amy said, with a straight face. "Free, this is Dr. Jacob Ross, professor of astronomy at the university."

"Assistant professor," Jake corrected as they stepped into the chaos of the room.

"Come on in," said Freeforall. "We can get started right away."

"What's your real name?" Jake asked.

Freeforall shot him an annoyed glance. "Doesn't matter."

"He won't use your name," Amy assured Jake. "And he won't mention the Tomlinson campaign, either. You'll be 'a reliable source.'"

They've got it all worked out, Jake realized.

Freeforall pulled a battered-looking rattan chair from the table by the sink and gestured for Jake to sit on it. He then settled himself in the wheeled padded chair in front of the computer and powered it up.

Turning to Jake, he began, "Okay, so what's this about a couple of murders that Senator Leeds is connected with?"

Looking around for a camera, Jake asked, "This isn't being videoed, is it?"

"Nope. Just audio," said Freeforall. "Then I'll transcribe it. Nobody'll even hear your voice. Now tell me about Senator Leeds and these murders."

Jake took in a deep breath, then started to unfold his story.

As he explained about Dr. McGruder, Freeforall interrupted him. "I understand somebody from Leeds's office was in Florida when the doctor died."

"That's right," said Jake.

"Who?"

"I thought we weren't going to mention any names."

"I'll protect your name," said the blogger, "but I want any names you can give me about the bad guys."

With a shake of his head, Jake replied, "Let's just say it was somebody who works in the senator's office. And he's connected with the gambling interests."

"Somebody named Perez?"

"You already know!" Jake blurted.

Freeforall grinned smugly. "I know many things. I even know the name of the graduate student who was sleeping with Professor Sinclair."

"You leave her out of it!" Jake snapped, half rising from his chair.

Freeforall put up his flabby arms to protect himself. "Hey, hey! Okay! I'm not gonna mention her name."

Amy gripped Jake's shoulder. "It's all right, Jake. Calm down."

Dropping back onto the creaking chair, Jake pointed at Freeforall. "I don't want any mention of any grad student. Get that straight!"

"Okay, okay," Freeforall said, his eyes wide, fearful. "I'll protect her identity."

"You won't mention that there's a grad student involved in this!" Jake insisted. "I'm your source. If that's not good enough, forget it."

"Okay, you're my source. I've got it."

The blogger resumed the interview, finally asking, "But what makes you say the professor was murdered? The police say it was suicide."

Jake replied evenly, "Professor Sinclair was killed by a bullet fired into his right temple. But he was left-handed. Somebody shot him. Somebody killed him and his wife, then went to Florida to murder Dr. McGruder so he couldn't reveal that Mrs. Sinclair didn't have cancer."

"Wow!" said Freeforall. "And that same guy from Leeds's office was in Vernon when the professor was shot and in Florida when the doctor died?"

"That's right. The same man. Who works for Senator Leeds."

Freeforall seemed to consider this for a long, thoughtful moment. Then he summed up, "So you're saying that Senator Leeds is involved in gambling, drugs, and three murders."

"I don't know if the senator is involved directly. But somebody who works for him sure is."

"The senator would have to know about it, dontcha think?"

Jake nodded. "Yes, I would think so."

"Great!" Freeforall banged his computer keyboard with a stubby finger, then turned back to Jake. "Great. This'll go out on the Net before lunchtime."

Amy got to her feet, beaming. "You did a good job, Jake."

Great job, Jake thought. Sure. It'll help Tomlinson, in an underhanded way. Maybe it'll help nail Nacho and Leeds and the rest of the bastards who're behind the murders. Maybe it'll make Glynis feel better. Maybe.

Jake stood up, shook hands with Freeforall, and left with Amy. He felt as if he needed another shower.

DOCUMENTARY

With some trepidation, Jake logged onto the Freeforall blog that afternoon, in his office.

And there was his interview, in print, scrolling down his computer screen. True to his word, the blogger identified his informant merely as "a reliable source." But there were all the other names: Senator Leeds, Nacho Perez, Professor and Mrs. Sinclair, Dr. McGruder in Florida, Captain Harraway in Vernon—and his insistence that Sinclair had committed suicide.

Now what? Jake asked himself. Does anybody read that grubby little guy's blatherings?

His phone rang.

"Jake, have you seen the b-school's student site?" Glynis asked, sounding excited.

"The business school—"

"They're running an interview somebody gave to a blogger. It's all about Arlan's murder!"

Jake hesitated a moment, then said as evenly as he could, "Is it?"

"It was you, Jake, wasn't it?" Glynis asked. "You gave the interview."

"Don't tell that to anybody else!" he snapped.

Glynis laughed. "Your secret is safe with me."

For how long? Jake wondered as he hung up.

He called up his calendar for the day and saw that he was scheduled to do a scene for the TV documentary that Tomlinson's public relations people were putting together about the promise of MHD. Nodding to himself, Jake thought, This'll be a good day to be off campus.

He had already arranged with a teaching assistant to handle his afternoon class, so Jake hurried down to the parking lot and drove to the utility company's power plant on the outskirts of the city, where Bob Rogers and the video crew were waiting for him. With Amy.

The power plant hummed and vibrated, huge turbines spinning endlessly, generating the electricity that lit the city and its environs. The turbines were taller than a basketball player, massive. Even though their metal housings were gleaming and spotless, somehow they looked old-fashioned to Jake, antiquated.

Bob Rogers was wearing an actual suit, dark brown, although he had a turquoise bolo at his throat rather than a normal necktie. Jake wondered if the sports jacket and open-necked shirt he was wearing would be good enough for the day.

Amy introduced them to the video director. "Jake, Bob, this is Wallace Ziegler, from Los Angeles."

Ziegler was an austere, tall, slim man with an outdoorsman's rugged, deeply tanned face and thinning silver hair. He was wearing a short-sleeved sport shirt and chinos.

"Call me Wally," he said, smiling genially as he shook hands with Rogers and Jake.

"Wally's worked a lot with Clint Eastwood," Amy said, obviously impressed.

"Assistant director," said Ziegler. "I handled some of his outdoor scenes."

"Wow," Rogers said. "What's he like to work with?"

"A real stickler. Same as me."

Jake asked, "Um, should I be wearing a tie?"

Ziegler gave him a fatherly smile. "No, you're fine."

A technician came up and clipped thumbtack-sized microphones to their shirts as Ziegler explained that they should just speak normally, stay relaxed, and pay no attention to the pair of cameras that would be trained on them.

"You just look at me, or each other. Talk as if you're having a normal conversation. We've got the script cued up on the teleprompters, but you don't have to follow it word for word. Just be your natural selves."

Jake wondered how natural he could be with a team of camera-men and technicians surrounding them.

As they walked over toward one of the big turbines to begin their scene, Bob Rogers asked Jake, "Did you look at the news blogs today? They've got Sinclair's murder splashed all over them."

"I took a look before driving out here," Jake said tightly.

"They're claiming Senator Leeds is mixed up in it." Rogers seemed to be eyeing Jake suspiciously.

He knows it was me, Jake thought. They all know it was me. Who else could give that interview, except for Glynis?

Amy Wexler stepped between them. "Ready for your moment of stardom?"

Jake forced a smile. "Yeah. It's showtime. Isn't it?"

They spent the whole afternoon going through a scene that would take up only a minute or two in the finished documentary, but it took more than three hours before the director was satisfied that they'd got it right.

Wally told the truth, all right, Jake thought. He's a stickler.

The idea of the scene was to show how big the ordinary turbine-driven power plant was, in contrast to the compactness of the MHD generator.

Rogers was saying, "So they boil water and use the steam to spin the turbine, and the turbine spins an armature that generates the electricity. That's the same way Edison did it, almost a hundred and fifty years ago."

Jake's line was, "And they get about the same efficiency as Edison got, don't they?"

"Right," Rogers came in on cue. "A little over forty percent."

"CUT!" Ziegler boomed.

The director came smiling kindly up to Rogers and said gently, "You said 'puhcent.' Could you pronounce it 'percent,' please?"

"Oh, sure," said Rogers.

"Okay, let's take it from Jake's line about the efficiency Edison got."

Again Rogers said, "puhcent." Again Ziegler roared, "CUT!"

"Gee, I'm sorry," Rogers said. "I never realized I pronounce it wrong."

"It's all right," Ziegler replied, a little tensely. "You'll get it."

Rogers finally said "percent" to Ziegler's satisfaction, but it took four takes. And then one of the camera operators announced that his batteries had hit the redline and he'd have to replace them before they started the next take.

Ziegler puffed out a weary breath. "Let's break for an early dinner."

Jake began to realize why it cost so much to make a movie.

Over the next few days the blogosphere erupted with stories about the Sinclair murders. The regular news media began to pick up on the story. Jake watched a local television station's interview with a very disgruntled Captain Harraway, in Vernon.

Looking like a dark thundercloud about to spit lightning, Harraway said grimly, "My forensics team decided it was a murder-suicide and the coroner's inquest came up with the same finding. End of story."

But the story would not end. CNN sent a reporter to Vernon, and the local news media began circulating a rumor that the FBI was investigating the case. The regional FBI office's director would neither confirm nor deny the rumor.

Jake wondered how long it would be before Freeforall or somebody outed him as the "reliable source" that got the story started. He wondered what Perez was doing about it. And Monster.

He stayed away from Glynis, although he phoned her daily, to make certain she was all right. She showed up at the big rig outside Lignite the day that Jake, Rogers, and the video team shot the scene for the documentary there.

Glynis stood beside Tim Younger while Jake and Rogers went before the cameras to show how much smaller and more efficient the MHD generator was compared to the standard turbine plants.

"No need to boil water and make steam," Rogers said, while Ziegler stood behind one of the cameras and smiled encouragingly. "No turbines. No moving parts at all. But this MHD generator is fifty *per*cent more efficient than turbine power plants. And bigger MHD plants will be even more efficient."

As the video crew wrapped up its equipment, and Ziegler complimented Rogers on his pronunciation, Amy grabbed Jake's arm.

"Isn't that Glynis Colwyn over there?" She nodded toward where Glynis and Tim Younger stood, deep in conversation.

"That's her," said Jake.

"I hadn't realized how good-looking she is." Amy cast a knowing eye at Jake. "Should I be jealous?"

Jake gaped at her. "Should *you* be . . . come on, Amy. What about you and Frank?"

She managed to look surprised. "Oh, Jake, you just don't understand, do you?"

"I understand," he said. "I understand perfectly."

But Amy shook her head, gave Jake a pitying smile, and walked away.

Two nights later the second debate between Tomlinson and Senator Leeds was staged at the Bok Planetarium. The two candidates stood at lecterns in the middle of the round, domed room, with the moderator—the blond, ebullient anchorwoman of the state's most popular TV news show—sat on a stool between them. The planetarium was filled, every seat occupied and standees jammed in shoulder to shoulder all around the circular wall.

The park outside was thick with people sitting on folding chairs or picnic blankets as they watched the big TV screens that Tomlinson's campaign staff had set up. A strong thundershower had soaked the grass earlier in the afternoon, but as the sun went down the skies cleared and a bright, nearly full moon rose in the east.

Aside from making the arrangements with Dr. Cardwell for using the planetarium, Jake had virtually nothing to do with the planning for the debate. He had tried to see Amy several times, but she avoided him, even stopped taking his phone calls.

He arrived early for the debate, hung out in Cardwell's office as the planetarium slowly filled with spectators. At five minutes before eight, Jake went down with Cardwell and took the front-row seats that had been reserved for them. He saw Amy across the central space where the planetarium projector was stowed neatly below the floor. She was sitting next to Tomlinson's father.

Bob Rogers sat behind Amy, and then Glynis came in with Tim Younger. They sat next to Rogers. Jake gave them a little wave. Rogers grinned at him, Glynis waved back, and Younger simply nodded. New England stone face, Jake thought.

Precisely at eight the candidates came in, entering the planetarium from opposite doors and striding down the sloping aisles like a pair of prizefighters heading for the ring. The TV anchorwoman came in with Senator Leeds.

Tomlinson looked rested and vigorous, beaming his killer smile at the audience. Leeds smiled, too, but to Jake his face looked puffy, baggy, faint rings beneath his eyes.

Perched on her stool while the candidates stood at their lecterns, the anchorwoman smoothed her skirt and went swiftly through the preliminaries and introductions.

"Mr. Tomlinson won the coin toss," she announced smilingly, "so he will give his opening remarks first."

Tomlinson gave her a megawatt smile, then turned a full circle to survey the audience.

"I want to thank you all for coming," he began. "And I want to thank Senator Leeds for graciously agreeing to this meeting."

Leeds dipped his chin and smiled his campaign poster smile back at his rival.

Tomlinson hesitated a heartbeat, then began, "You folks—you tax-payers and voters—have to make a choice in November. You must choose between change and progress, or the same old political system of the old-boys network that has failed to move our state forward."

Looking directly at Leeds, Tomlinson went on, "I don't want to see this state depending entirely on gambling and highway construc-tion for its economy. I don't want to see our citizens' money being funneled to Las Vegas and god knows where else. I want us to move forward, to build new industries, create thousands of new jobs, rein-vigorate our mining industry, and make this state the leader in bring-ing energy independence to America. I want us to break the chains that link our economy to organized crime."

They got to their feet and cheered. Jake was astounded, then re-alized that Amy must have learned from the first debate and packed the planetarium with Tomlinson backers.

Leeds scowled darkly at Tomlinson when it was his turn to speak.

"My opponent paints a pretty picture," he said, "but the truth is he has nothing to offer but fantasies and wishful thinking. He talks about energy and our coal mining industry. What he doesn't tell you is that it will take ten years, maybe twenty or even more, before his beautiful dreams can become reality. Maybe they never will."

Turning slowly as he spoke, Leeds told the audience, "New technology doesn't just spring up because you rub a magic lamp. I've asked the best scientists in Washington, men and women who work at the National Science Foundation and the National Academy of Sciences, what they think about my opponent's pipe dream. They tell me it won't work, not for many, many years. Maybe never. Is that what we should be pinning our hopes on? Is that what we should be spending our hard-earned tax dollars on?"

Tomlinson's rebuttal was simple. "The senator asks for advice from scientists who haven't worked in a laboratory for twenty years or more. But right here in this state we have scientists who are making MHD work! They're not sitting at desks and theorizing. They're getting their hands dirty and producing megawatts of electrical power for us. They lit up the whole county of Lignite on the Fourth of July. You all saw that. They can light up this entire state, this entire nation, if we give them the backing they need."

More cheers and applause.

Then, with an impish grin, Tomlinson added, "Remember the old adage: When a distinguished but elderly scientist says something is possible, he's almost always right. When he says something is impossible, he's almost always wrong."

Everyone laughed. Except Leeds.

Turning toward the senator again, Tomlinson said, "I invite your Washington desk-bound science advisors to come here, come to Lignite, and see the future of this state, of this country, at work."

And so it went. When it came time for questions from the audience only a half-dozen hands rose. Just like a classroom, Jake thought. Most of them are scared to stand out.

The blond moderator swiveled completely around, then selected a woman from the last row. She stood up, and Jake recognized her as one of the volunteers who had worked on the Fourth of July stunt at Lignite. One of Amy's plants, he thought.

"This is for either one of the candidates," she said, "or both of them, actually. There's been some talk about the professor who headed the MHD program being murdered. Is there anything to this rumor?"

Tomlinson spoke up before Leeds could open his mouth. "You're talking about Professor Arlan Sinclair. All we know for certain was that his wife had a gambling addiction, although the rumor claims she was a narcotics user, as well."

Leeds jumped in. "Those are totally unfounded rumors. The police report concluded that Professor Sinclair committed suicide after killing his wife."

"Yes, but why did he kill her?" Tomlinson asked. "And then himself—if he really did commit suicide."

"There's no reason to doubt the police report," Leeds insisted.

"Yes, there is," said Tomlinson. "Professor Sinclair was a noted and respected scientist. He was the head of the university's MHD program. His death and his wife's are certainly linked to gambling and perhaps to drugs. The case has the fingerprints of organized crime all over it."

His face reddening, Senator Leeds said, "My opponent is trying to turn a domestic tragedy into a political smear against me."

"Who said you're linked to this?" Tomlinson said, looking innocent, almost surprised. "I haven't." Turning to the seated moderator, he asked, "Have I mentioned the senator's name in connection with this tragedy?"

Instead of answering the loaded question, the moderator said, "Perhaps we should move on to another question." And she pointed to a man on the other side of the planetarium. "I believe you had your hand up, sir."

A middle-aged man rose slowly to his feet, potbellied and bald. "I was gonna ask about those killings, too. Professor Sinclair didn't seem like the kinda guy who'd shoot his own wife. And then kill hisself? No way."

Jake looked toward Amy. She was smiling like a cat who'd just feasted on several canaries. Even Tomlinson's father, sitting beside her, looked grimly satisfied. Behind them, Rogers looked puzzled, Younger inscrutable. But Glynis was glowing with triumph.

Once again, Tomlinson was the first to react. "If there are flaws with the report of the local police in this matter, then the state prosecutor's office should examine the case."

"I totally agree," Senator Leeds said.

"However," Tomlinson went on, "if there's any chance that the prosecutor's office is tainted by organized crime, then perhaps the federal Department of Justice should look into this."

Leeds's face grew darker than ever. For a moment the planetarium was absolutely still. It seemed to Jake that the entire crowd was holding its breath.

Then the senator said, slowly, "I have already asked the FBI to investigate the circumstances of Professor Sinclair's death."

The crowd gasped, then broke into applause. Senator Leeds dipped his chin in acknowledgment.

Once the applause died down, Tomlinson said to the senator, "I congratulate you on your action. It's the right thing to do."

Looking relieved, the moderator said, "Let's move on to another topic, shall we?"

The remainder of the Q-and-A period went fairly quietly, mostly questions about how the candidates intended to help the state's employment situation. Tomlinson hammered on new industrial growth, spearheaded by MHD. Leeds emphasized construction and education.

The debate ended at last. The moderator thanked the two candidates and the audience. The audience applauded appreciatively, then everyone got up from their chairs and started filing toward the planetarium's exits. Several campaign workers clustered around Senator Leeds, while Amy and the elder Tomlinson, together with Rogers, Glynis, and Younger, took turns shaking Tomlinson's hand.

Jake noticed that Tomlinson eyed Glynis smilingly. She didn't seem to notice, but Younger obviously bristled.

Standing beside Cardwell, watching the planetarium empty out, Jake said wearily, "Well, he let Leeds outmaneuver him again."

"Why do you say that?" Cardwell asked, his gray eyes curious.

"The senator said he's already put the FBI on the case."

Cardwell smiled. "Do you believe that?"

"He can call them in tomorrow. Nobody's going to check the date."

With a patient shake of his head, Cardwell said, "I don't think you understand, Jake."

"Understand what?"

Ticking points off on his fingers, Cardwell explained, "First, your boy definitely linked Leeds to organized crime. And murder. Second, he forced Leeds to retreat on his criticism of MHD. Third—and most important—he's put Leeds on the defensive."

Jake blinked at his mentor. "You think so?"

"Definitely. Leeds has been badly hurt. Tomlinson's going to win this election—barring some disaster."

OCTOBER

TOPPING PLANT

T he summer ended. While the election campaign heated up, cool winds swept down from the mountains. A mammoth rainstorm blew in from the west, soaking the state and swelling several rivers to flood stage. The town of Lignite was partially flooded for several days and operations at the big rig were temporarily halted because the roads were awash. Lignite's sole working coal mine had to suspend operations until the waters receded.

Tomlinson continued his exhausting travels around the state, speaking at every town, appearing at every occasion. He officiated at local beauty pageants, spoke at meetings of Elks and Moose associations, got himself photographed at local Boys and Girls Club activities.

The two candidates crossed paths at the state fair, Senator Leeds delivering a speech at the fair's opening, Tomlinson speaking on the closing day—to a noticeably larger crowd.

The fall semester started, and Jake had classes to teach. But he ran up to Lignite every week. Each time he visited the big rig Glynis was there, with Younger. Jake wondered if they were living together, but couldn't work up the nerve to ask either one of them.

Another major rainstorm drenched the state, and locals began eyeing the gray skies and telling one another, "Next one'll be snow."

Exactly one month before election day, Tomlinson surged ahead of Senator Leeds in the polls. He moved ahead by only a couple of percentage points, well within the pollsters' margin of error, but it was the first time he had taken the lead away from the senator.

"We're going to win!" Amy beamed when Jake visited the downtown campaign headquarters. "I know it!"

Tomlinson's father was less optimistic. "Don't count your chickens before they're hatched," he grumbled.

The FBI steadily refused to say anything about the Sinclair killings except to report, "The investigation is in progress." But Amy kept Tomlinson's publicity team driving hard on the links between gambling and organized crime—and by associating Senator Leeds with the state's casinos they associated him with narcotics and murder.

Jake's work on the NASA proposal had sunk out of sight. There isn't any time for it, he told himself. The truth was that he'd lost interest in it. Despite himself, the political campaign was absorbing all his energies. He worked closely with Bob Rogers, wrote pop-science pieces for the newspapers and television news shows, coached Rogers when Bob had to be interviewed or give a talk about MHD to some civic or social group.

One afternoon, as the October weather turned almost wintry, Jake popped into Rogers's office.

The physicist was poring over a huge blueprint that was draped over his desk, its corners drooping almost to the floor.

"What's this?" Jake asked, walking around the desk to stand beside Rogers.

"Topping plant," Rogers said. "I'm expecting—"

His phone buzzed. Rogers picked it up, nodded vigorously, and said, "Bring him right here, to my office."

Jake raised his brows questioningly.

"Guy from the NAEU," Rogers said.

"National . . ."

"The electric utilities gang. You know, O'Brien's people."

"What's he here for?"

Rogers tapped the blueprint. "He wants to see the topping plant."

Jake wondered what a topping plant might be, but before he could ask the office door opened and the department secretary ushered in a young, stocky fellow in a gray three-piece suit.

One of Francis X. O'Brien's people, Jake said to himself. They must get group discounts at Brooks Brothers.

"Hello," the young man said. "I'm Don Garza."

To Jake, Garza looked like a newly graduated student who'd

gone through college on an athletic scholarship. He was no taller than Jake himself, but his shoulders were wide and his body solid. He had a pleasant smile, bright teeth contrasting nicely with his olive complexion. Handsome kid, Jake thought. I wonder how smart he is.

Rogers came around the desk to shake hands with the kid. Turning, he introduced Jake. Then he led them both around his desk and the three of them looked down at the oversized blueprint.

Suddenly the smiling young man became all business, and quite knowledgeable.

"So what's the temperature of the gas when it exits the MHD channel?" Garza asked.

"About four thousand Fahrenheit," said Rogers.

Shaking his head, Garza muttered, "Way too hot for the turbines. You'll melt their blades off."

"No, no," Rogers countered, tapping the blueprint. "The exhaust gas goes through the heat exchanger, here. The heat boils water for your steam turbines, and by the time the plasma leaves the heat exchanger it's cool enough to run it through a set of gas turbines, here."

"I see," Garza muttered. "Very damned clever."

"It's like a meat processing factory," said Rogers, grinning. "We use everything but the oink."

Garza laughed, and Jake began to understand what Rogers had designed: a power-generating plant in which an MHD generator produces electricity, then feeds its still-hot exhaust gas to more conventional turbine systems that generate additional electrical power.

Pretty neat, Jake thought.

"How big can you make this system?" Garza asked, looking up from the blueprint.

Rogers waggled a hand. "Big as you want. The MHD generator gets more efficient with size."

"A thousand megawatts, total?"

Nodding, Rogers said, "The MHD generator could produce half, and the turbines the rest of it."

"Good. Fine." Garza broke into a satisfied smile. "I think you've really got something here."

Bending over the desk again, Rogers tapped the blueprint once more. "The heat exchanger is the trickiest part."

"We could talk to our people who've done exchangers for nuclear plants," said Garza.

"You'll have to deal with higher temperatures than the nukes use."

"Maybe NASA can give us some advice."

"Yeah. I hadn't thought of that."

"I know a couple of guys at the NASA center near Cleveland . . ."

Jake left the two of them huddled over the blueprint and almost tiptoed out of Rogers's office. Topping plant, he thought. I'll have to borrow Bob's blueprint and work it into a news release. Keep the MHD issue in the news, keep Tomlinson ahead.

THE BIG RIG

Younger actually looked happy.

Jake drove up to Lignite a few days after his meeting with Rogers and asked the engineer's opinion about the topping plant idea.

"Makes a lot of sense," Younger said, as he kept a careful eye on a trio of technicians who were removing worn electrodes from the innards of the big rig's central channel.

"You think?"

"Sure. There's a lot of heat energy in the plasma after it leaves the generator's channel. Why let it go up the smokestack? Instead of adding to global warming we can use the frigging heat to generate more electrical power."

"And the heat exchanger? Can you develop one to work at such high temperatures?"

Younger shrugged nonchalantly. "You find the right engineers and pay them enough, they'll design your heat exchanger for you."

Jake thought that it couldn't be that simple, but Younger seemed totally unworried about the problem.

Then Jake realized why Younger was so optimistic. Glynis came into the shed, pulling off a long fur-trimmed coat, smiling at Younger.

He broke into a positively boyish grin and rushed across the concrete floor to her.

Jake remembered the first time Glynis had come to the big rig, how Younger had practically thrown her out. He wasn't so inhospitable now. He walked arm in arm with her across the test cell, obviously showing off what his team of technicians were doing, grinning like a schoolboy. And Glynis was smiling up at him, seemingly just as happy as he was.

But a few minutes later, as Jake started for the door and Younger turned his attention back to his technicians, Glynis walked over toward Jake and fell in step with him.

"How are you, Jake?" she asked.

Miserable, he wanted to say, but instead he replied, "I'm okay. Pretty busy. How about you?"

"I've been talking to Sheila. They've taken her off the investigation."

"The FBI agent?" Jake asked. "She's off the case?"

"From what she tells me, a couple of more experienced agents have been assigned to look into Senator Leeds's connections to organized crime. It's all very hush-hush, of course."

They had reached the door. Jake said, "I wonder if we could get the FBI to make some kind of statement before election day."

"I doubt it," Glynis replied. "They're walking on eggs, you know."

"Probing a senator, yeah, I guess they're going to keep as quiet as they can."

Glynis looked thoughtful. "Unless someone does something to bring the investigation out into the open."

Jake snapped, "You stay out of it! Keep yourself out of this, Glyn. I don't want you in trouble with these guys."

"There you go again," she said, with a wry smile, "getting melodramatic."

"Glynis, I know these guys. I know how they operate. Perez warned us, remember?"

"And you take him seriously."

"Damned right I do. Let the FBI handle this. You steer clear of it."

She shook her head. "Jake, the FBI is going through a strictly pro forma routine. That's what Sheila told me. They're not going to find anything because they're not really looking for anything."

"Glyn . . ."

"For god's sake, Jake, Leeds *asked* them to investigate the link between Mrs. Sinclair's killing and organized gambling. They're not after Leeds; they're just making copies of that Captain Harraway's phony reports and calling that an investigation."

"Stay out of it," Jake repeated, trying to keep his voice low and forceful at the same time.

"Leeds is going to make a publicity splash about the FBI report finding nothing," she insisted.

Jake didn't know what to say about that.

"Unless we do something to stir them up," Glynis added.

Jake gripped her arm. "Glynis, I want you to go back to West Virginia and stay there until this election is over."

"I'll do nothing of the kind," she replied heatedly.

"I don't want you—"

"Hey, Glyn!" Younger called from across the test cell, his voice echoing off the metal walls. "Come on over here, I want to show you something."

Glynis pulled free of Jake's hand, gave him a perfunctory smile, and turned to hurry over to Younger, her boots clicking on the concrete and the coat in her arms dragging along the floor.

Jake stood there, worried, fearful, angry—and alone.

He drove straight to Tomlinson's campaign headquarters, calling Amy on his cell phone as he drove. A state highway patrol cruiser nosed alongside him on the interstate. Jake glanced at his speedometer, then realized that the cop was tapping his ear as he frowned at him from behind his mirrored sunglasses. He doesn't like me using the cell phone while I'm driving, Jake realized. There was talk in the capitol of making that illegal, but so far no law had been passed. Jake clicked his cell phone shut and put it on the seat beside him. The patrolman nodded once, then sped on up the highway.

Keeping just below the speed limit, Jake drove into the city and parked behind the former supermarket where Amy and the rest of Tomlinson's people were working.

The place was bustling with volunteers, people talking, phones ringing. A teenager pushing a cart piled high with Tomlinson posters nearly ran Jake over. He sniffed the odor of spicy food; sure enough, nearly a dozen empty cartons from a nearby Mandarin restaurant littered one of the long work tables.

Amy was in a huddle with a group of publicists at the far end of the big, cluttered room. She looked up as Jake approached, excused herself from the group, and led Jake through the rows of desks to one of the cubicles set up in the rear of the area, where it was a little quieter.

Once he had told Amy of Glynis's report on the FBI's inaction, Amy's first reaction was, "You see a lot of her, don't you?"

Jake felt his cheeks redden. "She works with the MHD guys," he temporized. "She and Tim Younger are going together."

"Are they?" Amy perched herself on the edge of the steel desk and eyed Jake with an arched eyebrow.

"Never mind her," Jake said. "What can we do to goose the FBI?"

Amy shrugged. "I don't know. I can ask Franklin's father about it, maybe he can put some pressure on them."

Jake glanced at the molded plastic chair in front of the desk, but remained standing. "Leeds could come out and claim that the FBI investigation confirms the Vernon police findings."

"That wouldn't be good."

"So?"

Thinking out loud, Amy said, "It wouldn't do us much good to accuse the FBI of dogging it. On the other hand, we'd benefit if they found some genuine links between Leeds and the crooks."

"I don't think that's going to happen," Jake admitted.

"Not unless this Glynis of yours stirs the pot."

"No!" Jake snapped. "I don't want her involved in this."

"Sounds to me as if she's already involved," Amy said, knowingly.

"That Perez guy warned us to back off," Jake said. "But Glynis wants to nail whoever it was that murdered Professor Sinclair."

"What's she after? What makes her tick?"

Jake hesitated a moment, then told Amy in a lowered voice, "She was involved with Sinclair."

"Involved? Sexually?"

Feeling ashamed of himself, Jake muttered, "Yeah. They were sleeping together."

Amy considered this for a moment, then said confidently, "Let me talk to her, Jake. Maybe I can talk some sense into her."

Brightening a bit, Jake said, "That would be good, Amy. I appreciate it."

"Think nothing of it."

HALLOWE'EN

With just nine days to go before the election, Senator Leeds threw a massive Hallowe'en rally in the city's National Guard armory. Everyone invited, bar none. Free food and drinks, courtesy of the Leeds campaign. Thousands were expected.

Jake watched the preliminaries on the television news as he dressed for the much smaller costume party that Tomlinson was hosting at his home. The TV news team was walking through the huge, open, high-ceilinged space inside the armory as volunteers, each one sporting red-white-and-blue Leeds buttons, were setting up long tables while caterers and workers from local bars were carting in crates of food and drink. Jake spotted waitresses from O'Brian's Irish Pub in their kelly green skirts and off-the-shoulder white blouses. They all wore Leeds buttons, too.

The TV commentator was saying, "Despite slipping slightly behind Franklin Tomlinson in the statewide polls, Senator Leeds is looking confident about the outcome of the election."

The screen cut to a pre-recorded interview of Leeds, standing in front of the city's cathedral steps at an earlier rally. He was wearing a dark blue overcoat with a burgundy muffler wrapped around his throat. Hatless, with his thick thatch of silver hair. The woman interviewing him had a knitted cap pulled over her golden curls.

"The polls don't mean a thing," the senator was saying, smiling heartily. "What counts is how people vote. And they'll vote for the better man, I'm sure."

"Meaning Senator Christopher Leeds?" the interviewer prompted.

"You said it," Leeds replied, laughing, "I didn't."

"But what about this FBI investigation? The Tomlinson campaign keeps harping on the links between the state's gambling casinos and organized crime."

The senator's face grew serious. "Nothing but insinuations and innuendos," he said. "It's all a smear, a desperate attempt by my opponent to cloud the real issues of this campaign."

"Which are?"

"The state's economy. Jobs, jobs, and jobs. Real jobs for real people. Not some pie-in-the-sky promises that'll only employ a handful of elite scientists and engineers for the next ten or twenty years."

The news show cut back to the live report from the armory. A German oompah band was warming up in one corner of the vast, echoing space; huge posters of Senator Leeds were draped on the brick walls behind them.

Jake picked up the remote and clicked off the TV. He knew that Tomlinson's Hallowe'en party was restricted to the monied elite, mostly old friends of his father's. Shaking his head worriedly, he stared at the costume he was going to wear for the party: He was going as Tycho Brahe, the great sixteenth-century astronomer. The costume consisted of a pair of light blue silk knee britches and white stockings, with a long, deep blue coat, elaborately embroidered in silver thread. Louise had made the costume years ago, for an earlier, happier Hallowe'en. Sewn it with her own hands. She'd even gone to an antique store to buy a sword to go with it.

Jake had added the finishing touch: a false nose of silver. Brahe had had his nose sliced off in a youthful duel and wore a silver one ever after.

He laboriously wriggled into the pantaloons, pulled on the stockings, and wormed his feet into the buckled shoes. He strapped the sword around his waist and then slid his arms into the jacket's silk-lined sleeves. Looking at himself in the mirror he marveled that the outfit still fit, after all these years.

And he burst into tears, remembering Louise and how much she had loved him.

.   .   .

It was starting to snow when Jake went down to the parking lot behind his apartment building. As he revved up the Mustang he turned on the radio and hunted for a weather report.

". . . with accumulations of a foot in the city and more in the western suburbs. Strong winds will produce blizzard-like conditions overnight, with clearing expected by sunrise. Low temperatures near zero . . ."

Jake clicked off the radio and headed for Tomlinson's place. The party's going to end early, he thought. Everybody'll want to get home before the storm gets bad.

By the time he stopped in front of the entrance to Tomlinson's mansion, Jake had to admit the snowfall looked pretty. Soft flakes drifting down into the lights lining the curving driveway. A thin blanket of white covering the drive, the shrubbery, outlining the bare branches of the trees. The snow hushed the traffic sounds out on the street, making the night seem peaceful and quiet.

The first snow of the year is always pretty, Jake thought. For the first hour or so.

He ducked back into the Mustang to get his sword and clip it to his belt, then let the valet drive the car away. The butler stood patiently at the front door, waiting for him in his usual black uniform. But tonight he had garish Tomlinson buttons pinned to both his lapels.

The house was nearly empty; Jake was a little early, as usual. The butler showed him to the ballroom, where the caterers had set up a well-stocked bar at the far end of the parqueted floor. Tomlinson Senior was standing there, a tumbler of whisky in his hand, dressed like George Washington, complete with a white powdered wig.

"And who might you be?" the elder Tomlinson asked, by way of greeting.

"Tycho Brahe," said Jake.

"Teeko who?"

"Danish astronomer. One of the great ones." Then Jake remembered that he hadn't tied on his silver nose. Feeling a little foolish, he fished in his jacket pocket for it.

Alexander Tomlinson gave him a look that was part curiosity and part contempt, then strode past Jake to welcome a pair of new arrivals.

Amy came in, alone. She was dressed as some sort of oriental harem girl, bare shoulders and midriff, slitted silk trousers showing plenty of leg, a jewel in her navel and a filmy veil over her face. She looked very sexy to Jake.

"Salaam," he said to her.

Amy smiled behind her veil and said, "Don't tell me. You're that astronomer who lost his nose in a duel, aren't you?"

"Tycho Brahe," Jake agreed.

They ordered drinks from the young bartender who grinned at Jake and ogled Amy; she took a flute of champagne, Jake opted for club soda, thinking about the drive home through the snow.

"How's our boy?" Jake asked.

"Franklin? He's fine. He'll be down in a few minutes; he's getting into his costume."

"What's he coming as?"

"You'll see," Amy said, with an impish smile.

Lowering his voice slightly, Jake asked, "How's his health? He's been looking pretty tired lately."

Amy took a sip of her champagne, then replied, "You'd be tired, too, Jake, if you had to run around the state the way he's been. But his health is fine."

"Really?"

Her mischievous smile returned. "I can tell you from firsthand experience, there's nothing wrong with his health."

"Really," Jake huffed.

Lots of people were arriving now, and Jake drifted away from Amy. His health is fine, Jake repeated to himself. She ought to know. She's in bed with him every chance she gets.

Bob Rogers and his wife came in, he in a fringed frontiersman's buckskins, complete with coonskin cap, she in a frilly colonial dress with voluminous skirts and a low neckline that showed off her plump bosom.

"Professor Ross, you look very handsome," said Mrs. Rogers, her round face dimpling with good humor. "But that false nose ruins the effect, don't you think?"

Jake explained the reason for the nose. Mrs. Rogers nodded

accommodatingly, then she and her husband moved away. A five-piece combo began playing soft dance music and Jake debated whether he should ask Amy for a dance.

Before he could make up his mind, though, Tomlinson entered the room. The band immediately broke into a brassy fanfare.

B. Franklin Tomlinson was dressed as Superman, in a blue muscle suit with a big S emblazoned on its chest, and a red cape hanging from his shoulders. Grinning from ear to ear, he planted his fists on his hips and shouted, "Up, up, and awaaay!"

Everyone laughed and applauded. Amy hurried to his side and even his father allowed a grin to crack his stern façade.

Tomlinson began working the room, shaking hands and chatting a few moments with each of the guests. With Amy close beside him. They make a great couple, Jake thought morosely: Superman and the blond harem girl. Terrific.

He slinked away and headed for a men's room.

As he came out, Tim Younger was being led by the butler toward the party room. Younger was dressed in a western square dance outfit: colorful checkered shirt, lean blue jeans, and tooled leather boots.

Younger stopped to gawk at Jake. "Who the hell are you supposed to be, Cyrano de Bergerac?"

"Tycho Brahe," Jake answered, suddenly weary of explaining.

"Nice sword," Younger allowed.

"Isn't Glynis with you?" Jake asked.

"She called me at the last minute, said she couldn't come."

"Why not?"

"She got a call from one of Leeds's people," Younger said, looking annoyed. "Said he wants to talk to her about this FBI business."

INTO THE SNOW

C old panic hit Jake like a blow to the pit of his stomach. "A call from one of Leeds's people?" he asked Younger. "Who? When?"

Younger shrugged. "Beats me. Glyn told me that one of Tomlinson's people set it up for her."

Amy! Jake realized.

He whirled away from Younger and sprinted back into the crowded, noisy party room. The band was playing a leisurely waltz, costumed people were chatting, laughing, drinking. Pushing through the couples dancing in the center of the room, Jake spotted Amy, still clinging to Tomlinson's arm.

He rushed up to her and demanded, "What'd you set up Glynis for?"

Amy blinked at him. "What?"

"Glynis Colwyn! What'd you tell her?"

Frowning at Jake's insistent tone, Tomlinson asked, "What's this all about?"

To Tomlinson, Amy replied, "That grad student who was involved with Professor Sinclair is trying to get somebody in Leeds's office to talk to her about the investigation."

Jake grabbed her arm. "And you set her up for a meeting?"

"With that Perez fellow," Amy said. "He said he wants to talk to her."

His frown turning puzzled, Tomlinson said, "Perez? You mean Leeds's Las Vegas connection?"

"That seedy little man, yes," Amy replied.

"Where?" Jake demanded, his voice shaking with fear. "Where are they meeting?"

"How should I know?" Amy said, nettled. "I talked to a couple of people in Leeds's office and said she had some new evidence about the killings. Less than an hour later Perez called me back and asked for her phone number."

"Jesus!" Jake turned and started to leave, only to bump into Younger.

"What the hell's going on?" the engineer asked.

"Glynis!" Jake snapped, hurrying for the door. "She's in trouble."

"Whattaya mean?"

Shouldering his way through the crowd, Jake said, "She's going to meet with the guy who told us to keep out of the investigation. And he thinks she's got evidence against him."

Keeping up with Jake stride for stride, Younger asked, "How the hell did that happen?"

"Long story. We've got to find her! Before—"

"Relax," Younger said, pulling his cell phone from his jeans pocket. "I'll get her."

As Younger tapped on the phone's keypad Jake towed him outside the ballroom. The foyer was quieter, empty of people except for one of the butler's assistants standing glumly at the front door.

Jake heard the phone buzz once, twice. . . .

"Glyn?" Younger's face lit up. "It's me. Jake's here, he wants to talk to you."

Jake grabbed at the phone so fast he nearly fumbled it out of his hand. Pressing it to his ear he said, "Where are you?"

"Jake?" Glynis's voice sounded calm, ordinary.

"Where are you? Where are you going?"

"I'm on the interstate. I'm heading for Senator Leeds's place by the lake."

"Stop right now! Turn around and go back home."

"Don't be ridiculous, Jake. The snow's getting heavier, but it's not bad enough to be a problem."

"Perez thinks you have new evidence!" Jake fairly yelled into the phone. "He's waiting for you so he can find out what the evidence is and then get rid of you!"

"That's why I'm carrying a microchip recorder. It will take down whatever Perez says and transmit it to my computer, in my apartment."

"They'll break into your apartment and tear your computer apart! They'll kill you!"

"They can't afford to have another body on their doorstep," Glynis said coolly.

"The hell they can't!" Jake shouted. "They'll make it look like an accident."

Younger yanked the phone out of Jake's hands. "Glyn, it's me again. Jake's right. Turn the car around and come on back home. I'll meet you at your—"

He took the phone from his ear and held it before his face, staring at it as if it had betrayed him.

"She hung up," Younger said, disbelief etching his face.

"Maybe the cellular service cut off," Jake suggested.

"Whatever." Younger started for the front door. "We've got to find her before she gets herself in trouble."

"Right!" Jake hurried after him.

"What're you driving?" Younger asked as they stepped outside. The snow was falling more thickly now, and a cold wind was swirling the white flakes past the lampposts.

"My Mustang," said Jake.

Younger gave a snort as he beckoned to the parking attendant, bundled in a puffy down-lined parka. Jake shuddered in the cold, then saw a boxy SUV lumber up the driveway. It was faded blue, and looked as if it had seen lots of miles.

"It's a Land Rover," Jake exclaimed. "Like Bob's."

"I bought it off Bob," Younger said as he went around the car, tipped the attendant, and climbed in behind the wheel. "When he got his new one."

Jake had to take off his sword before he could get into the right-hand side. He dumped it clanking on the floor behind the seats.

The snow looked even heavier in the headlights' glow.

"You know where this place is?" Younger asked as he put the van into gear.

"Yeah," said Jake. "I've been there before."

"Okay, you navigate."

And into the snow they drove.

THROUGH THE BLIZZARD

". . . expect blizzard conditions through most of the night," the radio commentator was saying. Jake had turned on the all-news station. "Drivers are advised to stay off the roads—"

"Turn that damned thing off," Younger growled. "I can see that it's snowing like hell."

The snow was coming down more thickly than ever, blowing almost horizontally across the highway by a howling wind. Younger was bent over the van's steering wheel, both hands gripping the wheel with white-knuckled intensity.

"You know where this place is?" Younger asked, for the fourth time.

"Yeah. I plugged its location into your GPS," Jake said, tapping the screen glowing in the middle of the dashboard. Its map showed the highway, but the female voice that gave directions had been silent for more than half an hour.

Jake was thinking, It's early for a blizzard. Not even November yet. Whatever happened to global warming?

There weren't any other cars on the highway. Nobody else is crazy enough to come out in this, Jake told himself. Then a big eighteen-wheeler roared past them, churning up blinding swirls of snow. The Land Rover shook in its wake and skidded slightly as Younger growled out a string of curses.

He corrected the van's skid and drove on in bleak silence.

After a dozen more miles, Jake asked, "How's the road?"

"Okay," Younger replied, staring straight ahead into the wind-swept white flakes. "Long as we don't come across any more cowboys in semis."

Jake nodded in the shadows.

"This buggy's got all sorts of traction," Younger added. "Your little Go-Kart would've spun out twenty miles back."

The wind was actually a help, driving the snow across the wide paved highway. Must be piling up drifts on the side of the road, Jake thought. He peered into the darkness but could make out nothing.

"Snowplow," Younger muttered, and Jake saw a big lumbering plow up ahead, its lights flashing. Younger settled in a respectful distance behind it and slowed to its pace. "Like a police escort," he muttered.

Jake felt antsy, though, wondering if Glynis had made it to Leeds's place and—if she had—what was happening to her.

After about half an hour the plow turned off at an exit ramp and they had to drive through steadily heavier snow. Younger kept their speed around fifty, pushing ahead steadily. Jake saw a semi rig jack-knifed on the shoulder of the median, its end projecting into the left lane.

"That's the asshole who zipped past us," Younger said. "Serves him frigging right."

"I didn't see the driver," Jake said. "I wonder if he's okay."

"Call the highway patrol, let them worry about it."

Jake pulled his cell phone from his ridiculous blue embroidered coat, but the screen said NO SERVICE.

"Cell towers must be down," he said.

"Or we're in an area with no service," Younger replied.

Then the roadside lights winked out. All of them. They were plunged into complete darkness, except for the Land Rover's headlights.

"Jesus Christ," Younger snapped. "Must be a blackout."

Without hesitating, Jake clicked on the dashboard radio. ". . . getting reports from across the state of a rolling blackout. Electrical power has gone off here in the capital, and as far east as Vernon. Adjoining states are reporting blackouts, as well, and we expect a statement from the state's utility board in a few minutes."

"Just what we need," Jake moaned.

Younger shook his head. "If the frigging phones worked I could get the guys in Lignite to fire up the big rig. Produce enough power to keep that half of the state alight."

"Really?"

"Really."

"If the cell phones worked."

"Yeah."

They drove on in dismal silence. The snow was too thick for Jake to make out the roadside signs. He hoped he had given the GPS system the right coordinates for the lakeside lodge.

Younger chuckled grimly. "Are we there yet?"

"Damned if I know," Jake admitted.

Then the female voice from the GPS said in its calm dulcet tone, "In point five mile, turn right onto exit ramp."

"We're almost there!" both men said in unison.

The side road was covered with several inches of snow but Younger doggedly mushed the Land Rover through. He nearly missed a turn and plowed into a drift. Cursing, he threw the transmission into reverse and rocked the SUV out of the piled-up snow. There were no lights anywhere, except for their headlamps. Younger drove slowly, cautiously, inching along the twisting road, careful not to slide off into another drift.

At last the headlights picked up a glint, a reflection off a window. Squinting into the wind-whipped snow, Jake barely made out the low silhouette of the lodge's roofline against the lighter background of the lake.

Younger inched the Land Rover through the open gate of the snow-covered wooden fence and gently slowed to a stop. The van slid sideways before coming to rest. He puffed out a relieved sigh.

"Made it," Younger said, his voice slightly shaky.

Jake was peering at the lodge. He couldn't see any lights inside. But then, in the glow from the Land Rover's headlamps, he saw Glynis's Jaguar, already thickly covered with snow. But its hood was up and a man was standing beside it, peering at the engine by the feeble glow of a flashlight.

He looked up and Jake recognized him. Monster.

Wearing a long black overcoat and a fur-trimmed hat with earflaps,

Monster trudged over to the SUV, shoulders bunched, looking truculent. Younger rolled down the driver-side window, but before he could say anything, Monster demanded, "Whattaya want?"

Jake leaned across and said as brightly as he could manage, "Hey, Monster, it's me, Jake."

"Jake?" Monster's heavy features registered surprise. Then he shook his head. "You ain't supposed to be here, Jake."

THE LAKESIDE LODGE

Monster led them through the snow and into the lodge, muttering about Glynis's Jaguar every step of the way.

"Fuckin' English cars're no fuckin' good. No way."

Except for Monster's flashlight it was dark in the entryway; all the lights in the lodge were out.

"Doesn't Leeds have an emergency generator?" Younger asked, sounding incredulous that a U.S. senator could be so short-sighted.

"That's the least of our troubles," Jake muttered as Monster led them into the lodge's main room, flicking the flashlight beam ahead of them.

One battery-powered hurricane lamp was lit, by the big window overlooking the lake. And there in front of the dark fireplace was Glynis, sitting in one of the rustic chairs, her body taut with tension, hands clasped on her lap, looking angry and fearful at the same time. She was dressed for Tomlinson's costume party in a pirate wench's outfit, lace-up black bodice, off-the-shoulder white blouse, ragged colorful skirt, and a scarlet red scarf knotted around her waist.

Jake felt the air gush out of him. She's all right. They haven't hurt her.

Not yet, he silently added.

As Younger rushed over to her, Jake saw Nacho Perez standing by the window, fidgeting nervously, his jacket flapping open, the black butt of a pistol showing at his belt. A pair of other men stood in the shadows by the bar, thickset, blank-faced, wearing dark suits. They had Mob written all over them, Jake thought.

"Who the hell are you supposed to be," Perez sneered, "the three musketeers or somethin'?"

Ignoring Nacho's sarcasm, Jake demanded, "What's going on here? Why are you holding her?"

"Me? Holdin' her?" Perez's lean face broke into a sardonic grin. "She came up here on her own. Di'n't you, babe?"

Glynis glared at him, said nothing.

Stepping closer to Jake, Perez fished in his jacket pocket as he said, "She came up here to talk to me about Sinclair and his wife. And that doc in Florida. With this in her purse." He waved a thumb-sized digital recorder in one hand.

Younger asked Glynis, "Are you okay?"

She nodded, her eyes riveted on Perez. Jake was looking at Perez, too, and the two hoods behind him. And Monster, looming in the shadows on the other side of the room. I'd need a machine gun to take on this mob, he said to himself. Wish I had at least brought the sword in with me from the Land Rover.

Younger said to Perez, "We've come to take her home."

"Yeah," Nacho replied. "Sure."

"I mean it!"

"So you mean it, so what? My pal here," he gestured toward Monster, "can't get her fuckin' car started."

"It's English," Monster grumbled, as if that explained anything.

Glynis spoke up. "They mean to kill me, Tim. They want to arrange an accident on the highway. I'll skid off the road and get killed."

Impulsively, Younger grabbed at Perez but before he could reach him, Monster gripped the engineer's shoulders in his massive paws and lifted Younger clear off his feet.

"You better siddown," Monster said. Softly. While he held Younger dangling in his hands.

The other two goons barely moved. One of them smiled a little.

Monster released Younger, then pointed to the chair near Glynis's. "Take it easy," he said to the engineer. Rubbing one of his shoulders, Younger sat.

Jake realized it was cold in the lodge. No electricity, no heat. The logs in the fireplace were phony, for decoration. Even if the place has an oil heater, the thermostat needs electricity to run it, he realized.

"So what happens now?" Jake asked.

Perez shrugged his narrow shoulders. "I'm waitin' for a phone call. Just take it easy for a while."

"You can't kill all of us," said Jake.

"Sez who? You two guys came up here 'cause her stupid English car wouldn't start. You drive off inta the blizzard. You have a smash-up." He shrugged again.

Jake thought, QED. Just like that. Problem solved. They kill all of us.

Glynis said, "You don't think three more deaths are going to pique the FBI's curiosity?"

"Hey, lady, you guys get yourselves killed in the snow, what's the FBI got to do with it?" He waved the miniaturized recorder again. "Long as I got this and you don't, we're okay."

Younger asked, "The phone's working?"

"The landline is," said Perez. "So what?"

"So let me call Lignite, get the generator working. We can end this blackout before it gets worse."

"Let you make a phone call? No way!"

Jake said, "Wait a minute. That could make your alibi airtight. Let Tim phone from here. It'll show that he was okay while he was here. You'll be in the clear when they investigate the accident."

It was the only thing Jake could think of. Let Tim call Lignite. Tell them he's at the senator's lodge with Glynis and me. Get them to start up the generator, and at the same time make it known where we are. It wasn't much, but it was something.

Perez stared at Jake. "You think I'm stupid? He yells for the cops over the phone."

"He won't," Jake promised. Turning to Younger, he said, "You won't tell them anything, will you, Tim?"

"The hell I won't," Younger growled.

Jake's shoulders slumped. There goes whatever chance we had to get out of this.

Jake stood in the middle of the shadow-filled room, trying desperately to think of some way to get out of this jam. *They're going to kill us!* he thought. *They're going to bundle us into Tim's Land Rover and drive it off a bridge, make it look like we skidded in the snow.*

"You can't just kill us all," Jake said.

Perez, still standing off to one side of the spacious room with the two Las Vegas musclemen behind him, chuckled dismissively. "I seen it done, kid."

Jake turned to Monster. "Are you going to let them do this?"

Monster shifted uneasily from one foot to the other. "Hey, Jake, you got yourself into this. Ain't my fault, what happens."

"You'll go to jail for it, just the same as they will."

"Nobody's goin' to jail," Perez said. "We're protected."

"By whom?" Glynis asked.

Perez glared at her. "None of yer business."

"It's Senator Leeds, isn't it? He's your protection."

"That cream puff?" Perez scoffed. "He's just the window dressin'."

"The front man," Jake said.

"Yeah."

"For who?"

With a shake of his head, Perez said, "Somebody you never heard of, kid. He don't even live in this state."

"From Nevada?" Glynis asked, eagerly.

Perez grinned at her.

"But why did you have to kill Professor Sinclair?" Jake asked. "I don't see why you did that."

"Wasn't me," Perez snapped. "The prof was fallin' apart. What with his wife's habit and all . . . he was gonna break up. So we put him out of his misery."

"And his wife," Jake said. "And that doctor."

Perez shrugged. "That's whatcha call collateral damage."

"Three murders—"

The phone rang.

Everyone froze where they were.

Perez crossed the room to the bar and picked up the phone. "Yeah?" He listened, then replied, "Yeah, it's snowin' like hell and we got no electricity. We're freezin' our cojones off up here."

Jake looked around the room. Younger was sitting beside Glynis, with Monster standing a few paces away, looking imperturbable. Perez was on the phone at the bar, along with the two sluggers from Las Vegas.

"We got two extra guys now," Perez was saying. "Yeah, they came up here to get the girl. Big heroes. Yeah . . . What choice do we have? Right."

Stepping closer to Monster, Jake whispered, "Are you going to let them do this to us? To me?" He was disgusted with the pleading whine of his own voice.

Monster looked uncomfortable, but replied, "Hey, it ain't my decision, Jake. I told you you shouldn'ta come here."

"But they're going to kill us!"

"It won't hurt none," said Monster. "Just a whack on the head to knock you out. Then we put you in the car and find a nice high overpass. No seat belts. You won't wake up."

"Monster, it's murder!"

"Yeah, I guess it is."

A weapon, Jake thought. I need a weapon, something to fight with. They've got guns. I've got nothing. They're going to kill us, kill the three of us and I'm standing here talking it over with one of the killers. If I had a gun, even that stupid sword from this dumb costume . . .

He saw the heavy brass lamp on the low table between the chairs where Younger and Glynis were sitting. If I could get to it, Jake thought, and take out Monster with it . . . Then he realized that Perez or one of the Nevada guys would gun him down.

Even so, he calculated, they'd have a hard time explaining a body with bullet holes in it as an accident. Yeah, sure, some plan. Get yourself killed. Brilliant strategy.

Perez hung up the phone. "Okay. That's it."

Younger started to get up, but Monster laid one paw on his shoulder and the engineer sat down again.

Perez asked Monster, "What was this guy drivin'?"

"Land Rover," Monster replied.

"Good." He turned to one of the gorillas and said, "Go outside and get it started."

The thug nodded, turned to his companion. "Come on."

They headed for the door. Jake thought, That leaves only Nacho and Monster.

Jake edged closer to Younger and the low table that bore the heavy-looking lamp. "Tim, could the big rig really stop this blackout?"

His brows rising slightly with surprise, Younger answered, "It could light up all of Lignite County, easy. Maybe more."

"The capital city?" Jake was standing in front of the table lamp now.

"If the fartbrains running the system pipe the juice that way, yes," Younger said, clearly unhappy with the executives in charge of the state's power grid.

"Uh-huh . . ." Jake grabbed the neck of the lamp with both hands and tugged as hard as he could. The lamp was indeed heavy, and for a moment the cord connecting it to the wall socket held fast. But only for a moment. Jake yanked it loose and, turning, banged it at Monster's surprised face.

"What the hell?" Perez snarled, fumbling for the pistol in his belt.

Monster tried to shield himself with his beefy arms, but Jake bashed him twice, three times, and the big guy went down to his knees. Jake bonked Monster squarely on the top of his head, then threw the heavy lamp at Perez.

Perez got off several shots before the lamp banged into him. Jake was right behind it, leaping at Perez, struggling for the gun. They crashed to the floor in a tangle of arms and legs. Glynis screamed.

Perez was wiry and stronger than he looked. Jake was gripping the gun with both hands, twisting it out of Perez's grasp. Perez butted Jake's face, punched with his free hand at Jake's ribs, his kidneys, but

Jake wrestled the automatic out of his hand and smashed it across his lean jaw. The man went limp.

Getting to his feet, Jake saw Monster pushing himself to his knees, blood streaming down his face from a gash on the top of his head.

"Tim's been shot!" Glynis cried, kneeling beside Younger, who sat slumped in his chair.

Jake pointed the automatic at Monster, who lurched toward him clumsily.

"Don't make me shoot you!" Jake begged.

Monster grinned crazily through the blood. "You ain't got a chance, Jake. When those two mooks come back they'll shoot you."

The two Las Vegas guys burst into the room, guns drawn.

"Hold it!" Jake snapped, in what he hoped was a believable imitation of countless TV cop shows.

Pointing the automatic at Perez, Jake yelled, "I'll blow his head off if you don't get the hell out of here."

The pair of thugs glanced at each other.

"Go on back to Las Vegas or wherever the hell you came from," Jake said, pointing the gun at the still-unconscious Perez.

They dithered. Jake cocked the automatic with his thumb. The click sounded very loud in the shadowy room.

"C'mon," said one of the goons to the other. They turned and left the room. Jake heard the lodge's front door slam.

Monster was sitting on the floor now, his knees drawn up. "They ain't gone," he said, in a low mumble. "They'll be waitin' for you out there."

"Then we'll stay right here," said Jake. "With our star witness."

"Jake, Tim's been shot!" Glynis repeated. "He's bleeding!"

"It's not bad," Younger said through gritted teeth. "Just nicked me, I think."

Younger had clamped one hand to his side. That half of his fancy western shirt was soaked with blood. But Tim seemed to be breathing all right, he was conscious, alive.

"Get on the phone, Glyn," he told her. "Call nine-one-one, tell them we've got a gunshot wound. We need an ambulance and the police."

Glynis got up from her chair and started for the phone. She made a swift detour, though, and filched her digital recorder from Perez's jacket pocket. Then she went to the telephone.

Perez moaned softly. His legs stirred, then his eyes opened. Focusing on Jake, he muttered, "The three fuckin' musketeers."

With the phone on her ear, Glynis reported from the bar, "They say they'll have a hard time getting here through the blizzard."

"But they're sending an ambulance?"

"And a highway patrol car."

"Did you tell them there's two armed men outside?"

But just as Jake asked that he heard the growl of a car engine starting up. They've decided to get out of here, he thought. I wonder how far they'll get through the snow.

"Bring that phone here," Younger said, wincing with pain. "I've got to call the big rig."

"You just sit there," Glynis said, "while I find something to use for bandages."

"Bring me the phone!" Younger insisted. He started to push himself up from the chair.

"No!" Glynis shouted. "Sit. Here's the phone." She crossed the room swiftly, the telephone cord trailing behind her. It didn't quite reach, so Glynis put the phone down on the floor and pushed Younger's chair close enough to it.

Jake stood in the middle of the room, keeping watch on Monster and Perez. Glancing at the cold stone fireplace, Jake wished the logs in it were real. We could use some heat in here, he said to himself.

Grimacing with pain, Younger was snapping orders into the phone. "Skeleton crew or no skeleton crew, you get that damned rig working! Start her up! Get your butt into the control booth and start the fire-up procedure. Stay on the line and I'll talk you through it."

Perez lay on his back on the floor, feeling his jaw where Jake had slugged him. It looked swollen.

"You busted my tooth," he mumbled. His lips were bloody.

Monster sat near him, sullenly mopping the blood off his face with a reddened sodden handkerchief. The brass table lamp was on its side, several paces away from him. Jake noticed a long gouge in it, where one of Perez's bullets had hit.

"I don't feel so good," Monster said, his head hanging between his knees.

Concussion, Jake thought. I banged him really hard.

All of a sudden Monster puked all over his shoes. The noise and stench made Jake's stomach turn.

"Hey, Jake," Younger called. "Turn on the fireplace before we turn into icicles, for chrissake."

Younger still had the phone in one hand. Glynis was off somewhere, looking for first-aid materials.

"It's not a real fireplace," Jake said, edging away from Monster and his mess.

"It's gas fed. See the knob over by the side? Turn it on and flick the ignition switch over the mantelpiece."

"Doesn't it need electricity?"

"No. It's natural gas."

Keeping the gun tightly gripped, Jake knelt by the fireplace and twisted the knob. It was stiff, but it gradually gave way and began to hiss. Standing, he clicked the switch.

Poof! Blue flames licked up among the artificial logs.

"It works!" Jake said, surprised. Not much heat, but it was better than nothing.

Younger was still on the phone, yelling at whoever was in charge of the skeleton crew at the big rig. Glynis came back from one of the bedrooms, dragging a bedsheet behind her. As she started to pull Younger's shirt off, Tim continued to bark orders into the phone.

It took nearly half an hour for the ambulance to arrive. Jake saw the flashing lights flickering through the lodge's curtained windows. While a pair of paramedics bandaged Younger properly, with Glynis hovering near them, a police cruiser pulled up.

Two state highway patrol officers came into the lodge, stamping snow off their boots. They looked around, scowling, saw Younger being attended to by the paramedics, saw Perez stretched out on the floor, saw Monster sitting with his head hung low and a pool of vomit at his feet, saw Jake in his sixteenth-century knee britches and embroidered jacket, the automatic pistol still tight in his hand.

"What the fuck has been going on here?" the first patrolman demanded.

His partner shook her head. "The senator's going to be damned sore about this."

Jake grinned wearily. "I'm sure he will be," he said.

FAIR PLAY

Once the highway patrol officers heard Jake's story, with Glynis and Younger nodding their agreement, they bundled Perez and Monster into their cruiser and told the paramedics to follow them to the highway patrol barracks off the interstate, with Younger, Jake, and Glynis.

As they drove through the swirling snow, the paramedic riding in back with them told Younger, "You're pretty lucky, man. Another inch and you would've been in real trouble."

"Yeah," said Younger, his face ashen now. He sat on the gurney, Glynis close beside him. She had helped him put his blood-soaked shirt back over his bandaged ribs. Jake sat on the opposite side of the ambulance, with the medic.

"Not even a broken rib," the guy said. "Bullet just grazed you."

The highway patrol barracks was ablaze with light in the wind-whipped snow. As Younger gingerly stepped down from the ambulance he muttered, "They must have an emergency generator."

Jake nodded and hustled Younger and Glynis into the building, out of the cold and snow. Inside, the barracks was warm and bright, but mostly empty. Rows of unoccupied desks, dark computer screens. Off in one corner of the main room an African American woman in the patrol's blue uniform sat at the communications console, a dozen phone screens flickering in front of her.

The two officers who'd come to the lodge were waiting for them, and ushered them into the office of their captain. He was a tall, stern-looking man with bloodshot gray eyes and close-cropped dirty blond hair, his shoulders wide and his stomach flat. Not the kind of man to take lightly.

He pointed at Jake before any of them could sit down and said, without preamble, "Those two men we've got in the infirmary claim you assaulted them both."

Jake nodded as Glynis helped Younger to ease into one of the plastic chairs in front of the captain's desk.

"I guess I did. But the older one, Perez, he shot my friend here."

Glynis blurted, "They're involved in three murders, maybe more."

The captain stared at her for a long, silent moment. Then, looking back at Jake, he asked, "What is this, a Hallowe'en party that got out of hand?"

It took a while for them to explain. Glynis took out her miniature recorder and the captain played it, listening in stolid, impassive silence. Jake saw his gray eyes narrow, though, whenever Senator Leeds's name was mentioned.

Once the recording ended, the captain asked, "Senator Leeds is involved in this?"

"He's mixed up with them," Jake said, "but I don't think he knew anything about their trying to kill us."

Glynis said, "He's mixed up in the murders of Professor Sinclair and his wife, over in Vernon."

"The senator?" Clear disbelief etched the captain's lean, angular face.

"The senator," Glynis said firmly.

Jake asked if he could phone Tomlinson.

"It's three in the morning, you know," said the captain.

"Then I guess I'll wake him up," Jake snapped.

The captain thought it over for a moment, then gestured to the phone console on his desk. Jake got Tomlinson's answering machine, with its cheery "Vote for change!" message. Trying to keep the annoyance out of his voice, Jake briefly told the machine where they were and what had happened.

"Phone machine?" Younger asked. He looked pale, drawn. Whatever the medics gave him for the pain is wearing off, Jake figured.

"Yeah. They're all asleep."

"But if his phone machine's working they must have electricity."

"You think the city hasn't been hit by the blackout?"

"Either that or he's got a backup generator at his house."

Thinking of the Tomlinson mansion, Jake was certain that there was an emergency generator chugging away somewhere on the grounds.

The captain slid his chair back from the desk. "You people better stay here tonight. We'll find bunks for you out back."

"What about Perez and . . ." Jake hesitated, feeling foolish about calling Monster by his nickname.

With a shrug, the captain said, "They're in the infirmary. Under guard. They're not going anyplace."

He got to his feet and Jake stood up, too, then helped Glynis to raise Younger from his chair.

"I'll get one of my men to pick up your car tomorrow morning, once the storm blows away."

"Thanks," said Jake.

The ghost of a smile curled the captain's thin lips slightly. "How much you want to bet there'll be a lawyer here for those two punks before we get your car back to you?"

It was nearly ten A.M. before Jake, Glynis, and Younger left the highway patrol barracks. Jake drove Younger's Land Rover back toward the lodge, to pick up Glynis's Jaguar.

"I hope I can get it started," she said.

"Do you have jumper cables?" Jake asked Younger.

Tim shook his head. "Never needed 'em."

"I have cables in my trunk," Glynis said. "I bought them last summer."

"Good," said Jake.

The sky had cleared to a cloudless brilliant blue, the interstate was plowed and sanded, big white banks of snow sparkled in the sunlight on either side of the road.

As he drove, with Glynis and Younger seated behind him, Jake turned on the radio and pecked buttons until a news station came on.

". . . several thousand households are still without electrical power in the wake of last night's surprise blizzard," a woman was saying, as cheerfully as if announcing a lottery winner.

Then she added, "But Lignite County and points west were only affected by the blackout for less than an hour. The experimental power generator operated by the university outside the town of Lignite provided electrical power for the entire western half of the state all through the storm."

Jake glanced at the rearview mirror. Younger was grinning tiredly, Glynis was beaming at him.

"Score one for MHD," Jake said.

Younger nodded happily and then broke into an enormous yawn.

By the time they reached the lodge Younger was snoring quietly, one arm wrapped protectively around Glynis's shoulders. Her head was resting on his shoulder.

Jake wished she were sitting beside him, with her head nuzzling his cheek.

Glynis's car was buried in snow. As Jake stopped the van and wondered if he could find a shovel inside the lodge, Glynis murmured, "They were going to kill me. You saved me, Jake. You and Tim."

"Your damned Jaguar saved you," Jake grumbled. "If Monster'd been able to start the car, they'd have taken you off before we got there."

"Still . . ." Glynis said softly, gazing at Younger's sleeping face.

Jake grimaced. I took out Monster and Perez, I was the hero last night. All Tim did was stop a bullet. But she's nestled with him like they're a pair of lovebirds.

Life isn't fair, he told himself. Not fair at all.

T he final week of the election campaign was a blurred furor of rallies, speeches, news media interviews.

The success of the MHD generator during the blackout made national headlines, while Senator Leeds's involvement with organized crime rattled the state's political structure.

Although neither Perez nor Monster would say a word to the police, the state's criminal prosecution office reopened the investigation into the Sinclair deaths, and even Florida ruled that Dr. McGruder's death was "suspicious."

Senator Leeds stoutly denied any connection with the murders, claiming it was all a political smear campaign, but as Tomlinson Senior gleefully pointed out, the senator was on the defensive now.

"We've got him on the run!" Amy boasted cheerfully. "His poll numbers are sinking out of sight!"

Jake was interviewed by each of the state's major TV news shows, and even a Public Broadcasting System team came in from New York to do a special report about the MHD generator.

With Bob Rogers feeding him details, Jake reeled off facts and figures about MHD power generation. Tim Younger, walking stiffly because of his bandaged ribs, groused and growled that he couldn't get much work done because of all the reporters and photographers prowling around the big rig.

"Don't worry about it," Jake told Younger, with a happy grin. "Each minute on TV is worth a thousand hours of running the rig."

Younger scowled at him.

Two days before the election, Senator Leeds called a major news conference.

"Maybe he's going to concede?" Jake wondered.

"When pigs fly," said the elder Tomlinson.

Jake was at the Tomlinson residence, in the library with the candidate's father and a few of his elderly cronies. A good percentage of the state's wealth is right here in this room, Jake said to himself as he watched the men—gray haired, white haired, no haired—settle themselves in armchairs to watch the televised news conference.

Tomlinson was on the other side of the state, where a mammoth rally was planned for the evening. With Amy. And Glynis is up in Lignite with Tim, Jake knew. I'm here with the rich and the arthritic.

Leeds's people had chosen the ballroom of the Sheridan Hotel, downtown. Every major news team in the state was there, and even reporters from several cable news networks had shown up. Jake saw CNN and Fox News cameras among the local crews. But the ballroom was so big that the audience of reporters and camera teams looked sparse. Not smart, Jake thought. Somebody in Leeds's organization didn't think this through. They should have partitioned the ballroom or used a smaller space to make the place look jammed.

A local anchorman was blathering about the campaign and Franklin Tomlinson's late surge to pass Leeds in the polls.

"Oddly enough, it was last week's Hallowe'en blackout that moved Tomlinson solidly ahead. He's been pushing for MHD power generation, and the experimental MHD generator in Lignite kept that whole region of the state alight and warm when most of the other power generators in the state failed."

Tomlinson Senior nodded vigorously at the TV screen. "Damned right," he said loudly. Then he turned to Jake and told the others, "And there's the man who advised my son about MHD."

Jake felt downright uncomfortable as the rest of the old men in the library smiled at him. All those expensive false teeth, he thought.

"And here comes Senator Leeds," the TV anchorman said, a note of excitement in his voice.

Jake saw that a stocky, middle-aged woman in a dark pants suit came up to the lectern with Leeds. Her complexion looked Hispanic to him. As the senator stood before the microphones, she took up a position behind him in a posture that reminded Jake of a soldier: chin high, spine straight, hands clasped behind her back.

Leeds smiled his toothy smile. "Thank you all for coming out on such short notice. I have an important announcement to make."

He hesitated, then half turned toward the gray-haired woman. "I'm sure you all know Ms. Yolanda Quintero, head of the regional office of the Federal Bureau of Investigation."

Jake leaned forward in his chair.

"Ms. Quintero has been investigating the deaths of Professor Arlan Sinclair and his wife. There's been a lot of insinuations made about these killings and the influence of organized crime in our state. I'm here today to tell you that the killers have been arrested and will be brought to trial."

Perez and Monster, Jake thought. They're going down for it.

His eyes narrowing, Leeds went on, "This election campaign has been marred by deliberate smears and outright falsehoods trying to link me with organized crime. I'm here to tell you that these smears are totally false. As Ms. Quintero will explain to you, my office has cooperated fully with the FBI and I have been cleared by the FBI of any connection with organized crime."

The elder Tomlinson laughed. "That's right, keep repeating it. That's what we want to hear."

Looking grim, Leeds was saying, "I have worked very hard for many years to make certain that this state's gaming industry is free of any criminal activity."

One of the old men in the library hooted with derision.

"And my opponent's attempts to smear me are actually thinly veiled attacks on the Native Americans in our state, loyal, hard-working men and women whose major source of income is from the state's five licensed gaming casinos."

Raising one finger in the air, Leeds added, "Now, I'm not accusing my opponent of racism. But his reckless attempts to smear me are harming our state's Native American population!"

"The racism card," muttered the old man sitting closest to Jake.

Dead silence among the reporters in the ballroom. Leeds glowered down at them from the lectern, then half turned toward the FBI chief once again.

"And now Ms. Quintero will give you the details of the FBI's investigation."

Tomlinson Senior clapped his hands together loudly. "The last act of a desperate man," he announced.

Jake wasn't so certain.

ELECTION DAY

It was snowing again. As Jake walked from his campus parking spot toward his office a gentle snow sifted down from the gray clouds overhead. It wasn't particularly cold and there was hardly any wind. Not enough snow to call off school for the day, Jake thought. Not enough for kids to go sledding.

"Jake! Wait up!"

Turning, he saw Amy Wexler hurrying toward him, bundled in a quilted parka, but bareheaded, her thick honey-blond hair bouncing off her shoulders as she jogged along the brick walkway.

"Hello, Amy," he said guardedly.

"Do you think this snow will keep people away from the polling places?" Amy asked, puffing slightly as she fell into step alongside him.

He shrugged. "Doesn't look like much. I guess not."

"Too bad," she said.

Jake pushed the door to the astronomy building open, asking, "Too bad?"

"Leeds has a lot of voting blocs lined up," Amy explained. "Those union people, they go through neighborhoods and drive people to the voting booths. Bad weather keeps the vote down. That could be good for us."

"Won't it keep our vote down, too?" He started up the concrete steps, with Amy beside him.

"It works better for the underdog," she said, her voice echoing slightly off the bare walls.

"We're not the underdog."

"Yes, we are," Amy insisted. "As far as delivering organized blocs of voters is concerned, Leeds is way ahead of us."

He led Amy down the corridor to his office, unlocked the door, and ushered her into the cluttered little room.

"I thought we were ahead," Jake said, pulling off his fleece-lined car coat.

"It ain't over till it's over," Amy said.

"Yogi Berra," said Jake. "Great political philosopher."

Amy unzipped her parka and shrugged out of it as she sat on the chair in front of Jake's desk. She let the parka droop over the chair's back. She was wearing a thick knitted off-white pullover and maroon slacks. Jake realized all over again what a beautiful woman she really was.

"Coffee?" he asked, glancing at the pot sitting on the hot plate atop the bookcase behind her.

"I can't stay long," Amy said. "I've got a million things to do."

"Don't forget to vote."

She beamed her cheerleader's smile at him. "Already did. Frank and I voted first thing this morning, as soon as the polls opened."

Jake nodded. Sure you did. You woke up with him, didn't you?

As if she could read the expression on his face, Amy said, "Jake, we couldn't have made it this far without you. Frank wants you to know that, win or lose, he's very grateful for your help and support."

"Uh-huh."

"I love him, Jake."

For a moment he didn't reply. He wasn't sure he'd heard her correctly. Amy, in love? He'd never thought that she'd fall in love with anyone. He realized that he'd thought of Amy only as a bed partner. Jesus Christ, Jake berated himself, I'm a male chauvinist pig!

"You love him?" he asked dully.

"I do. I truly do. At first I thought it was just a fling, you know, just for fun. . . ."

Like you thought of me, Jake realized.

"He's asked me to marry him."

Feeling totally stupid, Jake muttered, "Congratulations."

She smiled again, but this time it looked almost sad. Regretful. "I hope I haven't hurt you, Jake."

He shook his head, bewildered. "No . . . I'm okay."

"He wanted to get married right after the primary, but I told him to wait until after the election. I told Frank that if we got married during the campaign he'd lose half the women's vote."

Jake forced a weak smile. "Yeah. Guess so."

"I wanted to tell you myself," she said, "because . . . well, you know . . ."

"Yeah. I know. I understand."

She shot to her feet and grabbed the parka before it could fall to the floor. "Well, I've got to run. There's a million things I have to get done."

Jake stood up, but stayed behind his desk. "Thanks for telling me . . . and everything," he said. "I hope the two of you are very happy together. I really do."

"You're sweet, Jake." She rushed to the door, blew him a farewell kiss, and left, tugging on the parka.

Jake sank back into his chair, thinking, Well, what did you expect? You knew she was only playing around with you. He looked up at the partially open door. But getting married? I never thought she was that serious about him.

That's because you're an idiot, he told himself. A blind, stupid idiot.

And, like an idiot, he picked up the phone and called Glynis.

She picked up on the second ring. "Hello, Jake."

Caller ID, he realized. "Hi, Glyn. Uh, are you doing anything for lunch?"

"I'm driving up to Lignite. Want to have lunch with Tim and me?" She sounded cheerful, not a care in the world.

"I can't," he said. "Got a class this afternoon."

"Maybe some other time," said Glynis.

"Yeah, sure." He hesitated a heartbeat, then asked, "Are you coming to Tomlinson's party tonight?"

"At the Sheridan? Yes, we'll be there."

Jake heard the *we*. "Okay, see you then. Oh, don't forget to vote!"

"I will, Jake. I promise."

He hung up the phone, turned his little chair around, and watched the snow falling gently outside his window. I might as well go out and vote, Jake said to himself. I've got nothing better to do.

VICTORY

ake had to fight his way through the jam-packed lobby of the Sheridan Hotel. Senator Leeds's supporters were pouring into the ballroom, eagerly anticipating the election results.

Brilliant planning, he thought sourly while he squeezed into an elevator filled with laughing, chattering people. Leeds's party in the ballroom down on the ground floor, Tomlinson's in the auditorium on the top floor. In the whole damned city they both have to pick this hotel.

Well, he thought, no matter who loses, the Sheridan wins.

The hotel's rooftop auditorium was even more jammed. As the elevator doors opened, Jake was hit by a solid wall of bodies and deafening noise. Campaign workers, volunteers wearing garish sashes proclaiming TOMLINSON, news reporters, camera crews, a German brass band in lederhosen um-pahhing up on the stage, dignitaries from all over the state, call girls in low-cut dresses waving plastic glasses of champagne, everyone talking, laughing, tooting on plastic vuvuzelas; the noise was overpowering, the press of bodies crushing.

Wishing he were back at his apartment or off in the middle of the Sahara, Jake forced his way through the crowd. Big television screens hung from every wall, showing the vote tabulation. This close to midnight and the count was still too close to call a winner. He spotted Glynis and Younger, trying to dance in front of the stage to a waltz being played surprisingly gently by the brass band. They could barely move, the dance floor was so crowded, but neither of them seemed to mind. Dr. Cardwell and Alice were there, too, looking happily contented with each other.

Tomlinson's father stood off in one corner of the big room, talking animatedly with what looked like a pair of reporters. Jake pushed toward him. At least the crowd was hanging a respectful few feet away from the old man. Maybe he could breathe there.

The elder Tomlinson looked austere and dignified in his tuxedo, even though his bow tie was striped red, white, and blue. He held a cut-crystal glass of whiskey in one hand, while jabbing at the reporters with a forefinger of the other.

"I told him it's going to be a tight race," the elder Tomlinson was saying. "I'm not paying for a damned landslide!"

The reporters laughed dutifully. Jake remembered that old Joe Kennedy was supposed to have said something like that about his son's election in 1960.

The woman reporter prompted, "Interesting that both parties are here in the Sheridan." Even from five feet away Jake could hardly hear her over the babble of the crowd.

Tomlinson h'mmphed. "When they told me that Leeds had already booked the ballroom downstairs I just picked up the phone and talked to my old friend, Harry Hortenson."

"He's the owner of this hotel, isn't he?" the reporter asked, her voice barely under a shout.

"He is indeed. He gave us this lovely rooftop facility. When the good senator concedes, he'll have to ride the elevator up here to do it."

The reporters laughed again. Alexander Tomlinson allowed himself a thin smile.

Jake glanced up at the mammoth TV screen over the old man's head. FINAL RESULTS FROM CAPITAL CITY was printed along the bottom of the screen.

The auditorium suddenly went quiet. The whole crowd seemed to hold its breath. Jake watched the numbers from the tabulation adding up in a blurry whirl. Leeds was ahead . . . no, Tomlinson came from behind and edged him out!

The crowd roared. Even Tomlinson Senior broke into a pleased grin. Tomlinson's lead was slim, but he had taken the city's vote.

"That's it," the old man roared. "If the senator can't hold the capital, he's finished. My son will kick his butt out in the counties."

Jake stared at the screen. It's true, he told himself. We knew that

Leeds's main strength was here in the capital. If he's lost here, he's lost the state. Tomlinson's going to be our new senator!

As if on cue, B. Franklin Tomlinson entered the auditorium, with Amy at his side. He looked dashing in a hand-tailored tux; Amy wore a floor-length ball gown of pale gold. She was glowing.

Everyone applauded. Tomlinson smiled brilliantly, a boyish, almost bashful grin. He held up both hands, then sprinted to the stage and jumped up onto it in a single bound.

Gripping the edges of the lectern that had been set up onstage, Tomlinson said into the microphone, "It ain't over till it's over, remember."

A voice from the crowd roared, "It's over! Look at the numbers!"

Glancing up at the nearest TV screen, Tomlinson broke into a laugh, then said, "I've got to admit, it looks damned good!"

Everyone cheered.

It took nearly another hour before the TV finally announced that B. Franklin Tomlinson had won the election. The margin of victory was narrow, but undeniable. Leeds appeared on screen, looking more resentful than gracious, and made a brief concession speech, ending with:

"But this isn't the end of our efforts to make our state the best place in America to live and bring up families."

A few jeers and catcalls from the crowd. Then the victory party swung into high gear.

And Jake wanted to slink off and go home. It's over, he said to himself. We've won. So what?

Tomorrow I go back to my office and return to being an assistant professor of astronomy. Tomorrow I return to reality.

CONSEQUENCES

As he edged toward the exit, Jake felt a hand grip his shoulder. Turning, he saw Bob Rogers grinning at him.

"Where're you going, Jake?"

"Home, I guess."

"Not yet. He wants to see you," said Rogers. He looked slightly wobbly to Jake, as if he'd had too much to drink.

"He?"

"Our new senator. He sent me to find you. Rogers's Rangers, scouting through the wilderness, seeking . . . um, seeking . . ." Rogers shrugged good-naturedly. "Whatever. He wants to talk to you."

Jake allowed Rogers to lead him through the clamoring, celebrating throng to a metal door set in the wall off to one side of the stage.

It was a janitor's closet. Brooms and mops hung from clips on the wall. Metal shelves held cleaning solvents and detergents. A deep sink stood against the rear wall. Tomlinson, Amy, Glynis, and Younger were all crowded in, all looking happy, tired, drunk with victory and champagne.

"There you are!" Tomlinson said. He grabbed Jake's hand and pumped it vigorously.

"Congratulations," Jake said. Then, glancing at Amy, he added, "Double congratulations."

"I couldn't have done it without you, Jake," Tomlinson said.

Forcing a smile, Jake nodded toward Younger and Rogers and said, "These guys had something to do with it, too, you know."

"I know. I know. And I'm going to push for MHD as soon as I get on the Senate floor."

Rogers said, "Great." Even Younger looked pleased.

"I'm sorry to have such an informal setting for this conference," Tomlinson said, with a slight giggle. "It's the one place around here that my father won't think of looking for me."

Jake didn't know what to make of that.

More seriously, Tomlinson said, "I want you on my staff, Jake. I want you to be science advisor in Washington."

Jake felt his brows hike toward his scalp. "In Washington? I can't go to Washington. I've got my position here to—"

"I'm sure the university will grant you a leave of absence," said Tomlinson. "I'm going to need you in Washington."

"I don't know . . ."

"Come on, Jake," Tomlinson urged. "There's a lot to be done, and I need you to help me do it. MHD, the environment, NASA's budget . . . science is going to be an important part of my job, and I need the best scientific information I can get. That means you, Jake. I need you."

They were all staring at him: Tomlinson, Amy, Rogers, Tim Younger, and Glynis. I can't go to Washington, Jake told himself. I can't just pull up stakes at the university and trot off to Washington. He'll be in the Senate for six years, at least.

"What do you say, Jake?" Tomlinson asked, almost gently.

"I . . . this is kind of a surprise," Jake temporized. "I'll have to think about it."

Tomlinson gave him a dazzling smile. "You think about it, then." Turning to Amy, he went on, "And you find him an apartment in D.C."

Jake nodded numbly and slipped out of the broom closet as quickly as he could, his mind spinning. The party was ebbing, people were drifting toward the doors. A dance combo was still playing soft music, but the oompah band was packing up its brass instruments.

Tomlinson's father stalked by, looking nettled. "Have you seen my son?" he demanded of Jake. Without waiting for a reply he stamped past, muttering, "CBS News wants to interview him and he goes into hiding on me."

Jake held back an impulse to laugh. It's all so funny, he thought. Tomlinson's going to be our new senator. He's going to marry Amy and get out from under his father's thumb. Glynis is all wrapped up with Tim. And Tomlinson wants me to go to Washington with him.

I can't go to Washington, he repeated to himself. I can't. I don't know anybody there. I've never been out of this state in my life; all my friends are here.

All what friends? Jake asked himself. Bob Rogers? Tim? Glynis?

"Jake."

It was Dr. Cardwell's soft voice. Jake turned and saw his mentor smiling gently at him.

"Hello, Lev."

"Quite an evening, isn't it?" said Cardwell.

"Yeah."

"You did a fine job, Jake. I'm proud of you."

Ordinarily that would have made Jake's day. Instead, he heard himself say, "He wants me to work on his staff. In Washington."

Cardwell beamed. "That's wonderful! You'll be science advisor to a United States senator. Wonderful!"

"I can't go to Washington."

"Why not?"

"I've got my job at the university. . . ."

Cardwell waved a hand in the air. "Oh, the university will give you a leave of absence. It'll be quite a feather in their caps to have a member of the faculty on the staff of the state's new senator."

"I don't know anybody in Washington."

"So you'll make new friends. You won't be lonely for long."

Jake looked down at the older man's owlish face. I'm lonely here, he realized.

Cardwell gripped Jake's elbow and led him toward the row of French doors at the far side of the auditorium.

"Where's Mrs. Cee?" Jake asked as he reluctantly allowed Cardwell to steer him.

"Oh, Alice is chatting with some old friends. She won't miss us for a few minutes."

Before Jake could ask where they were going, Cardwell opened one of the glass doors. They stepped out onto the balcony, into the dark November night. It was cloudy and a chill breeze was blowing. Jake turned up his jacket collar.

"God must hate astronomers," Jake complained, leaning on the balcony's rail as he looked up at the sky. "All these cloudy nights."

Cardwell chuckled softly. "That's why astronomers have to move off the ground and get into orbit."

"I guess," Jake conceded.

"You could help to make that happen. In Washington."

"You think I should go, Lev?"

Cardwell seemed totally unaffected by the cold. He stood beside Jake at the balcony's rail, wearing nothing more than his usual gray suit and bow tie.

"I think you have to go, Jake," Cardwell said softly. "I think it will be good for you and good for Senator Tomlinson."

"Maybe."

"Pushing for MHD won't be easy," Cardwell added. "It's not a sure thing. The energy lobby has a lot of inertia built into it."

"Yeah."

"And there are all the other science issues: global warming, stem cell research, health . . . you'll have your hands full."

Nodding, Jake said, "You know, Tomlinson could be a real force in Washington. We need a senator who works for scientific progress."

"And the senator needs a science advisor who'll help him get things accomplished."

Suddenly Jake blurted, "I guess I don't have anything to keep me here. Not really. It's not like I'm Mr. Popularity or anything."

"You can work with your grad students on the Mars probe," Cardwell suggested. "What with e-mail and all, you don't have to be on campus to work with them. You don't have to be in the same state."

"It's not that easy, Lev."

"I know. I understand. But you can do it, Jake. I know you can."

Jake said nothing. His mind was churning, whirling. He got a mental image of a clothes dryer, with all the ideas and possibilities of the future tumbling over each other, spinning, stirring.

Cardwell pointed out toward the horizon. "Look!"

The clouds had parted and Jake saw a single ruddy point of light hanging in the night sky, a steady glowing light staring at him.

"Mars," he breathed.

Cardwell said softly, "Tomlinson could be in the Senate for a long time, Jake. Long enough to get human explorers to Mars. If he has the right science advice."

Jake grinned down at his mentor. "MHD's not enough for you, huh?"

"MHD is merely the beginning, my boy," said Cardwell. "Merely the beginning."